To my children,
Michael and Elisabeth

Above all, one must live as a full person at all times.

—Rosa Luxemburg, writing from prison in Germany, 1917

Wall Tappings

Wall Tappings

AN INTERNATIONAL ANTHOLOGY OF
WOMEN'S PRISON WRITINGS
200 TO THE PRESENT

Second Edition

Edited by Judith A. Scheffler

Foreword by Tracy Huling

The Feminist Press at the City University of New York
New York

Published by the Feminist Press at the City University of New York
The Graduate Center, 365 Fifth Avenue, Suite 5406, New York, NY 10016
feministpress.org

Second edition 2002

Library of Congress Cataloging-in-Publication Data
Wall tappings : an international anthology of women's prison writings,
200 to the present / edited by Judith A. Scheffler ; foreword by Tracy
Huling.— 2nd ed.
    p. cm.
Includes bibliographical references.
  ISBN 1-55861-272-6 (cloth) — ISBN 1-55861-273-4 (pbk.)
  1. Women prisoners—Biography. 2. Prisoners' writings. 3. Literature—Women authors.
4. Political prisoners—Biography. I. Scheffler, Judith A., 1949-
HV6245.W345 2002
365'.43'0922—dc21

                                                                           2002014631

Publication of this book is supported by public funds from the National Endowment for the Arts.

NATIONAL
ENDOWMENT
FOR THE ARTS

Publication of this book is also supported by public funds from the New York State Council on the Arts, a State Agency.

State of the Arts

NYSCA

The Feminist Press would like to thank the New York Community Trust and the Bydale Foundation and Jenny Warburg for supporting a program that makes *Wall Tappings* available to women in prison education programs.

The Feminist Press would also like to thank Janet E. Brown, Laura Brown and Barbara Danish, Mariam K. Chamberlain, Johnnetta B. Cole, Blanche Wiesen Cook, Barbara Grossman, Helene D. Goldfarb, Nancy Hoffman, Florence Howe, Yolanda T. Moses, and Genevieve Vaughan for supporting the publication of this book.

Text design by Dayna Navaro
Printed in Canada on acid-free paper by Transcontinental Printing

09 08 07 06 05 04 03 02   5 4 3 2 1

CONTENTS

PART 3

'Don't forget, you are a prisoner':
Prison Conditions and Deprivations   85

PART 4

'I have all the passion of life':
Psychological Survival Through Communication
and Relationships   123

FOREWORD

This new edition of *Wall Tappings* comes at a time when the prison experience threatens to become "normal" for whole segments of societies across the globe. Just as the American system of slavery once did, our current reliance on prisons can, even to nice people, seem inevitable, reasonable—even merciful.

The use of the criminal justice system to solve social problems has enjoyed unprecedented popularity in many countries over the last two decades. Detecting, arresting, trying, sentencing, imprisoning, guarding, feeding, clothing, and paroling the poor, the uneducated, the ill, and the disabled has become a giant and labor-intensive public works program. In the United States alone, over 4 million people (prisoners and justice system employees) are absorbed in the exercise of government-subsidized punishment.

At the center of this new enterprise are prisons. The last twenty years have seen an explosion in the use of imprisonment in a great number of countries. This rise has taken place in democratic countries and in totalitarian states. It has occurred in rich countries and in poor. It has happened in countries in the north and the south, the east and the west. The consequences have been profound. In some countries the explosion in prison populations has been matched by massive expenditure on prison building and upkeep. Other countries have not been able to afford to build more prisons; they have simply shoveled more prisoners into the space available, causing a dramatic increase in violence and disease.

In some societies imprisonment has become big business. There are powerful vested interests that see increased profit in more and larger prisons. Private prison corporations, banks and bond financiers, architects and construction companies, and political representatives of depressed rural areas where prisons are now used as "economic development" are just a few of the interests now actively engaged in lobbying for prison expansion divorced from penological need. Increased public expenditure on locking people up has resulted in less expenditure on other public services such as hospitals, schools, and care of the elderly.

The United States is now the world's leading jailer, according to the Sentencing Project, with 2 million people and a greater percentage of its residents behind bars than any other country in the world. Just in the last decade, the rate of Americans who are imprisoned has increased dramatically—from one in every 218 Americans to one in every 142. That translates to 1,585 additional inmates each week. The U.S. "prison-industrial complex," as it has aptly come to be called, is now the largest in the history of the world.

Black men in the United States are imprisoned at a rate far higher than they were in South Africa under Apartheid, reports the Sentencing Project.

Imprisonment has increasingly become the preferred method of punishment for nonwhite Americans. According to the U.S. Department of Justice, Bureau of Justice Statistics, as of June 30, 2000, the U.S. incarceration rate was 235 per 100,000 for whites compared with 1,815 per 100,000 for blacks; 709 per 100,000 for Native Americans; and 609 per 100,000 for Latinos.

While women remain a small percentage of those imprisoned worldwide and represent under 10 percent of the U.S. prison population, their rates of incarceration have been steadily increasing, with the weight of this alarming trend falling most heavily on women of color who are also poor. Most are incarcerated for nonviolent economic crimes such as theft and forgery, and in many countries involved in the so-called war on drugs, women convicted for nonviolent drug crimes under increasingly harsh mandatory prison sentencing laws make up the bulk of those recently sent to prison. During the 1990s alone, the number of women in prison in the United States doubled, to more than 90,000.

The conditions of women in prison have come under increasing scrutiny worldwide. Many are at risk of torture, including rape, and other forms of sexual violence. Many are denied health care that they desperately need. Many are singled out for cruel punishments, discriminated against, and treated as sub-human. On March 8, 1999, International Women's Day, Amnesty International launched a worldwide campaign to highlight the human rights of women prisoners. Once again, the United States stands out. Amnesty's report on the plight of women prisoners in the United States, *Breaking the Chain: The Human Rights of Women Prisoners*, charts a litany of human rights violations against incarcerated women, including rape and sexual abuse by prison staff, shackling of pregnant women, denial of adequate health care, and unlawful detention of female asylum-seekers.

In the late 1980s, the Correctional Association of New York, a nonprofit organization that monitors prison conditions and advocates criminal justice system reform, sent me, their new public policy director, to a women's correctional facility in New York City. It was my first time in a prison for women. I don't now recall the details of that visit—its precise purpose, the administrators with whom I met, even the name of the institution itself. What did stay with me from that first experience, what shocks and frightens and haunts me still, are the shadows of women I saw there: eyes devoid of light, faces without expression, listless bodies stripped of purpose. For most of that visit, I felt physically ill, followed by competing emotions of enormous relief and sadness when I left the prison.

It wasn't long before I learned that the "shadow women" I met at that awful place were on a variety of psychiatric medications as part of a behavior management strategy disguised as therapy—not an uncommon practice in women's prisons in the United States and other countries, where women's ways of being in the world seem to confound the mostly male-designed, male-administered, and male-staffed prison system. While appropriate therapy is warranted for women with serious mental illness inside and outside prisons, treating "bad" women as if they are "mad" is far too common.

The urge to make women in prison passive so that they will conform to the norms of male-imagined and -dominated life in these cages is pervasive and takes many more subtle forms than legalized drugging. I will never forget an incident that occurred at a women's prison in upstate New York when the security officer escorting me from one side of the prison compound to another stopped in front of a garden of flowers to complain that, unlike the men he had guarded at male institutions, the women at this prison couldn't seem to plant anything in a straight line. Sure enough, when I looked closely, I could see that curves defined the beds of that lovely garden. Moreover, as a hobby gardner myself, I knew those curves were not "mistakes." They made just the right design to complement both that area's landscape and the specific variety of flowers and other plants chosen for the beds. I couldn't help laughing out loud at the time—much to the guard's dismay.

As you might imagine, dear reader, particularly if you are a woman, this incident stood out for me as much more than funny. It opened my eyes to the essential and constant struggle for women in prison to find ways to assert and express themselves, not only as human beings but as women. As would many more experiences thereafter, it confirmed for me that far from being "shadow women," most women in prison are survivors, adept at finding ways to keep the human spirit and the female spirit alive despite seemingly insurmountable odds.

Wall Tappings is a testament both to the abilities of all women to survive the spirit-killing forces that confront us everywhere in our daily lives, and to the individual women who have survived the concentration of those forces in prison. The writings of the women here provide a guide for those of us who live both inside and outside prison walls. It is impossible to read this book without reflecting on what we ourselves make of the circumstances in which we find ourselves.

Wall Tappings also affirms the critical role of art—in this case, the art of writing—in the practice of survival and the transcendence of the prison experience. As someone who now practices the art of filmmaking, and whose work continues to be informed and inspired by prisoners, I am deeply moved by the shimmering beauty of what is contained in these pages. It takes talent and hard work to make something beautiful in the best of conditions, and I am awed by the achievement inherent in art-making in prison.

Finally, this book illustrates the partnerships that are necessary to enable our truths to be told. Without the Feminist Press, so much of women's experience in the world would remain unknown.

With heartfelt appreciation,
Tracy Huling
New York
July 2002

PREFACE

Publishing is part of the art of not bowing. —Carol Muske

The second edition of *Wall Tappings* offers the reader a broader selection of international prison works that proclaim their authors' humanity and refusal to bow. When poet Carol Muske conducted an early writing workshop for women imprisoned at Riker's Island in New York City, she noted this crucial function of prison writing. It was writing that mattered—if only to the imprisoned writer herself. But too often it did not matter to those outside the walls, because the public did not notice the works, had no access to them, and certainly did not respect them as "literature." The first edition of *Wall Tappings* proposed to address this information gap by foregrounding lost and previously unknown works by women prisoners. Since the publication of the first edition, increased rates of imprisonment worldwide and compelling recent or recently translated women's prison writings have prompted this new, very different *Wall Tappings*. To summarize the collective "mood" of this new edition: it does not bow.

Since publication of the first edition, prison writing has begun to command more attention and respect from publishers, the public, and the literary community. Recent anthologies of writing from America's prisons respond to this interest, as do prison writing–related sessions at major academic conferences, such as that of the Modern Language Association.[1] Some prison writing is now included in prison-related websites. The writing of imprisoned women contributes significantly to these successful avenues of dissemination. Almost always, though, women's prison writing appears in the context of general prison writing, assuming a relatively minor role, if considered in the most basic terms of numbers of pages devoted to women's works. Yet the writing of women prisoners constitutes a literary tradition that depicts the lives of silenced, imprisoned women and reveals a whole facet of women's experience usually considered too unpleasant or too atypical for attention. These are the marginal texts too often lost in the marginal "literature of the prison."

Wall Tappings invites the reader to discover the wealth of women's prison literature, a journey that may lead in many, varied directions. Sixteen of the thirty selections in this edition are new; an expanded scope suggests various paths readers might take for further reading or research. This second edition broadens the genres of selections, to include autobiography, memoir, letters, diary, essay, character sketch, fiction, poetry, and drama. Included are works from women's prisons in Argentina, ancient Carthage, Chile, Egypt, England, Eritrea, France, Germany, Iran, Malaysia, Malta, the Philippines,

South Africa, and the United States. Selections begin with Perpetua, a Christian martyred in third-century Carthage, and extend to the present. This expanded scope in time highlights the vitality of prison literature and the roots of contemporary texts. Nine of the sixteen new selections are international writings, which call the reader's attention to exciting new translations, particularly from Third World nations, and which have been published since the first edition. Regrettably, space constraints necessitate the deletion of twelve selections in order to make room for the new ones. A greatly expanded annotated bibliography of writings by women prisoners, including about 100 new entries, aids readers who wish to explore beyond the selections of this anthology. Works that were excerpted in the first edition but do not appear in the second are cited in entries in this bibliography.

Each selection begins with a biographical introduction to the author. Selections were written either during the woman's incarceration or at a later date about her incarceration, and each focuses on how the writer, as a woman, personally regarded imprisonment and adapted to her surroundings by work, special interests, or sheer mental effort, and especially by communicating with others both within prison and outside. Purely political treatises and works that do not discuss the prison experience are not included. The thematic organization of selections to highlight dominant concerns of women prisoners has been expanded in the second edition to include a new section on family relationships, often cited as a hallmark of women's prison experience. Finally, this edition emphasizes the *collective* nature of women's prison writing in diverse selections, such as those by Chilean political prisoners, Bahá'í prisoners of conscience, and women in an AIDS education program in a New York prison.

The fact that educated women and political activists figure prominently among the authors represented in this anthology requires explanation, since the majority of incarcerated women throughout history have been poor and uneducated. The vast majority of prisoners—whether men or women—do not write, and throughout the history of prisons, few works by the disadvantaged have survived, if indeed they ever *were* written. However, women imprisoned for political reasons often *do* write, and their works are doubly interesting, for they often discuss the plight of their sister prisoners with the same fervor and immediacy that they use in describing themselves. Frequently the prisoner's identification with her people leads to her imprisonment in the first place.

In the first edition of *Wall Tappings* I noted with regret the scarcity of firsthand accounts by poor and working-class imprisoned women. An exciting development since that publication is the increasing availability of material written by women imprisoned for nonpolitical reasons. Several new selections in this anthology are by women who are not political prisoners in the usual sense. When women prisoners write, they often reject the term "prisoner," with its connotation of shame, and they question the justice of the society that has imprisoned them. For example, some writers speak out against the increased imprisonment of poor and minority women in the United States. Those women who committed crimes, such as forgery, and who might even consider themselves deserving of punishment, assert their claim to decent treatment and boldly bear witness to human rights abuses. These prison writers unite to condemn an institution that labels them worthless and attempts to destroy their humanity in the name of justice. In this sense, each of the writers explicitly or implicitly considers herself a political prisoner, and writing itself becomes a part of her protest.

The researcher and general reader alike will discover in the largely unexplored body of women's prison writing a literary tradition that rewards investigation. From the perspective of many nations and eras, imprisoned women speak firsthand about the profound realities of their experience. Their works offer untapped primary source material for researchers in literature, sociology, criminal justice, legal studies, and women's studies. For those who are incarcerated, these readings offer the promise of conversation and communication.

NOTES

The epigraph to the preface is taken from Carol Muske, "The Art of Not Bowing: Writing by Women in Prison," *Heresies* I (January 1977): 30–34.

1. Two notable recent anthologies are Bell Gale Chevigny, ed., *Doing Time: 25 Years of Prison Writing* (New York: Arcade, 1999), and H. Bruce Franklin, ed., *Prison Writing in 20th-Century America* (New York: Penguin, 1998).

ACKNOWLEDGMENTS

In this new edition of *Wall Tappings*, my thanks go first to Jean Casella, publisher/director of the Feminist Press, who recognized that international women's prison writing has a vital message to communicate in this era of prison expansion. Her vision gave this project a welcome home with the Feminist Press.

Several people and organizations have assisted my work in compiling this new edition. Lynette McGrath, my friend and colleague at West Chester University, offered valued insight and support. I am indebted to the West Chester University Interlibrary Loan staff, especially Mary Sweeney and Kimberly Klaus, for their assistance with the research on the annotated bibliography; its value as a resource owes much to their professionalism. My students in the women's prison literature seminar at West Chester University shared their fresh perspective in many productive discussions on women's prison texts. I would also like to note the contributions to my research on this new edition of others who share an interest in issues of women's imprisonment or women's prison literature: Bell Gale Chevigny, Hettie Jones, June E. Licence, Quentin Miller, Aurora Levins Morales, Kathleen O'Shea, and Rosanna Warren.

I continue to appreciate the importance of the pathbreaking work done by H. Bruce Franklin and Elissa D. Gelfand in promoting the merits of prison literature for serious reading and study. During the 1970s and 1980s my volunteer work with the Pennsylvania Prison Society in the Philadelphia County Prisons gave me the idea to compile the first edition of this anthology and helped me to see the need for a humane approach to the ancient problem of imprisonment. H. Bruce Franklin and Elissa D. Gelfand generously supported the project of compiling the first edition of *Wall Tappings* at a time when women's prison writing still occupied the remotest regions of marginality.

For their assistance in providing biographical data and information on works by women prisoners for the first edition of *Wall Tappings*, I thank Grant Allen Anderson, Philip Balla, Jane Begos, Richard Binder, Susan L. Boone, David Braham, Joseph Bruchac, Nick Caistor, Pat Case, Sandra L. Chaff, Mara L. Crowell, Karlene Faith, Renny Golden, Paul Gordon, Axel Guwe, Nancy Halli, Ramon Hodel, James H. Hutson, Nicola Johnson, David King, J. Richard Kyle, Rita Lawn, Joan Leiby, Edward Lyon, Sally M. Miller, Aurora Levins Morales, David Rothenberg, Richard A. Schrader, Elizabeth Shenton, Gloria F. Waldman, Meta Winter, S. Wong, and Laura X. The following organizations and libraries provided information for the first edition: Amnesty International–International Secretariat; Amnesty International–U.S.A.; the Contemporary Culture Collection of

Temple University Library; the Fortune Society; the George Arents Research Library at Syracuse University; Greenfield Review Press; the Historical Department of the Church of Jesus Christ of Latter-day Saints, Salt Lake City; the Library of Congress Manuscript Division; the Medical College of Pennsylvania Archives; the New York Public Library Rare Books and Manuscripts Division and Newspaper Department; the Oswego County Historical Society (NY); PEN American Center; the Rare Book Department of the Free Library of Philadelphia; the Schlesinger Library; the Sophia Smith Collection, Smith College; the Southern Historical Collection at the University of North Carolina; the Suffragette Papers Collection at the Museum of London; the Swarthmore College Peace Collection; Women's History Research Center, Inc.; Women's International Resource Exchange (WIRE); Writers and Scholars Educational Trust, London. The Interlibrary Loan staff of Drexel University, especially Deidre Harper, Robin Barnes, and Merrill Stein, gave invaluable assistance in compiling the annotated bibliography for the first edition. I thank Peter Blood for providing research information for this new edition.

Jane Maher and Superintendent Elaine Lord of Bedford Hills Correctional Facility have contributed to this project through their interest in its potential use in programming for incarcerated women. I thank imprisoned poet Diane Hamill Metzger for her friendship and correspondence.

Molly Vaux, my editor at the Feminist Press, has influenced *Wall Tappings* in countless ways, and the project has benefited greatly from her association with it. I feel truly fortunate to have worked with her. I owe sincere thanks to the entire staff of the Feminist Press for their enthusiastic belief in the importance of this second edition. Dayna Navaro deserves special mention for her design of both the book and its cover, and I am grateful to Laura Whitehorn for her artwork that appears on the cover. *Wall Tappings* is a collective project in the true spirit of collaboration—a model of what a women's project can be.

My greatest debt is to my parents, Margaret and Carl Scheffler, and to my husband, Michael Neely. With love and encouragement they have supported me throughout this continuing project. Our children, Michael and Elisabeth, are a joyful personal development since publication of the first edition. Michael's computer skills have been particularly helpful with this edition, and Elisabeth has provided welcome comic relief.

To the many current or recently imprisoned women who have corresponded with me and shared their writings, I give my sincere thanks and appreciation, in the hope that this anthology gathers the audience they deserve.

INTRODUCTION

1 April 1957, Leningrad

In the fearful years of the Yezhov terror I spent seventeen months in prison queues in Leningrad. One day somebody "identified" me. Beside me, in the queue, there was a woman with blue lips. She had, of course, never heard of me: but she suddenly came out of that trance so common to us all and whispered in my ear (everybody spoke in whispers there): "Can you describe this?" And I said: "Yes, I can." And then something like the shadow of a smile crossed what had once been her face.   —Anna Akhmatova

Lesson #1. The first human right is to speak in one's own voice.
                                                                —Karlene Faith

Russian poet Anna Akhmatova (1889–1966), long suppressed and harassed by censors and police in her native land, was never imprisoned, but her senses were finely attuned to the suffering around her. In her long poem *Requiem,* she writes of her own anguished attempts to visit her son in Stalin's prisons. She voices the need of the silenced to communicate their experience, and stresses the invaluable function of the writer, whose words speak for those who cannot. The simple but powerful scene described above characterizes women's prison literature, with its clear link between the craft of writing and the society in which the writer lives and works.

Today women prisoners increasingly use their own voices to testify to their experiences and to affirm their continuing humanity in literary creations. Karlene Faith's profound statement suggests the need for this second edition of *Wall Tappings.* In the United States and internationally, the rising rate of women's incarceration and the abuses female prisoners suffer make it imperative that they tell their stories. Since the first edition of this anthology was published, the prison institution has changed markedly, becoming more remote to "decent" citizens while it simultaneously incarcerates increasing percentages of the general population. Publishing women's prison literature is one method of reminding society that incarcerated women exist.

All women's prison texts are political, each speaking uniquely for silenced women behind bars and prison walls. Many women prison writers are political activists who speak for fellow victims of society's repression.[1] Others, imprisoned for criminal offenses, express the plight of all incarcerated women through accounts of their own pain. Still others, despising the criminal women they have been forced to live with, seem absorbed in the task of justifying their own lives before society; yet, even their works reveal much about the social condition and status of women in prisons.

In the past twenty years, women's writing has gained increased notice and respect as literature, but that respect has not yet been extended to the writings of women prisoners. Although prison literature by men is often cited for its rich imagery and influence, works by women prisoners remain more obscure. Few people have access to these works or even know of them, and, consequently, a female prison author and her audience remain widely separated. She is doubly marginal: as a prisoner and as a female writer.

This "double marginality" makes the investigation of women's prison literature exciting from the standpoint of contemporary feminist scholars. The need to consider race and class as well as gender in revising the literary canon has been an ongoing concern among feminist literary critics, whose call for a reexamination of aesthetic and social assumptions behind our responses to works has made significant revisions to the literary canon. Feminist criminologists share these concerns about the dynamics of class, race, and gender in the criminal justice system. Women's prison literature lies at the heart of this issue, since its authors are the female dispossessed—in society, in the canon, and, until recently, even in feminist scholarship. Considerations of class, race, and gender are central to an understanding of these texts, which demonstrate that opening the canon to writing by women is not enough; authors who have been excluded by reason of race or low socioeconomic class must also share in the reconstruction of our concept of "great literature."

Feminist criticism and criticism of prison literature converge in a reading of women's prison literature, and highlight the need to reevaluate traditional aesthetic criteria. One of the first and most basic undertakings of feminist literary criticism, the recovery of lost texts, remains central to research in women's prison literature, where most works have been forgotten. To illustrate the neglect of women's prison literature, consider its status in the 1998 publication *The Oxford History of the Prison: The Practice of Punishment in Western Society.*[2] Despite chapters on women's imprisonment, political prisoners, and "The Literature of Confinement," minimal reference is made to writings *by* women. Another example is *Writers in Prison,* in which Ioan Davies gives scant attention to women's works. His generalization, "Prison writing is centrally about violence," excludes from consideration an entire segment of prison writing, for the "central" theme of violence is not central to women's texts.[3]

Female prison writers need an audience, and readers on the outside need to consider these forgotten authors. Historical writing by imprisoned women is especially difficult to identify and locate,[4] and this gap constitutes a cultural loss of undetermined scope. The more critical information gap, however, is the lack of access to recent prison writing—for readers inside as well as outside prison. Journalist and prison activist Christian Parenti describes the "TV therapy" administered in today's American prisons, in which communication with the outside world is discouraged and televisions placate and sedate prisoners.[5] Making women's prison writing more generally available is one step toward establishing two-way communication.

This information exchange is thwarted not only by prison restrictions, but also by a reluctance among readers to embrace works by women prisoners. Literary critic Linda Wagner-Martin's analysis of the difficulties facing biographers of marginalized subjects informs this discussion of women's prison literature: "Readership for biography wants the kind of comfort that comes with identification. If the subject comes from too remote a place, either geographically or financially, or from too different a culture, the oddity must be prestigious rather than threatening."[6] Rarely is the writing of an unknown female prisoner considered prestigious. Bringing works by women prisoners to the foreground does more than enrich our cultural and literary heritage; the works constitute a living testimony to counteract what scholar, activist, and former political prisoner Angela Davis has called the "hyperinvisibility of women prisoners."[7]

Women's prison literature is political, communal, and radical because women's prisons are paradigmatic of women's position in society. Michel Foucault, writing primarily of men's prisons, describes the modern trend toward objectification of the institutionalized prisoner, who is treated as a faulty mechanism that must be repaired.[8] Even more striking is prison's objectification of women, who are already treated as objects in the society outside. If women are generally vulnerable in society, their vulnerability is acute in prison. Critic Elissa Gelfand explains how writings by French women demonstrate this effect of imprisonment. She states that women's texts from French prisons, written "under explicitly sex-specific social conditions," show "an unusually clear interplay between society and text, or, more precisely, between social and literary representations of the same cultural myths surrounding criminal women."[9] In her recent study of the culture of women's prisons, Barbara Owen notes that "[p]ersonal relationships with other prisoners, both emotionally and physically intimate, connections to family and loved ones in the free community (or, 'on the street' in the language of the prison), and commitments to pre-prison identities continue to shape the core of prison culture among women."[10] In reflecting prisoners' views of this culture, prison texts simultaneously comment on women's position in society in general.

The Prison Institution and the Woman Prisoner

The "concrete womb" of prison, to use journalist Kathryn Watterson's telling metaphor, is a modern, paradoxical institution: "It is a place we send people for *change*. We expect them to grow and become responsible on literally concrete ground."[11] The concept of imprisonment has evolved over centuries, and prison as an institution is a relatively recent development. Social unrest in the 1960s made more Americans aware of this generally ignored institution and the grievances of prisoners, many of whom brought class action suits to protest their overcrowded, inhumane conditions. Since publication of the first edition of this anthology, however, increased incarceration rates and the growth of the prison industrial complex have appreciably worsened the prospects for imprisoned women and have created new barriers separating them from mainstream America. Drawing upon her extensive work with women at Bedford Hills Correctional Facility, Superintendent Elaine Lord states, "There are no 'good' prisons; some are simply more humane than others."[12]

Prisons before the eighteenth century were largely holding places for the condemned before execution; loss of liberty was not itself a punishment. Foucault describes the shifting locus of power from the king to society in the treatment of offenders in France.[13] Placing this shift in the eighteenth century's revolutionary ferment, he notes a transition from excessive demonstrations of the king's absolute power over the body of the offender during torture and execution, to society's discipline of the body of the offender by restriction of rights in prison.[14] Under either system, control over the body is the issue. And as prisons evolved as institutions reflecting and advancing an industrial society's goals, that control became more individualized. As society becomes more and more intent upon "normalizing" its members, explains Foucault, institutions such as schools, hospitals, the military, and prisons ensure this regulation at all levels. From the start, the purpose of prisons as institutions has been to reform deviants as well as to deprive them of liberty. The offender, no longer the enemy of the sovereign but rather a traitor or a social misfit, has to be made to conform.

With the establishment of a prison system, the individual offender became an object of scientific interest. Control of prisoner behavior was maintained by measuring the skull to identify criminal traits, classifying vices, probing social and psychological background, and observing every action.[15] In his classic study, *The Society of Captives*, Gresham Sykes presents prison as a totalitarian society that forces contact among many individuals. A "maximum security prison represents a social system in which an attempt is made to create and maintain total or almost total social control."[16]

A counterforce balancing prison's controls is reform. According to Foucault, this movement has proceeded simultaneously with prisons themselves: "The prison has always formed part of an active field in which projects, improvements, experiments, theoretical statements, personal evidence and investigations have proliferated. The prison institution has always been a focus of concern and debate."[17]

The history of reform in American prisons for women is distinctive in several ways. Historian Estelle Freedman explains that three principles characterized the independent movement for women's prison reform in the late nineteenth century: the separation of female from male prisoners, based upon the belief in women's moral superiority and men's corrupting influence; the provision of feminine care and facilities, based upon the concept of separate sexual spheres; and the management of women's prisons by female staff and administrators.[18]

Texts by women prisoners have played a part in the history of women's prison reform, with American Socialist Kate Richards O'Hare (*In Prison*) and British suffragette Lady Constance Lytton (*Prisons and Prisoners*) among the most notable writers who used their prison experience to advocate reform.[19] Recent, outspoken writings by female prisoners in America are part of this prison reform tradition that rejects stereotypes in an attempt to get to the heart of prison issues.

While reforms improved prison conditions for women, they also generated problems that continue to plague women's correctional institutions today. Training was restricted to moral and domestic education rather than useful occupational skills, even after twentieth-century criminologists began to discern the economic basis of female crime. To foster desirable domestic, maternal virtues, women's institutions were constructed as homelike cottages and located in rural areas far from urban corruption. This remoteness led to a lack of educational and training programs and isolation for prisoners whose families lived in the city.

During the past twenty years, increased rates of incarceration worldwide have inspired renewed energy in the movement to reform not just prisons, but the whole concept of imprisonment as the default solution to social problems. Angela Davis posits the rise of a "prison industrial complex," which generates income for those in power while it perpetuates the poverty/incarceration cycle that furnishes new prisoners for the system. She explains that this "complex" and the institutions it fosters are international:

> If I were to try to summarize my impressions of prison visits all over the world, and most of them have been to women's prisons, including three jails which I visited involuntarily, I would have to say that they are uncannily similar. I have always felt as if I am in the same place. No matter how far I have traveled across time and space—from 1970 to 2000, and from the Women's House of Detention in New York (where I was myself incarcerated) to the women's prison in Brasilia, Brazil—no matter how far, there is a strange sameness about prisons in general, and especially about women's prisons.[20]

The relative scarcity of prison texts by women can be partially explained by the historically small number of female prisoners. Internationally, women have always constituted a small segment of the total prison population. The significant point to note in the United States, however, is that the "imprisonment binge"[21] has resulted in rates of female incarceration that exceed those of men. The first edition of this anthology cited United States Department of Justice figures for 1981 showing that the 14,000 women in state and federal prisons accounted for only 4 percent of the total prison population.[22] Criminologist Meda Chesney-Lind reports that 1997 numbers are close to 80,000, and that women now represent 6.4 percent of the total prison population.[23] Whether or not this burgeoning incarceration rate increases the amount of women's prison writing remains to be seen; what is already clear is that its adverse effects on prison conditions for women have contributed to the increasingly politicized and assertive nature of recent women's prison writing.

Who is the female prisoner today? Chesney-Lind, among others, reports that she is likely to be a woman of color with a history of physical and sexual abuse, and a mother caring for her children at the time of her arrest. Her offense is most often nonviolent in nature, with drug-related offenses accounting for a large proportion of increased arrests.[24] Superintendent Elaine Lord explains that the situation of these women is complex, involving the impact of their separation from their children, as well as their own physical and mental health issues and the trend toward longer sentences.[25]

Historically, women prisoners have confronted adverse conditions as well as negative stereotypes. One prisoner who addressed the problem of stereotypes in her writing was Louise Michel, heroine of the Paris Commune of 1871. Imprisoned many times throughout her life as a political activist, Michel empathized with imprisoned women who suffered from poverty and the prejudices of a criminal justice system that based its judgments upon sexist stereotypes. Her memoirs describe the nineteenth-century woman's predicament:

> All the women reading these memoirs must remember that we women are not judged the same way men are. When men accuse some other man of a crime, they do not accuse him of such a stupid one that an observer wonders if they are serious. But that is how they deal with a woman; she is accused of things so stupid they defy belief. If she is not duped by the claims of popular sovereignty put forth to delude people, or if she is not fooled by the hypocritical concessions which hoodwink most women, she will be indicted. Then, if a woman is courageous, or if she grasps some bit of knowledge easily, men claim she is only a "pathological" case.[26]

Thus, women were viewed as inferior either morally or mentally, but in either case they were seen as controlled by their biology. The consequences of those stereotypes are still being felt by imprisoned women.

Classical studies of the female criminal, from that of Lombroso and Ferrero (1895) to that of Otto Pollak (1950; 1961), employ stereotypes.[27] Pollak is to be credited for bringing women's criminology to the attention of contemporary researchers, but even he accepted myths about women. The myth of women's emotional weakness and irrational nature led to several problems and inequities in their treatment within the criminal justice system. Writers like Pollak perpetuated the theory that males in control of court and correctional systems gave women chivalrous treatment. In his theory of the "masked character of female crime," he attributes women's low rate of reported crime to what he considers their innate ability to deceive, manifested, he contends, when they feign pleasure during sex.[28] His influence has been widespread; a rather sensational study of women's crime, *How Could She Do That?*, Edith deRahm made a similar statement in 1969:

> Among insects, the female of certain species is more deadly than the male; among human beings, her poison is of but equal potency, but when she chooses to use it, the victim is often caught unaware, for her sting is well concealed.[29]

Continuing in this tradition, journalist Patricia Pearson in 1997 published the sensationally titled *When She Was Bad: How and Why Women Get Away with Murder,* arguing that "the justice system has a host of exonerative excuses for female behavior," which justify its chivalrous approaches toward women's acts of violence.[30] Her foregrounding of a few high-profile, anomalous cases to prove the point that women are capable of violence diverts the public's attention from the daily violence done in the name of justice to families of a growing number of women imprisoned for nonviolent offenses.

The Convergence of Two Marginal Traditions— Women's Literature and Prison Literature

Readers must consider women's prison literature in the context of two separate traditions in order to understand the silence of most imprisoned women and the obscurity of most texts they have managed to write. The first tradition is that of women's literature, whose works have increasingly entered the accepted literary canon over the past twenty years. The second tradition is that of prison literature, whose "respectability" is far more problematic; despite a recent surge of interest in "prison literature," that term for most critics has denoted works by male prisoners or literature by nonprisoners who treat the subject of prison metaphorically. Discussing women's literature and prison literature in the same context offers possibilities for rich discoveries, for each helps to explain the historical marginality of the other.

Before the eighteenth century's establishment of imprisonment as a form of punishment, broadsides and pamphlets recorded the lives and executions of criminals and the condemned. Foucault notes the ambiguity of these texts. They served those in power as a form of ideological control over the people by presenting examples of crime, punishment, and repentance. On the other hand, they transformed criminals into folk heroes who achieved glory even in their infamy. With the rise of prisons and the changing perception of crime from offense against the ruler to betrayal of society, a new literature of crime supplanted these broadsides. Accounts of crimes by the masses were relegated to the newspapers, while the new literature glorified crime as a fine art, practiced by the great and powerful classes and epitomized by the intellectual confrontation between criminal and detective. As the institution of prison began to objectify prisoners in its discipline process, their biographies left the pages of heroic folk literature and entered the charts of case studies.[31]

Literature written in prison, like earlier works written in cells or dungeons that were holding places before punishment, was mostly written by educated political prisoners. Many of these works have become accepted as part of the world's great literature, and their authors, almost exclusively male, are noteworthy historical and literary figures: Mohandas Gandhi, Oscar Wilde, Silvio Pellico, Miguel de Cervantes, Saint Thomas More, François Villon, and Jean Genet. During World War II Isidore Abramowitz compiled *The Great Prisoners: The First Anthology of Literature Written in Prison;* he saw prison writing as an inspirational testimony to human endurance and hope: "If the great names appear here, and in some of the great papers and manifestos of the spirit, it is because what began as an experimental formula for exploring a bypath of literature flowered into an odd but effective commentary on our intellectual adventure in the west."[32] Abramowitz takes the traditional Western male perspective and gives little attention to women and Third World writers. However, his point may be adapted to explain the significance of women's prison writing, which makes "an odd but effective commentary" on women's intellectual adventure.

Analysis of women's prison literature is aided by H. Bruce Franklin's discussion of American prison literature by black males. This body of works combines two major streams of convict narrative in America: slave narratives and personal confessionals of an individual's life in crime. Few political prisoners before early twentieth-century anarchists wrote autobiographies, but Franklin finds that by the mid-nineteenth century, confessionals by common criminals had turned from their emphasis on moral example or mere entertainment to protests of social injustice. The choice of the term "prisoner" over the traditional label "criminal" and the objection to being identified by number demonstrate this awakening political consciousness. By the 1920s, works demonstrating prisoners' humanity, intelligence, and social concerns began to threaten prison authorities, who attempted to suppress prison writing during the Great Depression. Few works by women prisoners were published because, Franklin theorizes, few women were imprisoned, and their crimes, stemming from dismal poverty, did not lend themselves to descriptions of adventure.[33]

Until the twentieth century, the majority of prison narratives in America were written from white male perspectives. However, in the twentieth century, works by black American prisoners became prominent. In these works the white prison narrative tradition joined with black slave narratives that focused on the slave's awakening consciousness. Yet, the special perspective of the slaves' writings led to a basic difference in the prison works of black and white men. While white prison writers began with an emphasis on the individual "I" and later recognized the suppression of prison's social subclass and of workers in general, black prison writers began with the knowledge that prison was an updated form of slavery meant to control a whole people, not only an individual. The latter point of view generated a "collective aesthetic" that identifies the writer as a representative of the people rather than as a solitary artist. Franklin explains that this aesthetic often conflicts with generally accepted literary standards, for its emphasis is often on the power of the text to motivate its readers to action rather than on originality and literary artifice.[34]

To what extent are women's prison texts analogous to those of black men? Both differ from the white masculine mode of writing from a position of power. Though works by women prisoners before the twentieth century often turned inward to the self, women's contemporary prison texts have a strong similarity to black men's writing in the growing trend toward women's solidarity. However, while a comparison with the tradition of prison literature, especially that of blacks, gives insight into characteristics of women's prison literature, it should be noted that the most widely acclaimed works in the prison tradition are written by men. Therefore, attention to the *female* literary tradition, itself marginal, is needed to complement the perspective gained from reading prison texts by black men.

As a group, and to a large extent as individuals, women prison authors are among the most forgotten writers, epitomizing the plight of the silenced female writer. In the starkest sense the woman prisoner lacks Virginia Woolf's "room of one's own" and must contend with a lack of privacy, money, and education and the demoralizing effects of anonymity. The general lack of decent writing conditions for women is acute in a woman's prison, where regimentation and dreary routine sap creative energy, and where privacy loses all meaning. Most female prisoners, who generally have a below-average formal education, do not express themselves in writing. For most poor and minority women prisoners, writing was not seen as an option before imprisonment, and once released, these women usually face the same problems of basic survival that they knew before incarceration, and have little time, encouragement, or motivation to write their prison stories.

In *Silences* Tillie Olsen calls class, economic circumstance, and race "those other traditional silencers of humanity."[35] Women prisoners, with the exception of some political activists, display a unique combination of all those elements that work against expression and preclude acceptance of their work by the literary establishment, which has otherwise become more hospitable to women's works in general. Women prison writers have not, overall, shared in this more flexible canon or joined the conversation of women who consider themselves writers. Even if a woman prisoner from a background of poverty does succeed in publishing her work, she is likely to experience the "one-book phenomenon" Olsen describes. Ex-prisoners may be unproductive writers because, even when the prison experience gives the individual an unprecedented opportunity and the motivation to write, the released woman meets a hostile society that barely grants her employment or the means to survive; the writing of her memoirs has no place in this new life. She becomes the most extreme victim of Olsen's "discontinuity," the tendency of women to be easily distracted by everyday demands or others' needs.[36]

Just as the literary canon once admitted only a few elite women writers, so the prison writing of only famous women—Rosa Luxemburg, Emma Goldman, Dorothy Day—is readily acknowledged today as part of our cultural history. Feminist literary critics, however, have shown that beyond the works of the few elite writers lies a rich diversity of women's writing, and women's prison texts promise an analogous discovery of works that continue to be written today.

Feminist critics find that women writers who do break the silence often express their ideas through a deceptive code.[37] French women's prison texts, according to Gelfand, clearly demonstrate this coding technique. These female writers do not angrily challenge society, as in classic male prison texts:

> . . . rather than engage in an overt dialectic with the values of their times, women, who have never created those values, covertly subvert and contest them; instead of seeking to give wholeness to an incoherent world, women search within themselves for unity; and, far from attempting to conquer hostile space by appropriating it, women generally observe and respect it. Indirection and coded contestation, a search for self, and an acknowledgement of surroundings characterize women's prison writing.[38]

Increasingly, today's women prison writers do not code their images; the prison is direct and real. As the "titanic outcast," to use critic Nina Auerbach's term for the fallen woman in literature,[39] the imprisoned female writer assumes a sort of freedom and power in her ability to create without the deception of codes. The use of forthright, uncoded statements is found in the writings of many contemporary prisoners, as well as in works by earlier prisoners who wrote from a firm religious or political conviction. Consider the proclamation of Black Panther Ericka Huggins:

> How often do women awake
> in the prison of marriage,
> of solitary motherhood
> alone and forgotten [40]

Huggins's prison is a literal one, and she calls upon her sisters, black and white, to acknowledge that theirs is quite literal too. Ironically, if the woman prisoner is afforded the opportunity to write, her work often reveals her situation more directly than does that of the woman on the outside. She is, in a sense, more free to write truthfully. For imprisoned women, the example of other women who have described their prison experiences to the world can be especially meaningful, and from this female subculture, a body of literature with its own characteristics has arisen.

After a few days we were taken to prison, and I grew frightened, for I had never known such darkness. Oh grim day!—intense heat, because of the crowds, extortions by soldiers. Above all, I was tormented with anxiety there, on account of my child.

Then Tertius and Pomponius, those consecrated deacons who were looking after us, arranged by a bribe that they let us out into a better, cooler part of the prison for a few hours. Coming out of the dungeon, everyone began to move freely; I breast-fed my child, who was already weak with hunger.[41]

This passage from "The Passion of Saint Perpetua," a third-century Christian martyr from Carthage, vividly illustrates qualities that separate women's from men's prison writing. Perpetua's interest is in the concrete reality of the prison environment and especially in her relationship with those who are close to her. As one critic explains, hers is "the Christian woman's point of view, with its constant references to child-bearing, nursing, food, the drinking of milk, and so on."[42] Her focus is simultaneously upon eternity and the moment, with its physical discomforts and family responsibilities.

Most readers' impressions of prison writing come from the dominant tradition of the famous male prison authors, represented in general literature as well as in prison anthologies. Richard Lovelace's poem "To Althea from Prison," with its famous line "Stone walls do not a prison make," is a staple of British literature anthologies. It also graces the title page of John Alfred Langford's more specialized 1861 anthology, *Prison Books and Their Authors*. The editor includes only male writers and declares the works of these prisoners to be edifying reading: "Truly a noble record of the power of the mind to make its own kingdom—a perennial teaching of the benign influence of sorrow, and a glorious monument of genius are the world's Prison Books."[43] Langford's comment imitates the literature it praises in its elevated, cerebral tone. In the mental transformation of her prison to a palace, Perpetua to some extent shares Lovelace's triumph; however, men's prison writings in general are more concerned with images of transcendence and rebellion. Freedom has different meanings for Lovelace and Perpetua. Lovelace neglects the lover in his love poem in favor of a discourse on the abstract concept of freedom; freedom for Perpetua comes when she nurses her baby, as only then can she celebrate the paradox of a palatial prison.

A basic difference, then, separates male and female prison writers' treatment of the freedom/captivity opposition. The incarcerated male, aware of his separation from a distracting society, may view his imprisonment as a situation in which he is mentally free to write even though he is physically bound. He may claim that prison gives him genuine freedom. For the woman prisoner, this paradox is not at all a standard image, since she never knew on the outside the physical and social freedom that men enjoy. She does not share the luxury of verbal play with the word *freedom*. Instead, she records—perhaps for the first time—her understanding that she is and always has been a prisoner. While the male prisoner has exchanged literal freedom in society for a figurative freedom in prison, the female prisoner has traded virtual imprisonment in society for actual imprisonment. This explains the images of imprisonment and escape that are common in nineteenth-century literature by women who had never seen the inside of a prison,[44] and these images become quite literal in women's texts written behind bars and walls.

However, silenced by the lack of education and poverty that brought them to prison in the first place, and then by the sensory deprivation of the prison environment itself, the vast majority of women in prison do not write. "What are rights without means?" Tillie Olsen aptly quotes novelist Rebecca Harding Davis.[45] Estelle Freedman describes the problem this lack of a first person record presents for the researcher: "The most difficult problem in prison history is reconstructing the prisoner experience. Although quantitative data tell something about who went to prison and why, they do not record feelings. Most statements about prisoners come from reformers and officials, and thus must be read with care."[46] Kathryn Watterson explains that she hesitated to write *Women in Prison*, her study of daily life in women's correctional institutions, because she felt that this was a job for prisoners who could relate their experiences firsthand. But the women themselves encouraged her:

> As one older woman said, "Baby, you gotta be the voice for us. Cause according to society, we ain't got no voices. Numbers can't talk—everybody knows that. Besides that, we get so used to this whole thing we can't even see a lot of it. It's too close. You got some perspective.
>
> We haven't never had the chance to tell our side of the story," another jail-weary woman said. . . . "I always thought I'd try to write a book about all this but I never got past the title: *Jail Ain't Shit*."[47]

What, then, motivates the relatively few women prisoners who do write? Their work functions on personal, social, and political levels—sometimes simultaneously—and their intended audiences vary with their purposes. It is instructive to look in two directions simultaneously: at points that unify these texts, and at individual distinctions. Social and political circumstances and the woman's own background contribute to differences in writers' purposes. After experiencing several prison texts by women, however, a reader recognizes the special value of considering these writers as a *group* rather than as isolated authors of lost texts or as notable individuals. The sense of solidarity within the texts becomes increasingly strong in recent prison works, underscoring the communal nature of much of the writing.

On the most personal level, women prisoners write because they believe their experience is worth expressing, and they may or may not envision any outside reader among their contemporaries or posterity. They write to confirm their own sense of worth, which is essential for any woman writer, but especially empowering for the female outcast, relegated to one of society's most degrading institutions. For Patricia McConnel, imprisoned in a number of American jails and in the Federal Penitentiary for Women at Alderson, West Virginia, the impulse to write empowered her to advocate for prison reform. She did not come to prison as a political activist and she writes that she "deserved to be in jail." Witnessing the "extreme cruelty, both physical and psychological, of penal institutions" led her to write her short fiction long after her release: "I started writing these stories about 19 years ago to cleanse myself of horrors and to do a service for my society and women by bringing these conditions to light. . . . I have come to appreciate writing as a powerful tool for therapy and growth. I believe that in a very literal sense, it has saved me."[48]

The desire to vindicate herself before a hostile society motivates some authors. Texts written before the twentieth century, such as Madame Roland's memoirs from the French Revolution, tend to emphasize the writer's respectable femininity. Contemporary writers, like Egyptian feminist Nawal El Saadawi, on the other hand, may confront the prison system and declare their own integrity.

Commitment to a political, social, or religious cause inspires texts in which the writer's self receives little attention. These women enter prison with such self-confidence that they do not feel a need for self-justification. In this case, imprisonment encourages the woman to record her story, often to promote her cause. Nineteenth-century British suffragettes such as Lady Constance Lytton, for example, underwent frequent and often brutal imprisonment, which figured dramatically in the memoirs and histories they later wrote.[49] The work of women prisoners who write "resistance literature" from a standpoint of political consciousness is radical in its blurring of categories: political prisoners like Marilyn Buck and Assata Shakur regard nonpolitical prisoners as sisters who share the same grievances with respect to power.[50]

For some women, prison ironically opens doors to previously unrecognized talents. Precious Bedell, for example, discovered her voice in the Writing Workshop at Bedford Hills Correctional Facility, and her work exemplifies how prison can promote writing from silence. Writer Hettie Jones, who led that workshop, emphasized craft in the development of the writers; accepting that challenge, Bedell went on to win *Prison Life* magazine's First Prize for Drama in 1995 for her play, "Pieces."[51] For Diane Hamill Metzger, who is serving a life sentence in Pennsylvania, writing has been a constant companion and intellectual outlet over half a lifetime spent in prison. Her prose and poetry have won numerous awards and have provided an ongoing link with a world in which she courageously continues to participate: "I have made such a concerted effort not to let the world go on without me that I am probably more aware and informed of the happenings in the world than many of the people out there living in it!"[52]

The most basic reason for all prison writing is the human need to communicate. Choosing writing as a medium allows contact with a wider audience, but it stems from the same visceral need as do attempts to communicate through other means in prison. Although imprisonment itself forcibly separates the prisoner from her family, friends, and social environment, isolation can take much more extreme forms within the prison.

Human beings subjected to sensory deprivation and social isolation have always struggled to combat restricted communication. The panopticon, an early example of restriction, was an eighteenth-century architectural design by Jeremy Bentham that theorized a clever system of "communication" benefiting only the administration. From a central tower, all cells could be observed, but the prisoner could neither see the observer nor contact the prisoner in the next cell: "He is seen, but he does not see; he is the object of information, never a subject in communication," writes Foucault.[53] This isolation was a means of thought control as well as physical discipline, since the administration could monitor all ideas and messages conveyed to the prisoner—an architectural ideal implemented today in "supermax" prisons.

Wall tapping is the most ancient of all systems of prison communication. No mere cliché from romantic novels, this system has been responsible for saving the sanity, if not the lives, of prisoners throughout centuries around the globe. The British suffragettes defiantly tapped "No Surrender!" to encourage their sisters who were being forcibly fed. A striking story illustrating both the significance of wall tapping and the influence of one woman prison author on another comes from *Journey into the Whirlwind,* the memoirs of Eugenia Ginzburg, who was imprisoned in Stalin's prisons and camps for seventeen years. Ginzburg, at first ignorant of the code, could not benefit from the tapping of a fellow sufferer in the next cell. She launched her own life-sustaining communication after recalling an explanation of the code that she had read years earlier. Ginzburg's countrywoman Vera Figner had described in her memoirs the code she used to survive her twenty-year solitary confinement in the Schlüsselburg Fortress. Fifty years later, her message saved Ginzburg. In their memoirs, Vera Figner and Eugenia Ginzburg testify that wall tapping saved them by restoring the power to communicate. With communication came consciousness, strength, and pride in their intelligence. Writing, like the more basic medium of tapping, instills a sense of autonomy and pride.

For prisoners with the educational background, materials, and opportunity to write, communication may take a variety of forms, ranging in sophistication from the publishable book to the outlawed prison "kite," a communication medium in women's institutions.[54] Kites are notes that function as poetry, news, courtship, and political communication when they are passed between women.[55] The subversive nature of kites in the eyes of prison administrators became apparent in the trial of Ericka Huggins, when her messages to sister prisoners were exhibited in court as evidence against her.[56]

The woman who has the means to communicate through writing in prison must choose a form for her work. The overwhelming majority of women prisoners throughout the world and over the centuries have selected a form of life-writing—letters, diaries, memoirs, and autobiography. These forms are especially congenial if the woman did not write before imprisonment. For some, personal formats allow the self-justification that is their motivation for writing; for others, they enhance a bold affirmation of the writer's personality and beliefs.

In any case, life-writing displays a fascinating variety of ways that female prison writers create a "self" to sustain and express themselves during imprisonment.[57] In an environment where women too often are treated like children, the incarcerated woman writer can maintain some control over her world by ordering reality according to her own perceptions and organizing principles. In letters and memoirs she constructs a persona that, to varying degrees, can challenge the prevailing stereotypes of the woman prisoner.

Gelfand has shown that French women's prison texts generally follow confessional formats. Society often responds to female crime by accusing the woman of "desensitization" and a lack of femininity. An imprisoned woman can defend herself against unjust labels by writing a confessional text that presents a picture of an integrated, sensitive personality. In their defense before society, concludes Gelfand, many French women prison writers, from the eighteenth century to the present, actually reinforce female stereotypes to convey an impression of their social conformity to standards of acceptable female behavior. They *use* stereotypes for their own purposes, examining their own past lives and employing their knowledge of social conventions as a guide in their defense.[58]

Life-writing serves some imprisoned women as a means of working through the trauma of imprisonment and bearing witness to their experience.[59] The very fact of imprisonment impedes the prisoner's ability to work through the grief caused by her confinement and isolation from family. Sociologist P. J. Baunach explains that the institution of prison inhibits free expression and mutual support, constructing instead a contrary culture in which survival demands that prisoners "suspend emotional involvement."[60] Among society's institutions, prison demands a most extreme form of deception; prisoners must simultaneously deny and use their feelings to survive physically, emotionally, and mentally. "Jailface," Patricia McConnel explains, is the term prisoners use to describe the lack of affect with which the initiated protect themselves.[61] But writing helps some brave women to peel off the jailface and begin to come to terms with the private terror of their confinement. Explains Iris Bowen, imprisoned at Bedford Hills Correctional Facility, "I can disperse my pain through my pen."[62]

Two women prisoners facing execution—Krystyna Wituska, a Polish Resistance fighter, and Ethel Rosenberg, an American Communist accused of spying—chose the letter form for their writing. Condemned to the guillotine by the Nazis at age twenty-one, Wituska used correspondence to comfort her anxious family, and also to mature and develop mentally and spiritually. Readers encounter this young woman thinking through her philosophy of life and war, as death steadily approaches. During the Cold War in the United States, letters allowed Rosenberg to write her prison story boldly, under the guise of intimate communication with family and friends, with the expectation that the letters would be circulated among supporters and published to help support her children.

Besides life-writing, other forms are also used by women prison writers, particularly those who write to promote a cause or those who consider writing as their vocation or avocation. Journalism has provided one form, as in Agnes Smedley's 1918 account of her sister prisoners in the New York Tombs published in the socialist *New York Call*. Smedley's contemporary, American Socialist Kate Richards O'Hare, served a one-year sentence for protesting American involvement in World War I. O'Hare had clearly stated her intention to make a sociological study of her fellow prisoners, and in 1920 she published and submitted to the president of the United States her firsthand report on conditions and practices in the Missouri State Penitentiary.[63]

Impersonal approaches are a common choice of prisoners who write to advance a cause, such as the seventeenth-century Quaker women whose tracts detail their sufferings for their faith. Olya Roohizadegan offers a more contemporary example, in which her personal response to imprisonment in Iran is not nearly so important as her witness to the martyrdom of ten young Bahá'í women with whom she was imprisoned.

Many prisoners of both sexes have become conscious of the political aspects of the criminal justice system; in the United States, for example, a disproportionate number of male and female prisoners are black. Awareness of this fact leads some prison writers to abandon autobiographical forms and identify with the silenced prisoners around them. Such writers today often use literary genres of poetry, fiction, and drama, although over the centuries these have not generally been major forms of writing for women prisoners. In choosing these literary forms, as with expository writing, the author to some extent objectifies her personal experience of incarceration, this time projecting it onto a character or a scene or expressing it through the imaginative constructs of literature. Most women's prison poetry and fiction were written only recently, perhaps because prisoners today feel less need to justify or explore their lives in autobiographical forms.

Since the 1970s, poetry has become a popular genre for male as well as female prison writers, some of whom have had access to writing workshops sponsored by university or community groups. The poetry selections in this anthology by Carolyn Baxter (from the New York Correctional Facility for Women), Norma Stafford (from the California Institution for Women) and Bedell (from Bedford Hills) originated in workshops for women prisoners. The perspective of poetry written in the workshops varies with the personal styles and concerns of their members. The simple, declarative forms and vernacular diction of contemporary black poetry suit Baxter's purpose much more effectively than does the more self-directed mode of memoirs. In contrast, Stafford's poetry, closer to her personal pain, speaks for her sister prisoners by revealing her own struggles and victories.

Short fiction and novels are less common among women's prison texts, but fiction can be especially effective in helping the author achieve distance from her experience in order to communicate with those outside. McConnel, the recipient of a grant from the National Endowment for the Arts, published a collection of stories based upon her personal experiences as a prisoner in American prisons for women. It has taken years, she notes, to achieve the distance she feels is necessary to express her message, which, like that of Ericka Huggins' poetry, supports reform and declares unity with all who are oppressed.[64] McConnel's use of fiction rather than life-writing allows her to protest prison injustices as well as to affirm her faith in the survival of simple human decency in prison, without the risk of self-pity or self-absorption.

Life-writing, poetry, fiction, journalism—women's prison writing takes various forms. Form and content combine most powerfully in the collective voices of prison writing. Writing in her classic feminist study of motherhood, *Of Woman Born,* Adrienne Rich explains the potential power of women's shared experiences: "I believe increasingly that only the willingness to share private and sometimes painful experience can enable women to create a collective description of the world which will be truly ours."[65] Literary scholar Carolyn Heilbrun cites Rich's words and continues the conversation on the power of the collective female spirit:

> Women must turn to one another for stories; they must share the stories of their lives and their hopes and their unacceptable fantasies. . . . I do not believe that new stories will find their way into texts if they do not begin in oral exchanges among women in groups hearing and talking to one another. As long as women are isolated one from the other, not allowed to offer other women the most personal accounts of their lives, they will not be part of any narrative of their own.[66]

Heilbrun calls for women's mutual support as they exercise the "female impulse to power."[67] The prison application of this call to female community voiced by Rich and Heilbrun is profound. The community afforded by a writing workshop or women's program powerfully changes lives, if not circumstances, within the confines of prison. Selections in this anthology by Bedell, Stafford, Baxter, Chilean women prisoners, and Women of the AIDS Counseling and Education program at Bedford Hills all arise from writing done in community.

The theoretical basis for claiming literary merit for writing done in community has recently engaged critics of women's autobiographical writing. Using the term "resistance literature," Barbara Harlow describes, for example, political prisoners' memoirs as "collective documents, testimonies written by individuals to their common struggle."[68] The inherent paradox of considering autobiography—that most "individual" of genres—as a *communal* form is a crucial point.[69] Caren Kaplan calls women's prison memoirs an "out-law genre," threatening to destabilize the "power dynamics" of conventional autobiography.[70] This celebration of collaboration resounds in recent writing coming from today's women's prisons.

The varied selections in this anthology are organized thematically. Six parts highlight major concerns of women's prison writing, and selections are arranged chronologically within their respective parts. These six categories are by no means the only divisions appropriate to the study of women's prison literature, nor do the selections always fit neatly into one category. However, these parts are intended to highlight thematic differences among the selections; notes following each part cross-reference additional relevant titles from other parts in the anthology. Diversity in nationality, era, point of view, form, and style complements the unity of the six fundamental, recurring themes and concerns. The selections are further united by the writers' choice of realism over abstraction, whether the subject is prison food or spiritual growth.

Although contemporary women prisoners continue to write about each of the six themes, those highlighted in the first two parts have the oldest heritage. Part 1 focuses on women prisoners' attempts to oppose misogyny, set the record straight, and vindicate themselves before their families, their contemporaries, or posterity. In part 2 the writers' causes and beliefs take precedence over accounts of personal suffering or injustice.

Parts 3 through 6 deal directly with the writers' imprisonment. Part 3 offers several views of prison conditions, procedures, and deprivations in various countries. This topic is so basic that it forms the background for almost all prison writing. Part 4 examines coping strategies and methods of psychological survival within women's prisons. The writers here are concerned with combating attempts to break spirit and body. In part 5 writers explore the effects of their imprisonment on family relationships, particularly the mutual distress felt by divided mothers and children.

Part 6 concludes the anthology with a theme that receives increasing attention in recent prison writing: solidarity among sister prisoners. One intriguing aspect of women's prison literature is its theme of relationships among women, as opposed to the romance and marriage theme prominent in women's novels. Imprisoned women do, of course, write about their relationships with children, spouses, lovers, parents, prison guards, and administrators, but perhaps nowhere else in women's literature is the opportunity so rich to explore the dynamics of women's friendships, conflicts, prejudices, and mutual support.

The writing of women prisoners continues to reside in the margins of the literary canon—a curiosity, an anomaly, an oversight. Two considerations might serve to foreground these works: attention to the critical assessment of their quality, and recognition that, taken collectively, they constitute a literary tradition. Literary critics who venture beyond the scope of current scholarly interest in prison literature to acknowledge that writing from the world's prisons includes works by women too, might consider this line from James Joyce's *Ulysses:* "The supreme question about a work of art is out of how deep a life does it spring."[71] Readers would search far to find works springing from a deeper life than does women's prison writing.

The question of a literary tradition addresses the archival work that this anthology hopes to inspire. Two resources to guide the reader's research are the annotated bibliography of writings by women prisoners and a list of connections among women prison writers. The existence of linkages among women prison writers is a fact. A kind of solidarity, transcending time and place, links women prisoners through the works they have written or those that have been written about them. Names of earlier prisoners echo in later works, forming an informal *Who's Who* of women prisoners through the ages. Tracing the influences is fascinating. Ethel Rosenberg, referring to her martyrdom, compares herself to Joan of Arc, while Ericka Huggins and Socialist Elizabeth Gurley Flynn both are inspired by Rosenberg herself. Angela Davis and Huggins sustain each other through their writings while incarcerated in separate prisons. Eugenia Ginzburg is joined by British suffragette Evelyn Sharp and British-Hungarian physician Edith Bone in admiration of Vera Figner. While in New York's Tombs prison Agnes Smedley met Mollie Steimer and corresponded with Margaret Sanger, two activists whose work is also noted by Emma Goldman. Moreover, during her imprisonment, Goldman formed a supportive friendship with Kate Richards O'Hare and read an account of the tzar's prisons by Catherine Breshkovskaya, "Little Grandmother" of the Russian Revolution. In addition, Goldman was influenced by Figner and Louise Michel, and she regretted the brutal death of Rosa Luxemburg. Assata Shakur writes of her admiration and respect for Lolita Lebrón.

Researchers who examine women's prison texts, however, must look beyond these direct citations and traceable influences among writers. This literary tradition should be seen in terms of a community of women writers, perhaps modeled upon the communities of support that exist among writers in some women's prisons. Poet Norma Stafford, commenting upon the inclusion of her poems in this anthology, writes, "To have my work stand alongside the 'Great Ones' is incredible to me."[72] The hallmark of this tradition is resistance, sometimes expressed in the overt call to activism, sometimes more quietly demonstrated in the courageous act of writing itself.

Whether held in solitary confinement or meeting together in writing workshops, these female prisoners are obviously not alone. Their connections through writing argue for the existence of not only a *body* but also a *tradition* of women's prison literature. This anthology honors and itself testifies to the collective spirit of a tradition in women's prison literature: Each lost, scattered, or unknown selection printed here, and far more titles cited in the annotated bibliography, offer individual gifts to the reader. Considered *together* they testify powerfully to the real experience of imprisoned women worldwide. Vera Figner speaks for all women prison writers as she explains her motivation and the mutual benefits of writing: "Yet though my book speaks of the past and contributes nothing to the practical life of the present moment, a time will come when it will be of use. The dead do not rise, but there is resurrection in books."[73] Women prisoners have been writing a "narrative of their own"[74] for hundreds of years; they have been sharing that narrative, orally and in writing, within prison workshops for decades. It is now time for women *outside* prison walls to listen.

NOTES

The first epigraph to the introduction is taken from Anna Akhmatova, *Requiem and Poem without a Hero,* trans. D. M. Thomas (London: Paul Elek, 1976), 23. The second epigraph is taken from Karlene Faith, "Reflections on Inside/Out Organizing," *Social Justice* 27, no. 3 (2000): 158–67 (160).

1. Carolyn Forché, American poet and journalist, notes the dialectic of poetry as art and as social message and states that their division is false, in "Sensibility and Responsibility," in *The Writer and Human Rights,* ed. Toronto Arts Group for Human Rights (Garden City, N.Y.: Anchor/Doubleday, 1983), 22–25.

2. Norval Morris and David J. Rothman, eds. *The Oxford History of the Prison: The Practice of Punishment in Western Society* (New York: Oxford University Press, 1998).

3. Ioan Davies, *Writers in Prison* (Oxford: Basil Blackwell, 1990), 16.

4. Leslie Patrick, in "Ann Hinson: A Little-Known Woman in the Country's Premier Prison, Eastern State Penitentiary, 1831," *Pennsylvania History* 67, no. 3 (summer 2000) 361–72, states "The history of penal practices is and has been written almost exclusively from the perspective of those in a position of authority and those who were sympathetic to the use of imprisonment as a method to reduce criminal activity. Throughout the literature, prisoners remain either abstractions or absent—they have become imagined subjects confined by silence, yet victims first of circumstance and finally of history. Prisoners themselves did not help matters. Deliberately, perhaps, they left little to be discovered about their views on incarceration or about what they believed to be the causes of their criminality" (372).

5. Christian Parenti, *Lockdown America: Police and Prisons in the Age of Crisis.* (London: Verso, 2000), 181. Parenti quotes the term "TV therapy" from an article by prisoner Adrian Lomax, "Captive Audience," *In These Times,* 14 June 1998, 37–38.

6. Linda Wagner-Margin, *Telling Women's Lives: The New Biography.* (New Brunswick: Rutgers University Press, 1994), 132. See also Julia Watson's discussion of "unspeakable differences," in "Unspeakable Differences: The Politics of Gender in Lesbian and Heterosexual Women's Autobiography," in *De/Colonizing the Subject: The Politics of Gender in Women's Autobiography,* ed. Sidonie Smith and Julia Watson (Minneapolis: University of Minnesota Press, 1992), 139–68.

7. Angela Davis, foreword to *Behind the Razor Wire: Portrait of a Contemporary American Prison System,* by Michael Jacobson Hardy (New York: New York University Press, 1999), xi.

8. Michel Foucault, *Discipline and Punish: The Birth of the Prison,* trans. Alan Sheridan (New York: Vintage, 1979).

9. Elissa Gelfand, "Imprisoned Women: Toward a Socio-Literary Feminist Analysis," *Yale French Studies* 62 (1981): 185–203.

10. Barbara Owen, *"In the Mix": Struggle and Survival in a Women's Prison* (Albany: SUNY Press, 1998), 4. See also Andi Rierden, *The Farm: Life Inside a Women's Prison* (Amherst: University of Massachusetts Press, 1997), for a study of the lives of incarcerated women. A recent anthology offers articles on women's imprisonment: Sandy Cook and Susanne Davies, *Harsh Punishment: International Experiences of Women's Imprisonment* (Boston: Northeastern University Press, 1999). See also Barbara Raffel Price and Natalie J. Sokoloff's anthology of articles, *The Criminal Justice System and Women: Offenders, Victims, and Workers,* 2d ed. (New York: McGraw-Hill, 1995), in particular the following articles: Natalie J. Sokoloff and Barbara Raffel Price, "The Criminal Law and Women," 11–29; Dorie Klein, "The Etiology of Female Crime: A Review of the Literature," 30–53; Darrell Steffensmeier, "Trends in Female Crime: It's Still a Man's World," 89–104; Meda Chesney-Lind, "Rethinking Women's Imprisonment: A Critical Examination of Trends in Female Incarceration," 105–117; and Coramae Richey Mann, "Women of Color and the Criminal Justice System," 118–135.

11. Kathryn [Burkhart] Watterson, *Women in Prison: Inside the Concrete Womb* (Garden City, N.Y.: Doubleday, 1973, 425; rev. ed., Boston: Northeastern University Press, 1996).

12. Elaine Lord, "A Prison Superintendent's Perspective on Women in Prison," *Prison Journal* 75: 2 (June 1995) 257–69.

13. Foucault, *Discipline and Punish.*

14. *On Crimes and Punishments* (1764), by an aristocratic Italian, Cesare Beccaria, is acknowledged to have been a leading force in the movement toward humane punishment in the West. Beccaria concludes his treatise with this general theorem about appropriate punishment: "In order for punishment not to be, in every instance, an act of violence of one or of many against a private citizen, it must be essentially public, prompt, necessary, the least possible in the given circumstances, proportionate to the crimes, dictated by the laws." *On Crimes and Punishments,* trans. Henry Paolucci (Indianapolis: Bobbs-Merrill, 1963), 99.

15. Foucault, *Discipline and Punish.*

16. Gresham M. Sykes, *The Society of Captives: A Study of a Maximum Security Prison* (1958; reprint, New York: Atheneum, 1968), xii–xiv.

17. Foucault, *Discipline and Punish,* 235.

18. Estelle B. Freedman, *Their Sisters' Keepers: Women's Prison Reform in America, 1830–1930* (Ann Arbor: University of Michigan Press, 1981), 45–46. See also Nicole Rafter, *Partial Justice: Women, Prisons, and Social Control* (1985; 2d ed., New Brunswick: Transaction, 1990), for a discussion of women's prison reform.

19. See the annotated bibliography for full references to O'Hare and Lytton, and see the Lytton selection in this anthology. Foucault, in *Discipline and Punish,* 234–35, notes that there is a history of former prisoners taking a hand in prison reform through accounts of personal experience.

20. Angela Davis, "Prison as a Border: A Conversation on Gender, Globalization, and Punishment," interview by Gina Dent, *Signs* 26, no.4 (2001): 1235–41 (1237).

21. For a discussion of the "imprisonment binge," see Barbara Owen, "Women and Imprisonment in the United States: The Gendered Consequences of the U.S. Imprisonment Binge," in *Harsh Punishment: International Experiences of Women's Imprisonment,* ed. Sandy Cook and Susanne Davies (Boston: Northeastern University Press, 1999), 81, where she refers to John Irwin and James Austin, *It's about Time: America's Imprisonment Binge,* 2d ed. (Belmont, Calif.: Brooks Cole, 1997). Also see Joseph T. Hallinan, *Going Up the River: Travels in a Prison Nation* (New York: Random House, 2001). David Garland, in *The Culture of Control: Crime and Social Order in Contemporary Society* (Chicago: University of Chicago Press, 2001), discusses the increasingly punitive nature of contemporary society in the United States and Britain.

Lori B. Girshick, in *No Safe Haven: Stories of Women in Prison* (Boston: Northeastern University Press, 1999), presents results of her interviews with imprisoned women and argues for alternatives to incarceration. Russ Immarigeon and Meda Chesney-Lind, in *Women's Prisons: Overcrowded and Overused,* (San Francisco: National Council on Crime and Delinquency, 1992), report on the increased rates of women's imprisonment and call for community-based alternatives to incarceration.

22. Statistics are from Rafter, *Partial Justice: Women in State Prisons, 1800-1935,* 1st ed., (Boston: Northeastern University Press, 1985), 177.

23. Meda Chesney-Lind, "The Forgotten Offender," *Corrections Today* 60, no. 7 (December 1998): 1.

24. Chesney-Lind, "The Forgotten Offender." See also Owen, "Women and Imprisonment," 85, and Allen J. Beck, "Prison and Jail Inmates at Midyear 1999," *Bureau of Justice Statistics Bulletin* (Washington, D.C.: U. S. Dept. of Justice, Office of Justice Programs, April 2000).

25. Lord, "A Prison Superintendent's Perspective on Women in Prison," 257–69.

26. Louise Michel, *The Red Virgin: Memoirs of Louise Michel,* trans. Bullitt Lowry and Elizabeth Ellington Ganter (University, Ala. : University of Alabama Press, 1981), 139.

27. Carol Smart, *Women, Crime and Criminology: A Feminist Critique* (London: Routledge & Kegan Paul, 1976), 27.

28. Otto Pollak, *The Criminality of Women* (Philadelphia: University of Pennsylvania Press, 1950; reprint, New York: Barnes, 1961), 10.

29. Edith deRham, *How Could She Do That?: A Study of the Female Criminal* (New York: Potter, 1969), 337.

30. Patricia Pearson, *When She Was Bad: How and Why Women Get Away with Murder* (New York: Penguin, 1998), 62.

31. Foucault, *Discipline and Punish,* 66–69, 192–93.

32. Isidore Abramowitz, ed., *The Great Prisoners: The First Anthology of Literature Written in Prison* (1946; reprint, Salem, N.H.: Ayer, 1977), xviii.

33. H. Bruce Franklin, *Prison Literature in America: The Victim as Criminal and Artist* (Westport, Conn.: Lawrence Hill, 1982), 124–78, 236–37.

34. Franklin, *Prison Literature in America,* 100–101,142–49, 236–37, 243–51.

35. Tillie Olsen, *Silences* (New York: Dell, 1978), 24.

36. An excellent dramatization of the released female prisoner's economic and social plight is *Getting Out,* a play by Marsha Norman (New York: Dramatists Play Service, 1979).

37. See, for example, the classic literary study by Sandra M. Gilbert and Susan Gubar, *The Madwoman in the Attic: The Woman Writer and the Nineteenth-Century Literary Imagination* (New Haven: Yale University Press, 1979), 75. Gubar had direct experience teaching in a women's prison. See her account in Gubar and Ann Hedin, "A Jury of Our Peers: Teaching and Learning in the Indiana Women's Prison," *College English* 43, no. 8 (December 1981): 779–89.

38. Elissa Gelfand, *Imagination in Confinement: Women's Writings from French Prisons* (Ithaca, N.Y.: Cornell University Press, 1983), 110.

39. Nina Auerbach, *Woman and the Demon: The Life of a Victorian Myth* (Cambridge, Mass.: Harvard University Press, 1982), 159–61.

40. Ericka Huggins, see full text and reference in the Huggins selection in this anthology.

41. "Passion of Saint Perpetua," see full text and reference in the Saint Perpetua section in this anthology.

42. Herbert Musurillo, *The Acts of the Christian Martyrs* (Oxford: Clarendon Press, 1972), xxvi.

43. John Alfred Langford, *Prison Books and Their Authors* (London: William Tegg, 1861), 5.

44. See Victor Brombert, *The Romantic Prison: The French Tradition* (Princeton: Princeton University Press, 1978), for a discussion of the image of the prison as a paradoxical space of freedom, as used in French texts written by men from the Romantic era to the present. The image changed in the twentieth century to that of the prisoner as social rebel. See Gilbert and Gubar, *The Madwoman in the Attic*, on images of imprisonment and escape in nineteenth-century literature. The image may be that of the figurative prison of madness and domesticity.

45. Rebecca Harding Davis, quoted in Tillie Olsen, "Rebecca Harding Davis: Her Life and Times," afterword to *Life in the Iron Mills* (New York: The Feminist Press, 1972); reprinted in Olsen, *Silences* (New York: Delta, 1978), 49.

46. Freedman, *Their Sisters' Keepers*, 100.

47. Watterson, *Women in Prison*, 16.

48. Patricia McConnel, letter to Judith Scheffler, 2 March 1985.

49. For a discussion of the suffragettes' awareness of their own worth as their motivation for writing, see Kathleen Dehler, "The Need to Tell All: A Comparison of Historical and Modern Feminist 'Confessional' Writing," in *Feminist Criticism: Essays on Theory, Poetry and Prose*, ed. Cheryl L. Brown and K. Olson (Metuchen, N.J.: Scarecrow, 1978), 339–52. (Throughout this anthology *suffragette*, rather than *suffragist*, is used to refer to the women who worked in the militant arm of the British woman suffrage movement. *Suffragist* was a more general term used for supporters of woman suffrage. See Caroline J. Howlett, "Writing on the Body? Representation and Resistance in British Suffragette Accounts of Forcible Feeding," *Genders*, 23 (1996): 3–41, note 5, p. 37.

50. See Barbara Harlow, *Resistance Literature* (New York: Methuen, 1987), 140, for a discussion of "[t]he merging of the categories of common law prisoners and political detainees."

51. See the selection of Bedell's poetry and an excerpt from this play in this anthology.

52. Diane Hamill Metzger, "The Top of the Well." See full text and reference in the Metzger selection in this anthology.

53. Foucault, *Discipline and Punish*, 200.

54. Lee H. Bowker, "Gender Differences in Prison Subcultures," in *Women and Crime in America*, ed. Lee H. Bowker (New York: Macmillan, 1981), 41.

55. Rose Giallombardo, in *Society of Women: a Study of a Women's Prison* (New York: Wiley, 1966), 142–43, discusses the importance of these functions of kites.

56. Donald Freed, *Agony in New Haven* (New York: Simon & Schuster, 1973), 139–40.

57. Autobiography theory is currently a thriving area of literary criticism, and much of it is relevant to women's prison writing. Margo Culley, in her edited collection of essays on women's autobiography, *American Women's Autobiography: Fea(s)ts of Memory* (Madison: University of Wisconsin Press, 1992), 3, describes this area of criticism: "The most pressing concerns of contemporary scholars—genre and gender as culturally inscribed; the construction of the self within language systems; the referentiality of language itself; the nature of subjectivity, authority, and agency; the problematics of making meaning and making history; theories of time, memory, and narrative—all absorb critics of autobiography."

58. Gelfand, *Imagination in Confinement*, especially 120–21.

59. For a discussion of women's writing and trauma, see Suzette A. Henke, *Shattered Subjects: Trauma and Testimony in Women's Life-Writing* (New York: St. Martin's Press, 1998).

60. Phyllis Jo Baunach, "You Can't Be a Mother and Be in Prison . . . Can You?" in *The Criminal Justice System and Women*, ed. Barbara Raffel Price and Natalie J. Sokoloff (New York: Clark Boardman, 1982),158.

61. For a discussion of "jailface," see Patricia McConnel's short story "Sing Soft, Sing Loud" in this anthology.

62. Iris Bowen, quoted in "Sestina: Reflections on Writing," collaborative writing from the women of the Bedford Hills Writing Workshop, in *Doing Time: 25 Years of Prison Writing*, ed. Bell Gale Chevigny (New York: Arcade, 1999), 114–18.

63. See Smedley's character sketches in this anthology. The O'Hare reference is cited in the annotated bibliography. For a discussion of prison journalism history, see James McGrath Morris, *Jailhouse Journalism: The Fourth Estate Behind Bars* (Jefferson, N. C.: McFarland, 1998).

64. Patricia McConnel, letter to Judith Scheffler, 1 April 1983.

65. Adrienne Rich, *Of Woman Born: Motherhood as Experience and Institution* (1976; reprint, New York: Norton, 1986), 16.

66. Carolyn Heilbrun. *Writing a Woman's Life* (New York: Ballantine, 1988), 44, 46. Jane Adam, in "A Place of Adventure," *Concrete Garden* 4 (1996): 28–53, refers to Heilbrun's comments on women's collective exchange of their stories. She compares this to her observations as a volunteer at Paradise House, a halfway house for women in Buffalo, New York.

67. Heilbrun, *Writing a Woman's Life*, 44. Heilbrun states that she is quoting Nancy Miller.

68. Harlow, *Resistance Literature*, 120.

69. An influential early example of communal, activist writing, not from prisons, was *This Bridge Called My Back: Writings by Radical Women of Color*, ed. Cherríe Moraga and Gloria Anzaldúa (New York: Kitchen Table, 1983). See Julia Watson's analysis of *This Bridge Called My Back* as an important early contribution to collective autobiography in "Toward an Anti-Metaphysics of Autobiography," in *The Culture of Autobiography: Constructions of Self-Representation*, ed. Robert Folkenflik (Stanford: Stanford University Press, 1993), 57–79. Carol Boyce Davies, in "Collaboration and the Ordering Imperative in Life Story Production," in *De/Colonizing the Subject: The Politics of Gender in Women's Autobiography*, ed. Sidonie Smith and Julia Watson (Minneapolis: University of Minnesota Press, 1992), 3–19, discusses collaboration with respect to women's "life stories, orally narrated and transferred to print." She labels this a "*crossover genre* that challenges the oral/written separations and unites these forms [orality and writing] as they maintain their distinct textualities" (7). Philippe Lejeune, in "The Autobiography of Those Who Do Not Write," in *On Autobiography*, ed. Philippe Lejeune, trans. Katherine Leary (Minneapolis: University of Minnesota Press, 1989), 185–215, discusses the multiple authors involved in "autobiographical collaborations" (186) and ethnographies, and raises relevant questions about how readers identify and define authority in autobiographies.

70. Caren Kaplan, "Resisting Autobiography: Out-Law Genres and Transnational Feminist Subjects," in *Women, Autobiography, Theory: A Reader*, ed. Sidonie Smith and Julia Watson (Madison: University of Wisconsin Press, 1998), 208–16.

71. James Joyce, *Ulysses* (New York: Random House, 1961), 185.

72. Norma Stafford, letter to Judith Scheffler, 10 August 2001.

73. Vera Figner, *Memoirs of a Revolutionist*, trans. Camilla Chapin Daniels (New York: International, 1927), 5.

74. Heilbrun, 46.

PART 1

'PRESERVE THE REMEMBRANCE OF WHAT I WAS':

VINDICATION OF SELF

They were as obdurate as rocks. I have always observed that the female, who seems to have been made for tenderness, and piety, and moral courage, when really depraved and fallen, is not only the wickedest, but the most hard and unmanageable of beings. —James Bradley Finley

In 1846 the Reverend James Bradley Finley, chaplain of Ohio Penitentiary, wrote this stereotyped description of the female prisoners he visited. Finley was not alone in his opinions; misogynous characterizations of imprisoned women are as old as prisons themselves.[1] In the face of such hostility and sexist criticism, some women who write of their imprisonment focus on self-justification. In fact, it is primarily this need to vindicate the self that motivates some women prisoners to write in the first place. Ostensibly, they write privately to family and friends or to a public audience of their contemporaries, but often these women also seek to circumvent the power that oppresses them by addressing a presumably more enlightened and just posterity.

Before she became one of history's most notable monarchs, England's Princess Elizabeth was a prisoner. Her half sister, Queen Mary, imprisoned her in 1554 as a check on her possible rivalry. Elizabeth's assertion of her innocence, reputedly written with a diamond on her prison window, underscores her unequivocal vow of allegiance to her half sister, the queen: "Much suspected by me,/Nothing proved can be./Quoth Elizabeth prisoner."[2] The princess's identity is that of a faithful subject; those who malign and unjustly imprison her cannot change the essence of her loyal self. Elizabeth succeeds to power by identifying with it. Young and vulnerable, but politically savvy, Elizabeth responds to accusations with a self-confidence that resonates in prison writings from other countries, in other times.

To write in self-vindication is to resist authority; a woman prisoner's relationship to power determines the extent to which she may do this directly. Ranging from statements of support for those in power to overt opposition, these works share a conviction that, though imprisoned, the writer's self has a value that transcends questions of guilt or innocence. In the following selections, from the eighteenth through the twentieth centuries, Madame Roland, Nawal El Saadawi, Mila Aguilar, and the women of the AIDS Counseling and Education (ACE) Program at Bedford Hills Correctional Facility in New York use writing to address power and assert their identities as women, not prisoners.[3]

Many female prisoners have written to combat criticisms that they are monsters or fallen women. In her study of French women's prison writings, Elissa Gelfand proposes that this motivation, based upon a conflict between individual self-image and social stereotypes, explains the solipsism of most eighteenth- and nineteenth-century prison texts by French women.[4] An example from the French Revolution is Madame Roland, wife of the French minister of the interior. A refined and educated woman, Madame Roland was offended by her imprisonment "in the midst of murderers and women of the town." In her memoirs, *An Appeal to Impartial Posterity*, she deplores her forced association with "this scum of the earth" and carefully presents her case as a respectable, feminine woman, wrongfully thrown among genuine criminals whose acts shame their sex. Roland defends herself by denouncing the women around her and implying her own moral superiority. She responds to sexism with classism.

Madame Roland purports to tell the truth to posterity in her memoirs, knowing that she cannot expect justice in her time. Her strategy is to offer an account of her exemplary character and past. She implies that, because she has led a virtuous life according to the prevailing social definition of femininity, and because she is so obviously superior to imprisoned prostitutes and criminals, her current predicament must be unjust.[5] As an intellectual force behind her husband and the Girondists, moderate republicans during the French Revolution, Roland cannot argue that she lacks intellectual aspirations, but she is careful to show how she moderates and tailors them to conform to standards of appropriate female behavior. The proof is her own past and her unimpeachable method of educating her beloved daughter, for whom she desires a refined sensibility, judiciously chosen amusements, and modest accomplishments.

The need to defend herself against misogynous stereotypes persists for the modern woman prisoner as well, as demonstrated in the writings of Nawal El Saadawi. Like Roland, Saadawi was arrested for political crimes but was unofficially punished for overstepping her limits as a woman. Unlike Roland, however, Saadawi overtly contests the authorities' ability to define her as they imprison her. Saadawi's resistance begins at the most basic, physical level: she will exercise her body, which, after all, belongs to her and not to her jailers. This prisoner's refusal to relinquish control of her body is infectious. Soon other women join in the joyful combination of healthful exercise and political protest. "This is a provocation to revolt inside the prison!" exclaims the warden in alarm. The women have denied the state's power over the body of the prisoner, a power that is fundamental to imprisonment, according to French philosopher Michel Foucault.[6]

Saadawi explains, "Any organised group movement, even if it be merely bodily exercise or dancing, establishes a rhythm in the mind and body which resembles the pattern of revolution or revolt."[7]

Prison activist Karlene Faith's description of an "unruly woman" fits here: she is "undisciplined," "defiant," "offensive," "unmanageable."[8] Saadawi defies the Egyptian government that persecutes her. She responds to power with exercise and writing, in the spirit of Susannah Martin, who was hung for witchcraft in Salem, Massachusetts, in 1692. During her trial Martin laughed at her accusers. When asked why she laughed, Martin replied with dignity, "Well I may at such folly . . . I never hurt man woman or child," and she refused to speculate upon the cause of the ailments that her accusers attributed to her evil powers: "I do not desire to spend my judgm't upon it."[9]

To counter the inherent sexism of the charges against her and to vindicate herself, Saadawi does not resort to the classism used by some women prisoners who write in self-defense, as exemplified in the writings of Roland. Instead, Saadawi identifies with her outcast companions and uses imprisonment as an opportunity to continue the feminist leadership that got her into trouble with authorities on the outside. For Saadawi, vindication of self gives way to proudly proclaimed solidarity with her sister prisoners—a solidarity that resounds in the selections in part 6 of this anthology.

The prison writings of revolutionary Filipina poet and journalist Mila Aguilar create a tension in their blend of the personal and political. Commenting upon her writing and her political activity, Aguilar has made it clear that her goal is to support the welfare and freedom of her people.[10] During her detention as a political prisoner, Aguilar continued to write poems, which reflect the physical and emotional pain of her experience. Lyrical and sensitive, full of longing for her people and the beauty of her country's landscape, these poems serve to vindicate the poet in a unique fashion. Without directly addressing the brutal injustice of her situation, Aguilar evokes a vision of the life that she desires for herself and her people, thereby revealing herself to be a woman of justice and humanity, altogether superior to the power that confines her. Charged with the luminescence of her innate decency, Aguilar's poems testify in her defense and tell the world who she truly is.

And what of the majority of imprisoned women, who are not political prisoners, who have not committed acts that generate headlines or any public notice at all? Misogynous views of incarcerated women continue to breed fear and misconceptions about women in prison.[11] To counter stereotypes of hardened, incorrigible female prisoners, a writer may assert that she is more than her prison sentence, and offer her writing as evidence on her behalf.

The prisoner with AIDS, however, is an outcast among outcasts. She faces an even greater challenge to her identity, since negative images of imprisoned women are exacerbated by the stigma attached to AIDS by prisoners. The women of the ACE Program at Bedford Hills faced that challenge by empowering themselves through peer education about this dread illness.[12] They overcame their doubly outcast status by taking individual and collective responsibility for their health.[13] Through their actions they demanded the fundamental right to control the health of their own bodies, as Saadawi did with her exercises. The ACE Program, which provides HIV/AIDS orientation for new prisoners, as well as counseling and workshops, has served as a model for similar programs in other women's facilities.[14] Ironically, the experience of prison and even of AIDS offered these women the opportunity to discover a new respect for themselves and each other. Their message is that, though the prison institution and AIDS may restrict a woman, neither has the power to define her. Katrina Haslip explains how the program empowered her to contribute to society, and perhaps more significantly, to acknowledge to herself and others the value of that contribution: "We made a difference in our community behind the wall, and that difference has allowed me to survive and thrive as a person with AIDS."[15]

Writing that has emerged from the ACE Program comes full circle from Roland's classist memoirs. In *Breaking the Walls of Silence*, the collection of writing from the ACE Program from which the excerpts here are drawn, imprisoned women speak for themselves through their personal stories, the history of ACE, and curriculum materials that disseminate their program's information far beyond Bedford Hills. In form, their collective writing mirrors the communal spirit of the ACE Program itself. Moreover, their book's boldness in disrupting the individualism that characterizes traditional life-writing parallels the audacity of a program that dares to entrust prisoners with each other's welfare. Caren Kaplan, a scholar of women's life-writing, calls women's prison memoirs "out-law genres," and notes their use of collaborative techniques and "genre destabilization."[16] Carole Boyce Davies, who studies women's autobiography, describes the "multiply articulated text" of women's life-writing, which "can be read collectively as one story refracted through multiple lives, lives that share a common experience."[17] *Breaking the Walls of Silence* exemplifies both of these theories in its collective activism and committed writing. On several levels the writing sustains and nourishes these prison authors.

Whatever the stated charges against imprisoned women, sexist and classist stereotypes constitute some of the most damaging and least easily defeated criticisms. Writing in self-vindication may not reduce prison sentences, but to some extent it mitigates the pain of imprisonment for women prison authors.

NOTES

The quotation in the title of this section is taken from Madame Roland de la Platière, *An Appeal to Impartial Posterity* (New York: Robert Wilson, 1798), vol.1, part 2: 127. The epigraph to this section is taken from James Bradley Finley, *Memorials of Prison Life* (1855; reprint, New York: Arno, 1974), 60–61.

1. The particular criticisms may vary over time. For example, Nicole Hahn Rafter, in *Partial Justice: Women in State Prisons, 1800–1935* (1985; New Brunswick: Transaction, 1990) describes how reformatories in late-nineteenth- to early-twentieth-century

America proposed to make "promiscuous women" conform to ideals of "true woman-hood." Earlier in the nineteenth century, before reformatories were established, women in state prisons were regarded as monsters rather than as errant, redeemable fallen women. See also Rafter and Elizabeth A. Stanko, *Judge, Lawyer, Victim, Thief: Women, Gender Roles, and Criminal Justice* (Boston: Northeastern University Press, 1982), 2–7.

2. Raphael Holinshed, *Holinshed's Chronicles of England, Scotland, and Ireland*, vol. IV, *England* (1577; 1808; New York: AMS Press, 1965), 133.

3. Other selections in this anthology that illustrate women prisoners' writing in vindication of self include the writings by Henry, Lebrón, Metzger, Saubin, and Shakur.

4. Elissa D. Gelfand, *Imagination in Confinement: Women's Writings from French Prisons* (Ithaca, N.Y.: Cornell University Press, 1983), 28–30.

5. Gelfand, 130–52, 224. See also Gelfand, "A Response to the Void: Madame Roland's 'Mémoires Particuliers' and Her Imprisonment," *Romance Notes* (Fall 1979): 75–80.

6. Michel Foucault, *Discipline and Punish: The Birth of the Prison*, trans. Alan Sheridan (1975; New York: Vintage, 1979).

7. Nawal El Saadawi, *Memoirs from the Women's Prison*. (Berkeley: University of California Press, 1986; 1994), 96–97.

8. Karlene Faith, *Unruly Women: The Politics of Confinement and Resistance* (Vancouver: Press Gang, 1993), 1.

9. Susannah Martin, The Salem Witchcraft Papers, Case 36, Electronic Text Center, University of Virginia Library, online, available: http://www.etext.lib.virginia.edu/salem/ witchcraft/, January 29, 2002. Kathleen O'Shea discusses Martin's case and the witchcraft trials in the context of contemporary capital punishment debates in the Summer 2001 issue of *Women on the Row*, 3(3).

10. Mila Aguilar, interview, online, available: http:www.amazon.com, March 10, 2000.

11. An example of a work that presents a negative view of women and crime is Patricia Pearson, *When She Was Bad: How and Why Women Get Away with Murder* (New York: Penguin, 1998).

12. Ronald L. Braithwaite, Theordore M. Hammett, and Robert M. Mayberry, in *Prisons and AIDS: A Public Health Challenge* (San Francisco: Jossey-Bass, 1996), 123–26, describe a survey of women in a Midwestern county jail in which women stated their belief that the best instructor for an AIDS education program would be a person with AIDS who is knowledgeable and desires to help. Andi Rierden, in *The Farm: Life inside a Women's Prison* (Amherst: University of Massachusetts Press, 1997), 118–23, describes how women who are HIV-positive support each other in a drug treatment program at Niantic State Prison for Women in Connecticut.

13. The ACE Program is cited by Judy Greenspan, "Prisoners Respond to AIDS," and by rita d. brown, "White North American Political Prisoners," in Elihu Rosenblatt, ed. *Criminal Injustice: Confronting the Prison Crisis* (Boston: South End Press, 1996), 121, 286, and in *Prisons and AIDS*, 75–76. People with AIDS Coalition of New York, Inc. (PWACNY) includes an article about the annual ACE Walkathon at Bedford Hills, online, available: http://www.aidsinfonyc.org/pwac/9511/walk.html, October 4, 2001.

14. A program modeled on the ACE Program is Pleasanton AIDS Counseling and Education (PLACE) at the Federal Women's Prison in Dublin, California. Another prisoner AIDS peer education program is the Shawnee AIDS Awareness Group at the federal women's prison in Marianna, Florida. See Judy Greenspan, "Prisoners Respond to AIDS," in *Criminal Injustice*, 120–21.

15. Katrina Haslip, in Women of the ACE Program of the Bedford Hills Correctional Facility, *Breaking the Walls of Silence: AIDS and Women in a New York State Maximum Security Prison* (Woodstock: Overlook Press, 1998), 10.

16. Caren Kaplan, "Resisting Autobiography: Out-Law Genres and Transnational Subjects," in *Women, Autobiography, Theory: A Reader*, ed. Sidonie Smith and Julia Watson (Madison: University of Wisconsin Press, 1998), 208–16.

17. Carole Boyce Davies, "Collaboration and the Ordering Imperative in Life Story Production," in *De/Colonizing the Subject: The Politics of Gender in Women's Autobiography*, ed. Sidonie Smith and Julia Watson (Minneapolis: University of Minnesota Press, 1992), 3, 19.

MARIE JEANNE (MANON) PHLIPON, MADAME ROLAND DE LA PLATIÈRE

(1756–1793)

Manon Phlipon received an early appreciation for the arts from her father, an engraver. She began a "proper" female education in the arts in their bourgeois French home, and at the age of eleven completed her education in a convent. When she was twenty-five she married a middle-aged scholar, Jean Marie Roland. They had one daughter. Serving as secretary for her husband, who was minister of the interior, she met and entertained the most prominent political leaders of the day, including the Girondists, at her home.

Though she affirmed her republican sentiments and her hope for the French Revolution, on May 31, 1793, Madame Roland was arrested without a specific charge. She was taken from her Paris home and imprisoned in the Abbey and St. Pelagie prisons. While there, she wrote several works, including her memoirs, in which she took pains to clear her name for posterity by emphasizing her morality and normal femininity, despite the vicious charges that she had stepped outside her natural sphere by engaging in politics. She was taken to the Conciergerie prison on November 1, 1793, where she was tried and found guilty of conspiring with Girondists against the Republic. Observers praised her for her dignified bearing on the way to the guillotine. Her husband committed suicide shortly after hearing of her execution.

Note: Background information is from *An Appeal to Impartial Posterity: By Madame Roland, Wife of the Minister of the Interior: or, A Collection of Tracts Written by Her During Her Confinement in the Prisons of the Abbey, and St. Pelagie, in Paris,* translated from the French original, first American edition (corrected), 2 vols. (New York: Robert Wilson, 1798); Elissa D. Gelfand, *Imagination in Confinement: Women's Writings from French Prisons* (Ithaca, N.Y.: Cornell University Press, 1983); Winifred Stephens, *Women of the French Revolution* (London: Chapman & Hall, 1922).

MADAME ROLAND'S MEMOIRS

From An Appeal to Impartial Posterity, *1798.*

Abbey Prison, June 1793
Rising about noon, I considered how I should arrange my new apartment. With a clean napkin I covered a little paltry table, which I placed near my window, intending that it should serve me for a bureau, and resolved to eat my meals on a corner of the chimney-piece, that I might keep the table clean, and in order, for writing. Two large hat-pins, stuck into the boards, served me as a port manteau. In my pocket I had Thomson's Seasons, a

work which I was fond of on more than one account; and I made a memorandum of such other books as I should wish to procure. First, Plutarch's Lives of Illustrious Persons, which at eight years of age I used to carry to church instead of the Exercises of the holy week, and which I had not read regularly since that early period: then Hume's History of England, and Sheridan's Dictionary, in order to improve myself in the English language. I would rather have continued to read Mrs. Macaulay; but the person who had lent me some of the first volumes, was not at home; and I should not have known where to enquire for the work, as I had already tried in vain to get it from the booksellers. I could not avoid smiling at my peaceful preparations; for there was a great tumult in the town: the drums were continually beating to arms, and I knew not what might be the event. At any rate, said I to myself, they will not prevent my living to my last moment: more happy in my conscious innocence, than they can be with the rage that animates them. If they come, I will advance to meet them, and go to death as a man would go to repose.

The keeper's wife came to invite me to her apartment, where she had directed my cloth to be laid, that I might dine in better air. On repairing thither, I found my faithful maid, who threw herself into my arms, bathed in tears, and half suffocated by her sobs. I could not avoid melting into tenderness and sorrow. I almost upbraided myself with my previous tranquillity, when I reflected on the anxiety of those who were attached to me; and when I described to myself the anguish first of one friend, and then of another, my heart was rent by the keenest sensations of grief. Poor woman! how many tears have I caused her to shed! and for what does not an attachment like her's atone? In the common intercourse of life she sometimes treats me roughly, but it is when she thinks me too negligent of what may contribute to my health or happiness; and when I am in distress, the office of complaining is her's, and that of consoling mine. There was no getting rid of so inveterate a habit. I endeavoured to prove to her that, by giving way to her grief, she would be less capable of rendering me service; that she was more useful to me without, than within the walls of the prison, where she begged me to permit her to remain; and that, upon the whole, I was far from being so unfortunate as she imagined, which indeed was true. Whenever I have been ill, I have experienced a particular kind of serenity, unquestionably proceeding from my mode of contemplating things, and from the law I have laid down for myself, of always submitting quietly to necessity, instead of revolting against it. The moment I take to my bed, every duty seems at an end, and no solicitude whatever has any hold upon me: I am only bound to be there, and to remain there with resignation, which I do with a very good grace. I give freedom to my imagination; I call up agreeable impressions, pleasing remembrances, and ideas of happiness; all exertions, all reasonings, and all calculations, I discard; giving myself up entirely to nature, and, peaceful like her, I suffer pain without impatience, and seek repose or cheerfulness. I find that imprisonment produces on me nearly the same effect as disease; I am only bound to be in prison, and what great hardship is there in it? I am not such very bad company for myself. . . .

More than two months have I been imprisoned, because I am allied to a worthy man, who thought proper to retain his virtue in a revolution, and to give in exact accounts though a minister. For five months he solicited in vain the passing of those accounts, and the pronouncing of judgment on his administration. They have been examined; but, as they have afforded no room for blame, it has been deemed expedient to make no report on the subject, but to substitute calumny in its place. Roland's activity, his multifarious labours, and his instructive writings, had procured him a degree of consideration which appeared formidable; or so at least envious men would have it, in order to effect the downfall of a man whose integrity they detested. His ruin was resolved upon, and an attempt was made to take him into custody at the time of the insurrection of the 31st of May; the epoch of the complete debasement of the national representation, of its violation, and of the success of the decemvirate. He made his escape, and in their fury they fastened upon me; but I should have been arrested at any rate; for though our persecutors know that my name has not the same influence as his, they are persuaded that my temper is not less firm, and are almost equally desirous of my ruin.

The first part of my captivity I employed in writing. My pen proceeded with so much rapidity, and I was in so happy a disposition of mind, that in less than a month I had manuscripts sufficient to form a duodecimo volume. They were intitled Historical Notices [henceforth referred to as *Historic Notices*], and contained a variety of particulars relative to all the facts, and all the persons, connected with public affairs, that my situation had given me an opportunity of knowing. I related them with all the freedom and energy of my nature, with all the openness and unconstraint of an ingenuous mind, setting itself above selfish considerations, with all the pleasure which results from describing what we have experienced, or what we feel, and lastly with the confidence, that, happen what would, the collection would serve as my moral and political testament.

I had completed the whole, bringing things down to the present moment, and had entrusted it to a friend, who rated it at a high price. On a sudden the storm burst over his head. The instant he found himself put under arrest, he thought of nothing but the danger, he felt nothing but the necessity of averting it, and without casting about for expedients, threw my manuscript into the fire. This loss distressed me more than the severest trials have ever done. This will easily be conceived, when it is remembered that the crisis approaches, that I may be murdered tomorrow, or dragged, I know not how, before the tribunal which our rulers employ to rid them of the persons they find troublesome; and that these writings were the anchor to which I had committed my hopes of saving my own memory from reproach, as well as that of many deserving characters.

As we ought not, however, to sink under any event, I shall employ my leisure hours in setting down, without form or order, whatever may occur to my mind. These fragments will not make amends for what I have lost, but they will serve to recall it to my memory, and assist me in filling up the void on some future day, provided the means of doing so remain in my power.

Prison of St. Pelagie, Aug. 9, 1793
The daughter of an artist, the wife of a man of letters (who afterwards became a minister, and remained an honest man), now a prisoner, destined perhaps to a violent and unexpected death, I have been acquainted with happiness and with adversity, I have seen glory at hand, and I have experienced injustice.

Born in an obscure station, but of honest parents, I spent my youth in the bosom of the fine arts, nourished by the charms of study, and ignorant of all superiority but that of merit, of all greatness but that of virtue.

Arrived at years of maturity, I lost all hopes of that fortune, which might have placed me in a condition suitable to the education I had received. A marriage with a respectable man appeared to compensate this loss; it served to lay the foundation of new misfortunes.

A gentle disposition, a strong mind, a solid understanding, an extremely affectionate heart, and an exterior which announced these qualities, rendered me dear to all those with whom I was acquainted. The situation into which I have been thrown has created me enemies; personally I have none: to those who have spoken the worst of me I am utterly unknown.

It is so true that things are seldom what they appear to be, that the periods of my life in which I have felt the most pleasure, or experienced the greatest vexation, were often the very contrary of those that others might have supposed: the solution is, that happiness depends on the affections more than on events.

It is my purpose to employ the leisure of my captivity in retracing what has happened to me from my tenderest infancy to the present moment. Thus to tread over again all the steps of our career, is to live a second time; and what, in the gloom of a prison, can we do better than to transport our existence elsewhere by pleasing fictions, or by the recollection of interesting occurrences?

If we gain less experience by acting, than by reflecting on what we see and do, mine will be greatly augmented by my present undertaking.

Public affairs, and my own private sentiments, afforded me ample matter for thinking, and subjects enough for my pen during two months imprisonment, without obliging me to have recourse to distant times. Accordingly, the first five weeks were devoted to my *Historic Notices*, which formed perhaps no uninteresting collection. They have just been destroyed; and I have felt all the bitterness of a loss, which I shall never repair. But I should despise myself, could I suffer my mind to sink in any circumstances whatever. In all the troubles I have experienced, the most lively impression of sorrow has been almost immediately accompanied by the ambition of opposing my strength to the evil, and of surmounting it, either by doing good to others, or by exerting my own fortitude to the utmost. Thus misfortune may pursue, but cannot overwhelm me; tyrants may persecute, but never, no never shall they debase me. My *Historic Notices* are gone: I mean to write my *Memoirs*; and, prudently accommodating myself to my weakness, at a moment when my feelings are acute, I shall talk of my own person, that my thoughts may be the less at home. I shall exhibit my fair and my unfavourable side with equal freedom. He who dares not speak well of himself is almost always a coward, who knows and dreads the ill that may be said of him; and he who hesitates to confess his faults, has neither spirit to vindicate, nor virtue to repair them. Thus frank with respect to myself, I shall not be scrupulous in regard to others: father, mother, friends, husband, I shall paint them all in their proper colours, or in the colours, at least in which they appeared to me.

While I remained in a quiet and retired station, my natural sensibility so absorbed my other qualities, that it displayed itself alone, or governed all the rest. My first objects were to please and to do good. I was a little like that good man, Mr. de Gourville, of whom Madame de Sévigné said, that the love of his neighbour cut off half his words; nor was I undeserving of the character given me by Sainte-Lette, who said, that though possessed of wit to point an epigram, I never suffered one to escape my lips. Since the energy of my character has been unfolded by circumstances, by political and other storms, my frankness takes place of every thing, without considering too nicely the little scratches it may give in its way. Still, however, I deal not in epigrams; they indicate a mind pleased at irritating others by satirical observations; and, as to me, I never yet could find amusement in killing flies. But I love to do justice by the utterance of truths, and refrain not from the most severe, in presence of the parties concerned, without suffering myself to be alarmed, or moved, or angry, whatever may be the effects they produce. . . .

St. Pelagie, August 20, 1793
My courage did not sink under the new misfortunes I experienced;[1] but the refinement of cruelty with which they have given me a foretaste of liberty, only to load me with fresh chains, and the barbarous care with which they took advantage of a decree, by applying to me a false designation, as the mode of legalizing an arbitrary arrest, fired me with indignation. Feeling myself in that disposition of mind when every impression becomes stronger, and its effect more prejudicial to health, I went to bed; but as I could not sleep, it was impossible to avoid thinking. This violent state, however, never lasts long with me. Being accustomed to govern my mind, I felt the want of self-possession, and thought myself a fool for affording a triumph to my persecutors, by suffering their injustice to break my spirit. They were only bringing fresh odium on themselves, without making much alteration in the situation I had already found means so well to support: had I not books and leisure here as well as at the Abbey? I began indeed to be quite angry with myself for having allowed my peace of mind to be disturbed, and no longer thought of any thing, but of enjoying existence, and of employing my faculties with that independence of spirit

which a strong mind preserves in the midst of fetters, and which thus disappoints its most determined enemies. As I felt that it was necessary to vary my occupations, I bought crayons, and had recourse to drawing, which I had laid aside some time. Fortitude does not consist solely in rising superior to circumstances by an effort of the mind, but in maintaining that elevation by suitable conduct and care. Whenever unfortunate or irritating events take me by surprise, I am not content with calling up the maxims of philosophy to support my courage; but I provide agreeable amusements for my mind, and do not neglect the art of preserving health to keep myself in a just equilibrium. I laid out my days then with a certain sort of regularity. In the morning I studied the English language in Shaftsbury's Essay on Virtue, and in the poetry of Thomson. The sound metaphysics of the one, and the enchanting descriptions of the other, transported me by turns to the intellectual regions, and to the most touching scenes of nature. Shaftsbury's reason gave new strength to mine, and his thoughts invited meditation; while Thomson's sensibility, and his delightful and sublime pictures, went to my heart, and charmed my imagination. I afterwards sat down to my drawing till dinner time. Having been so long without handling the pencil, I could not expect to acquit myself with much skill; but we always preserve the power of repeating with pleasure, and of attempting with facility, whatever in our youth we have practised with success. Accordingly, the study of the fine arts, considered as a part of the education of young women, ought, in my opinion, to be less directed towards the acquisition of distinguished talents than to inspiring them with the love of employment, making them contract a habit of application, and multiplying their means of amusement; for it is thus we escape from that *ennui* which is the most cruel disease of man in society; and thus we avoid the quicksands of vice, and seductions still more to be feared than vice itself.

I will not then make my daughter a professor (*une virtuose*): I shall ever remember that my mother was afraid of my becoming too great a musician, or of my devoting myself entirely to painting, because she desired, above all things, that I should be fond of the duties of my sex, and learn to be a good housewife, in case of my becoming the mother of a family. My Eudora then shall learn to accompany herself in a pleasing manner on the harp, or to play with ease on the *forte piano*; and shall know enough of drawing, to enable her to contemplate the masterpieces of art with pleasure, to trace or imitate a flower which delights her, and to shew taste and elegant simplicity in the choice of her ornaments. It is my wish that the mediocrity of her talents may excite neither admiration in others, nor vanity in herself. It is my wish that she may please rather by her collective merit, than astonish at the first glance, and that she may rather gain affection by her good qualities, than applause by her brilliant accomplishments. But, good heavens! I am a prisoner and a great distance divides us! I dare not even send for her to receive my embraces; for hatred pursues the very children of those whom tyranny persecutes; and no sooner does my girl in her eleventh year appear in the streets with her virgin bashfulness, and her beautiful fair hair, than wretches, hired or seduced by falsehood, point her out as the offspring of a conspirator. Cruel wretches! they well know how to break a mother's heart.

Could not I have brought her with me?—I have not yet said what is the situation of a prisoner at Sainte Pelagie.

The wing appropriated to females, is divided into long and very narrow corridors, on one side of which are little cells like that which I have described as my lodging. There, under the same roof, upon the same line, and only separated by a thin plastered partition, I dwell in the midst of murderers and women of the town. By the side of me is one of those creatures who make a trade of seduction, and set up innocence to sale; and above me is a woman who forged assignats, and with a band of monsters to which she belongs, tore an individual of her own sex to pieces upon the highway. The door of each cell is secured by an enormous bolt, and opened every morning by a man who stares in impudently to see whether you be up or in bed: their inhabitants then assemble in the corridors, upon the staircases, or in a damp or noisome room, a worthy receptacle for this scum of the earth.

It will be readily believed that I confine myself constantly to my cell; but the distance is not great enough to save the ear from the expressions which such women may be supposed to utter, but which without hearing them it is impossible for any one to conceive.

This is not all: the wing where the men are confined, having windows in front of, and very near the building inhabited by the women, the individuals of the two sexes of analogous character, enter into conversation, which is the more dissolute, as those who hold it are unsusceptible of fear: gestures supply the place of actions, and the windows serve as the occasions of the most shameful scenes of infamous debauchery.

Such is the dwelling reserved for the worthy wife of an honest man!—If this be the reward of virtue on earth, who will be astonished at my contempt of life, and at the resolution with which I shall be able to look death in the face? It never appeared to me in a formidable shape; but at present is not without its charms; and I could embrace it with pleasure, if my daughter did not invite me to stay a little longer with her, and if my voluntary *exit* would not furnish calumny with weapons against my husband, whose glory I should support, if they should dare to carry me before a tribunal. . . .

October 18, 1793
To my daughter
I do not know, my dear girl, whether I shall be allowed to see, or to write to you again. REMEMBER YOUR MOTHER. In these few words is contained the best advice I can give you. You have seen me happy in fulfilling my duties, and in giving assistance to those who were in distress.—It is the only way of being happy.

You have seen me tranquil in misfortune and in confinement, because I was free from remorse, and because I enjoyed the pleasing recollections that good actions leave behind them. These are the only means that can enable us to support the evils of life, and the vicissitudes of fortune.

Perhaps you are not fated, and I hope you are not, to undergo trials so severe as mine; but there are others against which you ought to be equally on your guard. Serious and industrious habits are the best preservative against every danger; and necessity as well as prudence command you to persevere diligently in your studies.

Be worthy of your parents: they leave you great examples to follow; and if you are careful to avail yourself of them, your existence will not be useless to mankind.

FAREWELL, my beloved child, you who drew life from my bosom, and whom I wish to impress with all my sentiments. The time will come when you will be better able to judge of the efforts I make at this moment to repress the tender emotions excited by your dear image. I press you to my heart.

Farewell, my Eudora

To my faithful servant Fleury
My dear Fleury, you whose fidelity, services, and attachment, have been so grateful to me for thirteen years, receive my embraces, and my farewell.

PRESERVE the remembrance of what I was. It will console you for what I suffer: the good pass on to glory when they descend to the grave. My sorrows are about to terminate; lay aside yours, and think of the peace which I am about to enjoy, and which nobody will in future be able to disturb. Tell my Agatha that I carry with me to the grave the satisfaction of being beloved by her from my infancy, and the regret of not being able to give her proofs of my attachment. I could have wished to be of service to you—at least let me not afflict you.

Farewell, my poor Fleury, farewell!

NOTE

1. Madame Roland had been briefly released from prison, then rearrested.—*Ed.*

Nawal El Saadawi

(1931–)

"Danger has been a part of my life ever since I picked up a pen and wrote," writes Nawal El Saadawi in *Memoirs from the Women's Prison*. "There is no power in the world that can strip my writings from me" (203–204). Born in Egypt, Saadawi is an internationally known writer and feminist whose many publications on women in Egypt and the Arab world have been widely translated. A psychiatrist, she practiced medicine in Egypt and afterward served as director general of the Health Education Department of the Ministry of Health in Cairo until her dismissal in 1972 for her outspoken views expressed in her writings on women, among other subjects. She founded the Arab Women Solidarity Association and the feminist publication *Noon Magazine*, but in 1991 these were forced to close by the Egyptian government.

In September 1981 Saadawi, accused of alleged "crimes against the State," was one of over 1,500 people arrested by President Anwar Sadat's police. She was held in Qanatir Prison until late November 1981, when many detainees were released after the assassination of Sadat. In her earlier public health position she had visited that prison to conduct research for her study *Women and Neurosis in Egypt* (1976). Her release did not bring security, however; she went into exile after her name appeared on a fundamentalist death list in 1992. Since 1993 she has been a speaker and a visiting professor at universities in the United States, particularly Duke University.

Note: Background information is from *Memoirs from the Women's Prison*, trans. Marilyn Booth (Berkeley: University of California Press, 1986); *A Daughter of Isis: The Autobiography of Nawal El Saadawi*, trans. Sherif Hetata (London: Zed Books, 1999); "Nawal El Saadawi/Sherif Hetata," online, available: http://www.geocities.com/nawal-saadawi/bio.htm, November 6, 2001.

'RESIST AND LAUGH TOGETHER'

From Memoirs from the Women's Prison, *1986.*

From the moment I opened my eyes upon my first morning in prison, I understood from the motion of my body as I was rising and stretching the muscles of my neck and back, that I had made a firm decision: I would live in this place as I had lived in any other. It was a decision which appeared insane to me, for it would cancel out reality, logic, the walls and the steel doors.

Everywhere I had gone, wherever I had travelled, however far away the place, however unfamiliar, I would look around me in delighted wonder and concentration as if I had been born in that place and would die there, as if I had never known any other spot and never would. The faces around me, no matter how strange they might appear to me, seemed as if I had seen them before.

I found myself standing in front of the steel-barred door, jumping up and down on the tips of my toes and moving my arms and legs through the air, going through the physical exercises with which I had become accustomed to start every morning in my home or at the club. Between the steel bars I could see a piece of blue sky over the walls and wires, and I almost laughed out loud, like a child. Looking at the faces around me, I could smile and say, "Good morning," my voice ringing in my ears, merry and optimistic, announcing good news, resounding in the air around me as clearly as the ringing of pure silver—as if I were at home, as if these eyes around me were the eyes of my family.

To this day, I've never figured out the secret of the cheerfulness with which I greet any new morning. Does sleep wash the grief and pain from my mind? Or do I imagine with the naïvety of a child that the new day will bring something new? Or does my memory have an unusual capacity for rejecting sadness and pain? Sometimes I would accuse myself of naïvety or childishness, and I would wish to be free of these qualities. When my mother, and then my father, died, I tried to rid myself of this childlike demeanour, as I did when my daughter grew up to become a young woman, and when my son was no longer a child.

My mother used to scold me when I would laugh suddenly during a wake or funeral, while my father, too, would fix a sharp gaze on me and say, "You're a big girl now." Even my daughter said to me once, "Mama, really, you're a grown up."

Even in the midst of crises, in the hardest times and at moments which call for despair, this illogical optimism like that of an ingenuous child would spring from somewhere I could not fathom.

Sometimes matters would become even worse than they already were. Our circumstances inside the prison would sink to a new low, and we would hear news prophesying danger. Pessimism would darken the faces of all of the prisoners with me in the cell, and every one of us would feel surrounded by the most horrific dangers. We would sit together, silent, grave, pessimistic. Yet, something would move inside me suddenly, something built into me, the rebel, angry and revolting against this gravity, this submission to worry and grief. Rebelling against passivity and lack of movement, resisting defeat and pessimism, so that I would say: "We will not die, or if we are to die we won't die silently, we won't go off in the night without a row, we must rage and rage, we must beat the ground and make it shudder. We won't die without a revolution!" . . .

This was my first experience in prison, and I've always had an odd passion for "firsts." The first time I rode a donkey, as a child. The first time I went to school in the train. My first flight from Cairo to Aswan, and the first time I swam in the sea at Alexandria. The first time I lost my husband through divorce. The first time I lost my government job. My first experience of the pains of childbirth, those pains which would allow the head of my child to emerge from my body. The first time I placed a stethoscope to my ear and listened to a heart beating. The first time I saw the letters of my name printed in the press. The first step I took towards the first man in my life.

Every time I experienced a "first," I would react by trembling. I would feel heightened joy and intensified fear, both, but the joy always overcame the fear. Even this time, as they were leading me to gaol, joy got the better of fear. How? I don't know. But deep inside of me I would sense a hidden secret which was wary of appearing before others, as if it were a sort of crime.

For I was born into a world which despises joyousness and those who are high-spirited. Even my mother used to fix her eyes on me in irritation or repugnance when she would see me dancing with joy. I used to think at first that she did not want me to dance, but I understood later that she did not want me to be happy. But why not?

When I had grown older, I understood that she, like me, was born into a world which has an aversion to merriment and considers all human pleasures to be perversions. The pleasure of discovery? Since knowledge is forbidden, this pleasure is taboo, for only the gods may possess knowledge. Ignorance is the blessing which God granted to his human servants, and whoever yearns for knowledge is like one who wishes to commit crimes and offenses and longs for ill-gotten gains.

However, I was also born with a tempestuous and untameable impulse for knowledge. I want to know it all, everything, even death, and perhaps I have even been on the brink of death at times merely to satisfy childish curiosity.

As for prison, in my opinion it is like death in that it is worth discovering. All my life, I have regarded those entering and leaving prison as knowing something which I have not known, and living a life which I have not lived.

There is a difference, of course, between prison and death: it is possible for one to leave prison and return to a normal life, telling people what one has seen. As for death, no one returns or relates anything. Therefore, the experience of death has never lingered in my imagination. But how I had hoped to enter prison, on the condition that I would leave it in a sound state, and at the time I would wish! These are conditions which no one can guarantee, however. Prison remained in my imagination, like a nightmare, like death—the one who enters is lost forever, and the one who leaves is born anew.

In prison I came to know both extremes together. I experienced the height of grief and joy, the peaks of pain and pleasure, the greatest beauty and the most intense ugliness. At certain moments I imagined that I was living a new love story. In prison I found my heart opened to love—how I don't know—as if I were back in early adolescence. In prison, I remembered the way I had burst out laughing when a child, while the taste of tears from the harshest and hardest days of my life returned to my mouth.

In prison, I relived my entire childhood. At the sound of the spoon pouring sugar into a cup of tea, I would clap and dance with delight. The tea was like a mixture of black dirt and straw; the sugar consisted of brown bits over which ants crawled, but no sooner would I open my eyes in the morning and sniff the steam of tea from the pot than I would jump up from my spot. I'd pour the tea into a green plastic cup, and drink it slowly, sip by sip, its taste in my mouth sweeter than any tea I'd ever had, and all the faces around me beloved and near to my heart. Even those faces hidden under the black veils . . . when the *niqaabs* were lifted I could see faces that were shining, clear, overflowing with love, a cooperative spirit, and humanity.

Among the women and girls, I lived a communal life. I recaptured my happiness as a student at secondary school. Rejoicing, growing angry and fighting, mending our differences, feeling delight at the smallest things and growing sad for the simplest of reasons. Tears appearing in our eyes even as we smiled, and smiles breaking through while we still wept. From the disagreements among us in prison, one would have thought oceans separated one from another, and that each of us was an island unto herself. The dispute might grow yet more intense, but soon we would draw together, there would be harmony among us, and we would close ranks, a solid line facing the single power which had put us behind bars. . . .

It's after midnight, now, and I'm seated on top of the overturned bottom of the jerry can, ready to write. Since entering prison I've done my writing on toilet rolls and cigarette papers. Toilet paper isn't against the rules: we buy it from the canteen with our identity cards, like we do cigarettes.

I have not smoked at all since I have been in prison. Outside, I've smoked from time to time, but in here I've decided not to. I've heard of prisoners who've been weakened by a single cigarette, or by one puff of a cigarette. Also, the smoke cuts one's breathing short, and I need deep, long breaths, and all the patience I can muster here, for the struggle ahead of me is still a long one. . . .

A sharp pain is stabbing at the back of my head like a nail. Pains in my back, as I crouch over the jerry can. My fingers hurt. The pen is an uncomfortable, tiring one—it's so short, shorter than my fingers. The paper is lightweight, and almost transparent. If I press the pen down on it, it rips, and if I don't press down, no letters appear.

The light was dim, and I could barely see. I had put my aluminium plate under my feet to keep them away from the dampness of the floor. A black dung beetle climbed on to the plate to crawl over my leg, and I struck it off with my foot.

My *munaqqaba* cellmates rose habitually in time for the dawn prayers, whereupon I would hide my paper under the tiling in the corner of the toilet. . . .

Those eyes are looking straight at me through the slits of the *niqaab*. Boduur and Fawqiyya say she's a spy, working for the Internal Security police. Her eyes, though, are innocent, childish. Her name is Itidaal.

She approached me—in the manner of a child—and asked, "What are you writing?"

"A story."

Her eyes shone. "A love story?"

I laughed. "Yes."

A delighted smile. "I wish I could read it. I've been engaged to my cousin for three months now, and I started wearing this *niqaab* one month ago, for his sake. He reads the Qur'an, but I don't know how to read anything. I never went to school. I'd like to learn how to read—all the girls here except me can read. Can I learn?"

"Of course. You're still very young. How old are you, Itidaal?"

"Sixteen. How many days will it take for me to learn to read?" she asked anxiously, eagerly.

"Sixteen. One day for each year."

Her laugh was childish too. Long and unbroken, like a whinny. "Will you teach me?"

"I don't mind."

She gave me a hug, hopping up and down in delight. Happiness, like infection, spreads rapidly. I felt that I, too, had become a child, my heart filled with pleasure. The pains in my back disappeared, and my body felt strong and energetic. I went to the steel-barred door: the dawn breeze massaged my face with invigorating moisture. The sky was still black, but the early light was creeping in slowly.

Suddenly, I heard the voice of the curlew. My heart beat forcefully, and I jumped on to the bars, clambering up them with my bare feet, stretching my neck skyward, jamming my head between the two steel bars.

I can't see him. The voice, though, affects me as if it's me that he's calling. A sweet, sad voice, piercing the silence. A lone flute in the darkness. Singing like a mother's voice, like offering a prayer of supplication, like weeping, like a child's abrupt, long laugh, or like a single scream in the night. Or an uneven sobbing which goes on and on.

Every dawn, I wait for that voice, and I hear it. Every dusk, too, the curlew sings only in the stillness and the dark. Only in this moment which falls between night and day. A single bird in the universe . . . I raise my head toward the sky. I want to see him. Never in my life have I seen a curlew. The sky, though, is surrounded by walls and wires, and in prison we hear the curlew without seeing him. That's enough, to hear him without seeing him. Enough that I see a drop of dawn light, and a drop of dew. Enough that my fingers can take hold of my pen. I still have paper, too, over which the pen can move. It's not important for me to see the words. Nothing matters except the birth of words on paper, the dawn's birth, the gloom dissolving. . . .

I put on my sports shoes in preparation for my morning exercises. Moving the body means life, and bodily strength means strength of mind and soul. In prison, one needs all of one's forces.

Behind me, I heard the sound of bare feet jumping up and down, hitting the ground. It was Itidaal, who had finished her dawn prayers, removed her *niqaab* and cloak and begun to do exercises.

The sweat poured down, washing away my sleeplessness and fatigue. All my back and neck pains dwindled away. Exposing my body to the shower's spray, only now did I feel wonderfully refreshed, revived as if I had just been born, at this very moment. My appetite was ready for a new day. I was very hungry, and insanely thirsty for a cup of tea. . . .

The prisoners knew the time at which I usually exercised. At nine o'clock every morning, they gathered in front of the door to our enclosure in their long white *gallabiyyas* and bare feet, standing ready. No sooner had I begun than they would form themselves into a row to start, staying with me, movement by movement.

Warden Shukriyya would appear in the courtyard at the sound of hundreds of hands clapping in unison. The din scared her; quivering on her thin aluminium heels, she shouted, "Everyone into her own cell, quickly now!"

No one left the line. I han't finished my exercises yet, and I resumed my movements, as the row of prisoners followed me without a pause.

The warden stamped her feet on the ground in anger. She approached me and said to me through the bars: "This is a provocation to revolt inside the prison!" "The prison statutes," I replied, "do not prohibit physical exercise."

I didn't stop exercising, and neither did the row of prisoners. Every morning at nine o'clock precisely, I saw them standing there, waiting, smiling, bodies stretched, ready.

One day I was slightly late, and their voices called out to me. "Doctor, it's nine o'clock! Doctor!"

I ran towards them breathing hard, as if trying to make an appointment on time. I began my exercises. I moved my legs and arms in that regular rhythmic movement which resembles dancing. Before me I saw a long line of arms and legs, moving through the air, striking the ground with the same, regular rhythm.

As if my body and theirs are one. As if there are no bars or steel partitions between us. As if we are one body.

I was aware of my heart beating beneath my ribs and I could feel the sweat pouring down my face and into my mouth, the sharp bite of its touch pleasing to my tongue. In my head, I could still hear the echo of the voice and the words it had uttered: "This is a provocation to revolt inside the prison!" I could sense my brain cells opening to embrace a truth as if I were comprehending it, in fact, for the first time. Any organised group movement, even if it be merely bodily exercise or dancing, establishes a rhythm in the mind and body which resembles the pattern of revolution or revolt. . . .

'A PASSION FOR SOLITUDE'

From Memoirs from the Women's Prison, 1986.

I had imagined prison to be solitude and total silence, the isolated cell in which one lives alone, talking to oneself, rapping at the wall to hear the responding knock of one's neighbour. Here, though, I enjoyed neither solitude nor silence, except in the space after midnight and before the dawn call to prayer. I could not pull a door shut between me and the others, even when I was in the toilet.

If Boduur ceased quarrelling with her colleagues, she would begin reciting the Qur'an out loud. And if Boduur went to sleep, Fawqiyya would wake up and begin to discuss and orate. If Fawqiyya went to sleep, Boduur would wake up to announce prayertime and the onset of night.

One night, the quarrel between Boduur and one of her comrades continued until dawn, ending only when Boduur fainted after she'd been hit by violent nervous convulsions. She tore at her hair and face with her fingernails, screaming until she lost consciousness.

As soon as the *shawisha* had opened the cell door in the morning, I called out to her. "I want to be transferred to a solitary cell. I don't want to stay in this cell any longer."

But the prison administration rejected my request. I came to understand that in prison, torture occurs not through solitude and silence but in a far more forceful way through uproar and noise. The solitary cell continued to float before me like a dream unlikely to be realised.

Since childhood, I've had a passion for solitude. I've not had a room in which I could shut myself off, for the number of individuals in every stage of my life has been greater than the number of rooms in the house. But I have always wrested for myself a place in which I could be alone to write. My ability to write has been linked to the possibility of complete seclusion, of being alone with myself, for I am incapable of writing when I am unable to give myself completely to solitude.

After midnight, when the atmosphere grows calm and I hear only the sound of sleep's regular breathing, I rise from my bed and tiptoe to the corner of the toilet, turn the empty jerry can upside down and sit on its bottom. I rest the aluminium plate on my knees, place against it the long, tape-like toilet paper, and begin to write.

MILA D. AGUILAR

(c. 1952–)

In the words of poet Audre Lorde, "Mila Aguilar is a revolutionary woman poet, and in her strongest work, her militancy is enhanced by her tenderness, her pain, and her love, by the female power of deep feeling." A Filipina poet, journalist, and university professor, Aguilar worked from 1969 to 1971 on the national weekly magazine *Graphic*, but went underground in the 1970s because of her opposition to President Ferdinand Marcos's regime. Aguilar was arrested by the Philippine military on August 6, 1984. Charged with "subversion," she was held in solitary confinement for a month in Camp Crame military prison in Quezon City, and afterward imprisoned in Bicutan. Further charges included membership in the National Executive Committee and Politburo of the Communist Party of the Philippines, an accusation she denied. Her imprisonment drew international protest, including that of the PEN American Center, which stated, "In her life and work she has symbolized the overwhelming desire of her people for an end to arbitrary arrest and censorship."

Aguilar, who has published under the name Clarita Roja, says of her writing, "I have always written with one and only one purpose in mind: to help my country and my people" (interview, 2000). Currently, she is a writer, producer, and director of video documentaries and a columnist for the *Manila Standard*. Her column, "Pinoy Tok," (Filipino Talk), is now on the World Wide Web, with a link to Aguilar's own Web page.

Note: Background information is from Aguilar, "Message on the Launching of *Why Cage Pigeons*," and Audre Lorde, "Introduction" in *A Comrade Is as Precious as a Rice Seedling* (Latham, N.Y.: Kitchen Table / Women of Color Press, 1984); interview with Mila D. Aguilar, online, available: http://www.amazon.com, March 10, 2000; PEN American Center, Case Sheet and Protocol for Mila Aguilar, October 24, 1984; E. San Juan, *Crisis in the Philippines* (South Hadley, Mass.: Bergin & Garvey, 1986); "Mila D. Aguilar on the Web," online, available: http://www.info.com.ph/~pinoytok/milarez.htm, October 30, 2001.

SIX POEMS

"Haikus in Solitary Confinement," "Prison," and "As the Dust" are from A Comrade Is as Precious as a Rice Seedling, *1987; "Lizard of Bicutan," "Pigeons for My Son," and "Freed Pigeon I Shall Be," are from* Journey: An Autobiography in Verse (1964–1995), *1996*

Haikus in Solitary Confinement

I

The sea
even by the light of the quarter moon
shines.

II

The tree lives
by the sun's rays.
But under the tree's shade
I will always find my comfort.

III

A lone flower
once kept in memory
never wilts.

IV

A rose
is a rose
by whatever name.

V

Sometimes it seems
the only defense left
is to return to the silence
of a mother's womb.

Prison

Prison is
a double wall
one of adobe
the other
so many layers
of barbed wire
both formidable.
The outer wall
is guarded
from watchtowers.

The other
is the prison
within,
where they will
hammer you
into the image
of their own likeness,
whoever they are.

As The Dust

You ask
why the sadness.

I would be
as coal
by the infinite
load of the earth
reduced
to a single
precious diamond.

But the infernal dust
permits it not.
The most radiant
inner light
could be lost
in one brush
with the wind

carrying this
ungodly mantle.
It creeps
through closed doors
in the dead of night,
I would have you know,
after you've so diligently

swept and husked
and cleansed your soul.
You would think
it were a breeze,
imprisoned here
but ah, that breeze
has its designs,

so vulgarly obvious
weaving dastardly tales
with the dry devilish dirt.
With wet cloth
we keep wiping,
trying desperately

to put some sheen
into our dulled lives,
but they would not
permit it.
Cowardly they creep in
with their petty intrigues
designed

to envelop and mummify
rendering us
friendless and forgotten.
Yes, they would have me
roll in the dust
the better to bite it.
So you asked:

As the dust, I say,
so my interminable sadness.

Lizard of Bicutan

A new-found friend
surprised me once some weeks ago.
He asked, do I believe
in territoriality.
What's that again? I said
dumbfounded.
He then explained he'd painted red
upon a lizard's back, one
that he'd seen so often in his room.
And then he'd brought it
to another hall to stay.
Next day he saw it once again
upon his desk, the lizard with
the red dot on its back.
I sat amazed.
Paint red upon some more,
I said, and see what happens.
Today I asked about our plot,

but he'd been busy with his cards[1]
and so he answered,
the first lizard is still there
carousing in my room.

I wondered then—if he'd
sent back the lizard to the hall
again and once again,
and somehow it got a mind
all of its own,
what it could have done
with such injustice.
Would it have stayed away
forever, I said to myself,
as any person would
who'd been thrown out of house and home
so often?

Pigeons for My Son

I gave the boy
a pair of pigeons
born and bred
in my harsh prison.
They had taped wings,
and the instructions were
specifically
to keep them on for weeks
until they'd gotten used
to their new cages.
He never liked
the thought of me
in prison, his own mother,
and would never
stay for long
to visit.
So perhaps I thought
of souvenirs.
But the tape from his pigeons
he removed one day,
and set them free.
You'd think
that would have angered me,
or made me sad at least
but I guess we're of one mind.
Why cage pigeons

who prefer free flight
in the vaster, bluer skies?

Freed Pigeon I Shall Be

(For Sylvia Mayuga)

Her Christmas gift to me
was a tiny yellow pigeon
trying to fly free
from a knitted and starched
white cage.
More apt than she had thought
(I guess),

for put up,
the bird's weight
carries its cage along,
tail caught in the door.
Freed pigeon shall I
also be
cage caught in my tail?

I shall wonder then
whether it's because
of the narrow door
or the smallness of my
forever-prison-now
or the color of the mantle
on me—

or, for that matter,
the starching.

NOTE

1. Greeting cards handcrafted by political detainees in Bicutan.

THE WOMEN OF THE AIDS COUNSELING AND EDUCATION (ACE) PROGRAM

BEDFORD HILLS CORRECTIONAL FACILITY, NEW YORK

The ACE Program was begun in 1988 at the Bedford Hills Correctional Facility, a maximum-security prison for women in New York State. *Breaking the Walls of Silence*, published in 1998, is the women's record of their peer education program, including an account of its origins and selected writings by individual women prisoners associated with ACE. This innovative, courageous program was begun, the women explain, because

> we lived in a state of constant anxiety over whether or not we would test positive for HIV. Locked up with one another, sharing the same showers, kitchen, and living space, we felt panic. . . . We knew that we would have to help ourselves and each other. We started ACE because we felt that as prisoners, we would be the most effective in educating, counseling, and building a community of support. (19)

In *Breaking the Walls of Silence*, the women of the ACE Program demonstrate the many facets of their achievement. Their program has served the population at Bedford Hills and has offered a model for others struggling with AIDS issues. Perhaps most significantly the program has supported the women of Bedford Hills in their determination to assume personal responsibility for each other and themselves—to build community: "We are women, convicted of crimes, who, in spite of it all, created something that is making a difference in many people's lives. Out of tragedy came one of the most positive experiences in our lives"(20).

As testimony to this value of community, *Breaking the Walls of Silence* itself is a collaborative product of many writers and perspectives. Women prisoners, a traditionally silenced group, claim their right to a voice in its pages. "Most of us," they explain, "were never writers. What we had to say was of little or no importance to anyone. Ironically, it took the tragedy of AIDS and imprisonment for us to be heard. Now our stories matter" (27).

Included below are selections by five women of the ACE Program: Katrina Haslip, Kathy Boudin, Doris Moices, Aida Rivera, and Gloria Boyd.

Note: Background information is from The Women of the ACE Program of the Bedford Hills Correctional Facility, *Breaking the Walls of Silence* (Woodstock, N.Y.: Overlook Press, 1998); Kathy Boudin et al., "ACE: A Peer Education and Counseling Program Meets the Needs of Incarcerated Women with HIV/AIDS Issues," *Journal of the Association of Nurses in AIDS Care*" 10, no. 6 (1999): 90.

A COMMUNITY OF WOMEN: LIVING WITH AIDS

From Breaking the Walls of Silence, *1998.*

Foreword

I often ask myself how it is that I came to be open about my status. For me, AIDS had been one of my best-kept secrets. It took me approximately fifteen months to discuss this issue openly. I could not bring myself to say it out loud. As if not saying it would make it go away. I watched other people with AIDS, who were much more open than I was at the time, reveal to audiences their status and their vulnerability. I wanted to be a part of what they were building, what they were doing, their statement, "I am a person with AIDS," "a PWA," because I was.

Somewhere behind a prison wall in Bedford Hills a movement or community was being built. It was a diverse group of women teaming together to meet the needs and fears that had developed with this new epidemic, AIDS. These women believed that none of their peers should be discriminated against, isolated, or treated cruelly merely because they were ill. They believed that it was necessary for this prison to build an environment of support, comfort, education, and trust. I was a part of this process. In the center of its establishment I stood, struggling with my own personal issues of HIV infection.

While held in some sort of limbo, I felt as if the women of ACE had built a cocoon around me, for me. I felt warmed by them and so totally understood. These were the women who understood my silence and yet felt my need to be heard. They gave me comfort when I needed it and an ear when I needed a listener. They helped me to grow stronger with hopes that one day I would be able to stand alone and still feel as safe. Empowered! I took from them all that they were capable of putting out. I gave back to them what I was given. It was as if I mirrored back what they put out. I had never before noticed in my peers this ability to care so deeply. For I too had labeled them prisoners, cold and uncaring. Yet they had managed to build a community of women: black, white, Hispanic, learned, illiterate, robbers, murderers, forgers, rich, poor, Christian, Muslim, Jewish, bisexual, gay, heterosexual—all putting aside their differences and egos for a collective cause, to help themselves. I could not believe my eyes. Right before me lay a model of how we, as a whole, needed to combat all the issues AIDS brought, and we were building it from behind a wall, from prison. We were the community that no one thought would help itself. Social outcasts, because of our crimes against society, in spite of what society inflicted upon some of us.

We emerged from the nothingness with a need to build consciousness and to save lives. We made a difference in our community behind the wall, and that difference has allowed me to survive and thrive as a person with AIDS. To my peers in Bedford Hills Correctional Facility, you have truly made a difference. I can now go anywhere, and stand openly, alone without the silence.

—Katrina Haslip

Last Will and Testament, written upon leaving Bedford Hills on parole in September 1990.

I, Katrina Haslip, being of sound mind, except when suffering from dementia, or half-himers, do swear that the following are my wishes, to be duly executed upon my departure from Bedford Hills. That I leave my worldly possessions to the following:

TO KATHY BOUDIN AND JUDY CLARK: For all the times that you asked me questions about myself, my personal life, and my own growth.

To you I leave my condensed version of the story of my life, which should answer all your questions, to be divided equally between the two of you.

TO AIDA RIVERA: I bequest to you my treasured Vaseline case, so that you will never forget how it looks, and for all the times that you hid it from me. Now grease your lips!

TO DEE (DEBRA IRVING): I leave to you my medium-size replicate doll, Dreads, as a reminder to you that I am your dreaded sister.

TO MARIA HERNANDEZ: ACE has acknowledged your worrying ability. In honor of that recognition, I leave you with my official pendant, my pink worry stone. Worry much!

TO PEARL WARD: I leave you with my name, Katrina Haslip, in exchange for yours, which I will be using on job applications, since you hold a bachelor's degree. Thank you kindly.

TO ROMEO (DORIS ROMEO): I leave you with a gift certificate of unlimited value for your use to use only at Bricetti's for gum on a regular basis. Send Elaine for it—it's only right down the street.

TO AGNES ALVAREZ: For your assistance with any/all of my problems, in regards to this office, my personal affairs, and your attentive ear, I leave to you a set of earphones, so that you will not have to listen to the others when I'm gone. Block them out, honey!

TO BARBARA FORD: To you I leave a manual on how to run ACE. Please use it.

TO LINDA MALMBERG: To you I leave population, for which you will be doing a lot of counseling. Good luck!

TO ALL THE PWAS: I leave you with hope, that you, too, are capable of becoming empowered and strong. Lean on ACE, they are the key to your empowerment and strength. Thanks to them, I can now go anywhere and stand openly alone as a PWA and feel wonderful about myself. Know that the same experience lies ahead of you. Be well!

TO ALL THE OTHER ACE MEMBERS that I have not listed by name, I have not forgotten you. Continue your commitment, and know that I will go away torn but strong.

—Katrina Haslip

A Harsh Poem, an Angry Poem, a Hard Poem

Two sisters died this week . . . of AIDS!
How dare they call it AIDS!
"To aid" is to help, to lend assistance
An aid—someone or thing which helps.
But there is no help, no cure, no vaccine
What a cruel name
Cruel as the name of the town Liberty, Alabama
Where so many black people have been lynched.

—Kathy B.

[It's difficult getting out of bed]

It's difficult getting out
of Bed. These Days.
Yet I know what lies ahead
will require me to force
the muscles to me
standing on these painful leg bones.
I'm remembering when I was
the best on my feet.
I could dance
on the tip of my toes!
I grasp on to those moments
I'm on stage with the lead
part, of *Grease*.
Wow!! Whee!!
There I go, I'm without
limits, without the pain.
The dance of the 50's,
Do you love me? Do you love me?
Now that I can dance
Watch me now. I do the
mashed potatoes, I'll do the twist.
I could shake, shake. Do you like
it like this?
It's difficult getting out of bed
These days.
But not in my head.

—Doris Moices

[I was conscious of women]

I was conscious of women before I came in here, but not on that level. ACE has made it deeper. ACE made me realize that AIDS is bigger than each individual woman, that it's going to take all of us coming together. I never knew so many things affected just women. I had looked at issues as a black woman—religious issues, being a single parent or not—but I had never reflected on being a woman in society.

The Beauty of It All

I've become a walking game of connect the dots, from the scars I've accumulated from many ongoing viruses, fungi, and bacteria. My tongue has become a mass production of cotton fields. Enough to dress a few. I have an abundance of hair; jealous of my two strands?
I was once called pretty, but now I'm called Beautiful.
Jealous, are you?
I was fast on my feet and great on my toes, now I let others do the walking for me, just like the Yellow Pages. I've developed a genuine sense of humor, and so I hide, I hide and wait.
Jealous, are you?
Even as I walk through the corridors at St. Clare's prison ward, I see so many, yet they can't see me. They've lost their sight. Where did it go?
Jealous, are you?
Just like me, we're on a permanent diet of anorexia.
Jealous, are you?
Don't be. I've just gained eleven pounds. I'm an overweight 96 pounds. I'm the beauty of it all.
Jealous, are you?
I thought you might be. . . .

—Doris Moices

[In 1983, I was arrested in Brooklyn]

In 1983, I was arrested in Brooklyn and charged with the sale and possession of drugs. I was sent to Rikers Island, and a year later I was sentenced to fifteen years to life. On December 10, 1984, I was sent to Bedford Hills to serve my time.

I grew up in Brooklyn, in Coney Island, and with eight brothers and four sisters, life wasn't easy. We were on public assistance. My mother, in a way, was the one who kept order in the house. She was the one who disciplined us. My dad was the easygoing one. I love both my parents very much, but my dad was my teacher and my soulmate. He taught me to see things through his eyes.

There were two things I enjoyed doing with my dad, and those were fishing and going to the junkyard. I remember going fishing with my dad. He always woke up at five in the morning, started the coffee, and got the gear together, and by six-thirty we were on our way. My dad considered himself a real live fisherman. The man would fish anything out of the water.

My father wasn't just a fisherman, he was also a junkyard man. The junkyard was his paradise. Everything and anything he found was good. Our first blender came from the junkyard, but it burned out after a week. One of the things we never ran out of were combs, because it didn't matter where my father found a comb, he always picked it up and brought it home. He used to go fishing and come back with a couple of fish and a pocket full of combs. He would say, "Why bother to buy them, when I can find them? Why pay for them? He would put the combs in hot water and soap and say, "See? Now we have combs." So we never ran out of combs.

My parents are both from Puerto Rico. My dad spoke a little English. My mother didn't speak it at all. We grew up talking English to them. In turn, they answered us in Spanish.

When I was in high school, things were hard, times were hard. We didn't have enough money for so many people. And at sixteen, I decided one day, instead of going to school, to drop out and find a job. And I found a job where my father used to work, in a yarn factory. I got hired, and every day I'd start out for school but I really went to work. They knew my father. And finally I had to tell my mother, and she was upset, but I was sixteen so there was nothing she could do. After there I worked in a doll factory in Bay Ridge, and it was then that I found a way to make better money—drugs. As for me and drugs, I was a casual user—I wasn't into shooting and sniffing. I had a habit, although I didn't see it as that at the time. It took me till I got here to figure out that that was true. When I was arrested, I had five kids. I was selling drugs for the easy money.

When I first arrived at Bedford Hills, my attitude was to take care of myself and the hell with everyone else. The bottom line was that I just wanted to do my time and not concern myself with anyone else. I had my own problems, which were my sentence and the fact that I wanted to see my five children that I left behind. Anyone with a problem was on their own. Whatever problem they had was their own, not mine.

When I was in the street, it was very different. If anybody needed my help, I was there for them. I was dealing drugs, so it was easy for me to do whatever I had to do for whomever. I had the money. I remember one time my mother called me about some lady. Her infant baby had just died and they didn't have money to bury her, to lay her out in the funeral, and I just went and gave the lady her money. And I didn't know her. It was like I cared enough to do that. But once I came into the prison, I didn't want to be bothered with anybody's feelings.

Then, in 1987, I found out that my sister was HIV-positive. I had no understanding nor any knowledge of what HIV/AIDS was. I decided that it was time to get off the merry-go-round completely, step back and take a real good look at myself. I had to figure out what I really wanted to do with myself. Did I want to continue living the life I was leading or make a change for the better? I realized that instead of my sister being HIV-positive, it could have been me. In prison, arts and crafts was the first place I went to when I came here. I remember making this ugly cup—to me it looked so beautiful. Then I made a vase. And I realized that I could do things. I was amazed that I could do all these things, it was a whole different experience for me. And I guess every time I had a problem or crisis, ceramics became a way of expressing what I felt. I actually won first prize with a vase that was called *A Sandwich*. It wasn't even supposed to be in the competition. I had made it for a friend, and when I went in to pick it up, I found out it had been sent to an art show, a Department of Corrections art show. I was amazed that not only had it won first prize but someone had bought it.

In 1988, I joined ACE. I wanted to learn more about the virus that my sister had. To do so I knew that I had to get an education, so I went back to school. After nine years as a high school drop-out, I found that going back was not easy. Getting involved in ACE changed my life. I began to look at things differently. I started caring about other people, even people I did not know and might never see again in life. In 1989, I received my GED. Today, in 1992, I'm about ready to get my associate's degree and I'm working on my bachelor's degree. Today I know who I am and what I want to do with my life as well as where I'm going in life.

—*Aida Rivera*

[It don't matter now]

It don't matter now, how or why or who.

It don't matter now when
  the year of the virus entered my life
    and my body
      and my bloodstream
      and my brain.

In the name of the indifference, who cares?

The life flow of my existence speaks loudly
in many tongues.

See me,
  Hear me,
    Hold me.

Now for a second I ponder,
  then I let it go.

In my world there is no time
   for idle thought
      nor space
         nor room to roam.

Only to gather as I go in a relentless
pursuit to the rhythm of my own pace
         is miracle indeed.

To hold my world—never to relinquish
   my power
      my presence,
         my heart felt struggle with
         conflict through change.

Until the end

   Past tomorrow

   Forever more

   I am Gloria B.
                              —*Gloria Boyd*

PART 2

'WE WERE STRONGER AFTERWARD THAN BEFORE':

TRANSCENDENCE THROUGH CAUSES AND
BELIEFS BEYOND THE SELF

*If a person does not know his or her standpoint, that person can be sup-
pressed—silenced. But if you know where you stand, if you know the people
support you, you will keep on resisting, wherever you are.*
—Caesarina Kona Makhoere

During her thirty-year confinement in the Tour de Constance in Aigues-
Morte, France, Marie Durand carved the word *"Resister"* (To resist) in the
stones of her tower prison.[1] One simple, profound word—this message from
Durand, an eighteenth-century French Protestant prisoner of conscience,
echoes a timeless call to commitment that continues to inspire and support
those who repeat it today. The message links prisoners of conscience worldwide, throughout history. It is a message the writer sends to others as well
as to herself, and in one word it reveals how dynamic and full of purpose
prison literature can be.

Most women's prison literature explores the writer's personal response to
incarceration or describes her prison environment and lifestyle. Whether
the writer focuses directly on herself or shifts her gaze to her sister prisoners, the basic subject is the reality of imprisonment. Some writers, however,
transcend this focus on the immediate situation to discuss another topic:
the cause or belief that brought them to prison in the first place. In these
works, the fact of imprisonment is decidedly secondary and is mentioned
only to enhance the argument by demonstrating the prisoner's professed
dedication to a political, social, or religious cause. And, as is the case with
other prison literature by women, this type of writing firmly grasps the concrete; the writer transcends imprisonment without ethereal flights into theory or abstract philosophical arguments.[2]

Both male and female prisoners who write about a cause usually intend to
support an audience of other believers or to persuade a neutral or hostile
audience. Imprisonment underscores the merit of a cause that can elicit such
commitment despite injustice and hardship. The five selections in this section demonstrate the authors' overriding sense of a larger, external purpose

that eclipses the self. The selections show, however, that women writers often stress the concerns of *women* working for a cause, even while they downplay their own personal histories.

Focusing on an external cause at the expense of self is a centuries-old theme in women's prison literature. "The Passion of Saint Perpetua" offers an early and vivid illustration. In this early Christian's account of a vision on the day before her martyrdom in the amphitheater at Carthage in 203 A.D., confidence in the truth for which she dies makes her a victor; an anonymous chosen daughter of God triumphs, and not Perpetua the individual. In fact, it is the truth, and not a person at all, that triumphs in Perpetua's testimony. Her narrative is remarkable for its omission of references to her personal identity; even her sex is changed, though the female pronoun continues to be used. The text does not, however, launch into an abstract discussion of Perpetua's Christian philosophy. Instead, she chooses to convince her reader through recitation of visions recounted with simplicity and dignity.[3]

British Quaker Katharine Evans uses similar techniques in her account of her religious trials in seventeenth-century Malta.[4] The works of Evans and Sarah Cheevers, Evans's companion in the ministry, belong to the early Quaker movement's literature of "sufferings," which emphasized the cause rather than the writer. Written explanations of the principles for which they suffered enabled members of the Religious Society of Friends to combat religious intolerance without violating their peace testimony, which led them to affirm good and deny evil through nonviolent means. Since the form of sufferings tracts was quite standardized and, after 1672, subject to approval by the London Yearly Meeting (the largest central body of Quakers), there was relatively little room for expression of the writer's personality.[5] Still, the spiritual and physical power that these Quaker women possessed shines through their writings even though they used impersonal, standard forms of expression.

High drama charges Evans's account of the classic battle between good and evil that she and Cheevers lived. The lines are clearly and absolutely drawn: the Lord Inquisitor and his accomplices "with a black Rod" represent the Devil, while Evans and Cheevers stand fast in the Light. Although we see little of Evans's *self,* she is far more than a cardboard figure. She demonstrates the toughness that made leaders of so many seventeenth-century Quaker women. Despite failing health, she refuses to be moved from her airless "inner Room" and separated from Cheevers, but her joy in her strength bears no trace of ego: "We were stronger afterward than before, the Lord God did fit us for every Condition."

Prison writing about a cause often employs public formats, such as that of Quaker sufferings tracts, rather than the personal, confessional formats of diaries or memoirs. The author wishes to announce rather than to justify her imprisonment. Madame Roland's need to justify herself before an impartial posterity is absent from these confident but relatively selfless prison writings. Some women imprisoned for a cause, however, write both works that advertise the cause as well as more autobiographical accounts of how incarceration affected them personally. An example is Margaret Sanger (see the annotated bibliography), noted American birth control activist.

The selections in part 2 from the Chilean resistance movement of the 1970s are testimonies of the authors' experiences as representative of the collective experience of their people. Anonymity is more than a security measure for the writer: it is a reinforcement of the message that the writer belongs to a community of imprisoned and oppressed women who speak collectively through her. She provides the voice; the experience is shared by all.[6]

The testimonies of most Latin American women prisoners take the form of oral interviews, or begin as interviews that are later written as narratives by collaborating authors.[7] Many testimonies have not been recorded because of fear of reprisal or because the woman, tortured and physically humiliated, found it difficult to publicize her painful experience within a society that considers her somehow to blame for the violation of her body.[8] Ana Guadalupe Martínez of El Salvador's Revolutionary Democratic Front (RDF) explains the psychological aspect of women's physical torture:

> In the case of women, sexual abuse, the constant pawing, and the threat of rape are among the principal ways used by the repressive apparatus to demoralize. The mere fact of feeling an assassin's hands on your body causes revulsion and anguish. Even though I had known that all this would happen, it was a brutal, horrible experience.[9]

The testimonies that have been recorded proclaim that the pain and humiliation of torture are by no means the whole story of political prisoners. When women who endured this trauma were afterward imprisoned in camps such as Tres Alamos in Chile, they put their revolutionary theory to practice in the most inauspicious of environments. Communal organization of work, leisure, domestic tasks, and childcare made prison existence bearable while it created, in microcosm, the society that the women and their *compañeros* (male comrades) struggled to build. The challenge these women faced was to maintain morale and momentum upon release, despite exile's disruption, grief over comrades who had disappeared, and resistance by *compañeros* who were uneasy with new female roles. Since publication of the first edition of this anthology, English translations of Latin American women's prison writing have become somewhat more available to readers, as noted in the annotated bibliography.[10]

All writings by prisoners of conscience speak to their willingness to pay the ultimate price for a cause or belief. The selections in part 2 are grim and their endings are often disconcerting: torture figures prominently in three selections, and three end with an execution. In 203 A.D., Perpetua chooses martyrdom; Iranian prisoner Olya Roohizadegan describes how, in 1980, ten young Bahá'í women make the same decision. Even their words are strikingly similar: "I am a Christian." "I am a Bahá'í." Most fundamental of all are the life-affirming words of Polish resistance fighter Krystyna Wituska, who was guillotined by the Nazis in 1944: "I am first a human being."

Olya Roohizadegan is a survivor of the Bahá'í persecution in Iran. Her description of her life, her own prison experience, and her release is subordinated to her primary goal: to tell her sister prisoners' story. Her testimony has special resonance with readers because Roohizadegan is more than a sensitive witness and recorder of events. She, too, is committed to the cause for which her sisters were imprisoned and executed, and she aims to honor their message as well as the memory of their individual lives. The horror of their deaths is juxtaposed with the beauty expressed in their youthful biographies. "Remember this," recites Roohizadegan to herself upon her release; for this prison writer, each word fulfills a promise and the text becomes a living memorial.

Twenty-three-year-old Krystyna Wituska was executed by the Nazis following a two-year imprisonment during World War II. She wrote letters from prison to her parents and to the teenage daughter of a cooperative German guard. Unpretentious and hopeful, her letters state the condemned writer's practical requests for the few simple supplies and comforts allowed her, and comment on events in the lives of loved ones within the prison and outside. This quotidian aspect of Wituska's correspondence serves as a foil for the somber but never morbid consideration of her own approaching death. With impressive maturity she speculates upon the practical arrangements for her beheading as well as the larger significance of her sacrifice. Like other women prisoners of conscience, Wituska perceives the cause as more important than her own situation. Identifying with humanity and disavowing nationalism as too narrow and restrictive, she recognizes her resistance to Nazism as a battle for civilization itself: "On the day that I will die, I would prefer to tell myself that I am dying for freedom and justice, rather than that I die just for my own Poland. Consciousness of a universal humanity will comfort me."

Literature of commitment is among the most articulate, unambiguous, and positive of all women's prison writings.[11] Many of the causes supported in this literature are shared by men and women alike, so that gender differences are not always prominent in this type of prison writing. Still, the unique aspects of women's experiences as activists and as prisoners underscore the perspective of each selection in this section.

NOTES

The quotation in the title of this section is taken from Katharine Evans, "Isle of Malta, Anno 1661," in chap. 13 of *A Collection of the Sufferings of the People Called Quakers,* ed. Joseph Besse, vol. 2 (London: Luke Hinde, 1753). The epigraph to this section is taken from Caesarina Kona Makhoere, *No Child's Play: In Prison under Apartheid* (London: The Women's Press, 1988), 47.

1. See Marie Durand, *Lettres de Marie Durand (1711–1776): Prisonnière à la Tour de Constance de 1730 à 1768,* ed. Étienne Gammonet (Montpellier, France: Les Presses du Languedoc, 1986; 1998), 5.

2. Selections in this anthology by the following writers are also relevant to the discussion of women's imprisonment for causes and beliefs: Aguilar, Baxley, Buck, Figner, Huggins, Lebrón, Lytton, Makhoere, Partnoy, Saadawi, Shakur, Smedley, and Tesfagiorgis.

3. Joyce E. Salisbury's *Perpetua's Passion: The Death and Memory of a Young Roman Woman* (New York: Routledge, 1997), presents an extended analysis of Perpetua's life and death in the context of the early Christian church and women's position within it.

4. See Judith Scheffler, "Prison Writings of Early Quaker Women," *Quaker History* 73, no. 2 (Fall 1984): 25–37.

5. For a discussion of Quaker sufferings literature, see Luella Wright, *The Literary Life of the Early Friends, 1650–1725* (New York: Columbia University Press, 1932), 74–97; John R. Knott, "Joseph Besse and the Quaker Culture of Suffering," *Prose Studies* (Great Britain) 17, no. 3 (1994): 126–41; Rosemary Kegl, "Women's Preaching, Absolute Property, and the Cruel . . .," *Women's Studies* 24, nos. 1/2 (November 1994): 51–84.

6. A similar message is stated in the preface to *Slave of Slaves: The Challenge of Latin American Women*, by the Latin American and Caribbean Women's Collective, trans. Michael Pallis (London: Zed Press, 1980), 5: "We have sought to show that it is quite possible to write as a group and that ideas are no one's private property."

7. See, for example, Domitila Barrios de Chungara with Moema Viezzer, *Let Me Speak! Testimony of Domitila, a Woman of the Bolivian Mines*, trans. Victoria Ortiz (New York: Monthly Review Press, 1978); Margaret Randall, *Sandino's Daughters: Testimonies of Nicaraguan Women in Struggle*, ed. Lynda Yanz (1981; New Brunswick: Rutgers University Press, 1995); Margaret Randall, *Sandino's Daughters Revisted: Feminism in Nicaragua* (New Brunswick: Rutgers University Press, 1994); Comite Jane Vanini, *Women in Resistance* (Berkeley, Calif.: Support Committee for Women in the Chilean and Latin American Resistance, n.d.), which includes an interview with Gladys Diaz; Rigoberta Menchú, *I, Rigoberta Menchú: An Indian Woman in Guatemala*, ed. Elisabeth Burgos-Debray, trans. Ann Wright (New York: Verso/ Schocken, 1984); Ana Guadalupe Martínez, *Las Cárceles Clandestinas de El Salvador* (Libertad por El Secuestro de un Oligarca, 1978).

8. Ximena Bunster, presentation in the "Women and Human Rights" session, Women's Studies Conference, University of Pennsylvania, Philadelphia, March 1985. Oppression of women is also seen in harsh antiabortion laws. *Women behind Bars: Chile's Abortion Laws, A Human Rights Analysis* (New York: The Center for Reproductive Law and Policy and The Open Forum on Reproductive Health and Rights, 1998) reports that women in Chile face prosecution and imprisonment for choosing abortion.

9. Ana Guadalupe Martínez, *Las Cárceles Clandestinas de El Salvador*, excerpt translated in *Women and War: El Salvador* (New York: Women's International Resource Exchange Service, 1981) 24–26.

10. See the annotated bibliography for these entries, some of which are new entries: Cassidy; Diaz, Gladys; Diaz, Nidia; Kozameh; Partnoy; Talamante; Varela. Note that this bibliography includes only works written entirely by the prisoner herself, so that some testimonies are not included.

11. Barbara Harlow, in *Barred Visions: Women, Writing, and Political Detention* (Middletown, Conn.: Wesleyan University Press, 1992), discusses the writing of women imprisoned for political reasons. Caren Kaplan refers to this writing as an "out-law genre," in "Resisting Autobiography: Out-law Genres and Transnational Feminist Subjects," in *Women, Autobiography, Theory: A Reader*, ed. Sidonie Smith and Julia Watson (Madison: University of Wisconsin Press, 1998) 208–16. Alicia Partnoy collects the writing of "Latin American Women Writing in Exile" (not all of them imprisoned) in *You Can't Drown the Fire* (Pittsburgh: Cleis Press, 1988). Elihu Rosenblatt, ed., *Criminal Injustice: Confronting the Prison Crisis* (Boston: South End Press, 1996) discusses political imprisonment and includes some writing by political prisoners, and Aryeh Neier discusses political prisoners in "Confining Dissent," in *The Oxford History of the Prison*, ed. Norval Morris and David J. Rothman (New York: Oxford, 1998) 350–80. Websites to visit for information about international political prisoners, including writers, are Pen American Center, http://www.pen.org; Amnesty International On-line, http://www.amnesty.org/; and Amnesty International USA, http://www.aiusa.org/.

SAINT PERPETUA

(d. A.D. 203)

Vibia Perpetua, a twenty-two-year-old Carthaginian woman, was arrested and imprisoned in A.D. 203 for her refusal to sacrifice to the Roman gods for the welfare of the emperor, Septimius Severus. This well-born young woman was a nursing mother at the time of her arrest. As an early Christian catechumen, a follower preparing herself for baptism into the church, she was persecuted under the emperor's decree forbidding Christians to practice their faith. She and other Christians were baptized while under house arrest. Scholars believe that she was a leader in the Christian community as well as in prison. Perpetua was martyred on March 7, A.D. 203, in the arena at Carthage during games held to celebrate the birthday of Severus's son. She was sacrificed together with male Christian prisoners and the slave Felicitas (Felicity), who gave birth to a baby girl in prison two days before the games.

Perpetua's story is told by the narrator of the *Passio SS. Perpetuae et Felicitatis*, identified by some scholars as i.d. Tertullian. He records the martyrdom of both young mothers and tells the reader that he has faithfully included the text of Perpetua's prison diary. This Latin narrative, translated below, is remarkable for its simplicity of style and content. Perpetua gives a detailed description of four dreams or visions she had while in prison and an unadorned account of the effect these events had upon her family relationships. The diary concludes immediately before Perpetua's death in the arena.

Perpetua's execution is described by the narrator of the *Passio*, who states that she refused to wear the required ritual costume of the goddess Ceres as she entered the arena. Inside the arena a mad heifer tossed but failed to kill the women. As in Perpetua's fourth dream, which she describes in the diary below, she was called away from the heifer to the Gate of the Living, the arena exit used by those who survived their contests. However, Perpetua and her companions were eventually taken to a gladiator to be executed by sword. When the young gladiator missed at the first strike, Perpetua herself guided his hand to her throat. The narrator of the *Passio* suggests that her greatness prevented anyone from killing her without her own assistance.

Over the centuries, the church was not always comfortable with the contents of Perpetua's diary; the power and independence emanating from her self-portrait were not always considered to be consistent with cultural expectations for female behavior. But Saint Perpetua became an important figure in the early church in Carthage and March 7 became her feast day in the calendar of the Roman Church.

Note: Background information is from Peter Dronke, *Women Writers of the Middle Ages* (Cambridge: Cambridge University Press, 1988); David Hugh Farmer, *The Oxford Dictionary of Saints* (Oxford: Oxford University Press, 1978); Joyce E. Salisbury, *Perpetua's Passion* (New York: Routledge, 1997).

THE PASSION OF SAINT PERPETUA

From Women Writers of the Middle Ages, *1984*

When we were as yet only under legal surveillance, and my father, out of love for me, kept trying to refute me by argument and to break my resolve, I said: "Father, do you see that container over there, for instance—a jug or something?" And he said: "Yes, I do." And I said to him: "It can't be anything other than it is, can it?" And he said: "No." "So too, I can't call myself anything other than I am: a Christian."

Then my father, angry at this word, bore down on me as if he would pluck out my eyes. But he only fumed, and went away, defeated, along with the devil's sophistries. Then, for the few days that I was without my father, I gave thanks to God—I felt relieved at his not being there. In that short space of time we were baptized. But the Spirit enjoined me not to seek from that water any favour except physical endurance. After a few days we were taken to prison, and I grew frightened, for I had never known such darkness. Oh grim day!—intense heat, because of the crowds, extortions by soldiers. Above all, I was tormented with anxiety there, on account of my child.

Then Tertius and Pomponius, the consecrated deacons who were looking after us, arranged by a bribe that they let us out into a better, cooler part of the prison for a few hours. Coming out of the dungeon, everyone began to move freely; I breast-fed my child, who was already weak with hunger. Anxiously I spoke to my mother about him, I consoled my brother, I gave them charge of my son. I was worn out, seeing them so worn because of me. Such were my fearful thoughts for many days. Then I managed to have the child allowed to stay with me in prison. And at once I grew well again, relieved of the strain and anguish for him. And suddenly the prison became a palace to me, where I would rather be than anywhere.

Then my brother said to me: "My lady, my sister, you are now greatly blessed: so much that you can ask for a vision, and you will be shown if it is to be suffering unto death or a passing thing." And I, who knew I was in dialogue with God, whose great benefits I had experienced, promised him faithfully, saying: "Tomorrow I'll tell you." And I asked for a vision, and this was shown to me:

I saw a bronze ladder, marvellously long, reaching as far as heaven, and narrow too: people could climb it only one at a time. And on the sides of the ladder every kind of iron implement was fixed: there were swords, lances, hooks, cutlasses, javelins, so that if anyone went up carelessly or not looking upwards, he would be torn and his flesh caught on the sharp iron. And beneath the ladder lurked a serpent of wondrous size, who laid ambushes for those mounting, making them terrified of the ascent. But Saturus climbed up first (he was the one who at a later stage gave himself up spontaneously on account of us—he had built up our courage and then, when we were arrested, had been away). And he reached the top of the ladder, and turned and said to me: "Perpetua, I'm waiting for you—but watch out that the serpent doesn't bite you!" And I said: "He won't hurt me, in Christ's name!" And under that ladder, almost, it seemed, afraid of me, the serpent slowly thrust out its head—and, as if I were treading on the first rung, I trod on it, and I climbed. And I saw an immense space of garden, and in the middle of it a white-haired man sitting in shepherd's garb, vast, milking sheep, with many thousands of people dressed in shining white standing all round. And he raised his head, looked at me, and said: "You are welcome, child." And he called me, and gave me, it seemed, a mouthful of the cheese he was milking; and I accepted it in both my hands together, and ate it, and all those standing around said: "Amen." And at the sound of that word I awoke, still chewing something indefinable and sweet. And at once I told my brother, and we understood that it would be mortal suffering; and we began to have no more hope in the world.

A few days later the rumour ran that our hearing would take place. My father came over from the city worn out with exhaustion, and he went up to me in order to deflect me, saying: "My daughter, have pity on my white hairs! Show some compassion to your father, if I deserve to be called father by you. If with these hands I have helped you to the flower of your youth, if I favoured you beyond all your brothers—do not bring me into disgrace in all men's eyes! Look at your brothers, look at your mother and your aunt—look at your son, who won't be able to live if you die. Don't flaunt your insistence, or you'll destroy us all: for if anything happens to you, none of us will ever be able to speak freely and openly again."

This is what my father said, out of devotion to me, kissing my hands and flinging himself at my feet; and amid his tears he called me not "daughter" but "*domina*." And I grieved for my father's condition—for he alone of all my family would not gain joy from my ordeal. And I comforted him, saying: "At the tribunal things will go as God wills: for you must know we are no longer in our own hands, but in God's." And he left me, griefstricken.

Another day, whilst we were eating our midday meal, we were suddenly taken away to the hearing, and arrived at the forum. At once the rumour swept the neighborhood, and an immense crowd formed. We mounted the tribunal. The others, when interrogated, confessed. Then my turn came. And my father appeared there with my son, and pulled me off the step, saying: "Perform the sacrifice! Have pity on your child!" So too the governor, Hilarianus, who had been given judiciary power in place of the late proconsul Minucius Timinianus: "Spare your father's old age, spare your little boy's infancy! Perform the ritual for the Emperor's welfare." And I answered: "I will not perform it." Hilarianus: "You are a Christian then?" And I answered: "I am a Christian." And as my father still hovered, trying to deflect me, Hilarianus ordered him to be thrown out, and he was struck with a rod. And I grieved for my father's downfall as if I'd been struck myself: that's how I mourned for his pitiful old age.

Then the governor sentenced us all and condemned us to the beasts of the arena. And joyful we went back to prison.

Then, as the baby was used to breast-feeding and staying in the prison with me, I at once sent the deacon Pomponius to my father, imploring to have it back. But my father did not want to let it go. And somehow, through God's will, it no longer needed the breast, nor did my breasts become inflamed—so I was not tormented with worry for the child, or with soreness.

A few days later, while we were all praying, suddenly in the middle of my prayer I let slip a word: the name, Dinocrates. And I was amazed, for he had never entered my thoughts except just then. And I grieved, remembering his plight. Then at once I realized that I was entitled to ask for a vision about him, and that I ought to; and I began to pray for him a lot, and plaintively, to God. That very night, this is what I was shown: I saw Dinocrates coming out of a dark place, where there were many people. He was very hot and thirsty, his clothes dirty and his looks pallid—he still had on his face the same wound as when he died. When alive he had been my brother, who at the age of seven died wretchedly, of a cancer of the face, in such a way that everyone saw his death with revulsion. So I prayed for him, and between me and him there was a great gap, such that we could not come near each other. Beside Dinocrates was a pool full of water, with a rim that was higher than he. And Dinocrates stretched up as if to drink. I was full of sorrow that, even though the pool had water, the rim was so high that he could not drink. And I awoke, and realized that my brother was struggling. Yet I was confident that I could help him in his struggle, and I prayed for him every day, till we moved to the military prison—for we were destined to fight in the garrison-games: they were on Emperor Geta's birthday. Day and night I prayed for Dinocrates, groaning and weeping that my prayer be granted.

On a day when we remained in fetters, I was shown this: I saw the place I'd seen before, and there was Dinocrates, clean, well-dressed, refreshed; and where the wound had been I saw a scar; and the pool I'd seen previously had its rim lowered: it was down to the boy's navel. And he was drinking from the pool incessantly. Above the rim was a golden bowl full of water. Dinocrates came near it and began to drink from that, and the bowl never ran dry. And when he had drunk his fill, he began to play with the water, as children do, full of happiness. And I awoke: I realized then that he'd been freed from pain.

A few days after that, the adjutant, Pudens, provost of the prison, began to show us honour, perceiving that there was a rare power in us. He allowed us many visitors, so that we could comfort one another. But when the day of the spectacle drew near, my father came in to me, wasted and worn. He began to tear out the hair of his beard and fling it on the ground, he hurled himself headlong and cursed his life, and said such things as would move every living creature. I ached for his unhappy old age.

The day before our fight, this is what I saw in vision: Pomponius the deacon was coming to the prison gate and knocking urgently. And I went out to him and opened for him. He was wearing a loose, gleaming white tunic, and damasked sandals, and he said: "Perpetua, we are waiting for you: come!" He took my hand and we began to go over rough, winding ways. We had hardly reached the amphitheatre, breathless, when he took me into the middle of the arena, and said: "Don't be afraid; here I am, beside you, sharing your toil." And he vanished. And I saw the immense, astonished crowd. And as I knew I had been condemned to the wild beasts, I was amazed they did not send them out at me. Out against me came an Egyptian, foul of aspect, with his seconds: he was to fight with me. And some handsome young men came up beside me: my own seconds and supporters. And I was stripped naked, and became a man. And my supporters began to rub me with oil, as they do for a wrestling match; and on the other side I saw the Egyptian rolling himself in the dust. And a man of amazing size came out—he towered even over the vault of the amphitheatre. He was wearing the purple, loosely, with two stripes crossing his chest, and patterned sandals made of gold and silver, carrying a baton like a fencing-master and a green bough laden with golden apples. He asked for silence, and said: "This Egyptian, if he defeats her, will kill her with his sword; she, if she defeats him, will receive this bough." And he drew back.

And we joined combat, and fists began to fly. He tried to grab my feet, but I struck him in the face with my heels. And I felt airborne, and began to strike him as if I were not touching ground. But when I saw there was a lull, I locked my hands, clenching my fingers together, and so caught hold of his head; and he fell on his face, and I trod upon his head. The populace began to shout, and my supporters to sing jubilantly. And I went to the fencing-master and received the bough. He kissed me and said: "Daughter, peace be with you!" And triumphantly I began to walk towards the Gate of the Living. And I awoke. And I knew I should have to fight not against wild beasts but against the Fiend; but I knew the victory would be mine.

This is what I have done till the day before the contest; if anyone wants to write of its outcome, let them do so.

KATHARINE EVANS

(?–1692)

English Quaker Katharine Evans and her husband, John, "a Man of considerable Estate," lived near Bath in Englishbatch, Somerset. She was a housewife whose fervent commitment to the beliefs of the Religious Society of Friends inspired her traveling ministry. As was the custom in the early years of this religious movement, husband and wife traveled separately, and Evans's frequent companion in the ministry was Sarah Cheevers (or Chevers), a housewife from Wiltshire. Like other early Quakers, Evans was persecuted throughout her extensive travels. Between 1655 and 1658 she was jailed in Exeter, banished from the Isle of Wight and the Isle of Man, whipped in Salisbury, and attacked in Warminster.

While on a journey to Alexandria and Jerusalem in 1659, Evans and Cheevers were arrested by the Inquisition when their ship stopped at Malta and they boldly preached there. They were initially confined in the English consul's house, but were later transferred to the Inquisition's prison and pressured to convert to Roman Catholicism. Defying their captors, Evans and Cheevers instead preached to the other prisoners. Their most severe test came when Evans, whose fragile health was suffering from the lack of air in their small room, was offered a separate, cooler room. They refused to be parted, but after nine months they were forced to separate. To earn money for expenses in prison, Evans and Cheevers were allowed to knit and darn clothes for other prisoners, and, more important, they were permitted to write letters of spiritual encouragement to family and other Friends at home.

Meanwhile, in England, attempts were being made to secure the women's release. Sea captain Daniel Baker traveled to Malta but was unable to help them. However, when George Fox, founder of the Society of Friends, appealed to powerful English nobles, the release followed promptly. While at the consul's house awaiting passage home, Evans and Cheevers continued to proclaim their message. They arrived home in 1662, after three and a half years. Cheevers died shortly afterward, in 1664, and Evans's husband died in prison the same year, but Katharine Evans lived many more years and continued in the ministry.

Note: Background information is from Joseph Besse, ed., *A Collection of the Sufferings of the People Called Quakers* (London: Luke Hinde, 1753); Mable R. Brailsford, *Quaker Women 1650–1690* (London: Duckworth, 1915); William C. Braithwaite, *The Beginnings of Quakerism*, 2d ed. (Cambridge: Cambridge University Press, 1955); Cicely Veronica Wedgewood, "The Converstion of Malta," *Velvet Studies* (London: J. Cape, 1946).

A Sufferings Tract

From "Isle of Malta, Anno 1661."

The Day that we were had from the *English* Consul's to the Inquisition, there came a Man with a black Rod, and the Chancellor and Council, and had us before their Lord Inquisitor, and he asked us, *Whether we had changed our Minds yet?* We said, *Nay we should not change from the Truth.* He asked, *What new Light we talked of?* We said, *No new Light, but the same the Prophets and Apostles bore Testimony to.* Then he said, *How came this Light to be lost ever since the Apostles Time?* We said, *It was not lost, Men had it still in them, but they did not know it, by reason the Night of Apostacy had and hath overspread the Nations.* Then he said, *If we would change our Minds, and do as they would have us do, we should say so, or else they would use us as they pleased.* We said, *The Will of the Lord be done.* And he rose up, and went his Way with the Consul, and left us there. And the Man with the black Rod, and the Keeper, took us and put us into an inner Room in the Inquisition, which had but two little Holes in it for Light or Air; but the Glory of the Lord did shine round about us. . . .

But he did thirst daily for our Blood, because we would not turn, and urged us much about our Faith and the Sacrament, to bring us under their Law, but the Lord preserved us. They said, *It was impossible we could live long in that hot Room*; for the Room was so hot and so close, that we were fain to rise often out of our Bed, and lie down at a Chink of the Door for Air to fetch Breath, and with the Fire within, and the Heat without, our Skin was like Sheep's Leather, and the Hair did fall off our Heads, and we did fail often; our Afflictions and Burdens were so great, that when it was Day we wished for Night, and when it was Night we wished for Day, we sought Death, but could not find it. We desired to die, but Death fled from us. We did eat our Bread with Weeping, and mingled our Drink with our Tears. We did write to the Inquisitor, and laid before him our Innocency and our Faithfulness in giving our Testimony for the Lord amongst them, and I told him, *If it were our Blood they did thirst after, they might take it any other Way, as well as smother us up in that hot Room.* So he sent for the Friar, and he took away our Inkhorns, (they had our Bibles before). We asked, *Why they took away our Goods?* They said, *It was all theirs, and our Lives too if they would.* We asked, *How we had forfeited our Lives to them?* They said, *For bringing Books and Papers.* We said, *If there was any Thing in them that was not true, they might write against it.* They said, *They did scorn to write to Fools and Asses, that did not know true* Latin. And told us, *The Inquisitor would have us separated because I was weak, and I should go into a cooler Room, but* Sarah *should abide there.* I took her by the Arm, and said, *The Lord hath joined us together, and Wo be to them that shall part us: I chuse rather to die here with my Friend, than to part from her.* The Friar was smitten, and went away, and came no more in five Weeks, and the Door was not opened in all that Time. Then they came again to part us, but I was sick, and broke out from Head to Foot. They sent for a Doctor, who said, *We must have Air, or else we must die.* So the Lord compelled them to go to the Inquisitor, and he gave Order for the Door to be set open six Hours in the Day. They did not part us in ten Weeks after. But O the dark Clouds, and the sharp Showers, the Lord did carry us through! Death itself had been better than to have parted in that Place. They said, *We corrupted each other, and that they thought when we were parted, we would bow to them,* but they found it otherwise. We were stronger afterward than before, the Lord our God did fit us for every Condition. They came and brought a Scourge of small Hemp, and asked us, *If we would have any of it?* They said, *They did whip themselves till the Blood came.* We said, *That could not reach the Devil, he sat upon the Heart.* They said, *All the Men and Women of* Malta *were for us if we would be* Catholicks, *for there would be none like unto us.* We said, *The Lord had changed us into that which changeth not.* They said, *All their holy Women did pray for us, and we should be honoured of all the World, if we would turn.* We said, *We were of God, and the whole World did lie in Wickedness, and we denied the Honour of the World, and the Glory too.* They said, *We should be honoured of God too, but now we were hated of all.* We said, *It is an evident Token whose Servants we are, the Servant is not greater than the Lord, and that the Scripture was fulfilled, which saith,* All this will I give thee, if thou wilt fall down and worship me.

At Another Time the *English* Friar shewed us his Crucifix, and bade us *Look there.* We said, *The Lord saith,* thou shalt not make to thyself the Likeness of any Thing that is in Heaven above, or in the Earth beneath, or in the Waters under the Earth, thou shalt not bow down to them, nor worship them, but me the Lord thy God only. He (the Friar) was so mad, that he called for Irons to chain *Sarah,* because she spake so boldly to him: She bowed her Head, and said, *Not only my Feet, but my Hands and my Head also for the Testimony of Jesus.*

They fought three Quarters of a Year to part us, before they could bring it to pass, and when they did part us, they prepared a Bed for *Sarah,* and removed her to another Room. When we were parted, they went from one to another, thinking to intangle us in our Talk, but we were guided by the same Spirit, and spake one and the same Thing in Effect, so that they had not a Jot or a Tittle against us, but for Righteousness-sake. Our God did keep us by his Power and Holiness out of their Hands. . . .

There was a poor *Englishman,* who hearing that *Sarah* was in a Room with a Window next the Street, which was high, got up and spoke a few Words to her: They came violently and haled him down, and cast him into Prison upon Life and Death. And the Friars came to know of us, *Whether he had brought us any Letters?* We said, *No.* I did not see him. They said, *They did think he would be hanged for it.* He was one they had taken from the *Turks,* and made a *Catholick* of. *Sarah* wrote a few Lines to me about it, and said, *She did think the* English *Friars were the chief Actors of it.* We had a private Way to send to each other. I wrote to her again, and after my Salutation, I said, *Whereas she said,* the Friars were the chief Actors, *she* might be sure of that, *for they did hasten to fill up their Measures; but I did believe the Lord would preserve the poor Man for his Love,* and that *I was made willing to seek the Lord for him with Tears.* And I desired she would *send him something once or twice a Day, if the Keeper would carry it.* And I told her of the *glorious Manifestations of God to my Soul,* for her Comfort. I told her, *It was much they did not tempt us with-Money.*[1] I bade her *take Heed, the Light would discover it, and many more Things.*

This Letter came to the Friar's Hands, he translated it into *Italian*, and laid it before the Lord Inquisitor, and got the Inquisitor's Lieutenant, and came to me with both the Papers in his Hand, and asked me, *If I could read it?* I told him, *Yea, I writ it. O did you indeed,* says he, *and what is it you say of me here? That which is Truth,* saith I. Then he said, *Where is the Paper* Sarah *sent, bring it, or else I will search the Trunk, and every where else.* I bade him, *Search where he would.* He said, *I must tell what Man it was that brought me the Ink, or else I should be tied with Chains presently.* I told him, *I had done nothing but what was just and right in the Sight of God, and what I did suffer would be for the Truth's Sake, and I did not care*: I would not meddle nor make with the poor Workmen. He said, *For God's Sake tell me what* Sarah *did write.* I told him a few words, and he said, *It was Truth.* Said he, *You say, it is much we do not tempt you with Money.* And in a few Hours they came and tempted us with Money often. So the Lieutenant took my Ink, and threw it away; and they were smitten, as if they would have fallen to the Ground, and went their Way. I saw them no more in three Weeks; but the poor Man was set free the next Morning.

NOTE

1. Their own Money, which had now served them about a Year and seven Weeks, was almost exhausted.

KRYSTYNA WITUSKA

(1920–1943)

Born to a Catholic family of the landed gentry, Krystyna Wituska and her sister Halina enjoyed a happy, sheltered childhood in western Poland. Wituska became engaged to marry Zbyszek Walc, the son of family friends, and was sent to a Swiss private school, but she returned home when war threatened in 1939. After Poland fell to Germany, the Nazis evicted Wituska's family from their estate. Krystyna's parents, whose marriage had been unhappy, decided to separate. Her father moved to a German-occupied estate where he found work. Krystyna and her mother settled in Warsaw, where she witnessed the brutal treatment of the Jews. While in Warsaw Wituska, who had never felt more than friendship for Walc, fell in love with a Jewish student in hiding named Karol Szapiro.

In November 1941 Wituska joined the Union for Armed Resistance (ZWZ), an organization of the Polish underground. She engaged in espionage in Warsaw, conveying information about the movement of German troops. Arrested by the Gestapo in 1942, she was taken to Pawiak, a prison in Warsaw, interrogated at Gestapo headquarters, and transferred to Alexanderplatz Prison and then to Alt-Moabit Prison, both in Berlin. There she was given a trial together with Walc, who was also active in the resistance; he served a prison sentence and was transferred to the Nazi concentration camp at Buchenwald, where he was killed in a barn fire. Karol Szapiro was arrested in 1943 and shot. Wituska never learned the fate of either young man. In April 1943 she was sentenced to death for spying and treason. She was executed by guillotine at the Halle-Salle prison on June 26, 1944.

Wituska's letters over the two-year period of her imprisonment reveal her great love for her parents and the women who were her cellmates and friends. These women lived with the weekly threat that their death sentences would be carried out, since executions occurred on Wednesdays. Particularly remarkable is Wituska's correspondence with Helga Grimpe, the sixteen-year-old daughter of Hedwig Grimpe, a beloved German prison guard. Hedwig Grimpe, whom the women called *Sonnenschein* (Sunshine), comforted the prisoners in any way she could, delivering notes between them and allowing her own daughter to become their clandestine correspondent. Although they lived apart, Krystyna's parents shared her letters, which are often addressed to both of them.

The 1995 documentary film *A Web of War*, written by Brian and Terence McKenna and produced in Canada, draws upon Wituska's writings and her story in its account of the Polish resistance.

Note: Background information is from Irene Tomaszewski, introduction to *I Am First a Human Being: The Prison Letters of Krystyna Wituska* (Montreal: Véhicule Press, 1997); "Chronicle of Polish Valour during Second World War," National Film Board of Canada press release, December 14, 1995.

PRISON LETTERS, 1943: LIVING WITH A DEATH SENTENCE

From I Am First a Human Being, *1997*

Alt-Moabit, Berlin,
14 March, 1943
Dearest parents,[1]
Thank you for your letters and parcels. I got two packages from Father and three from Mummy—with shampoo, toothpaste, postage stamps and a pretty postcard. Mummy, please send me some Camelia sanitary napkins, a little mirror, my old blue silk blouse, and buy me some blue—navy blue —sandals—but make sure they're not too ugly!

Dear, kind Mummy, I feel less lonely now that I get so many loving letters from you; if only I could enclose my heart with this letter, and cheer you a little. I would love to tell you more about my situation but I am afraid to because everything was secret. You knew nothing about what I was doing because I told you nothing. Nor do you know about Military Law. It seems to be very severe. I am now in a Military (War) Court. If it is possible, perhaps you should get me a private lawyer, but this must be arranged quite quickly, if one indeed could help me. I didn't want to tell you about this before so as not to worry you, but the matter is now quite serious.

[Note to her beloved Karol Szapiro, enclosed with the letter to her parents] How delighted I was to recognize your handwriting dear, kind friend! You are for me someone from another world, someone who will soon forget about me. What am I to you, Karol? A thought, a memory? But in your world there is no time for reflection and memories. I, on the other hand, am lost in the past and like a stern judge, I examine my life. Here, in prison, one can recognize the important things in life. In freedom, one can get lost in daily cares and all kinds of details. Here we acquire some distance and so we see life as a whole. Life can only be understood if one believes in God but even then one often asks—why? Sometimes I find it so hard. You know so well how spoiled I was, how much love and understanding I demanded from everybody. Now I tell myself: can't you finally teach yourself to settle everything with God by yourself? Do you have to always have someone who will comfort and cheer you? You must learn to be independent!

When I get a letter, I want to laugh and to cry. At first I feel so close to you, and then I feel myself painfully abandoned. But letters are really the only comfort and joy. At Alexanderplatz, my friend [Mimi Terwiel] and I were so in tune. We never cried together: if one was depressed and cried—the other comforted her.

This week, I was put to work packing medicines—pleasant and light work. Spring arrives earlier here than at home. The spring shrubs are big, budding. I saw them when I was washing windows.

•

Dear Father, you must tell me how your work in the garden is coming along. The weather here is splendid, making this prison desert harder for me to bear.

Don't worry about my health, Mummy. That is not, at the moment, so very important. When *Pani*Wanda[2] writes to Zbyszek, tell her to send him my love. I am sure that he is sad that we are separated again. He is still so in love with me. I am glad that your money worries are over, dear Mummy, and that things are going better for Janek.[3] At night, in my bed, I compose endless, long letters to you in my mind. Far too long for the sheet of paper I get. You can't possibly imagine how much I love you.

I kiss you with all my heart and send my love to all my friends, especially Alina,[4] Karol, and Zbyszek's family.

Your Tina

Alt-Moabit, Berlin
25 April, 1943
Beloved parents,
No doubt by now you have been informed by our defence counsel that on April 19 I was sentenced to death for spying and for treason. I did not lose my courage, I maintained my dignity. For many long months I prepared myself for the possibility that I will have to die. My heart only aches for you, knowing how you must be suffering.

But you shouldn't lose all hope. I spoke two days ago with my lawyer who reassured me that there may be some way out of my situation and there still remains the possibility of clemency. There are still about three months left before the sentence is executed so I will have time to write more than one long letter to you.

I will ask permission to send you all the things which I will no longer need. I am so glad that the other two girls got lighter sentences. I love them both like sisters. People on the outside imagine that someone sentenced to death must go mad from fear and anguish. In fact, it's quite the contrary. Maybe that's because it's beyond comprehension. I couldn't sleep the first night and I cried a bit, but only because of you, my best and most beloved Mummy. I didn't even consider suicide—I will not take on myself the responsibility for my death.

I am not alone right now and that is wonderful. With me is a Polish woman from Warsaw who was on the same train with me to Berlin, was at the Alex the whole time I was there and now is sharing my sad fate with me. She is my age, a good, dignified young woman. We talk all day long, we have so much to tell one another, all the things we experienced and felt while we were in solitary. We discovered that we have mutual friends in Poland; our country is so small that everybody knows everybody else. Today is Easter, the day of the Resurrection, and on this day I must write about such sad things.

We now have permission to go to church and this morning we sang in the chapel: "Gone now are the terrors of the grave. Death, where now is your victory?" I want to believe that someday we shall all be together again, that I won't be alone there where I will go. So many of my young friends will be with me: Lolo, Stas, Tomek, Zbyszek. Death is the salvation of all people and in this life I believe only in this one great truth that one sees so often etched into prison walls: "And this too shall pass." I am not afraid of death, at least no more than I would be before some serious operation; it takes, after all, just a moment—and then it's all over.

You must be brave, my best Mummy, chin up and forgive me for putting you through this. Maybe . . . maybe it will still turn out all right. There is always plenty of time for sadness. . . .

Dear Karol. So our friendship is coming to an end. I wanted so much to know how your life would unfold. You know, on the wall of my cell at the Alex someone wrote in big letters: "Everything because of your great love." So I realized that I was not really alone.

Mummy, I no longer need money, of course, just send me my navy silk dress and some shampoo. I will always be vain and I will curl my hair even on the last day. They took away my little doll. Pity, because I wanted to send her to you as a memento. We are not allowed to play here, we must only work and atone for our sins. I could, of course, still appeal for clemency; in that case maybe Daddy could remind them that back in the days when he was in Warsaw, he once saved the lives of a German family.

Once again I beg of you: hold your heads high and write often. I think of you all the time and send kisses from the bottom of my heart. I didn't get the medicines you sent, such things are forbidden.

Your Tina

Dearest, beloved Mummy, don't cry so much!

Alt-Moabit, Berlin,
9 May, 1943
Beloved parents,

I hope that the censors will not have anything against these last few letters being written in Polish. I would like you to understand them too, my dearest Mummy. I've received your wonderful, heartfelt letters. Naturally, on such an occasion I had to cry a little because I feel so terribly sorry for you and feel so guilty because I've never brought you much joy, only worries. I breathed a sigh of relief that you are not in despair and have not given up hope.

Thank you for all your words of encouragement and reassurance that you think of me. I feel very well and I am so cheerful that I feel guilty. Here I am perfectly happy while there you are all worried and thinking heavens know what. We are now three and we all have the same concerns. Olga [Jedrkiewicz] is from Warsaw and is my age, while Monika [Dymska], from Torun, is twenty-five. Olga is very beautiful and both are awfully nice. You can't imagine how wonderful it is, after a few months of solitary confinement, to once again have young friends and be able to talk as much as we like. I hardly ever think about what awaits me because I simply don't have time for that. All day long we sing, joke, and behave very much like playful girls at boarding school. We feel like we are in boarding school because there are so many things forbidden here and we're afraid we will get a scolding. All three of us have a sewing machine, Monika for making buttonholes, I for hemstitching, while Olga sews very pretty dresses. All night we have to put the machines out into the corridor so we have enough room for sleeping. I sleep on the bed and they on mattresses on the floor, but they are not at all upset by that because the bed is just as hard as the floor. In any case, we sleep very well. It's the month of May, so every evening we sing hymns to our Blessed Mother, and in the daytime all the folksongs, army songs and popular songs that we know. You know, Alina [her young aunt] it is as cheerful here as it used to be in the shop.

Beloved parents, I have one final, difficult duty ahead of me, to remain brave and dignified until the end. Pray for me, dearest Mummy, that in the event that I do not get clemency and one beautiful day they take me away to the place where I will die, pray that I can do this. I didn't write my appeal until today because the lawyer said he would come to help me, but he didn't get here until now. Thank you from the bottom of my heart for all your efforts. I pray every day for God to save me, not just for myself but for you. The act of beheading lasts one second, and then I will be free of all fear and worries, but you will never be able to forget my death.

About your visit here, dearest little Mummy, I wrote a *Wunschzettel* [a list of requests] to the military court. But think about this carefully. A 10-minute visit might cause you even greater heartache. Would you not return to Warsaw even more broken-hearted? At least now, you have grown accustomed to my not being near you.

My best loved Daddy. Your brief letter revealed to me how much you think about me and how terribly worried you are about the latest news. I know that you didn't entirely realize how serious my situation was and it tore me apart whenever I had to write to you about it. I was thrilled to get all your parcels. . .

My beloved parents, I often wish you could get a glimpse of me, at least for a moment; I am sure that would ease some of the pain in your hearts. It is pleasant now during *Freistund* [free time], because it's warm and the four trees in the courtyard are in full leaf. Forget-me-nots, lily-of-the-valley and other wonderful things are in full bloom in the flowerbeds. If you come to visit me, Mummy, then you will see this courtyard where I walk everyday, head held high. Every two weeks we get clean towels, dishcloths and shirts. We look very funny in these shirts because they are very thick, long and so wide that I could get two of me in them. I seem lost inside, which makes Olga once again roar with laughter. That's when I think of that lovely silk lingerie Daddy gave me—what ironic fate! Now I am always wearing the navy skirt and blue jersey blouse; it is quite cool in our cell because the walls are incredibly thick and the sun peeps in only for an hour in the morning. It is dry here compared to the Alex, where it was so damp you could get stuck to the walls, and hygienic conditions in general are first rate. There are very nice bathrooms here with bathtubs where we bathe every two weeks.

Chin up! dearest Mummy, and don't worry about me. My peerless father—it's not for nothing that I am your daughter; I can bear the ups and downs of life very bravely.

I kiss you a thousand times, and all those whom I love. Little brother-in-law, Janusz, thank you for your note.

[Note in the margin] Oh, my dearest, sweetest Karol, do you know what? I am writing with the pen that you gave me for my Name Day.[5] I also used it to write my *Gnadengesuch* [appeal].

[unsigned]

Alt-Moabit, Berlin,
June 6, 1943

Dear Halinka.[6] Yesterday I got your letter in which you write about your happy family and how well you are managing. It amazes us, here, so cut off from normal life, that there are places on this earth where life goes on so smoothly, happily as before. To us it seems that the whole world must be engulfed in the flames of war, that everywhere people are fighting and killing, or weeping and in agony. Lucky Halinka, may your family's nest, sheltered in a distant village, escape this unhappy fate. It seems to me that I was never intended for such a serene life. I was always drawn to extremes, and this continues, even here. No doubt you will be surprised if I tell you that I would like to live so I could continue studying and I regret terribly the time that I have wasted. Dear Olenka and I often talk far into the night, after the ever-sleepy Monika has fallen asleep, about every possible subject and we have come to the conclusion that if we were ever able to return to normal life, our outlook on life and the world would be very different from that of other people. We feel as though we are standing on a ship's plank, over the deep ocean and it's amazing that in this position instead of getting dizzy, it's quite the opposite, we are clear-headed and can evaluate everything and everybody objectively. We are no longer part of a crowd whose spirit could influence our feelings or our judgement.

Lots of kisses to you Halinka, and to Jan and the little one. And you, beloved parents, I kiss most of all and think of you always. Best regards to all those whom I love,

Your Tina

Please send me a little mirror, Mummy, because I gave mine to Mimi and please, pray for me.

Alt-Moabit, Berlin
August 17, 1943
Gelesen: _____
To be signed by: Sonnenschein

[This smuggled letter to Helga was written on official prison stationery so the instruction for *Sonnenschein*'s signature is a joke. "Gelesen"—"Read by," is the space for the censor's name.]

Dear Helga,

Today was, without question, the most unbelievably happy day. My head still can't fully absorb the fact that today I actually saw my father. Looking at him sitting across from me, I felt that my year in prison and my death sentence were just a bad dream. I managed to maintain my happy disposition the whole time he was here, Helga, and I am sure that my father left me convinced that I am getting along here very well. He even managed to exchange a few words with our *Sonnenschein*, and that reassured him that I am getting good care here. Unfortunately, they took away the sweets, the cigarettes and the flowers he brought me. But that doesn't matter! During our conversation, he expressed the hope that before too long we will be able to return to our family estate in Wartheland, our home from which the Germans evicted us. But it is not the estate that is important, but only that we are all together at last. I gave him Mimi's family address and asked him to go see them and give them my kindest regards. The only thing, it was such a short visit and there was so much to say. I want to believe that someday I will be able to tell him about everything. And, oh, I was able to hug him! How comforting that was. . . .

Best regards from your *Kleeblatt.*[7]

Alt-Moabit, Berlin,
22 August 1943

Dear *Pani*Wanda,

You were once interested in the effect that prison life has had on my disposition and my character. I now have a strange desire to tell you about this, what my thoughts are at this time. Perhaps that is because it seems to me that you will understand this best, and you will see it objectively—not like Mummy who is blinded by her great love for me. I wish to be very sincere. Now that some of your anxiety is eased about Zbyszek, I'm not afraid that I would add to your worries.

Maybe this is completely unnecessary but I would like someone to know more about me, though in the end, it really doesn't matter. It's hard to write this, because it's hard, almost impossible, to find the words to describe all these contradictory thoughts and feelings. Every time I think about Zbyszek, I feel an immense debt of gratitude to fate that he was saved. I doubt that my death will have any long term effect on his life in the future; he is so young. I know now from my own experience how quickly a person can accept and get used to things, which at first seemed impossible to bear.

Thinking about Mummy's despair is far more painful for me than abandoning all my plans for the future, but there's nothing I can do for her. I know that she will never forget this, but I hope that she will not break down, that she will find comfort in religion, in her love for Halinka and her grandson. It will be so hard for her; her love for me is without bounds.

I wouldn't want to exploit the idea that I am a patriot who died for her country. For one thing, I was initially propelled into the conspiracy by curiosity and a sense of adventure. Only later by love of my country. Still, I do not regret a single step I took, not even now.

However, I did not become a nationalist here, quite the contrary. I consider strong nationalism to be a serious limitation and I always consider myself first a human being and only then a Pole. On the day that I will die, I would prefer to tell myself that I am dying for freedom and justice, rather than that I die just for my own Poland. Consciousness of a universal humanity will comfort me. But please don't misunderstand—it is not that I don't love my country, but I would relinquish my country's objectives if they were not also good for all of Europe and all of humanity.

I am not distressed that I must die. We all know that we must die; the difference is that most people don't know when their hour will come. Death is as natural as life, and that is how one should approach it. If you have a good understanding of life, you know how to accept death. The important thing is to maintain one's human dignity to the end, not to give in at the last moment to an animal-like survival instinct, not to be frightened by that moment of physical pain. But I am sure that we can overcome that, we must summon all our strength for that. We will die free, so free—because prison life taught us to detach ourselves from the minor things that enslave people on the outside. Nobody can imprison our souls unless we ourselves lock them behind the bars of narrow prejudice.

In prison I became—how awful!—much less religious. That is rather odd, but I can't be religious just because there is no other way out. I would think it presumptuous to ask God to save my life, which after all is of no great importance in the universal scheme of things. Why should I have a greater right to life than those millions who have already perished in this terrible war? What will come next, I can't and don't try to imagine. I do believe, though, that the best and the most noble that is in us will not perish, that through this we will unite with something greater than ourselves, that we will approach perfection. It is nice to think that I will meet, in another world, all those I have loved—after all, is it possible that such a powerful feeling as love could just cease to be? Yet to be completely free, one must not love individually but dedicate one's life to the greater common good. But that is for exceptional people, not for me. Because I loved Mimi too much, I now suffer unnecessarily. I can't forget my little Mimi, I can't get over her death even though I have known so many others who were killed.

I have read over my letter and all my conclusions, after so many long months of thinking, struck me as a collection of platitudes. What I had to do, was to arrive at some kind of personal philosophy for my daily use. I had to find a way to achieve this objective: not to lapse into despair, not to lose our spirit even under the most tragic circumstances, and to comfort others. As for death, it is a great comfort to know that when we are gone from this earth, nothing will end or change. The sun will continue to shine, the flowers will blossom, autumn will follow summer, everything will be as it should and always be. What value is one life? Today, it has the least value of anything.

Dear *Pani*Wanda, please believe me that I accept my fate without fear. I am well, and my father's visit gave me great joy. Please kiss all my dear aunts for me, also *Pan* Lucjan[8] and the boys, and I hope that Roza,[9] whom I barely know, will get well and return to Warsaw soon. Heartfelt kisses . . .Tina

Alt-Moabit, Berlin
18 September 1943
[This letter was given to *Sonnenschein* to keep and then forward to the Wituska family after Krystyna's death. Mrs. Grimpe did this after the war.]
Dearest parents,
You will receive this letter after my death. It will be sent to you by a person to whom we are immeasurably indebted. She has been our friend, and our guardian. At great personal risk, she tried as much as possible to ease our difficult fate; she shared with us whatever she could, never asking for anything in return. We called her our "Ray of Sunshine," because whenever she came into our cell, she brought her joy and laughter. We became friends with her daughter. You saw her once, Daddy; do you remember?

I only regret that I will never be able to repay her for everything that she did for us, for her dear heart of gold. She was especially fond of me and I loved her as one can only love one who offers a hand when you are truly in need and never thinks of this as charity, but only as something normal. Please don't forget her.

Dearest parents, writing this letter, I still don't know what will be the outcome of my application for clemency, but believe me that I am completely ready for death and I don't entertain any false hopes. Our long separation has deepened my feelings for you, and it pains me to leave you in such sorrow. But believe me, I am prepared to go to my death with head held high, without fear. This is my last obligation to you and to my country. Prison was for me a good, often difficult school of life, but there were nevertheless joyful, sunny days. My friendship with Mimi will remain with me, an unforgettable and wonderful memory until the end. She taught me to never lose my humour, to laugh at "them," and to die bravely. We will die on the eve of our victory knowing that we did not resist in vain against injustice and brute force.

Don't despair beloved parents, be brave dearest Mummy. Remember that I watch over you and grieve over every one of your tears. But when you smile, I smile with you.

May God reward you for the love and care with which you have enveloped me. Farewell, dearest parents, farewell Halinka.
Your Tina

Halle/Saale,
23 April 1944
Mummy,

You are the best and the most loved Mummy. Every letter and package from you reminds me of this. I know that many people are thinking of me, but you, it's as though you are always with me. Don't you agree? I could lose faith in everything in the world, except your love for me. The comb and the sanitary pads arrived; nothing is missing. I love the sweet smelling soap and the colourful card. Set on my little table during Easter, it cheered up this monotonous cell. You can't imagine how much I liked looking at the little yellow chicks. And at the sight of the little Pascal Lamb I cried thinking how much you love me and I can't even kiss you. Oh Mummy, sometimes it's not so easy to be brave, especially at moments when I am overcome with homesickness. I'm sure you feel the same way. But we shall overcome this—right, dear, brave Mummy? I received your letters of March 20 and April 9. For two weeks, including the holidays, I was alone. Now I have company again. I'm almost finished my Italian book—it's amazing how much I learned in such a short time. I can see the top of a chestnut tree outside my window; what a pleasure to watch the leaves grow and the flowers bud. The sun peeks in after dinner. April 19 marked a year since my death sentence; my friends are probably thinking of me as I am of them. When do you expect Wanek to visit? Where is he now? Thank you Janek, for your loving letters. I kiss you dearest Mummy, and you Halinka, Janek and little Kola. Best wishes to Mr. and Mrs. Mierkowski, Leszek and Janusz.

Beloved, wonderful Father. I received your letter of April 2 and I was so pleased to read your words of praise for my endurance. Admiration from you is doubly pleasing because I know that your standards of behaviour are very high. You see, I never forget that I have courageous parents; how I wish that someday I could bring you happiness. You know, there was a time when I wanted everything, but not anymore. I don't miss anyone but you and Mother. I have lived through enough and I learned a lot about human nature. Now I want only you, my parents, and to walk together with you over the broad meadows at home. And I am fully aware that nobody in the world can help me now and I must deal with my sorrows myself.

Dear *Pani* Wanda. Mummy told me such sad news and I can imagine the sorrow in your face. If only I could comfort you. I desperately want to believe that *Pan* Lucjan [Walc] survived his illness; and perhaps you've had news from Zbyszek by now. It was inevitable that after he served his sentence he would be transferred to *Staatspolizei*, and if he is in the *Polizeiprasidium*, he will only be able to write after four weeks. He might be sent for forced labour which is infinitely better than to be sent to a camp. If you happen to have a chance, please forward the following words to him.

My dear friend, I fear you may remain behind prison walls for a while yet, though I would be so happy to hear that you had better luck. My dear, good, faithful friend, thinking of you helps me through many difficult hours. It is foolish to be thinking about the future while I remain on the abyss. You know yourself how often in moments of despair one must hold on to something strong as a rock just to survive. My rock was your love. Thank you, dear Zbyszek. I worry about you sometimes, but I want to believe that everything will turn out fine. Stay well. All my best,

Your Krystyna

Halle/Saale,
26 June 44
Beloved parents,
How hard it is to write this last letter. But you must believe me—I am not afraid of death, I do not regret my life. I only think how much sorrow I give you, how you will grieve during the last hours of my life. I want to thank you again for your care and your love, for your unconditional dedication, my dearest Mummy! I can never thank you enough for everything you have done for me, for my joyful, carefree childhood. Don't cry, Mummy, may God ease your pain. I know that you long ago forgave me all the trouble and worry I caused you. I am looking for words that would help me cheer you but I can only think of one sentence that *Pani*Wanda said when she lost Lolek: "God's best-loved die young."

I am completely at peace, believe me, and I will remain serene to the end. My last obligation to Poland and to you—is to die bravely.

Beloved Daddy, dearest Mummy, I feel you are with me today and I am so conscious of my great love for you. I dedicate my last thoughts to you. Be brave! Bid me farewell.

Your Tina.

NOTES

1. Krystyna had to write in German to pass the prison censor. The letters went first to her father, who translated them for her mother. *–Ed.*

2. *Pani*Wanda is Dr. Wanda Walc, a dermatologist and mother of Krystyna's fiancé, Zbyszek.—*Ed.*

3. A fellow prisoner who was in an adjacent cell at the Alex. He fell in love with Krystyna's voice. Originally from Suwalk, he was an escapee from Auschwitz, wounded in the leg during his escape. He expected a death sentence and disappeared one day without a trace.

4. Her aunt, only slightly older than Krystyna, with whom she stayed and worked in Warsaw. Alina's husband, Stanislaw Golebiowski, was killed in battle on Sept 5, 1939.

5. Celebrated like a birthday.

6. Halinka is the diminutive for Halina, Krystyna's older sister, who was married and mother to a young son.—*Ed.*

7. Kleeblatt, meaning Cloverleaf, was Krystyna's symbol for herself and her two cell-mates, Marysia and Lena. Sometimes instead of signing off with her name, Krystyna drew a cloverleaf, with each one's initials in each of the three petals. Helga collected all their letters and drawings in an album which she called the *Kleeblattalbum*. It is now in

the archives of the Main Commission for the Investigation of Crimes Against the Polish Nation, in Warsaw.

8. Dr. Lucjan Walc, *Pani*Wanda's husband and Zbyszek's father.

9. Zbyszek's brother's fiancée.

CHILEAN WOMEN POLITICAL PRISONERS OF THE 1970S

In Latin American countries an important function of literature has traditionally been to reflect the social reality of the people—a social reality that often, during periods of political repression, cannot be expressed through established institutions. Literature is regarded as a source of truth opposing official lies, and as such it is often regarded as a threat to totalitarian regimes. Their lives endangered, writers and artists, along with other intellectuals, often find it necessary to continue their work in exile.

Political prisoners, even if they have not been writers by vocation, often write of their experiences to protest their countries' violations of human rights. In Chile, intellectual freedom was repressed after the 1973 military coup against President Salvador Allende's socialist government brought army general Augusto Pinochet into power. Male and female resistance workers were imprisoned and sadistically tortured. For women the experience was doubly traumatic: because women in the Chilean culture are socialized to consider feminine purity essential, a female prisoner who has been sexually tortured may feel unmerited guilt over her own victimization.

The writings of Chilean women political prisoners are generally collective in nature; the individual writer's life or experience is not emphasized, except as an illustration of the experience of her sister prisoners. The testimony is the prevailing genre, with its descriptions of prison conditions and institutionalized brutality. Thus, the excerpts below do not stress the authors' individuality. The poetry selections come from "Sonia," the pseudonym of a prisoner in Santiago Prison and a participant in a Chilean women prisoners' writing collective. The description of Tres Alamos prison camp is the testimony of "Marta Vera," the pseudonym of a prisoner who spent fifteen months there and wrote of her experiences from exile in 1976. The selection by Chilean resistance worker Gladys Diaz was written with the collaboration of other women prisoners. Diaz had been arrested, brutally tortured and imprisoned in Villa Grimaldi, and finally released into exile as the result of an international campaign on her behalf.

Note: Background information is from Mario Vargas Llosa, "The Writer in Latin America," *Index on Censorship* 1, no. 6 (November–December 1978): 34–40; Robert Pring-Mill, "Poems at Curfew," *Index on Censorship* 7, no. 1 (January –February 1978): 43–44; Comite Jane Vanini, *Women in Resistance* (Berkeley, Calif.: Support Committee for Women in the Chilean and Latin American Resistance, n.d.); Ximena Bunster, presentation at the "Women and Human Rights" session, Women's Studies Conference, University of Pennsylvania, Philadelphia, March 1985.

POEMS BY SONIA

Translated by Aurora Levins Morales.

To Celia, A Disappeared Comrade[1]

The roses will bloom once again in Europe
while back there, far away, they have stopped time

decreeing hunger
decreeing fear
decreeing a state of death.
The aromos bloomed
. . . and no one saw them.

She Disappeared

Brother, sister, you who survived the horror
of the stadium, Tres Alamos or Ritoque,
Tejas Verdes or Chaiguin[2]
have you seen my daughter, my brother,
my father, my beloved husband,
my daughter, my sweet daughter.

Wasn't your hand chained to hers—
you must have heard her call me in her pain
when the lash fell on her heart
when the executioner stained her innocence.
Don't you remember her?
I will describe her for you:
She was more beautiful than the sun and the stars
and gave out hope with full hands.
Her eyes flashed like sparks when she dreamed of her country
without flags, the happiness of its people
no longer in chains.
She said goodbye one afternoon (what an afternoon it was)
her smile bleeding, and with a sweet kiss
"See you soon, querida madre"[3]
Since then, pain is my companion.
Cradling my hope I walk the roadside
with this question on my lips and in my conscience
killing me with blows, day after day.

Poem

They take off the bandage
and the light
wounds my eyes.
The world spins dizzily . . .
stops, then a sheltering hand, a voice
whispers a strange name evoking
stories lost in my childhood. A name
with a smell.
The smell of dampness of the south.
The smell of forests

and fires made with wet wood,
dispersing
the stench of fear.

She was in front of me
sitting at the foot of the cot.
She had long white hands, blonde hair
tied in two braids, and the eyes of a frightened girl:
such a contrast with her words.

Then came days and days of dead
afternoons, of little figures made from mashed bread,
fragments of sad poetry, tangos,
boleros, sorrows and laughter.

Nights of sudden assault.
Terror.
Terror breathing always through the walls,
through the bars, through the door
that opened from the outside.
Voices far away and close by,
always howling
hope.

On a day like any other they took her away.
Hours later it was my turn. For me
freedom. The freedom of exile (and the world
shattered like a pumpkin).

Today (time is counted now in years)
I found her again: the same timid smile,
her hair loose, the hands hidden
in the folds of a skirt
already old. . .
frozen forever in a blurry photograph.

Under it
a name
    Muriel
a last name, two last names
an age
    22 years
Detained in August of 1974
in Santiago de Chile.
DISAPPEARED.

LIFE INSIDE THE WOMEN'S SECTION

From "Marta Vera," Political Prisoners, Chilean Women No. 2, *1976.*

Prison life brings together people of different ages in this case from 17 to almost 60 years old. And from different walks of life: workers, students, housewives, professional women—some are mothers and others are not.

In spite of the differences there are many factors that fundamentally unite them. In the first place they have been detained for struggling for a fairer society which would allow for human development and permit the emergence of a better human being, a whole person. In the second place they share the uncertainty in which they find themselves—not knowing what those who arrested them intend to do with them. Thirdly, and by no means least important, they are united in their refusal to acquiesce, determined to uphold till the last the remnants of human dignity that are left to them. In spite of overcrowding, suffering constant humiliation and nervous strain, being dragged to the lowest levels of human degradation, in spite of imprisonment and torture, the moral resistance of the detainees of the political prisoners has not been worn down.

Imprisonment and torture has not been able to break down the resistance of the Chilean prisoners who collectively benefit as much as they can from the "minimum freedom" that they have in organising their food and leisure. Inside the camp they have managed to solve their material needs by working collectively and through discussion and study have built up morale establishing a fellowship that makes living together a pleasant experience, forming friendships which makes leaving difficult. All this happens under the watchful scrutiny of the gaolers who see everything, but fail to understand that the political prisoners' determination to carry on their struggle and to continue living has been strengthened rather than weakened.

One might ask what relevance this has to the situation of the political prisoners? How does it manifest itself from day to day?

The uncertainty of the rules of the internal regime permits an elementary level of organisation which is expressed in sporadic meetings to discuss domestic problems such as cleaning, for making a decision with which they [the prisoners] are sometimes presented by the authorities, and in planning and organising their lives in productive and cultural activity. The solidarity between political prisoners is of immense importance in the activities described below. Each person takes on the problems of the others as a practical expression of the political prisoners' concept of the needs and the potential of human beings. . . .

The 'Food Kitty'

In November 1974 we had started to discuss the problems of nutrition. It was clear that the food provided by the camp was deficient in every respect and that eating it for a year or more led to a severe deterioration of health, leaving the prisoners wide open to all kinds of sickness. By this time food was allowed to be brought into the camp. Some of the compañeras [female comrades]came from the provinces and therefore rarely had visitors. There were others whose families were in such difficult economic straits that they were unable to bring anything. Other compañeras had relatives also in detention. All these situations together with the general need for a balanced diet, were decisive factors in the creation of the "Food Kitty." Yet it would not have happened without the solidarity of the prisoners and their collective determination not to give in to defeat.

The "Food Kitty" had the following objectives:

a) to improve the prisoners' diet with fresh fruit, vegetables, eggs, etc., that is, with basic foods. For this they pool all the food that prisoners receive individually and share it out in equal portions prepared from whatever there is in the "kitty." More often than not these were salads.
b) to work as a team, treating it as a way to get to know each other better, and developing collective and community feeling.

The Food Collective was organised and structured in this way: four compañeras are democratically elected as food organisers and everyone else is then organised into groups of 8 or 9 called "kitchen hands." The food organisers receive the food on the visiting days when food is allowed to be brought in; they store, preserve and distribute the food for the rest of the week, and they formulate the meals. The kitchen hands help in the collection, storage and preparation of the food whenever it is their turn (the rota would depend upon the number of kitchen groups). Both groups work together, daily assessing what [is] to be done, and collectively discussing how to improve the group.

The Food Collective began in this way, and after periodic assessment decided in April 1975 that it should give priority to looking after compañeras who were sick, pregnant or breast-feeding, and young children. They did this by reserving for them the most nourishing food.

In May 1975 the new team of food organisers initiated a discussion amongst all the kitchen groups about "tit-bits." These are the sorts of food that are not essential and therefore were not included in the kitty (chocolates, cakes, etc.). Political prisoners have families whose incomes vary substantially, so some receive a much greater quantity and quality of food than others. In terms of the basic objectives of the food collective everyone has the same right to enjoy these delicacies, and it was agreed after frank discussion that these should be shared as well. This meant that all food that came into the camp went into the Food Kitty. Also in May the number of food organisers was increased, electing a chief organiser who reports to the Elders' Council[4] to co-ordinate the work of the food collective with the other activities of the camp.

In June and July there was a discussion about whether the "tit bits" were really necessary. In the light of the grave economic situation suffered by the people in Chile, and hence of course the prisoners' families, it was agreed to ask our relatives not to incur this sort of expenditure on our behalf.

The food collective still functions, evaluating its work, improving its techniques, revising its objectives and paying constant attention to the working relationships between the compañeras, emphasising the solidarity and the collective enterprise.

The Workshops Committee

In January 1975, a regular course in English was being held, organised by one of the compañeras and with 9 percent of the prisoners participating. Earlier in 1974 classes in gymnastics and the plastic arts had been set up but they had been discontinued by the end of the year because of lack of participation. Only the English course had survived.

At the beginning of 1975 the idea arose in a general meeting of forming an organisation which would take charge of activities that could be organised in the camp. The idea was approved and three compañeras volunteered to implement it. Their job was to consider the physical limitations, the human and material conditions and to work out a programme and present it to the other prisoners. After discussion this programme was accepted, and a Workshops Committee was created to harmonise and develop the cultural, artistic and recreational activities and also to encourage general participation in these workshops. There were workshops in: English, German, Gymnastics, Folklore, Theatre, Plastic Arts, Literature and a Discussion group.[5] Each workshop has the compañera who is most accomplished in the activity and therefore in charge of the development of the workshop.

Thus we began to take part in other activities outside the cell besides that of the Food Collective. Time was short and space was minimal for there were at this time 150 with less than a square yard per person in the interior courtyard; and conditions were difficult.

Yet the activity of the workshops grew and in May 1975 a choral group and a production workshop were formed (more will be said about the latter later on). A study was made of the time available and the workshops were divided into recreational activity, cultural activity and the production workshop. After a deep and lengthy discussion it was agreed that the Production Workshop was the most important and so the hours were reduced for the other's [sic] workshops to give more time to the Production Workshop.

When we moved to Pirque, the workshops had to suspend their activities because physical conditions had changed, and there was a delay of two weeks before they recommenced.

The Discussion Group organised a Talk-in on nutrition during a week specifically devoted to the Food Collective. Later the literary group prepared an analysis of the women's magazine *Vanidades* (similar to *Cosmopolitan*) and together with the Theatre Workshop presented this analysis in the form of a play. They chose this magazine as being the most representative of its type. The study sets out to expose the many subtle ways in which women are ideologically controlled, setting up woman as a sexual symbol, as a consumer package or a marketable article, trivialising women with meaningless quizzes, making "love" a commercial focal point, distorting reality through the news they present in third rate journalism.

A Sports Group was also organised and every fortnight there was a joint group day when each group displayed its work and everyone joined in the games and songs.

In July 1975 the Library Group was started to organise reading, and making books accessible to everybody. Before this some compañeras had received books which they and others who shared their cells had read; but others who wanted to read had no access to books. These books we had were pooled and the majority of books received afterwards were given to the library group. This group organised a system of borrowing and storage and started archives of the daily and weekly press (newspapers and magazines).

During September and October the workshop programme began to even itself out; some lapsed while others survived and grew, developing workshops representing the stronger interests of the group in that they had the greatest support on the return to Tres Alamos. The governor of the camp accelerated this process by banning the Discussion and Choral groups because he considered them to be political. Since intellectual activity is essential, given the importance of maintaining a high morale and good mental health, the library group began to give out weekly press summaries of national and international events, thus giving a broad spectrum of the news and also treating one theme in depth each time. These summaries were given to all the compañeras, but after issue No. 6 they were banned because they were considered to be political. For the authorities, the simple fact of thinking or reading a paper together constitutes a political act which must be suppressed.

We carried on until the end of the year, resisting attack from the authorities, when time began to be given to the preparation of presents for relatives who were not in detention, for children and husbands. This began to have an effect on the attendance and activities of the workshop groups.

In January 1976 the general discrepancy in the level of education among the political prisoners necessitated setting up a course of elementary education in Maths, Spanish, Natural Sciences, and Social Sciences and some of the former groups such as French, German and the plastic arts disappeared. Thus the workshops still continued to respond to the needs of the group, having highs and lows depending on the level of repression and the mental and psychological state of the compañeras. The Workshops Committee continuing the struggle to develop was reinforced by a realisation of its relevance and importance in maintaining cultural and intellectual activity so that women would not leave the prison having also deteriorated in this respect. . . .

The Production Workshop

Discussion began in May 1975 about the situation of relatives and families outside the camp: some did not have many problems, but others had not enough money for even the basic necessities. There were two types of work done in the camp: the one a permanent and daily and absolute necessity, based on the need to provide money for food for children left outside the camp. The other was voluntary and was combined with cultural and recreational activity as a form of therapy or means of distraction. It was decided after some discussion of this situation that everyone would share the responsibility for providing for the children of the imprisoned compañeras. In the earlier discussion three fundamental factors were taken into account; first, the economic situation worsening from day to day; secondly the solidarity which should be manifest in the life shared by the prisoners; and finally to attempt to find the positive aspects of being a political prisoner with the given limitations. A form of organisation was sought to best meet the following objectives:

a) to ease the economic burden of the families of detainees;
b) to supply products to those families with the lowest incomes, more or less defining which products could be made;
c) to create a discipline for working with set hours of work, and maintaining standards of quality and efficiency. In other words developing a respect for manual work.

After further discussion it was agreed to set up:

a) an Administrative Committee made up of three compañeras who, as well as working, also had the responsibility of looking after the finances, sales and work routine. These compañeras worked on the committee for three months;
b) a large work section to make the products, with three monitors responsible for technical advice and quality control;
c) a Workshop Assembly in which all the compañeras participated and which was the only group with the power to make decisions about the objectives of the production workshop.

It was agreed to work two hours a day from Monday to Friday, making knitted products such as gloves, mittens, scarves, shawls and hats. As far as wages were concerned, it was decided to pay a wage to all the members of the workshop. A minimum wage was calculated to cover the monthly outlay on soap, toothpaste, shampoo, toilet paper and detergents. Special unemployment allowance was allocated to those compañeras whose husbands were out of work, and another compensatory allowance allocated for those whose families were in difficult economic straits and not receiving enough to live on. It was further decided to fix a family allowance for the children left outside the prison. This meant that a prisoner without serious economic problems would receive the minimum wage while another prisoner with a husband out of work and eight children would receive a wage of *twenty times as much*, while both women worked the same hours, under the same conditions, and with the same degree of concentration. That is from each according to her abilities and to each according to her needs. . . .

Conclusion

There is no conclusion while the arrests continue in Chile, along with the disappearances and the deaths. Torture has become institutionalised.

The above account describes the life of Chilean women political prisoners, explaining the development of their internal organisation and some of the factors which influenced this. Its intention is to show how a small community hemmed in by barbed wire and guns, has evolved a way of life where the collective interests are put first and how women who have been imprisoned for their political ideas strive even in prison to live in accordance with what they believe.

Many human beings whose position is particularly difficult are living their lives this way. To know this reality must deeply wound the conscience of humanity. The lack of conclusion is a call to all peoples and organisations who respect humanity and wish to see the complete restoration of human rights in Chile.

COLLECTIVE REFLECTIONS

From "Roles and Contradictions of Chilean Women in the Resistance and in Exile: Collective Reflections of a Group of Militant Prisoners" 1979.

Yes, our compañeras are winning space, but it has not been easy and it is not enough. There is still a very, very long road to be traveled. Now we have women in the front lines of the working class; there are now women among those who tomorrow will be the vanguard and who will lead decisive battles. And this role has been won fundamentally during these six years of struggle against the dictatorship. Thus we are witnessing the enormous revolutionary potential of the 50 percent of us who are women. Nor has it been a linear process. Like the struggle of the masses, it is a process which advances irregularly. In 1975, only 8 percent of the first women prisoners in Tres Alamos had really done sustained mass work as party members, and only 5 percent had been in high or immediate leadership positions. The majority of the women had only had experience in rank-and-file conspiratorial activities, or in the reproduction of materials and ideas which others had elaborated. We know that today the situation has improved considerably, but we also know that it could be even better.

The party women have now proved themselves in many battles; like their male comrades, they have had their ordeal by fire. This was at the moment of torture. In the case of the women, this was a difficult moment, but also one of a brutal encounter with the role to which the capitalistic system has assigned us, and one of an equally brutal and cruel encounter with all the contradictions yet to be overcome; all of this we women had to carry with us in the interrogation with the enemy.

Like us, the military have a deep class hatred, but they despise doubly those of us who have committed ourselves to the people's cause. They despise us because we are their class enemies; they despise us because we have dared to break out of the roles to which we had been assigned. Because we have dared to think, because we have dared to rebel against the system. And the ferocity of the military is redoubled in angry and attacking response to the women's emancipation from that traditional role.

They would threaten to bring a woman's children and kill them in her presence, if she did not speak. Or they would already have them there and would make them cry in a neighboring room in order to remind the woman of her basic maternal function. They undressed the women, they ran their hands over their bodies, they raped them, they gave them electric shocks on their naked bodies which had been developed in a context of modesty and virginity. They beat women on the face and on the body in order to mutilate them, because within the conception of femininity, society has given great importance to symmetry, to bourgeois models of beauty. Some women were forced to confront their bleeding, dying compañeros; the torturers hoped that this would demoralize the men, that the women would beg their men to confess. Thus they were forced to weigh their love for their compañeros against their love for the people and the cause of freedom.

This is why we women prisoners in Tres Alamos were proud that 95 percent of us had heroically resisted torture. This sense of proletarian pride was not because we thought ourselves braver, stronger, or as strong as our male compañeros. The sense of pride came from having been able to reject our traditional role at a critical moment. Of having been able to see the priorities clearly as committed and fearless fighters, transcending the tears which we all held back in order not to show weakness.

The women prisoners, despite the fact that most had not had leadership positions, despite the fact that most were very young and inexperienced politically, mastered their limitations, their weaknesses, and took a qualitative leap in their emancipation as women as well as in their revolutionary commitment. Once they lived through the first stage on this second battle front which prison represents, the women went on to live another enriching experience, out of solitary confinement and into the prison community.

There, there were no male compañeros, always so good at organizing and at organizing us; in spite of this, the task of organizing was carried out rigorously and carefully. Discipline, a spirit of sacrifice, solidarity, dignity in the face of the enemy, the creation of activities and workshops to fill the lives of the women and avoid stagnation. Each woman had to contribute what she knew, each one had to be generous with her knowledge, with her experience, and with the maturity she had already achieved. If there was anything of importance learned there, it was how to share, to share food, joys, tasks, knowledge, and pain. And there we did exactly what political prisoners all over the world have done; we converted the prison into a school for well-trained cadres, for combatants, for human beings who were free even behind bars to love more than ever, in those conditions, the freedom which had been so cruelly torn from them.

Just like our compañeros, we women prisoners built our freedom every day. In the absence of freedom of the press, we created wall-newspapers which would be put up and taken down, depending on the degree of vigilance. In the absence of freedom of expression, we responded by creating poems, songs, theatrical works, dances which reflected our lives and hopes. We learned that children are not individual property but rather the children of the collectivity. Miguelito was born in the prison and was freed when he was sixteen months old, when he was already dancing to the song about "el negro José"[6] and would clap his hands to announce the arrival of the daily meals. Miguelito, along with Amanda, Alejandrito, and so many others lived a new conception of the family. They were the children of one mother and of a hundred aunts. Their feeding, education, entertainment, clothing, bathing, etc., were tasks and responsibilities of the collectivity. The mother's responsibilities toward her child were the same as those of each one of us.

The majority of women reached exile with this cumulus of experience. With the mutilation inherent in the loss of loved ones, with the traumas remaining from the moments of horror lived while in the hands of the brutal enemy; but also with their hearts overflowing with solidarity received and shared. Externally we were older, but inside we felt renewed by having been able to meet our responsibilities. We arrived at an obligatory but temporary exile, another battle front, less comforting, less gratifying, but as useful as the previous front—as useful and as necessary. This is the temporal space in which the rearguard is constructed and developed, a rearguard which nourishes, which denounces, which propagandizes, which accumulates international forces while basing itself on the actions carried out on the front lines of the battle. An exile in which we must also prepare the conditions for returning to Chile, improved, renewed, strengthened, better than before.

But, what we have just defined as our task is being accomplished with difficulty, with advances and retreats. Once again, in exile, party women face the daily contradictions implicit in being a woman, a worker, a mother, a housewife, and a party militant.

In prison, after having thrown off our traditional role in the torture chamber, we reflected at length on our lives, became aware of many things, wrote to our compañeros who were also in prison or on the outside, in order to communicate our thoughts. We questioned the unproletarian relationship which existed between men and women; we wanted to develop an ideological discussion on that theme. And the debate, which often became collective, began. In the light of the growth achieved, the whole concept of the couple was reformulated. In exile, the topic has been brought up more energetically, sometimes advancing the discussion, at other times hampering it, and at still others leading to the breakup of the couple. Because women and men emerged from a rich but difficult experience and because both had grown, but not always in parallel ways. Exile has tended to create an inhospitable framework for discussion.

NOTES

1. A former prison mate.—*Ed.*
2. Prisons and concentration camps.—*Trans.*
3. Dear Mother.—*Trans.*
4. A representative body, elected by the prisoners.—*Ed.*
5. The Discussion Group was the first to hold discussions on general themes such as abortion, christianity, and its role in society, women and the significance of International Women's Year, and so on. Such discussions played an important part in general development of our ideas.
6. "El negro José" is a traditional Chilean song which came to be extremely significant, in a symbolic manner, in the prisons, where it would be sung each time a prisoner or a group of prisoners was released.

OLYA ROOHIZADEGAN

On June 18, 1983, the following ten women were executed by hanging in Shiraz, Iran: Nusrat Yaldá'í, 'Izzat Ishráqí, Roya Ishráqí, Táhirih Síyávushí, Mahshíd Nírúmand, Símín Sábirí, Akhtar Sabet, Zarrín Muqímí, Shírín Dlvand, and Mona Mahmúdnizhád. Among them were a mother and daughter, the Ishráqís—the father had been executed two days earlier. Mahmúdnizhád, the youngest of the ten, was only seventeen years old. The crime of all these women was their Bahá'í faith. Other specific charges included teaching Bahá'ísm to children and, for the young women, not being married. The women had been arrested in November 1982 and imprisoned in Sepah and Adelabad Prisons, where they had endured interrogation and torture as part of the persecution of Bahá'ís by the Iranian government. It was regular practice during interrogation to offer freedom in exchange for recanting and accepting Islam, but the prisoners had refused.

Bahá'ísm is a world religion that began in nineteenth-century Persia under its founder, Bahá'u'llá (1817 –92) and an earlier leader, the Bab (1819–50). Drawing upon its roots in Islam, it was considered heretical by Islamic clergy and fiercely persecuted in Persia. Its central tenet is that of unification among all the world's peoples; other teachings include the equality of men and women. An early female leader of the religion was Tahirih, a Persian poet, who announced the radical message of women's equality by unveiling in public; she was confined under house arrest and executed by strangling. Persecution of Bahá'ís continued into the twentieth century. After the fall of the Shah the coming to power of Áyatu'lláh Khomeini in the late 1970s, persecution of this religious minority in Iran escalated. Despite world protests and election of a moderate president in 1997, Bahá'ís continue to be persecuted to some degree.

Olya Roohizedegan, the author of the following selection, had been employed by the National Iranian Oil Company, but had lost her job in May 1992 because of her Bahá'í faith. Imprisoned with these women, she had been released shortly before their execution. With the publication of *Olya's Story*, she fulfilled her promise to tell the truth about her martyred Bahá'í friends. The stories of Zarrín Muqímí, Mahshíd Nírúmand, and Roya Ishráqí are told below.

Notes: Background information is from William S. Hatcher and J. Douglas Martin, *The Bahá'í Faith: The Emerging Global Religion* (San Francisco: Harper & Row, 1985); H. M. Balyuzi, *The Báb* (Oxford: George Ronald, 1973); Amberin Zamin, "Iranian Bahais," *Los Angeles Times,* October 28, 2000; "The Bahá'í World," online, available: http://www.bahai.org, November 10, 2001.

PROLOGUE

From Olya's Story, *1993.*

It was 10:30 a.m., 19 January 1983 when I heard the sound of my name echo throughout the prison. They were calling me for release over the loudspeakers. Or at least, I hoped they were.

I wouldn't be the only one to be put through their cruel game. It was a familiar trick. Bails had been paid in vain and false promises made on other occasions. Friends and relatives of prisoners would be forced to surrender their homes in the hope of being reunited with their loved ones, only to discover that the prisoners had been led to execution.

The day before, the prosecutor had offered to set me free—so long as my husband Morad could come up with 800,000 tuman. There was no way of telling if the order for my release was genuine, but I had to believe it was.

At the announcement of my name, everyone rushed out of their cells and gathered round. In the excitement each began to talk over the others' voices. "Take this with you," said Táhirih, handing me a bar of soap. "If you *are* released, give it to the guard and tell him it belongs to me. If not—"

"Then you can be sure I am dead."

She tightened her grip on my hand. I looked at her and at the others— Mona was there and so was Shírín and Roya and Nusrat and Túbá and Zarrín and Mahshíd and Akhtar and Símín and 'Izzat. Every face wore a smile that whispered: "Remember us."

My name was announced for a second time.

I had rehearsed this moment a thousand times in my head and now I was barely able to speak a word. These women were my dearest sisters. We had shared the same food, the same cell, the same air, the same pain.

And now I was leaving them.

But there was a purpose in my going. I had often sworn to them—as they had to me—that if I was ever to get out of Adelabad Prison I would tell the world their story, our story.

Nusrat threw her arms around me. "If only I could sneak into your pocket and come with you," she said, tears streaming down her face. I couldn't bear to look into her eyes; I was scared I might not be able to tear my gaze away from them. But how could I turn away from those eyes? I had to keep this moment with me.

She was still embracing me when I heard my name called for a third and final time. If you failed to show up after the third call, your release was cancelled. Fakhrí, one of the political prisoners who had come out from the cell opposite, tried to loosen Nusrat's hold. "Let her go. Olya will be too late for her release," she urged. In the end Fakhrí practically bundled me down the stairs.

I mechanically descended the steps, but at the same time I felt myself being pulled back towards my friends. The conflicting emotions were almost paralysing. Remember this, I kept telling myself. Remember this. My feet became rooted to the spot as though in a dream. By now the women above me were all imploring me to go. "Run. Before it's too late," they cried.

I took one last look from the foot of the stairs. Oh God, would I ever see those dear faces again? Would they ever be free?

ZARRÍN MUQÍMÍ, AGE 29

From Olya's Story, *1993*

Zarrín Muqímí was born in 1954, in a village near Isfahán called Abíyánih. She was the third child in a Bahá'í family. She obtained a degree in English Literature from the University of Tehran, and was an excellent student all through her academic years.

After she finished her studies she moved to Shíráz with her parents, who were involved in the maintenance of the House of the Báb and its surrounding buildings. They lived in one of the houses in that alley. She worked as a translator and accountant in a petrochemical company near Marvdasht, but at the end of 1981 she was fired for being a Bahá'í. She was always proud of the fact that she had lost her job because of her Faith.

Zarrín was tall and slim, and always dressed simply. Unlike other girls of her age, she was never a follower of fashion. She loved studying, had a wide knowledge of the Bahá'í writings and the Qur'án, and knew the book of Aqdas by heart.

She taught Bahá'í children's classes, was a member of the Youth Committee and just before her arrest was appointed as a member of the Publishing Committee and an assistant, as I was. While the Bahá'ís were being subjected to fierce opposition and their every move was closely watched, she fearlessly put her books under her arm and travelled from house to house, encouraging the Bahá'í youth. . . .

Zarrín was under tremendous pressure for five years prior to her arrest, particularly because of her involvement with efforts to protect the House of the Báb. I remember seeing Zarrín and her father speaking kindly to fanatical Muslims and explaining Bahá'í teachings to them while they were in the act of destroying the holy house. Zarrín and her parents were among the first group of Bahá'ís arrested in October in 1982. I never saw Zarrín in Sepah, but I heard from some of the prisoners about her direct and brave response to the questions of the guards and the interrogators, and how impressive her strength had seemed to them. Later, when I was transferred to Adelabad, I got a chance to speak to her, and she described her experiences to me.

> When I was in Sepah the investigators put me on trial every day for long hours, asking me questions about my beliefs. I was on trial with Bahrám Yaldá'í, because we were both members of the Education Committee.
>
> One day, they put me in a room on my own and kept me blind-

folded for seven hours while they asked questions. I answered the questions from my knowledge of the Qur'án and the Bahá'í writings. Then the investigator suddenly said, "Now Brothers, what do you have to say to this girl? I myself have nothing more to say. She claims she is a Bahá'í, and that the promised one whom we are all waiting for has come. If you have any questions, you can ask her yourself."

There was a moment of silence and then I heard the sound of several people leaving the room one after another. I said to the investigator, "I don't know what is going on here. How many people were here during my trial?"

"I have asked you questions many times, and I told them all about your bravery, your perseverance and your knowledge but they didn't believe me, so I asked them to come here today and see for themselves."

He asked me what I thought my sentence would be.

"Ultimately, execution, but I would prefer to die and have told you the truth rather than be guilty in the divine court of justice."

Another day the investigator was insisting that I recant. I said, "I am a Bahá'í, and under no circumstances will I recant my faith."

He said, "Up to what point will you adhere to your beliefs? To the moment of execution?" I replied that I would, but he wouldn't give up and kept repeating that I must recant.

"Your honour," I said, "for days you have been asking me the same questions. I have written and signed numerous statements that I would prefer to die rather than recant. I don't think it is necessary to keep repeating the same question! I gave you a definite answer the first day. If you propose the same thing for years to come, I will still give you the same answer. Why don't you leave me alone?" I began to sob. "In what language must I tell you, my being is Bahá'u'lláh, my love is Bahá'u'lláh, my whole heart is Bahá'u'lláh."

"I will tear your heart from your chest!" he shouted angrily.

"Then my heart will call out and cry, 'Bahá'u'lláh, Bahá'u'lláh.'"

He rushed out of the room, moved by my display of emotion, and when he came back he found me still sobbing.

"You are still crying, Miss? We are human beings too, you know—we have feelings too."

They used every trick to torment us and to try and break the trust between us. One day after a long trial in Adelabad, the investigator called on me and my parents to go to Sepah, and there they confronted us with Suhayl Húshmand. I could tell he had been tortured, although we were blindfolded during the entire trial; it was obvious they had forced him to confirm false charges against us. They said, "Suhayl here has admitted that Mr. and Mrs. Muqímí went to Israel a few years ago on a spying mission; the three of you must admit to the fact that you are spies for Israel and the Universal House of Justice."

I was very naive about their devious methods at that time and I believed them. I said, "Suhayl, I hope God forgives your lies. We are not spies and we don't have anything to hide. Every individual Bahá'í is forbidden to take part in politics. Anyone who breaks this rule and becomes involved in political activities is not a Bahá'í. We have been ordered to abide by the laws of the government of the country we live in. My parents went to Israel years ago, purely on a pilgrimage."

"Your honour," my mother said, "I am an old and uneducated woman. I don't know anything about spying and politics. Once I went to Israel to visit the Bahá'í holy places, just as you go to Iraq to visit the grave of Imám Husayn. Does that make you a spy for Iraq?"

Zarrín's mother was released shortly afterwards, without any security bond being demanded, but Zarrín and her father remained in prison.

Because of Zarrín's extensive knowledge of religion, she was especially at risk. The more learning we revealed, the harder they leant on us and the more guilty we became in their eyes. I specifically mentioned to Zarrín, the night before her final trial, that she should be careful. "The prosecutor is a very prejudiced man, and if he finds out how knowledgeable you are, it will antagonize him and he will order your execution."

She looked at me and smiled. The last thing on her mind was her freedom. "Now that we have this opportunity, we must teach them the truth and help them to understand it. We can't afford to be scared of what they might do. We have to be honest, answer every question they ask us in detail and not leave anything unexplained. We have to put the Faith before ourselves and our own lives, and sacrifice absolutely everything for the truth."

A few minutes later she returned to my cell holding a piece of elastic, a needle, some thread and her black chador which we had to wear every day. "I must sew this piece of elastic to my chador so I can easily put it around my neck and not worry about it slipping from my head. Then I can concentrate on what they have to say to me tomorrow and not be distracted." This was how she prepared herself, calmly and decisively, for the next day.

She woke up at 4 a.m. to pray, and then kissed us goodbye. At five o'clock they called her to the lobby, and it was 8 P.M. when she returned. She had been charged with participation in the Bahá'í administration, being a spy for Israel, a Bahá'í class teacher, a member of various local committees, not being married, and refusing to recant her faith. She had been sentenced to be hanged unless she recanted, and she had courageously told the prosecutor: "I have found the truth, and I will not give it away at any price." She was twenty-eight.

MASHÍD NÍRÚMAND, AGE 28

From Olya's Story, *1993*

Another of the young prisoners was Mahshíd Nírúmand. Mahshíd was born into a Bahá'í family in Shíráz in 1955. Her father was a technical worker, and though they were not a wealthy family, they had a comfortable life. Mahshíd was a quiet person who normally kept to herself, but at times she could be very funny. She had a naive, childlike quality about her, but was also very mature and intelligent.

Mahshíd was a good student and passed her exams every year with good marks. Túbá Zá'irpúr was one of her teachers for a while. She went on to Pahlaví University to study physics, but because of her special interest in geophysics, she took extra courses in geology as well. Had university policy permitted it, she would have liked to have stayed on after her graduation, and in another six months she would have achieved a double major and received her second Bachelor of Science degree.

As well as English, which was the working language at university, Mahshíd learned French and German by attending optional courses. After finishing all her studies so successfully, and even though she had paid back her student loan in full, the authorities refused to give a degree certificate because she was a Bahá'í.

Mahshíd was a very conscientious person, both in her work and her private life. She believed that the opportunity to serve was God's favour to the individual, so one had to take full advantage of this favour and always give of one's best. Her mother later told me that she used to wake herself up in the middle of the night to pray and meditate. She found it easier to concentrate when everyone else was asleep and all was quiet.

Before she was arrested she always said, "I wish I could trade places with someone in prison." Just before her arrest, as if she could foresee what would happen, she prepared herself by reviewing the prayers she had memorized, and studied some new writings so she would be able to answer the investigators with actual quotations. She kept a set of clean clothes ready so she would be prepared to go to prison at any time. She even started to sleep on the floor without a pillow, telling her mother, "I must build up my tolerance to hardship. If one day I am arrested and have to go to prison, I must be able to sleep on the floor."

It was not long before her premonitions were realized, and she was arrested and taken to Sepah. We were arrested on the same night, and then transferred to Adelabad together just over a month later, so I came to know her very well, although by nature she was shy and retiring.

Mahshíd was as hard-working in prison as she had been at home. The younger Bahá'ís took responsibility for the tasks we had been given. "You are like our mothers," they argued. "How can we sit and watch you work? Let us do it." Mahshíd took on the job of washing all the dishes.

Although we were very close and united in prison, and shared the same beliefs, it didn't mean we were all alike. Quite the contrary. Mahshíd, for example, was a very serious young woman, always neat and tidy. Roya Ishráqí, on the other hand, had a very bubbly, easy-going personality, and couldn't resist playing practical jokes on her in Adelabad to cheer her up. One of her favourite pranks was to slip into Mahshíd's cell just after she had finished tidying it, and mess it all up again. When Mahshíd got back from her interrogation or visiting one of the other prisoners, everyone would laugh as she tried to find where Roya was hiding.

Roya was always the first to wake up, and another of he[r]
sneak into Mahshíd's cell in the morning and strip her blanke[t]
"Wake up, lazy bones!" Mahshíd feigned a long-suffering attitu[de]
it all in good spirit.

Mahshíd had great inner strength, and she always comforted her p[arents]
during family visits, and urged them to be patient and firm. I remem[ber]
that during her first visit with her parents she brought out her hand fro[m]
under her chador and showed them her clenched fist as a symbol of
strength and steadfastness.

She was incredibly brave and honest during her interrogations in Sepah,
which were usually conducted at the same time as mine; she always avoided
mentioning any names, but explained in detail her own activities and services. Mahshíd's replies to the interrogators were always calm and meas-
ured, in contrast with my own impulsive desire to shout back at them. She
was always worried I would get myself into trouble with my quick tongue,
and used to say, "Olya, be careful! Don't talk back to them."

Once they took Mahshíd alone to the basement where they tortured prisoners. Hours later they brought her back to join us in the interrogation room,
and then sent us all back to the cell. Mahshíd told us what had happened.

> When they separated me from you I was blindfolded and taken to the
> basement, and they made me sit on a wooden table they use when they
> whip people. I could hear people screaming and crying all around me.
> The guards swore at me and insulted me. Later they uncovered my
> eyes. There were chains hanging from the four corners of the table, and
> two investigators wearing masks were standing in front of me.
>
> There was also a man who called himself 'Abdu'lláh—he was
> the one who tortured the prisoners. He had a wire cable in his
> hand and was threatening to whip me. Sometimes they yelled at
> me and sometimes they begged me to recant and to give them the
> names of the other committee members. I simply told them, "I will
> not recant or give you any names even if you tear me apart."
>
> 'Abdu'lláh began to get angry and kept playing with the wire
> cable in his hands and threatening me. I said, "I have told you every-
> thing you wanted to know." They were so inhuman that I was sure I
> would be flogged. I asked as calmly as I could, "On which side
> would you like me to lie down? Do you want to whip my back first
> or the soles of my feet?" My composure just made them laugh.

One day I came across Mahshíd lying on the floor of her cell staring at the
ceiling, deep in thought. I went to her and asked, "What's wrong,
Mahshíd, has something happened?"

She simply smiled, replying, "No, nothing important," but I persisted
and she said, "For two nights running now I've had the same dream. I
know they will execute me. Even if they let everyone else go, I know they
will execute me. But I am not afraid. I have surrendered to His will."

e you saying this? We all hope that these misunder-
e put right and our innocence will be proved to the

en I am executed," replied Mah<u>sh</u>íd with a smile,
ue dream."

ed with us to Adelabad after over a month of non-
1 16 January she was taken to the Revolutionary
ır days later she faced her final trial before the
one was charged with being a Bahá'í, attending
as a child, being a Bahá'í class teacher, being a member of the
th Committee, giving money to the Bahá'í fund, being unmarried, and
being a supporter of Zionism. She, too, was condemned to death.

Roya I<u>sh</u>ráqí, Age 22

From Olya's Story, *1993*

Roya had just turned twenty-two and was a vivacious, happy girl. She sacrificed every bit of comfort she had in prison to help others. Her character
and the strength of her faith made her very popular among all the prisoners, but especially with Fa<u>kh</u>rí Imámí, the political prisoner who was in
charge of the cell at Sepah. Roya willingly helped her keep the records of
who was supposed to go for questioning and who had to clean the floors
or toilets on our cell rota. With so many prisoners in the cell block at that
time, Fa<u>kh</u>rí had found it very difficult to cope, and she really appreciated
Roya's help. In return, whenever she heard of a new order or any other
news she immediately shared it with Roya, and out of respect and affection
for her she was kind to all of us.

'Izzat went through a rough time. Most nights she sat up by the young
girls, worrying about them and praying for their freedom. She daredn't
sleep in case the guards came to take one of the girls in the middle of the
night—she wanted to be there to comfort them. She and I became very
close, and we used to talk for hours, sharing all our inner feelings.

I remember once 'Izzat was telling us how popular Roya was among the
Bahá'í families, and how many young men had asked her to marry them.
But Roya had always said it was not the time to get married, but the time
to support the Bahá'í in their difficulties. She turned to Roya: "Now see, if
you had got married and moved away, this wouldn't have happened, and
you wouldn't be here."

Roya smiled and replied, "But Mother, being here is much sweeter."

Roya was calm and firm at all times, even under the most severe pressure. I never saw her crying or upset except once, when her mother was
very distressed and said to Roya through her tears, "I fear only one thing
in prison—if it happens to you, I am afraid I wouldn't be able to bear it,
and just the thought of it makes me tremble." 'Izzat had every right to be

concerned; the political prisoners had told of assaults and rapes, in stories we could hardly bear to listen to.

That was the only time I saw Roya with tears running down her face. "Mama, I don't want you even to think about that, but you must know even in that situation I would surrender to whatever was ordained for me." Luckily, since we Bahá'ís were regarded as unclean by the guards, that test never arose for us.

At last we were told we could receive visitors. After over three weeks without any news of Rosita, 'Izzat and Roya were so excited they counted the minutes to visiting time. Rosita was the first to enter, rushing into the room as soon as the door opened, her face lit up with a lovely smile. Before we were connected on the telephones she had gestured to Roya that she hadn't seen their father, and asked how he was. Roya gestured back that she shouldn't worry and he was fine. Then the connection was turned on and we all talked.

Rosita had to make the long journey by bus from the city to the prison twice a week for the visiting days, each time bringing two plastic bags full of fresh fruit and clean clothes, and some money for their needs in prison. Every time we saw her she was as cheerful and charming as ever. One day, Roya wrote a small note for her sister and cleverly sewed it into the sleeve of a shirt she was sending out. On the note she wrote: "Rosita, don't wait for Mother and Father's freedom, nor mine. You are alone now. Marry the man you love and start your own family." She gave the clothes to the guard to give to Rosita, and during the visit that day, pointed to her sleeve to let Rosita know that there was a message hidden in it.

Rosita also used her visits to pass messages between her mother and sister, and her father. The second time she came to visit 'Izzat and Roya, she said, "Last week I saw Dad. He was strong and firm. He asked how you were!"

Her mother replied, "Next time you see him, tell him that I miss him very much." Although the Ishráqís were under investigation in the same room every day, they hadn't seen or spoken to each other since the night they were arrested, because in the trial room we were not allowed even to look at each other.

One day Roya said to the investigator, "Today is the thirtieth day that my parents and I have been in prison. In all this time I haven't seen my father once. I would be very grateful if you would let me turn my head and glance at him, just to see his face."

The investigator paused for a moment, then evidently touched by her request, took Roya and her father to the adjoining room together; then he gave 'Izzat a chance to be with her husband for five minutes. As soon as Roya saw her father she held him in her arms and kissed him and said, "Father, I love you very much. Please stay strong." She looked at her father's pale and tired face and asked, "Father, why is your beard so long?"

He explained that they were not allowed to shave in prison. Lovingly she kissed her father over and over again. The investigator took advantage of this moment and said to Roya, "Isn't it a shame! Even though you love your father so much, by refusing to say one word you deprive yourselves of the chance of being together. By simply saying that you are not Bahá'ís you could free yourselves from all of this. I would even unfreeze your family's assets and restore your father's pension."

Roya smiled at him and firmly replied, "Your honour, my love for my parents is only natural; my love for Bahá'u'lláh, however, is much greater. Perhaps you should stop and think about what kind of truth this must be that makes a young girl like me refuse to exchange this love even for the love of my parents, even for the whole world."

PART 3

'DON'T FORGET, YOU ARE A PRISONER':
PRISON CONDITIONS AND DEPRIVATIONS

Bright shiny bracelets
jangling on my arm
wide leather belt
snug about my waist
chains dangling seductively
between my legs.
I am captured
but not subdued
—Judee Norton

Guarded. Counted. Observed. Being on the downside of a huge power imbalance is the essence of being incarcerated, and guards personify the many restrictions of a prisoner's condition. In 1787 Jeremy Bentham theorized his ideal prison architecture: the panopticon, "a new mode of obtaining power of mind over mind."[1] In this circular structure, with cells lining the circumference, an inspector's "lodge" serves as the central observation point. The prisoner is perpetually under inspection by the omnipresent guard, whose power manifests itself in the position of "seeing without being seen."[2] Whether or not women's prisons literally apply the panopticon structure, the gaze of prison authority is omnipresent in the form of restrictions and deprivations.

Control and deprivation characterize the woman prisoner's life. In his classic 1958 study of a male maximum-security prison Gresham Sykes cites five general areas of deprivation: liberty, goods and services, security, heterosexual relationships, and autonomy.[3] Early researchers who studied American women's prisons noted that Sykes's "pains of imprisonment" also held true for female prisoners.[4] Sykes's categories, balanced by findings of current sociological studies, can be used as a general framework for discussing major concerns in women's prison writings. Allowing for differences in gender, time period, nationality, and social and political climate, these studies offer insight about women's descriptions of prison conditions.

Since publication of the first edition of this anthology, basic conditions in American women's prisons have changed, mostly for the worse.[5] Private corporations have entered the field of corrections. The construction of supermax prisons and the upsurge of the prison-industrial complex[6] have confirmed what women prisoners have long known: that the rehabilitation of female offenders can no longer be claimed as a justification for their incarceration.[7] Although far fewer women than men are imprisoned, their numbers are rising at a much higher rate, as a result of mandatory sentencing and arrests for drug-related offenses. "With a few exceptions, prisons are pretty much back to the custodial mode," criminologist and historian of women's prisons Nicole Hahn Rafter explains. "It's very punitive, and it's being driven by the tremendous growth in the women's prison population as a result of drug laws."[8] Poems by Diane Hamill Metzger and Barbara Saunders in this section offer glimpses into this new, soul-deadening prison environment.[9]

"Reception"—this corrections euphemism is incapable of masking the raw reality of a woman prisoner's experience. The admissions process introduces the new prisoner to prison rules and conditions and holds so much strangeness, fear, and degradation[10] that it is almost universally described in prison memoirs. Readers quickly identify with these descriptions and participate in the prison initiation. It epitomizes the woman's complete loss of autonomy and even identity, if the institution has its way. Typically, the prisoner is physically stripped and searched, then relieved of all material belongings and given a number in exchange. Joan Henry's autobiographical narrative in this section mixes humor with pain to illustrate the alienation of her first days in an English prison. Henry came from a civilized London world that respected privacy to the regulated, utterly impersonal world of Holloway Prison. Her account jars the reader with a hint of the culture shock she felt.

Prison food, at best unvaried and bland, is a constant reminder to the prisoner that she has lost control over the basics of her own existence. For many prison writers, nutrition is a critical issue. Caesarina Makhoere, for example, knew that the inadequate food in her South African prison jeopardized health and life; even more galling was the fact that her race determined the quality of her diet. Refusing to obey authority, Makhoere led the first hunger strike by women in South African prisons, and secured a better diet for herself and other prisoners. Their victory won more than better, healthful food; it emboldened the women collectively to boycott parading and clothing regulations. Makhoere's example speaks for all women prisoners oppressed by inhumane conditions: "If a person does not know his or her standpoint, that person can be suppressed—silenced. But if you know where you stand, if you know the people support you, you will keep on resisting, wherever you are."[11]

Scandalous health conditions are too often a "given" of prison life, in the United States as well as in countries worldwide. The privatization of American prison health-care systems, overcrowding, and increased numbers of mentally ill and aging prisoners as well as those with substance abuse problems significantly undermine the quality of medical attention, often with serious consequences.[12] Within this context of inadequate health care, indicted in Barbara Saunders' poem, "A Life Worth Living," the AIDS counseling and education peer education program at Bedford Hills Correctional Facility, discussed in part 1 of this anthology, stands out as a bold and responsible prisoner action.

Changed relationships with others disturb the female prisoner; in particular, her anxiety over separation from supportive relationships with those on the outside and from family is acute and for many prisoners is the most devastating of prison deprivations.[13] A concern voiced by some women prison writers through the ages has been the lack of heterosexual relationships and the forced association in prison with other females. Black Panther Assata Shakur, during her imprisonment at the New York City Correctional Institution for Women, stated, "Women prisoners rarely refer to each other as sister. Instead, 'bitch' and 'whore' are the common terms of reference."[14] Carolyn Baxter's poems in this section seem to bear this out, but they also display women's genuine concern for each other and a level of kindness toward fellow prisoners that, according to Shakur, is greater than that in men's prisons. Negative attitudes of some female prisoners toward other imprisoned women raise complex questions concerning class, race, and gender issues. These negative attitudes are balanced, however, by other women prisoners' positive expressions of solidarity, as seen in the selections in part 6 of this anthology, and by expressions of sexual attraction and love, as seen in the selections in part 4. Diane Hamill Metzger writes:

> I have had to co-exist in close quarters with people I thought to be so unlike myself that I couldn't imagine how I could share space and time with them. I have shed prejudices and gained understanding and empathy. I have found a courage within myself that I never knew I had. I have learned who and what are important in my life and have questioned everything that I thought I once believed.[15]

Another prison deprivation is loss of autonomy. In contemporary American prisons this loss is difficult for male as well as female prisoners. However, it takes a unique form in a women's prison, where a woman not only loses decision-making power, but is also often treated like a child, encouraged to be dependent, and called a girl by the prison administration.[16] Carolyn Baxter's poems tell the frank reality of a woman's loss of autonomy in an institution where racism and sexism are too often the rule. "Whatever its purported purpose," writes Patricia McConnel, who spent time in six jails and in the Federal Reformatory for Women in Alderson, West Virginia, its [prison's] actual effect is to destroy all those qualities in a person that might enable her to become an effective human being. Initiative and self-assertion are usually severely punished. The prisoner has no control over any aspect of her existence; she is expected to surrender any will to direct her own life.[17]

Concerns about guards' control pervade women's prison writing. As Patricia McConnel writes, "[P]risoners in fact are obsessed with them [guards], and their [prisoners'] day-to-day life has *everything* to do with their relations to those people."[18] Most references to guards are negative, although not always presented in graphic scenes of actual conflict.[19] Correctional officers may be a woman prisoner's central subject, as in Barbara Saunders' poem "Wrong," which is charged with the tension of latent violence, or in Caesarina Makhoere's account of her relationship with a racist wardress who abuses power. More typically, guards play a background role as the omnipresent agent supervising imprisoned women's lives. If prison food is the writer's subject, a guard is there to serve it. In descriptions of the prison intake ritual, a guard initiates the neophyte. In accounts of discipline, a guard is the enforcer, the very essence of institutional control. Positive accounts of guards are rare and therefore often touching.[20]

The power and control exerted by the prison institution may cross the line to violate a woman's human rights. Torture is part of imprisonment for some women—even in the United States.[21] In her article "Telling Someone," political activist Susan Saxe testifies to the mental and physical abuse of institutionalized women and men: "Frankly, I don't think most of us care. We don't know or don't want to know. We want 'those people' kept out of sight and out of mind."[22] A prison writer's need to tell someone gives voice to the too often nameless, voiceless pain of prisoners around the world.[23]

Although lacking in physical torture, the American courtroom scene generates psychological violence against poor, minority female defendants, as New York poet Carolyn Baxter reminds us. Within American prisons, that violence too often becomes blatant sexual abuse, in rape by guards and strip searches—the sort of violence that is about to erupt in Saunders' poem, "Wrong."[24] The Human Rights Watch Women's Rights Project, monitoring violence against women since 1990, reported bluntly in 1996: "Our findings indicate that being a woman prisoner in U.S. state prisons can be a terrifying experience."[25]

Underlying all the deprivations explored in the following selections, the most fundamental is the loss of liberty itself, a loss for which most people would be psychologically unprepared. Every selection in this section, and, indeed, in this entire anthology and its bibliography, has the loss of liberty at its core. That elemental loss, shared by each prisoner worldwide, is to some degree the impetus for the creation of all prison literature, since the communication implied by writing is a way out of prison walls. A woman prisoner's decision to write is itself a statement of hope and a refusal to give in to intolerable conditions. As

Diane Hamill Metzger writes," I often live vicariously, but I still live. I still feel the sun on my face and the wind in my hair as I walk from one building to another. The fences cannot deprive me of these things."[26]

NOTES

The quotation in the title of this section is taken from Caesarina Kona Makhoere, *No Child's Play: In Prison under Apartheid* (London: The Women's Press, 1988), 19. The epigraph to this section is taken from Judee Norton, "Arrival," in *Doing Time: 25 Years of Prison Writing*, ed. Bell Gale Chevigny (New York: Arcade, 1999), 22.

1. Jeremy Bentham, "Panopticon; or The Inspection-House," in *The Works of Jeremy Bentham*, vol. 4 (New York: Russell & Russell, 1962), 39.

2. Bentham, "Panopticon," 44.

3. Gresham M. Sykes, *The Society of Captives: A Study of a Maximum Security Prison* (1958; reprint, New York: Atheneum, 1968), 63–83. A 1977 study by Toch listing seven similar "environmental concerns"—privacy, safety, structure, support, emotional feedback, activity, and freedom—is cited in Nicolette Parisi, "The Prisoner's Pressures and Responses," in *Coping with Imprisonment*, ed. N. Parisi (Beverly Hills, Calif.: Sage, 1982), 10–11.

4. Rose Giallombardo, *Society of Women: A Study of a Women's Prison* (New York: Wiley, 1966), 93–102; David A. Ward and Gene G. Kassebaum, *Women's Prison: Sex and Social Structure* (Chicago: Aldine, 1965), 3–28.

5. Currently there is much discussion about prison reform and resistance to prison abuses. See Angela Y. Davis, "Incarcerated Women: Transformative Strategies," *Black Renaissance/Renaissance Noire* 1, no. 1, online, available: http://www.iupjournals.org/ blackren/brn1-1.html, August 7, 2001, and Russ Immarigeon, "Why a Moratorium on Prison Construction Is Critical to Real Reform," *Fortune Society News*, online, available: http://www.fortunesociety.org/summer00-04.htm, August 18, 2001. See also Pat Carlen, *Alternatives to Women's Imprisonment*, Milton Keynes, U.K.: Open University Press, 1990, and Bell Gale Chevigny, "Prison Activists Come of Age," *Nation*, 24 July, 2000, 27–30. Critical Resistance is an activist organization holding annual conferences on issues of prison reform. They are available at *http://www.criticalresistance.org*.

6. Angela Davis has recently devoted much research to discussion of the prison-industrial complex. The prison-industrial complex is defined by Eric Schlosser in "The Prison-Industrial Complex," *The Atlantic Online*, December 1998, available at http://www.theatlantic.com/ issues/98dec/prisons.html: "It is a confluence of special interests that has given prison construction in the United States a seemingly unstoppable momentum," January 5, 2002.

7. See Joseph T. Hallinan, *Going Up the River* on the growth of private prisons in the United States since 1983 and on prison overcrowding. See the essays in *Criminal Injustice: Confronting the Prison Crisis*, ed. Elihu Rosenblatt(Boston: South End Press, 1996), on the growth of supermax prisons and the prison industrial complex. David Shichor, in *Punishment for Profit*, Thousand Oaks, Calif.: Sage, 1995), 218–19, summarizes findings of a federal study of three women's prisons, including a privately run institution. Daniel Burton-Rose, Dan Pens, and Paul Wright, in *The Celling of America: An Inside Look at the U.S. Prison Industry*, (Monroe, Me.: Common Courage Press, 1998) edit a collection of articles discussing current conditions in American prisons. Christian Parenti, in *Lockdown America: Police and Prisons in the Age of Crisis* (London: Verso, 1999), discusses the prison-industrial complex and the need for control over prisoners by such means as "therapy" with television. Amanda George describes the use of private prisons for women in Australia in "The New Prison Culture: Making Millions from Misery," 189–210, in *Harsh Punishment: International Experiences of Women's Imprisonment*, ed. Sandy Cook and Susanne Davies (Boston: Northeastern University

Press, 1999). Russ Immarigeon and Meda Chesney-Lind discuss the unnecessary growth of women's prisons and suggest ways to use community resources as alternatives to incarceration in *Women's Prisons: Overcrowded and Overused* (San Francisco: National Council on Crime and Delinquency, 1992).

8. Nicole Hahn Rafter, "The More Things Change . . .," *Women's Review of Books* 14: 10–11 (July 1997), 3–4.

9. Other selections in this anthology dealing with prison conditions include those by Baxley, Chilean women, Evans, Figner, Lytton, McConnel, Norton, Partnoy, Roland, Saubin, and Wituska.

10. For a different perspective, see the selection by Nawal El Saadawi, in part 1 of this anthology.

11. Makhoere, *No Child's Play*, p. 47.

12. See Corey Weinstein, "Systematic Abuse of Women Prisoners," *Concrete Garden* 4 (1996): 173–75, on inadequate medical care for women prisoners in California. See Nicole Hahn Rafter and Debra L. Stanley, *Prisons in America: A Reference Handbook* (Santa Barbara, Calif.: ABC-CLIO, 1999), for a discussion of issues concerning prison health care.

13. Meda Chesney-Lind discusses the situation of imprisoned mothers in *The Female Offender: Girls, Women, and Crime* (Thousand Oaks, Calif.: Sage, 1997), 158. See part 5 of this anthology for selections and discussion of imprisoned women and their family concerns.

14. Assata Shakur, "Women in Prison: How We Are," *Black Scholar* 12: 6 (November–December 1981): 54–55, reprinted from 9: 7 (April 1978).

15. Diane Hamill Metzger, "The Top of the Well," p. 120 in this volume.

16. See Shakur, "Women in Prison," 52–53; Angela Davis, *An Autobiography* (New York: Random House, 1974).

17. Patricia McConnel to Judith Scheffler, 6 July 1983.

18. Patricia McConnel to Judith Scheffler, 23 July 1987.

19. For negative accounts of prison authority, including guards, physicians, and administrators, see selections in this anthology by Bedell, Chilean women, Evans, Figner, Lytton, McConnel, Norton, Partnoy, Roohizadegan, and Saadawi.

20. For positive accounts of prison authority, see selections in this anthology by Saubin, Tesfagiorgis, Wituska, and the women of the ACE Program. Baxley 's diary expresses both positive and negative associations with guards. In "Ramblings of a C.O." in *Concrete Garden*, 4 (1996) 215–16, a guard named "J.T.S." explains the point of view of some correctional officers: "We, as Correction Officers, are in a position of control over human beings, but we also work under strict rules and regulations that restrain and tend to harden our human nature. . . . All of our time seems to be spent on solving tangible problems like taking counts or noting who is moving to what block or who violates what rule. We never get to the major problems or things that will really help somebody."

21. See Holly J. Burkhalter, "Torture in U.S. Prisons," *Nation* 3 July 1995, 17.

22. Susan Saxe, "Telling Someone," in *Cages of Steel: The Politics of Imprisonment in the United States*, ed. Ward Churchill and J. J.Vander Wall (Washington, D.C.: Maisonneuve Press, 1992), 359–61.

23. Additional selections in this anthology dealing with torture include the writings by Chilean women, Evans, Figner, Lytton, McConnel, Partnoy, and Roohizadegan. Two organizations dedicated to promoting the Universal Declaration of Human Rights are Amnesty International (www.amnesty.org) and Amnesty International USA (www.aiusa.org). Elaine Scarry, in *The Body in Pain: The Making and Unmaking of the World* (New York: Oxford, 1985), theorizes that the "display of the fiction of power" is "the final product and outcome of torture" (57).

24. For a discussion of sexual abuse in women's prisons in the United States, see Chesney-Lind, *The Female Offender*; Parenti, *Lockdown America*; Barbara Owen, "Women and Imprisonment in the United States," in *Harsh Punishment*, 81–98.

25. Human Rights Watch Women's Rights Project, *All Too Familiar: Sexual Abuse of Women in U.S. State Prisons* (New York: Human Rights Watch, 1996), 1.

26. Metzger, "The Top of the Well," p. 121 in this volume.

JOAN HENRY

(1914–2000)

Joan Henry was born in London to a "rather illustrious," though not wealthy family. Descended from two British prime ministers and related to the British philosopher Bertrand Russell, the former debutante had the "usual over protected childhood and adolescence of that period," but was "shattered" by her twin sister's death at the age of twenty-one.

In 1938 she married an army officer and they had one daughter. The marriage ended during the war. Her twelve-month sentence in 1951 for passing bad checks resulted from her financial troubles following the end of the marriage. She had not realized that she had accepted a forged check when she accepted a friend's offer of financial help.

Her first book, *Women in Prison*, was based on her own prison experiences. The title of its first edition, published in Britain, was *Who Lie in Gaol*, from a line in Oscar Wilde's "Ballad of Reading Gaol." The book exposed the brutal treatment women received in English prisons and was criticized by the prison service for sensationalism. A best seller, it helped to effect gradual changes. The book was the basis of a 1954 film, *The Weak and the Wicked,* starring Glynis Johns. Henry's second prison book, *Yield to the Night,* is a novel about a woman condemned to death. Henry worked on the screenplay for the 1958 film that starred Diana Dors and was released in Britain as *Yield to the Night* and in the United States as *Blonde Sinner.* Henry also wrote plays for television and theater and three other novels.

In 1957 Henry married J. Lee Thompson, director of the two film versions of her books. They divorced in the late 1960s. She spent her final years in London, enjoying poetry, painting, theater, and family.

In the following selection from *Women in Prison*, Henry recalls her eight months' imprisonment in England's Holloway and Askham Grange prisons, portraying a naive inmate adjusting to the jargon, inhabitants, and inflexible routine of a different world.

Note: Background information is from Henry's letter to Judith Scheffler, October 21, 1982; letter from Anne Maycock, Henry's daughter, to Scheffler August 17, 2001; obituary, *The Daily Telegraph* (London) 1 January 2001.

AT HOLLOWAY PRISON

From Women in Prison, *1952.*

In a few minutes I was back in the cell.[1] I found a single sheet of lined paper with "H. M. Prison" on the top and a few words telling the recipient to quote my name and number when replying. I wondered how I obtained a pen and ink. In a little while the cell door was unlocked and I was given to understand that it was lunch time; it involved a similar procedure as at breakfast. This time it was stew in a tin bowl; mostly soup with a few pieces of meat and a lot of potato, more bread, and a slab of pudding. I supposed that in a few days I would be hungry, but at the moment I could only swallow a few mouthfuls. I washed up the plates and lay down on the bed and tried to think what I would say in my letter when I eventually got a pen, and to calculate how long it would be before I received an answer.

Time passed by. The cell doors were unlocked, and the pail emptying took place again. Then I was told to pack up my things, which did not take long, as I was moving.

I followed an officer along the passages and through a door. Everything looked just the same, only slightly smaller. I was taken upstairs to the first floor, to the far end. The cell was a bit smaller than my previous one, and the bed was even lower on the ground. The cell was warmer, though, as hot pipes ran through the back of it. I had been given a pen and ink, and when the door was locked once more I sat down to write my letter. There was so much I wanted to say, but so little space on which to say it. I discovered afterward that the fortnightly letter permitted by the regulations consisted of a double sheet, but any special letters—for which you had to book for the governor[2] and which were granted only in cases of necessity—consisted, like the reception letter, of just one sheet. All correspondence was subject to the strictest censorship, and you never received a letter in its envelope.

In the next-door cell a woman began to scream.

"I shall soon get used to it," I wrote. "Naturally everything is very strange at first . . ."

The screams continued, and I heard the next-door cell being unlocked. After a while there was silence.

". . . very strange indeed. You will be able to come and see me in a month from now. . . ."

I made up my bed. The mattress seemed worse than the other one. I heard the other women being let out to go to work. I wished I could go too. Anything would be better than just sitting here.

The hours passed by, and then I heard,

"Exercise! EXERCISE!" The door opened, and I was told to go downstairs. I gave the officer my letter.

The women were lining up in twos on the ground floor. I imagined they were mostly "new girls," like myself. All had red ties. I noticed the girl with the swept-up coiffure, and two very old ladies with white hair, who were standing talking together. I learned later that both were abortionists. They had cells next door to one another and seldom spoke to any of the other prisoners. They were known as "Arsenic" and "Old Lace." Arsenic had a very long, thin nose with a permanent drop on the end of it, and Old Lace had a large, coarse face strangely out of proportion to her narrow, stooping body. She always wore her gray cardigan thrown carelessly over her shoulders in the manner of one accustomed to a sable stole. She was constantly being reprimanded for this. Both of them appeared to have an endless supply of small, gilt safety pins with which they pinned their ties. These were articles much sought after by the other women and sometimes bequeathed to the specially favored by outgoing prisoners. You were not allowed to have such things sent in, and it remained a mystery to me how Arsenic and Old Lace came by their store.

I walked round with a young Indian girl. She was a friendly, naughty little thing with beautiful white teeth in her thin brown face and the large, dark, mournful eyes of her race. Her name was Marie. She had been sentenced to eighteen months.

As we walked round the exercise ground in the cold wind she told me that she was the mother of a baby of six months.

Three officers stood at different points around us.

"Those are the workrooms," said Marie, pointing to a large building ahead of us where a lot of other women were emerging to join us. "I'm going to be a cleaner."

"Will you like that?"

She shrugged her lean shoulders. "Not bad . . . and sometimes you can pick up things . . . I've got a friend in the hospital, she's got T.B. . . . lucky dog . . . Maybe I'll think of some way of going sick myself." Her black eyes twinkled. "It depends which doctor you see . . . One of them is a bit soft."

A woman behind us moved up to say something to Marie.

"In TWOS . . ." yelled one of the officers.

"F . . . . . g mare," said the woman in a loud voice. "Wots it to 'er if we go on all fours like the animals we are now . . . Who she think she is . . . Queen Mary?"

I giggled for the first time since my entry into prison. Arsenic and Old Lace sailed by us, smiling ingratiatingly at the wardress nearest to us.

"Smarmy bitches," growled our friend behind. "Sucking up to them screws . . . Abortion ain't no better than murder in my opinion . . . Respectable women didn't ought to speak to them. . . . I don't know wot my ole man would say at the kind of people I 'ave to mix with here . . . I didn't ought to be among 'em in the first place . . . just for receiving a couple of blankets."

Marie began to walk very fast, and I had almost to run to catch up with her.

"The girl with her killed her baby," she said. "But I don't suppose the old witch knows it . . . It doesn't do to talk about people's crimes here . . . Half the time you don't know what they're in for."

"I suppose not." I felt rather sick.

"What time do we get shut up for the night?" I asked Marie.

"Four o'clock, when we have tea. Fill your pail when you get back to the cell. There's only one hot tap for the whole of this wing. It's hardly worth queuing for that, and you haven't any fags or sweets to bribe someone to get it for you, have you? Ask Miss Mack—she's quite decent—if you can have a couple of books from the library. You *may* get them, though they aren't due till next week. If not, I'll lend you one tomorrow, but don't lose it . . . You can lose remission for that. . . ."

"Thank you very much." It seemed hardly worth the responsibility.

There seemed no opportunity to ask for library books, and I did not know which officer was Miss Mack. I filled my pail as advised and stood in the doorway of my cell waiting for tea. Presently the familiar procession appeared. Warm hay-water, and bread and margarine.

As the cell door closed behind me, I remembered that it was only 4:00 in the afternoon. My door would not be reopened, except for me to be handed a mug of cocoa, until 6:45 the following morning.

Tomorrow would be Sunday. At home I would lie in bed late reading the morning papers. I would see . . . No, NO, had I not resolved to think of nothing that would remind me of the life I had lost? This was to be my existence for eight months . . . until October ninth . . . It had already been worked out on my card, and all I could do was put up with it.

"Thank you." I took the mug of tea and the great slices of bread. I had discovered a bucket on the landing where you could throw unused food.

I drank a little of the tea and ate half a slice of bread and margarine. I rinsed the mug and put the things tidily together. I washed my handkerchief and hung it over the hot pipe to dry. I wondered if I would be given anything to keep my cell clean with. I must ask about it tomorrow. Tomorrow seemed about a month away. I lay down on the bed. I might just as well undress and get under the bedclothes. There was nothing to stay up for.

I remembered that the previous evening, very shortly after they had been round with cocoa, I heard a voice shouting what I took to be "Teas . . . Teas . . ." It had seemed odd, so soon after cocoa, but I decided that tonight I would refuse the cocoa and have another cup of warm hay-water—anything was preferable to that bitter-tasting stuff.

I lay on my back staring at the ceiling. I thought, This is no dream, this is happening. Even if you sleep, you will wake up and find yourself enclosed in these four walls, and there is nothing in the world you can do about it . . . So what? Nothing is here for tears; self-pity is the least comforting of emotions; it can only lead you back by a road littered with bogus philosophies under a pall of sentimentality to yourself. Maybe there are lucky ones who can pray . . . yet God has always seemed nearer to me in happiness and sunshine than He has in despair. . . . I closed my eyes. . . . "Our Father which art in heaven, Hallowed be thy name. Thy kingdom come. Thy will be done in earth, as it is in heaven. Give us this day our daily bread. And forgive us our trespasses, as we forgive them that trespass against us . . . but deliver us from evil . . . Amen." . . .

In years to come I knew I would be able to look back and my own tragedy would seem a little comic. I must look so funny in my enormous white nightgown, with my hair tied back with a bit of string, and all of us in blue cotton dresses and ties, like overgrown Girl Guides or Damon Runyon's broken-down Dolls. . . .

At that moment, to my surprise, I heard the sounds of a piano, very badly played, coming from downstairs and raucous voices singing, "Is it true what they say about Dixie?" I learned later that these came from the

"Brownies," or young prisoners under twenty-one, and so-called because they wore brown dresses in contrast to our blue ones. They gave more trouble—most of them were ex-Borstal girls—than all the rest of the prison put together, but they were allowed out a bit later than the rest of the women. Strumming on an ancient piano was their favorite form of recreation and a constant source of irritation to the older prisoners.

However, I was amazed at hearing a piano at the moment.

"'There's just one place for me, near Y-E-U. It's like heaven to be, near Y-E-U . . .'" screamed the girls.

"'Times when we're apart, I just can't face my heart . . . never stray more than just teu lips away. . . .'"

I shall never hear this tune without thinking of Holloway, for "Near You" haunted my prison days: it seemed to be on everybody's lips, though I had never heard it outside.

After some time the noise—I can hardly call it anything else—ceased and I heard the jangle of keys. I imagined the songsters were being locked up for the night.

Soon came the cry of "Cocoa." I refused it when it came to my cell. I was reserving my strength for a cup of tea.

"Teas . . . Teas . . ."Ah. I rose and went to my cell door. I had not long to wait. I held out my mug with an expectant air . . . A sanitary towel was pushed at me through the door, and I was once more alone. . . .

Light dawned slowly and painfully. "S.T.s" was the cry.

No tea, no cocoa for 6425: she sat down on the bed, a forlorn figure. I could not swear to it, but I think two large tears gathered and fell on the white pad in her hand.

This is a story still enjoyed by the inmates of Holloway, but to me it was one of the most frustrating moments of all time. So in all circumstances is tragedy intermingled with comedy.

Notes

1. This excerpt begins on the second day of Henry's imprisonment in Holloway Prison.—*Ed.*

2. Prisoners had to petition the prison administrator, or warden, for privileges.—*Ed.*

CAESARINA KONA MAKHOERE

(1955–)

South African Caesarina Kona Makhoere, one of seven children, lived with her family in a township near Pretoria. Her mother worked as a domestic servant for whites, and her father was a policeman. At age sixteen, Makhoere gave birth to a son, whom her mother cared for so that Caesarina could continue her education at Vlakfontein Technical High School. Her experience of the inequities of Bantu education and of the racism at her school inspired her as a young woman to join the resistance movement, Umkhonto We Sizwe, part of the African National Congress, which fought the South African government's apartheid policy of racial segregation. Following the Soweto uprising of 1976, Makhoere was arrested as an "agitator" and held in solitary confinement without trial. A year after her arrest, she was tried and received a five-year sentence, which she served in several South African prisons.

While incarcerated, Makhoere refused to submit quietly to prison rules and she noted glaring racial inequities. She organized women prisoners in resisting the human rights violations in their prison conditions. "It had never happened in the history of South Africa that women prisoners had been on a hunger strike," she writes in her memoir, *No Child's Play*, but their strike resulted in improved food (30). She subsequently led the women in protests against parading, prison clothes, and unfair labor practices. She makes it clear that the women prisoners drew strength from their collective spirit and pride. When her protests led to solitary confinement, Makhoere suffered greatly but endured that, too: "At times I think I am tough. They did not break me then, either" (75).

After her release in 1982, Makhoere was reunited with her family and son, then eleven years old. She was afterward forced to live in hiding because the South African government had declared a state of emergency and she had learned that her "name had appeared on the death squad hit list" (120). She later served in the Black Sash organization, advising those charged with pass law violations or facing workplace discrimination, and she worked in the African National Congress's cultural department. By the late 1980s she was studying for a business degree. Information from interviews with Makhoere has become part of the records of the resistance movement in South Africa (see the annotated bibliography in this volume.)

Note: Background information is from Caesarina Kona Makhoere, *No Child's Play: In Prison under Apartheid* (London: The Women's Press, 1988).

RACIAL DISCRIMINATION IN PRISON

From No Child's Play, *1988.*

The physical conditions of Kroonstad were supplemented by the staff. Warrant Officer Smith was a real bitch. She was a bully, clumsy, and most of the time when she came to work she was drunk. She believed her juniors should idolise her. She was especially on top of the world when her captain was not around. She would prance around like a peacock, ordering everyone around as though she owned the whole prison. We prisoners were worst off with her. She would look at us as if we were things coughed up and splashed against a dirty wall. A black person was not expected to talk back to her. Blacks were supposed to shuffle around and nod their heads all the time, but they had to jump when she called. She hated political prisoners most of all. . . .

There was Captain Callitz, who must be the most stupid person I have ever come across. A tall Afrikaner woman, she kept repeating again and again that there were rules and regulations to be observed. I'm sure she even repeated this in her sleep. No matter how you would try to look for reason from her—you wouldn't get it. That's the kind of fool I was trapped with for my entire stay in Kroonstad Prison.

Then there was Erasmus Junior, whom we used to call Tomboy. She was another fool. She just could not reason. She would start, "Whatever I tell you *die kaptein sê julle moet so iets doen* [the captain says you must do it]." We would retort, "Please, can't you talk straight English? It sounds funny and incomprehensible when you start mixing the languages like that." Like a fool she would try, "Well the captain said, the captain said . . . agh! *los julle my* [let me go]," and she'd storm away and leave us laughing. She was one of those people who left school too early in their lives. And all because she failed a standard. In South Africa it seems, a white is not supposed to repeat a standard because every Afrikaner should be born intelligent. So if you have to repeat they chase you away.

Later, there was this wardress that we called Mbomvana. Hey, Thixo! I have never come across such a problem. But this one we dealt with, quite effectively. She was a stout woman who could pass for a rugby scrum-half. Her face and arms were so red, like beetroot, she was blonde and around 23 or 24. I was told she was not married yet and I believed this immediately; who would marry a woman who was so sadistic? But such things do happen in this crazy world; I learned she had a boyfriend who was also a warder in the same prison. It was true! I finally saw the boyfriend. Poor Boer boy. He was as thin as a bean stick. I was afraid to imagine how she would throw him around in her fits of anger. Whew!

And of course there was the head of the prison, Brigadier Venter. He is hard to describe. He was a diplomatic, maybe even a cunning person. He was so tactful; he agreed with most of the complaints we raised against his staff and usually promised to solve any one of our problems. And, honestly, he did. His attitude towards the comrades seemed warm and acceptable. He always tried to put himself across as only a servant of the government and promised that if he could help he would. He said he did not believe in some of the laws; for instance, he would say there was no reason why some human beings should discriminate against other human beings. But, he would go on, he just had no power to do anything about it, the power lay in Pretoria. If he was able to change some of the things he would try to do so, but most things he could not change. Of all the prison staff members, he was the one most of the comrades would speak to and be open with. And they would get satisfactory answers, of course—given that they would have to understand that at this stage action would be beyond his powers. When the staff behaved badly towards prisoners, he would stop them and even remove them from the section. Being head of the whole prison he worried about his good record, I suppose.

Brigadier Venter was in his fifties, about six foot tall, hefty, with brown hair, hazy blue eyes and a handsome face. His manners towards people gained him a lot of respect. He regarded other people as human beings, with the result that whatever he said was not lightly taken. At no stage did he use an iron hand towards a prisoner; instead he preferred to talk to and understand a person. . . .

The prisons gave us work to do like ironing and crocheting. I was expected to iron, together with Mama Dorothy. To be honest, I did not know whose clothes they were, and that made me angry. They would bring the clothes from the other section of the prison, black prisoners' uniforms, and say: "Here, this is your amount of work to be ironed today." They were telling me and Mama Dorothy, and the other four were to do crocheting. Mama Aminah only repeated, "I don't care whether I'm going to finish this thing after my release or what; I'm just passing time." In some cases they would bring wet clothes and expect us to dry them. At first I told them, "Listen, we want to know the procedure. I also want to know crocheting. I'm not going to iron for the rest of my sentence." And they responded, "Don't worry. We are going to make arrangements." But the original set-up continued, and when I complained that these people were continuing to give us ironing, although they had promised we would take turns, they reminded me: "Don't forget, you are a prisoner."

It has always been my tendency to study the situation first, quietly. I don't just attack immediately. Thus in October 1977 I studied the situation. We continued to work through November. Day after day, we worked from eight o'clock to eleven o'clock, then we had lunch. At twenty to twelve, they would lock us up, then unlock us again for work at one. We would work until two o'clock, often we would go for exercise, after exercise we had our supper. They locked us up at three. And it continued like that.

The exercise they expected us to perform was to walk around the yard in circles; they called it exercise. It was just a big yard, with cement walls surrounding it, and a cement pavement skirting the wall, an edge of flower beds, a square lawn in the middle, and one tree, smack in the centre, a peach tree. We decided that peach tree belonged to the people, meaning us. It would bear peaches, golden, round and juicy. And as far as we were concerned the peaches were ours, only. We got no fruit in our official diet. We agreed that black male prisoners who mowed the lawn should take the peaches with the understanding that we were suffering the same fate. But let any white warder or wardress try it and we would scream through the windows: "Hey! What are you doing? Leave our peaches alone!" Eventually even the wardresses accepted that it was more peaceful to ask our permission to eat those peaches.

Once Mbomvana decided that she would assume control of our beautiful peach tree. We screamed at her. Was she not ashamed, stealing the prisoners' peaches? And we told her to stop it. When she didn't, we lodged a complaint with the captain, to stop Mbomvana stealing from our beautiful peach tree, a full-scale formal complaint which brought down Mbomvana from her high and mighty imaginary perch. She had to ask permission from us, which we often refused, to get near that peach tree. The supervisor in charge of our tree was Mama Dorothy. We gave permission to all prisoners only. We very rarely gave permission to prison officials. Agh, those peaches were nice.

The walls of the exercise yard were something like ten metres high, so there was no point thinking about escaping. You just had to forget about it. Normally at supper time we were locked into the small section first, and the big section would be locked up later. One day, for some reason, Mbomvana went straight to the big section and started to have a friendly chat with Mama Dorothy and Thandisa. After some time she left in a hurry without locking the grille, leaving us outside!

It grew dark. We looked up at the stars. It was the only time in six years in prison that I was able to gaze at the stars. Being outside my cell, standing beneath the stars, dreaming, dreaming of freedom. If only we could climb that wall, if they could find us gone, if we could touch the sky, if . . . We talked about freedom and a possible way out of there. But then there were guards patrolling the prison accompanied by guard dogs. Escaping is always in the prisoner's mind. It's natural, I suppose. You just cannot help dreaming sometimes, can you? But look at the security—maybe it was a trap and they wanted to shoot us. Maybe . . . Oh well, at all events we spent the night beneath the stars.

We were expected to parade daily when we were locked up. You had to stand at attention, inside your cell, about a metre from the grille, with your hands clasped behind you. They were just never too tired to recite or read the prison rules and regulations At times they did that before lock-up. I was getting annoyed with all this. Nobody has ever consulted us about these rules and regulations when they were planned and made law, anyway.

They gave us clothes, according to some bureaucratic whim of long ago. Each of us had two denim overalls, two *doeks* (turbans), and two pairs of panties. Let me describe the panties. They were baggy white shorts with no elastic where they ended, which was somewhere mid-thigh; they had elastic only at the waist. They were the thick, old-fashioned cotton type. How could the Prisons Department expect us to use pads with that type of panties? They would look very good on soccer players on the field.

Somebody came up with a bright idea. Mama Aminah had varicose veins and they gave her pantie-hose to cover her legs. When these became old (the pantie-hose, that is), instead of throwing them away she would give them to us. We discovered that we could take the elastic from Mama Aminah's pantie-hose and sew them to the legs of the panties so a person could be more comfortable, if not precisely in style.

We were expected to wear men's shoes, solid, clomping tough shoes meant to last for the whole five years. They did not give us any polish for the shoes, either. To round off our wardrobe, we were given two khaki-grey nighties, one with long sleeves, one with short sleeves; V-neck jerseys, two each; men's socks; and a white apron, as well as a red and yellow *doek*. Looking at this ensemble, a normal, reasonable person could see that this was insane. The place looked like a mental asylum when we appeared in these crazy combinations of clothes. White apron, sky-blue denim overalls, navy-blue jersey, brown shoes, navy-blue socks and red *doek*! These people had decided to treat us like mad people, but all identically mad, a uniform insanity.

When it came to white prisoners, things were different. We could see some white prisoners; they were feeling at home. All white prisoners had the chance to choose what type of shoes they wanted. They had stylish shoes and sandals, shoes you might get at Cuthberts or any decent shoe shop in town, and the dresses were all smart. Different dresses they chose; no uniforms for the white ladies. You would not be able to identify any one of them as a prisoner. Also they did not have to wear *doeks* to cover their heads like housemaids. They might have been mistaken for newly employed wardresses or visitors.

And the food again. On Mondays for breakfast we got porridge with weak black coffee or tea. Black, as milk counted as a privilege. The prison staff admitted that they did not know the type of coffee we were drinking. Some of the older women maintained they would take some mealies, *braai* (grill) them, grind them, and boil the grounds to make coffee. The tea was like red *muti* (medicine) that some *nnyangas* (African traditional doctors) use. The prison staff did not know the name of that tea, either. I think this tea made us ill, or perhaps all of the diet made us ill.

At lunchtime we ate mealies (maize), with either rotten cabbage with insects and black spots on it, or carrots cooked until brown in some sort of syrup, and a mug of *phuzamandla*. This is a drink I've only found in prison, and have never seen outside. It is a yellow powder they mix with water and give to the prisoners. They claimed it would make us strong—as the Zulu name *phuzamandla*, meaning drink strength.

And for supper—this is still Monday's food—we were given *somos*, soya beans. Imagine taking the stuff as it is, putting it into a pot, pouring on salt and then serving. I bet the people you are serving might think you are trying to poison them. So we were given *somos* with soft porridge and a slice of bread: bread to us was like cake. And they would give us something made from some brown powder and water which they called soup.

Breakfast was the same all week, the whole month, the whole year through. Maize porridge with either coffee or that *muti* tea. Lunch was the same, except when they changed to *samp* (a form of maize that is only partially grinded rather like what Americans call hominy) on Sundays. And that *samp*, I'm sure they boiled it a little and then served it; it was terrible.

With supper they went to town; Monday was *somos*; Tuesday, fish; Wednesday, meat with a slice of bread; Thursday, *somos* again; Friday, fish; Saturday, *somos*, yet again; Sunday, meat. This was repeated week after week.

Even with that overly familiar menu, the food was prepared in indescribably awful ways. Their recipe for fish, for example: mix it up, bones and all, and put on to boil. Recipe for *somos:* do the same and add salt. They wanted to make life unbearable for us. They would often remind us not to forget that we were prisoners—as if we could forget.

We were three in my section, and the other three comrades stayed in the other section. During breakfast, lunch and supper, each group of three would receive their food together. In our section, Mama Dorothy could not eat mealies or soft porridge. She got bread for breakfast, lunch and supper—four slices. The doctor had prescribed bread for her serious stomach problems. Aminah Desai's diet was completely different. Her breakfast was bread with jam or syrup, coffee or tea with a dash of milk; lunch, bread and well prepared vegetables; supper, mealie rice with meat or fish. She was getting meat three times a week, fish twice a week and *somos* also twice a week. When we questioned her different diet the answer was: "She is Coloured. So she's getting a Coloured diet." So it goes without saying that what Aminah Desai ate was considered too good for us blacks.

If you want to find out what racial discrimination is, just go to any South African prison. The reality is very hard. Here are three people sharing the same table. Yet what they eat is divided on racial lines. And you are expected not to be hurt. Mama Aminah has a "Coloured" diet and Mama Dorothy another different diet, while the four of us—Aus Joyce, Aus Esther, Mama Edith and myself have to eat rubbish food. That was not acceptable to us. We could not let that kind of madness continue unchallenged.

I was a bit fortunate because Mama Dorothy and Mama Aminah always shared their bread with me. At that time, staying with grown-up people, since I was the youngest, I got a little spoiled. Here I was sharing bread with these two beautiful people and yet our other comrades, in the other cell, could not have the same bread we were enjoying. That made me feel bad. Even though at times we managed to leave them some.

This was Kroonstad Prison where I started to serve my sentence in 1977. . . .

The farce in the internal courts went on; meanwhile the struggle continued in our daily lives as well.

During this time there was the wardress called Mbomvana. You know, I hated her like hell. I don't even remember her real surname. Because she was so red, we just called her Mbomvana, which means red. She had this attitude, that she would deal with us brutally. Here was one thing about us: if a person decided to be difficult, to show an iron hand, we would retaliate the same way. I think she made us more stubborn, and for sure we were already stubborn.

The Price of Being a 'Lady'

From No Child's Play, *1988*

Before the internal trials, on 8 June, in the morning, they brought breakfast. She [Mbomvana] brought us porridge which was not properly prepared, stiff and raw; I think they cooked it for three minutes and served it up. And they came in a big crowd. We were wondering, uh, what is happening? Because here are so many of these people, men and women, just to bring the porridge. They just stood around in the passage. It was clearly not all right.

We called to them; "This porridge is not okay." Mbomvana said she had prepared the porridge that morning and she was satisfied that it was okay. We told her, "You are talking nonsense, man. How can you say this porridge is okay? Have you eaten it? She replied that she was not a prisoner, she was not going to eat prisoners' food.

So I spelt it out: "Then you are cooking shit and coming to tell us it is prisoners' food. You are not a prisoner. So you are doing all this deliberately." We picked up the quarrel; everybody was after her. Suddenly they changed their line, "Thandisa must take her stuff, because she is going." We demanded, "Where to?" even before Thandisa could ask "Where?", because we felt she was just part of us. We asked them, "Where is she going?"

Her cell was unlocked. They got two men, huge men, tall and healthy, who just grabbed her, beating her on the way. I saw them: ta ta ta! Banging on her throat. They dragged her to the isolation section and dumped her there.

I was the next victim. I was not expecting this, standing in my cell and cursing them for their treatment of Thandisa. Not knowing that they were coming for me. And they just bundled me, too, took me to the cells. On the way I was telling them a lot of things. That they were afraid of our brothers on the borders, let them go to Angola, SWAPO would shoot them to pieces, the bloody fucking cowards, they were just ill-treating women, knowing that we did not have weapons, anything; I'd just smash them to pieces anyway—after liberation. I would just show them. They started beating me. They were hitting me with a baton, seriously hitting, yo! I was dragged into a cell and dropped.

My old cell was stripped. Most of my things were taken away. They only brought the clothes. That was in the morning. They brought lunch. After lunch they left the cells and went away.

That afternoon this Mbomvana came again, in the company of one we called Yita. I don't remember her surname, either. She unlocked the cell. The men were standing in the courtyard. She said to me I could go and have my bath. She took Thandisa for her exercise and locked her into the small courtyard.

I was hardly three minutes in the bath when she came and told me, "Come, your time is up." I objected. "*Au, o a hlanya*; you are insane. How can you say time is up, I have not even washed my face? How long do you provide for bathtime?" And she said "Fifteen minutes." Then I asked her, "Do you know the meaning of 15 minutes? Because I have not even started to wash my face and you are telling me my time is up." By that time I was sitting in the bath, naked. She locked the grille, went to call the men. And they came.

You know, Mbomvana, this stupid wardress, had a boyfriend, one of the warders at Kroonstad. And her boyfriend, whose name was Roet, came with another man called Else. They swaggered into the bathroom, lugged me out of the bath, naked, water running off me. And they started smashing into me with batons. All over my body. They pulled me to my cell, one on each side, hammering me with their batons. They dumped me there like a sack of potatoes.

That day I was raving mad. In my anger, I swore that I would never forgive these people. Actually I made it very clear to them that after takeover, if I happen to be alive, they are the people I am going to kill. I am going to hunt for them, to make sure. After liberation, if I happen to see it. No, I won't die before killing you. It cannot be otherwise.

Of course, it was not solely her fault, this Mbomvana; brought up with the idea that you are a superior being, that you have to be on top of the black woman or man's head, that a black woman or man cannot say anything, she or he must take what you give because you are the *baas*. These characters are brought up like that; but still she's one of those I can't forgive.

The following day Brigadier Venter came. In fact, immediately after the beating I rang the bell and said I wanted to see the doctor. Because I must record proof, to lay a charge against them. They told me the doctor was not there. And I reminded them that the doctor himself had said to us that if we wanted him to see us he was willing to come at any time. So I didn't see any reason why they said the doctor was not there.

The next day, before the doctor came, I saw Brigadier Venter and made the complaint about the beating. He defended the assault: according to him, I had refused to go into the cell, and he had given instructions that if anyone refused to go into her cell she had to be taken by force. I said: "I never refused to go into the cell. This woman has a bad attitude towards us, particularly towards me. She thinks she is in a position to discipline us. I had not been long in the bath and yet she came to say time was up. This was done deliberately. And she decided to call her boyfriend and a friend to beat me up." And I informed Venter that I wanted to lay a charge against them. Then I saw the doctor, who gave me a thorough examination. He wrote down everything. I was really ill.

I want to make it clear that this Mbomvana was a real sadist. We—
Thandisa and I—decided to plot against Mbomvana. Because, with all our
sufferings in prison, this sadist managed to make life even more miserable
than it normally was. . . .

To be honest I can be a very decent lady if you are a lady to me; but if
you decide to be difficult, I am also willing to be quite difficult. I refuse to
be a lady when other people are not ladies. It is too expensive.

CAROLYN BAXTER

(1953–)

Harlem-born Carolyn Baxter is a published writer who draws from her experiences as an African American woman, a former participant in the original Harlem chapter of the Black Panthers' School Breakfast program, and a person who has been incarcerated. While at the New York City Correctional Institution for Women at Riker's Island, she participated in the Free Space Writing Project, which featured her work in an anthology.

Baxter attended Bard College and has worked for the National Association for the Advancement of Colored People (NAACP) and the New York City Board of Education in programs for ex-offenders and adolescent offenders. A member of the United Federation of Teachers and the Screen Actors Guild, she has worked for the New York Shakespeare Festival and recently completed a memoir, *Raw Knuckles*. Baxter lives in New York State and has worked in New York City as a high-technology intensive care nurse.

Note: Background information is from Judith Scheffler's interviews with Carolyn Baxter, March 1985 and August 2001; Joseph Bruchac, ed., *The Light from Another Country: Poetry from American Prisons* (Greenfield Center, N.Y.: Greenfield Review Press, 1984).

FOUR POEMS

From Prison Solitary and Other Free Government Services, *1979.*

Lower Court

She opens her mouth, a switchblade falls out, along
with a .22 automatic, a few shells, crumpled one
dollar bills, some change in attitude (she's uncomfortable)
now.
Her pimp steps in,　　　slaps her,　　　see jugular
vein separate from neck muscle.

She opens her mouth wider, crumpled one dollar bills
fall out, along with prophylactics, 10¢ perfume, lipstick,
a newspaper clipping for a pair of $30 boots, a whip,
an explanation for the forged driver's license/a

picture of her favorite group, "The Shantells."
She closes her mouth,   The lights dim
in the courtroom.   As her pimp turns her left ear
with his fist, activating last night's streetreel of how
hot it was on the hoe stroll, projected out her eyeballs,
/smell of tricks.

> Legal Aid Lawyer says: Cop Out!
>   She does.

Another nite.
Trapped between gavel/wood.   Making it possible for
her to hit the streets.
Sound of her heels cut grey morning air,
/recite her life back, (in the) same order.

Toilet Bowl Congregation

(Holding cell in Criminal Courthouse, 100 Centre St.)

I

The toilet bowl congregation, preaches sounds of a
cheap hotel, pacing, bitching, broken neon hopes,
pictured in steelbars/cracked wht. paint,
contrasting 2 transients in red/blk. micro miniskirts,
racing words from each other's mouth, on who's pimp
will show/up with bail money first.

"Fas'll be here first!"
"Uhhahh! Smokey will."
"Bitch, you tryin to say my niggah ain't good as yours?"
An ain't on his J.O.B.!"
"Huh! Thas rite Hoe."

As they convince cheap perfumed falseness off each other
with their hands. First the platinum, then red/blonde
streaked wig flies off, while adhesive eyelashes fall like
lead rose petals, a blouse cut off rolling on the
floor, a dress slashed quickly, as officers enter backward, slow motion,
stopping the fight.

On the floor, blk, bloody, bald, a 90 lb knock-kneed
deception of a cheap prostitute.

Congregations expression; unchanged still as innocent bystander,
the stud broad, flinched a shoulder, holding her
zipper—juvenile still sleeping,
the nut, never stopped pacing,
murderer, extremely bored.

I tossed a wad of toilet paper by her hand,
waited a min, extended a hand (to help her up.)
got cussed out, sat back down on the bench,
thought—Dizzy Bitch!

(walking out)
handcuffed/belly chained, on our way to Riker's Island.
Another slave's
blood christened cement . . . Again!

35 Years a Correctional Officer

Ms. Goodall does not drink, swear, or masturbate.
"It's against God's will," she says.

Ms. Goodall does not gamble, gets paid to be slick
an' creep around after 1:00 AM to listen for
creaking beds, so she can give out incident reports

to anyone she catches by the creaks
of their bed "Masturbating!"
"It's against God's will," she says.

So I lay naked on floor, along with cold
tile, I feel like a private under the bunk,
hiding from the enemy.

/as her Sears/Roebuck crepe soles creep by the door—
I wanted to ask, what's the difference between a
creaking bed/a manic breathing heavy under the door.

On Being Counted

Standing next to the radiator, watching the room,
Do my tarot cards for the 1000th time.
I hear the radiator whispering, how stupid I was to
trade your warmth for his.
And I brood over you not letting me steal your hands.
To dry up my pains.

I smell lemon powder, thinking of my name.
Trying to remember femininity.
I can't sleep until I pay my personal digits to
Washington.

2

It's lights out,
yawns, coughs, and dreams from different realities.
Pack up the day, and seek refuge in the night.
Traveling down dark invisible roads.
Hoping to tap a stranger on the back.
Only to find it's their old friend.
Freedom.

I lay down, thinking thoughts that
were one time real,
But are now like houses that have been torn down,
and families that have moved away.

3

I smell the questioning flashlights,
walking down the hall, closing the storage doors
on dead lives,

demanding I recite the patented number, stamped on
my ass,
which is presently subletting the space
my soul used to own.
I'm also asked where I got my map of the justice system.
I say the judge traded it for my birth certificate.
The interrogator smiles, saying he'd never trade his,

and that I'm getting prettier with age.
Not mentioning ugly with time.

4

The dark highlights my barren existence,
that's gushed from me so far.
And I wonder, how there's even a corpuscle of patience
left.
The closing door joins the lock in the key
of finality, in three years from today time.

5

Spotlight invades my public privacy.
Like a peeping tom, inspiring me to sleep insomnia.
I turn to the radiator for some warmth, as I mumble
I feel like I gotta vomit.
The cold radiator yells, not on me bitch.
I have to live here too.

Joining the moon singing do you know the way to
San Jose.
In two part cruelty.

Asking do I know the words to nobody knows da
trouble I seen.

6

So I hum, off key thoughts, that were one time,
real.
But are now like houses that have been torn down
and families that have moved away.

BARBARA SAUNDERS

(1944–)

Born in Texas, Barbara Saunders moved frequently throughout the Southwest and Midwest, following the work of her father, an oil driller. Her educational achievements include a master's degree in art education and a second master's degree in counseling psychology. She has served as a nurse in the U.S. Navy.

A writer since the age of five, Saunders states, "I have been journaling since my release. . . . I am an artist working primarily in watercolor and oils, a poetess, a reader and a writer. I have been a student and a teacher, a prisoner and a free woman. I am passionate about the empowerment of women who have traditionally been considered disenfranchised. I am currently involved in prison ministry helping others transition back into the free world" (letters to Scheffler).

In the 1990s Saunders spent time in the Eddie Warrior Correctional Center in Taft, Oklahoma. She has received two PEN Prison Writing Awards for her poetry about her prison experience: "The Red Dress" (second prize, 1996) and "Wolf" (second prize, 1998).

Note: Background information is from Barbara Saunders, letters to Judith Scheffler, October 15, 2000 and August 10, 2001; Bell Gale Chevigny, *Doing Time: 25 Years of Prison Writing* (New York: Arcade, 1999).

THREE POEMS

[8-8-98]

8-8-98
Wrong
there's something wrong
What is it?
Where is it coming from?
I spin, picking up velocity
a deep unrelieved brain itch
requiring readiness
action
movement.
Waiting, watchful
signaling
Look

feel the tension knotting the air
oppressive
the weight of it
compressing me into
a tattered shred of skin.
Listen!
Can you hear the testosterone poisoned, key flipping, handcuff popping
rookie corrections officers
pacing off the cells.
There's gonna be a beating tonight
somewhere on the yard,
a rape, maybe.
Someone in this community
of incarcerated women
will act out the tension,
someone will break
the spell of fear.
Can you hear it gathering
the copper taste of blood
fills your mouth
cries danger as the crack of someone's fist
breaks bone.
Like flint against a fracture line.

The Grievance

She is tough, small and wiry
so tough she's damn near stringy.
She is looking for comfort in a routine
a routine so precise it's a small ritual
of practical magic to keep the day contained,
the fear contained
to keep the losses at bay.

Economical movements, almost as if she is afraid
of occupying too much space.
Folding, brushing off the tops of things,
straightening it out, tearing the flaps off boxes for easy access.
She "plays it close to the vest."
Pull it, tighten it, tug it, smooth it, make it perfect.
Folding, creasing, lining things up,
getting it right, getting it straight, getting it tight, controlled,
working spells to keep the danger away.

Making offerings to the capricious gods of bureaucracy,
the authority, the power and control freaks.

Fiercely protective of this small space, these few things
grateful for the comfort of feeling safe in this cubical.
Courteous, thoughtful, looking for ways to please.
Quick to anger and to protect what is important to her.

Each morning choreographed.
I, the early riser, drink coffee and enjoy the quiet
turn to peace within and elsewhere.
She sleeps on, deeply, soundly, snoring.
Able to relax enough to sleep that way.
I offer no threat, only acceptance and what she needs to feel secure.

I, who lounge, spread out, occupy my space and more
and leave things out, lying around, filling up chairs and counters.
I, used to broad, grand gestures, expansive, exuberant, sloppy,
provide the contrast she needs to define who she is becoming.
She with her tight curls and pursed lips
Me with hair down my back and crooked smile.
I, who listen and watch,
as she writes and rewrites her justification,
her defense, her indignation,
her woundedness, her anger, her fury
at the arbitrary, unilateral judgment handed down with cavalier detachment
that keeps her here in this hell-hole longer,
that extends her time, that lengthens her days.
If she writes it right, if she words it right,
if it makes a difference, if she just gets it right.
Small rituals, practical magic,
when she can't take it anymore
there has to be magic.

A Life Worth Living

We have walked our own roads, kept our own ledgers.
Risk is no stranger here.
We do what we must for our lives.
We must make a life worth living.
And the headline said: API~Boston, Massachusetts: "HIV Affects
    Primarily the Marginalized, Stigmatized and Discriminated Against."

We are women.
Women stigmatized who when released from prison
or singled out by our difference
deny the existence of the disease
in our own community.
Trying to make a life worth living.

And the headline said: UPI~Tulsa, Oklahoma: "Incidence of HIV
Among Incarcerated Women Increasing."

We are women, some gay
when geographically confined
bi much of the rest of the time;
we are women, lesbians perhaps.
We are women of color, already in crisis
trying to beat the odds.
Looking to make a life worth living.
And the headline said: API~Bedford Hills, New York: "Rate of
HIV/AIDS Among Prisoners 6 Times That of the Public."

We are women denied the most basic comforts
existing in famine for fragrance, color, texture, taste
who when released will risk anything
to feed the emptiness of the years.
Trying to make a life worth living.
And the headline said: UPI~Muskogee, Oklahoma: "Woman Murdered
by Boyfriend After Revealing Self Positive for HIV."

We are women used to domestic violence,
social vulnerability and power differentials within relationships.
Familiar with control freaks insulting and abusing us.
For many it is the norm.
Trying to have a life worth living.
And the headline said: UPI~Loveland, Colorado: "AIDS Is The
Leading Cause of Death in Prisons Across the United States."

We are women who have lost friends
lovers, husbands, children, parents.
Fall-partners, abusers, roadies to the scourge
of sex and drugs and HIV.
A life worth living could halt this disease
in this community of women.
And the headline said: API~Atlanta, Georgia: "HIV Stopped by
Women Demanding a Life Worth Living."

DIANE HAMILL METZGER

(1949–)

Diane Hamill Metzger has been serving a life sentence in Pennsylvania and Delaware state prisons since 1975. Her extraordinary achievements during that time have been recognized in educational, political, and cultural forums. She is a widely published creative writer. The first woman prisoner in Pennsylvania to earn her bachelor's degree while incarcerated, she has also earned an associate's degree in business administration and a master's degree in humanities/history. She is a certified paralegal and has completed training and apprenticeships in computer operation and electrical maintenance. In 1988 she was recognized by the Pennsylvania Association of Adult Continuing Education as the Outstanding Adult Student in Continuing Higher Education and by the Pennsylvania Prison Society as Prisoner of the Year. That same year, the Pennsylvania House of Representatives and Senate awarded her citations for outstanding achievement.

In 1974 Metzger and her infant son sat outside in the family car while, unknown to Metzger, her husband entered his ex-wife's home and killed her during an argument. Metzger then aided her husband in a cover-up and went into hiding with him and their infant son. When they were apprehended, both Metzger and her husband testified that she knew nothing of the crime until afterward. But Pennsylvania's law of accomplice liability gave Metzger and her husband the same life sentence without parole for first-degree murder. Metzger's applications for clemency have not yet met with success.

During her more than twenty-five years in prison, Metzger's parents raised her son. He has now grown to manhood, and mother and son share a good relationship. Metzger has been transferred to a Delaware prison that is closer to her family in order to make visiting easier.

Writing has been an important outlet for Metzger since her imprisonment at age 26. She explains, "If nothing else, prison has given me insight into myself that I never had before. As a result, I began to write about the things I had begun to see for the first time in my life, and about the things most important to me" (*Coralline Ornaments*.) Metzger has received numerous literary awards, including *Writer's Digest*, National Creative Writing Contest, and PEN Writing awards.

Note: Background information is from Metzger's correspondence with Judith Scheffler, 2000–2001; *Frontiers of Justice*, vol. 3 (Brunswick, Me.: Biddle Publishing, 2000); Diane Hamill Metzger, *Coralline Ornaments* (Sedona, Ariz.: Weed Patch Press, 1980).

From The Long Islander, *1989;* Pearl, *1989;* Anima, *1991; and* Collages & Bricolages, *1992.*

M.I.: Circa 1980

Her name was Dorothy, fiftyish,
Apple-red chubby cheeks, granny-laughed
Nurturing mama of the house.
Loved her coffee, made two cups for
Herself and gruff-girl Bert every night.
We heard the awful crash clear up on
The second floor. Me and Carol
Ran down the stairs two at a time.
She was lying on her back, black-lipped,
Coffee everywhere in brown puddles,
Bert keening wild-eyed, rocking and
Inconsolable. We did our
Best at CPR; the sergeant came
And helped us, shaking his head, pulling
Us away, saying she must have
Been gone before she hit the floor.
I didn't know what we would ever tell
Her husband, alone and waiting for her.
She was only in for forgery.

Panopticon

So again this vista is eroding.
The buildings dim. The women doze in their
Steel and stone barns, their toil
Having been state approved, the sheets
Bleached harmless and stacked on the tables
By numbers, as the lambent stars emerge.
This is the desolation of
Similitude and recurrence.
And the ones not yet hardened
Sometimes nod in passing, with
Their eyes averted as in deference,
And the tree-bedded crows,
Ebon, latrant, mocking,
"Again!" Always again it begins.
And the years
Seep out of the wind.

Tapwater Coffee

They took away our coffee pots;
You know the type:
Big forty-cup, with chrome,
Black plastic spigot and feet;
The kind you'd never use at home.
They said a weapon
Potentially lurked there,
Were it heaved or water thrown.
Now in the land of synthetic dreams,
Of cup-a-soup and instant tea,
Another compromise
Slips in to burden me.
I may suck the caffeine
Of paper packets and sleepless nights
And write endless narratives
Of wasted years and trampled rights,
But, try as I may, as I burn midnight oil,
And heat up my verses and curse my toil,
My thirst is room temperature—
My water won't boil.
Ah, what emotional masturbation
Brews in the grounds of this pleasure dome;
Drinking tapwater coffee,
And thinking of home.

The Getaway

The distance between the buildings is not
that long. I walk slowly so I can fill
my lungs completely with rationed night air.
The forecast calls for thick, cloaking clouds, but
the sky glows. Damn the underhanded moon.
Even it deceives me.
In moments the door will steal my brief leave.
Indecision bodes my road not taken.
It is not the years that make me waver;
It is the bone-chill of uncertainty
That has lasted far too many winters
And made me doubt the sun.

From Frontiers of Justice, *2000.*

It's in these early hours of the morning when the virus of fear begins to multiply in my stomach. These stark hours, still quiet, when another day is about to begin. I can't explain why it is the morning and not the night that creeps in like an intruder and gets a hold of my throat. Perhaps it is because at night that protective blanket of darkness allows my mind to sneak away into fantasy where I am with my family, or driving down the highway, or sitting on a starlit beach with someone who loves me.

In my fantasies, I am free.

How do I describe a descent into hell and the slow, agonizing climb back out? Truth is, I'm not even back out yet, but I hope I'm getting closer. I keep trying to glimpse a light at the top of the well, something to let me know that it's going to be over eventually.

I came to prison at the age of 25 with no previous criminal record and a life sentence, co-defendant to my husband, a man twelve years my senior. I met him when I was only 18; by the time I was 20, we were married. He came with plenty of baggage: an ex-wife with whom he bickered constantly, children by that marriage and severe custody/child-support problems. I came with plenty of baggage of my own, not the least of which was a serious lack of self-esteem.

"Lack of self-esteem"—you hear that so much now that sometimes it's considered a joke, a catch-word in the lexicon of "psycho-babble." But it's very, very real, and I believe that the lack of it accounts for a great majority of the social ills in this country, from the most miniscule to the most horrifying. Almost without exception, women in prison suffer from an overwhelming lack of self-esteem; at least they come in that way.

Most women doing time for homicide fall into two categories—those who were accomplices in a crime of violence committed by a man, or those who killed an abusive spouse or boyfriend. Women usually don't commit random violence, multiple murders or rape-related killings; it is also rare for women to commit other crimes that include violence (armed robberies, aggravated assault, etc.). Though a large percentage (75–80 percent) of women doing time are doing so for drug-related crime (i.e., committing crime to get money to buy drugs), the crimes that women commit to support a drug habit are usually nonviolent in nature, such as forgery, shop lifting or prostitution.

This is still a man's world. Maybe, with our generation of "baby boomers" gaining some wisdom and passing it on to our children, things are beginning to change. But growing up, I never had any doubts about whose world it was. I knew at a young age that my father had wanted me to be a boy, so my first impression of myself was that I was a disappointment. My dad is from the "old school" where men are macho, girl-children are their mother's responsibility, and fathers don't invest much emotion or affection in their little girls. I hold no animosity toward him; that was just the way things were back then, and my dad is a good man and a good provider. I know now that he loves me, in fact we've become very close. But growing up, all I felt was starved for male affection, attention and approval. And, as is so typical in so many females of my generation, I went looking for a "daddy" to love me.

I had another problem as well. I was not physically attractive, never the cutesie-pie cheerleader type. I was plain, athletic and a "brainiac," not exactly the type that attracted boys. Never mind that as compensation I became witty, creative, resourceful, compassionate and a good friend. None of these things brought me what I wanted most—a boyfriend. Oh, now and then there would be a boy who liked me, who found that I was great fun to be with and who liked being with me. But inevitably, he'd get teased (more often than not by the girls) for being with a girl who wasn't pretty or part of the "in crowd," and he'd stop coming around. Girls can be terribly cruel to other girls and are often socialized to dislike and distrust one another. Where boys compete in sports and for career opportunities as well as dates, girls compete for just one thing and that's boys! So despite the fact that I was smart in school, talented in many areas and capable of getting into just about any college I chose, I wanted only one thing, the only thing that would make me a success in my own eyes—a man to love me.

As a result, I chose not to go to college. In the year after I graduated from high school, I met the man who would become my husband. He was older, the father figure I'd been searching for, and intelligent, someone I could look up to. He was experienced and told me everything I wanted to hear. He said I was beautiful, something I'd never heard from a male in my life, and he told me he loved me. He was a dream come true. I would have done anything for him, anything to make sure he never left my life. I never saw that my husband's age, experience and intelligence allowed him to manipulate me in every way possible. I endured deceit and emotional abuse that I rationalized as necessary evils that every woman endures to keep her man. I knew, as a woman who would never be thought of as beautiful in a world where physical beauty is everything, I had to hold onto what I had, no matter how much pain went along with it.

It was at that point in my life that the unspeakable happened. On a summer night in 1974, while I and our six-month-old son were outside waiting in the car, my husband killed his ex-wife during a fight over child custody. The decisions that I made from that point on forever changed my life and the lives of the people I loved. I helped my husband in the attempted cover-up of what he had done. My infant son and I were fugitives with him for nearly a year afterward, and when we were finally arrested, I made it very clear to the authorities that I would be telling them nothing. And they made it very clear to me that, as an uncooperative accomplice to my husband, under Pennsylvania's law of accomplice liability, I would be given a sentence identical to his, though I had done violence to no one. And that's exactly what happened. On the fateful day of my arrest, I was 25 years old. I am 50 years old now as I write this from prison where I have been for almost 25 years, serving a life sentence.

When I was arrested, my son was 17 months old. The night of our arrest by FBI agents in Boise, Idaho, my baby son was literally ripped, screaming, from my arms by a brusque child-welfare worker. I didn't see my son again for six months when my parents were finally able to wrest custody of him from a system eager to see him kept from me forever. Thus began years of seeing my son for only a few hours a month in prison visiting rooms, talking to him in cost-limiting 15-minute collect phone calls, and exchanging with him hundreds of letters that were opened and read by prison mail censors first. My son grew from a toddler to a schoolboy to a teenager to the adult man he is now, and I missed all of it. My parents gave him love, safety, security and all of his material needs, but they couldn't give him me.

My son and I have a loving relationship today, but not without much effort and much heartache. Who knows what our relationship could have been were we together all these years? Yet, as much sadness and regret as I feel about the loss of years with my son, I am relieved and grateful that my parents were there to raise him. So many children of incarcerated mothers tragically fall victim to the foster care system and are shifted from guardian to guardian. Their mothers in prison rarely, if ever, get to see them or form any relationship with them at all. It is agonizing for the mothers and their children and leaves both sides scarred forever. People should never assume that because a woman is in prison, she is a bad mother, that she doesn't love her children or that she doesn't deserve a loving relationship with them. A woman serving a life sentence in Pennsylvania endures a double-edged nightmare: that of doing a possibly endless sentence in prison, and that of knowing she may never be with her children again.

In Pennsylvania, all life sentences are without parole eligibility. Our only hope for freedom is via clemency and commutation of sentence from Pennsylvania's Board of Pardons and Governor. The past two decades in Pennsylvania have been ones of increasing "lock 'em up and throw away the key" hysteria, resulting in an almost automatic denial of commutations/ clemency for lifers. We can only hope that the new millennium brings with it a softening of the harsh attitudes that have robbed us of our hope.

The past two-and-a-half decades of my life have often been filled with anguish and despair, but they have also been ones of introspection, growth, maturation, learning, and the acquisition of much wisdom. I often wonder if the passage of years outside would have brought me the degree and depth of these qualities that these years of imprisonment have brought me! I have been forced to face myself, to know myself and to learn to be true to myself. I have endured an environment of deprivation, regimentation, and loss of personal freedoms that I always took for granted. I have had to co-exist in close quarters with people I thought to be so unlike myself that I couldn't imagine how I could share space and time with them. I have shed prejudices and gained understanding and empathy. I have found a courage within myself that I never knew I had. I have learned who and what are important in my life and have questioned everything that I thought I once believed. I have made such a concerted effort not to let the world go on without me that I am probably more aware and informed of the happenings in the world than many of the people out there living in it! I have educated myself to the most attainable degree possible within the confines of prison.

Some people look at me with pity and exclaim, "Oh! you've missed everything!" But I haven't, you see. I've missed many things, particularly the joy of physically being able to be there at events and with people. But I absorb everything from life that I can, from the TV, radio, books, newspapers, magazines and from the accounts of family, friends, acquaintances and strangers who relate to me the details of their lives and experiences. I often live vicariously, but I live. I still feel the sun on my face and the wind in my hair as I walk from one building to another. The fences cannot deprive me of these things. I still write poetry, sing a song, laugh at a joke. There are days when despair threatens to envelope me, when I decry the loss of these years and yearn to hold a child, to pet a dog, to see and smell the ocean. Sometimes the abject need to be free and the overwhelming frustration of not being able to be almost swallow me up and the yearning is almost too much to bear. But I bear each sorrow one day at a time, knowing that the next day will bring a new joy, a new enlightenment, a new reason to be grateful for what I yet have.

My most fervent hope is to be free again, to enjoy my loved ones and to give back to them some of what they have so selflessly given me. My spirit can sometimes be bruised by those who feel that their job and duty and right is to punish, but my spirit is resilient and strong. No one yet has been able to crush it. I believe that the best restitution I can give to those I have hurt in this life is to live life the very best I can and to help anyone I can along the way, wherever I may be.

It's not ever easy. Make no mistake—these walls are cruel. But each day I'm still making that climb out of the well to the top, one step and one day at a time. If I stop climbing, then those who wish to keep me encased behind walls have won. That won't happen.

I don't know what the future will bring. But I do know that I, and thousands of prisoners like me, fervently hope that the politicians and administrators and the people who live each day in society and take their freedom for granted will come to see that without the belief that people can change, there can be no hope. Hope is the foundation upon which all life is built, that which allows us all to face each day with courage and positive anticipation.

Let there be hope for us all.

PART 4

'I HAVE ALL THE PASSION OF LIFE':

PSYCHOLOGICAL SURVIVAL THROUGH COMMUNICATION AND RELATIONSHIPS

During my two final years in solitary confinement, the wall took up the most important part of my time. There I had a curious experience. I realized that one's manner of tapping is just as expressive as the timbre of one's voice. As one's handwriting. Sometimes even more so. For it is unaffected by the conscious censorship of the voice. Or the acquired control of gestures and facial expression. —Lena Constante

I lived a full, almost complete life during this eternal year. Acquaintances were timidly struck up, friendships developed, even love affairs ensued—all through the thick prison walls. —Erica Glaser Wallach

The dramatic changes imposed on a woman's life by imprisonment challenge her psychologically as well as physically. The image of a woman relentlessly tapping on an unyielding stone wall epitomizes the will to survive psychologically. Through communication and relationships, women prisoners express a "passion of life" that refuses to succumb to prison, for prisoners' passive acceptance of institutionalization is not a given. According to prison activist Karlene Faith, incarceration does not necessarily destroy women's egos: "The prevailing, time-worn assumption that female prisoners have low self-esteem may well be a blaming or condescending projection by class-biased people who can't imagine that women with so many problems could think well of themselves."[1] Through the act of writing, women prison authors articulate a sense of self that is also felt by prisoners who are not educated or politically oriented.[2]

Since publication of the first edition of this anthology, conditions in women's prison in the United States have changed in important ways: increasing numbers of women are being imprisoned, with a disproportionate number of minorities represented, and the number of women arrested for drug-related offenses has grown.[3] Further complicating issues surrounding prison conditions is the greater incidence of mental illness in the prison population.[4] Recent studies of women's prisons examine the impact of these developments upon the experience of prisoners.[5] In her 1998 ethnographic study of women in the massive Central California Women's Facility, Barbara Owen observes that "the world of the women's prison is shaped by pre-prison experiences, the role of women in contemporary society, and the ways in which women rely on personalized relationships to survive their prison terms. Women's prison culture, then, is decidedly personal, a network of meanings and relationships that create and reproduce the ways women do their time."[6] Owen explains that women survive the destructive effects of imprisonment in two ways: they take some measure of control over their own lives by structuring their experience, and they create a sense of "belonging" through relationships.[7]

Writings by women prisoners confirm Owen's findings by depicting two major coping strategies: the formation of relationships and the establishment of communication. These strategies are not unique to prisoners, of course, but the acute stress of a prison environment increases the pressure to adjust. Whether alone in "the hole" or with others in a "campus" institution, the incarcerated woman shares all prisoners' need to withstand the "pains of imprisonment."[8] The process of surviving psychologically and maintaining self-respect and integrity figures prominently among topics in women's prison literature.[9]

Writing itself can be a prisoner's act of affirmation. The research of Cohen and Taylor on methods of psychological survival of long-term prisoners in an English maximum-security men's prison sheds light on women's as well as men's motivation to write as a means of coping through communication.[10] These researchers found that reading and writing are particularly important to long-term prisoners because such activities provide goals for achievement and an outlet for expressing what is happening to them. Prisoners do not automatically and totally accept society's demeaning labels, nor do they accept "prisoner" as their only role, according to the study. Instead, they achieve their perspective through considering the prison experience and what it means to them. Cohen and Taylor quote Hilde Bluhm's study of the autobiographies of concentration camp survivors:

> Those . . . who embarked on a study of the concentration camp proper, turned towards that very reality which had threatened to overpower them: and they rendered that reality into an object of their "creation." This turn from a passive suffering to an active undertaking indicated that the ego was regaining control.
> . . . [T]he association between self-observation and self-expression became a most successful means of survival.[11]

Applicable to prisoners as well as concentration camp victims, this survival mechanism explains much about prisoners' motivation to confront and express the pains of imprisonment through writing and their rejection of the all-encompassing label of "prisoner."

Writing opens a substitute universe to the prisoner, as demonstrated vividly in the selections that follow. Some of the authors in this section were permitted to write in prison, although the amount of writing was sometimes restricted and the content censored. Others, like Russian prisoner Eugenia Ginzburg, were not so fortunate. Yet even without the means to write they discovered their strength by mentally composing poetry.[12] When faced with absolute isolation and denied any reading or writing material, some prisoners demonstrate the mind's incredible capacity to maintain alertness and power and discover latent intellectual resources.

Solitary confinement carries the threat of double imprisonment. This ultimate challenge to a woman's psychological survival undermines the essence of her humanity, but the impulse to communicate is not to be suppressed by isolation or lack of writing materials. Women's prison memoirs, such as those by Lena Constante and Ericka Glaser Wallach, address this challenge by disclosing the mystery of wall tapping, the powerful, ancient medium of prison communication in which prisoners spell out messages to each other on prison walls. The "language" of wall tapping may be considered symbolic of women prisoners' more general response to the human need to communicate. Both male and female prisoners held in isolation have been mentally and emotionally sustained by this means of expanding their sense of self. Tapping episodes are among the most vivid and riveting events in prison literature, and those narrated by Constante, Wallach, Eugenia Ginzburg, and Vera Figner rank among the most compelling.[13] Learning the prison alphabet allowed these women to establish contact with other sufferers, thus escaping through imagination during long periods of solitude and gaining a psychological victory over their captors. Russian revolutionary Figner explains that her very sanity was saved when she dared to defy the ban on tapping and later overheard comments of awed respect from her comrades.

The stark poverty of the senses, imposed universally in solitary confinement, does not eliminate "class" distinctions in communication. Constante notes the "penitentiary illiteracy" of those women whose difficulty in quickly mastering Morse code rendered them incapable of deciphering the tappings; political prisoners, usually well educated, were more likely to communicate by this means, she observed.[14] It seems that even this basic antidote to "hard time" in the starkest of prison settings has not been available to all.[15]

A woman's impulse to survive incarceration by maintaining communication with the world is aided considerably by the existence of prisoner-centered programs. Prisons in the United States offer varying amounts of education and vocational training to women.[16] Programs emphasizing the arts have been among the most effective in empowering women. One of the earliest was the Santa Cruz Women's Prison Project, established in the 1970s at the California Institution for Women. In this program poet

Norma Stafford first discovered her artistic gift.[17] The Writing Workshop at Bedford Hills Correctional Facility, led by Hettie Jones, and the poetry workshop at the Massachusetts Correctional Institute in Framingham, led by Rosanna Warren, are two recent, successful examples.[18] "The world we created at Framingham Prison was a world that felt free," says Jean Trounstine, who led a drama program at Framingham. "It was a place where [women prisoners] came to feel safe and to be challenged creatively, a time when the prison did not intrude. For the hours that we gathered each evening, a space behind bars became, in a sense, sanctified. . . . Art at Framingham was a catalyst for transformation."[19]

The desire for beauty as a means of self-expression and communication with the world takes many forms for women prisoners. In "Slick and the Beanstalk," Judee Norton shows that by sheer will and creative energy a woman may generate new life out of prison's sterile bureaucracy. The creation in this case is not a poem, but a living bean sprout—a testament to Norton's uncompromising love of life and refusal to be defined or limited by her prison sentence.[20] In the poetry of Puerto Rican Nationalist Lolita Lebrón, imprisoned for twenty-five years in the Federal Reformatory for Women in Alderson, West Virginia, a deep loneliness for her homeland and her people is mitigated by love for her sister prisoners and joy in retaining the freshness of life's passion, even in prison. "Lolita, what do you see of any beauty?" asks the world. The poet's response is a determination, against all logic, to experience life richly, to refuse to be institutionalized.

Relationships are the primary means of coping with deprivations for most female prisoners, including those without the background to communicate through writing. Since the 1960s, researchers on women's prisons in the United States have studied the forms those relationships take. In her classic study of women's prisons, Giallombardo explained that male prisoners establish a rigid "inmate code" of behavior and a defined system of social roles. "In contrast to the male prison," she says,

> the evolution of an informal social structure in the female prison
> to withstand the deleterious effects of physical and social isolation
> is in many respects an attempt to resist the destructive effects of
> imprisonment by creating a substitute universe—a world in which
> the inmates may preserve an identity which is relevant to life out-
> side the prison.[21]

Researchers identify the characteristic system of interpersonal relationships among American female prisoners as the "kinship group," with prisoners assuming pseudofamily roles of both sexes, including parents, children, grandparents, aunts, and cousins.[22]

The social structure may take the form of various support systems consistent with relationships the women knew on the outside. Friendships between women are one form of relationship, as are lesbian alliances, or "same-sex relationships," to use Barbara Owen's term for prisoners' intimate bonding

that may or may not be sexual.[23] In general, homosexual contact in male institutions tends to be coercive and power-oriented, whereas women's alliances
often have complex origins, including the need for affection and support.[24]

Writing by women prisoners clearly exhibits the concern for personal
relationships demonstrated by the general female prison population.
Women prisoners' lack of, need for, and joy in human companionship are
major themes in their literature. Their works show the many paths taken
to fulfill this need. French writer Beatrice Saubin, for example, describes
the sustaining power of women's bonding, both sexual and emotional, during her ten-year imprisonment in Malaysia. A naive and reckless love affair
with a man she barely knew had led to Saubin's arrest for drug smuggling
and her unjust imprisonment under Malaysia's draconian drug laws. In her
account of how she coped with this injustice, women's love and friendship,
experienced on several levels, dominate the story.[25]

During her twenty years of virtual isolation, Vera Figner took comfort
in her intense friendship with another imprisoned woman revolutionary.
Her loving description of their close bond leaves no doubt that this cher-
ished friend transformed prison life for Figner. Judee Norton's story
"Gerta's Story" depicts another kind of female support. The lesson taught
by the mysterious "Crazy Gert" brings all women together to protest
crimes against humanity and to testify that those inside and outside prison
walls are affected, universally.[26]

Through communication and interpersonal relationships, women prison
writers cope with the pains of incarceration and gather strength to proclaim their personal identity and integrity. Giving birth to self and freedom is Norma Stafford's image of the female prisoner's power to survive.
It is a birthing process that only a woman prisoner could envision:

> blessed relief   the emergence of me
> when i finally walk out those gates.[27]

NOTES

The quotation in the title of this section is taken from Lolita Lebrón, "I Have All the
Passion of Life," trans. Gloria Waldman, in *Voices of Women: Poetry by and About Third
World Women* (New York: Women's International Research Exchange (WIRE), 1982.
The first epigraph to this section is taken from Lena Constante, *The Silent Escape:
Three Thousand Days in Romanian Prisons*, trans. Franklin Philip (Berkeley: University
of California Press, 1995), 235. The second epigraph is taken from Erica Glaser
Wallach, *Light at Midnight* (Garden City, N.Y.: Doubleday, 1967), 129–30.

1. Karlene Faith, "The Politics of Confinement and Resistance: The Imprisonment
of Women," in *Criminal Injustice: Confronting the Prison Crisis*, ed. Elihu Rosenblatt
(Boston: South End Press, 1996), 165–83.

2. In their quest to survive psychologically, women may encounter opposition from
the prison system. Criminologist Nancy Stoller Shaw states, "It is ironically tragic that
prisons aim to crush the very characteristics that women need in the struggle for a dignified existence," in "Female Patients and the Medical Profession in Jails and Prisons,"

in *Judge, Lawyer, Victim, Thief: Women, Gender Roles, and Criminal Justice,* ed. Nicole Hahn Rafter and Elizabeth A. Stanko (Boston: Northeastern University Press, 1982), 266. See Adrian Lomax, "Captive Audience," *In These Times* (14 June 1998): 37–38, for a discussion of "TV therapy," the practice of using television to numb prisoners to the realities of imprisonment.

3. For a discussion of issues related to female prisoners and addiction, see Stephanie S. Covington, "Women in Prison: Approaches in the Treatment of Our Most Invisible Population," in *Breaking the Rules: Women in Prison and Feminist Therapy,* ed. Judy Harden and Marcia Hill, (Binghamton, N. Y.: Harrington Park Press, 1998), 141–55.

4. For a discussion of mental illness in prisons in the United States, see Nicole Hahn Rafter and Debra L. Stanley, *Prisons in America: A Reference Handbook* (Santa Barbara, Calif.: ABC-CLIO, 1999) and Terry Allen Kupers, *Prison Madness: The Mental Health Crisis behind Bars,* (Somerset, N. J.: Jossey-Bass, 1999). Catherine I. Fogel and Sandra L. Martin, in "The Mental Health of Incarcerated Women," *Western Journal of Nursing Research* 14, no. 1 (February 1992): 30–47, report a study of the stress of maternal incarceration.

5. See Barbara Owen, *In the Mix: Struggle and Survival in a Women's Prison* (Albany: SUNY Press, 1998); Andi Rierden, *The Farm: Life Inside a Women's Prison* (Amherst: University of Massachusetts Press, 1997); Lori B. Girshick, *No Safe Haven: Stories of Women in Prison* (Boston: Northeastern University Press, 1999), and articles in *Harsh Punishment: International Experiences of Women's Imprisonment,* ed. Sandy Cook and Susanne Davies (Boston: Northeastern University Press, 1999). A review of the literature on women's coping with imprisonment is Sharon McQuaide and John H. Ehrenreich, "Women in Prison: Approaches to Understanding the Lives of a Forgotten Population," *Affilia: Journal of Women & Social Work* 13, no. 2 (Summer 1998): 233–47. For classic discussions of women's responses to imprisonment, see David A. Ward and Gene G. Kassebaum, *Women's Prison: Sex and Social Structure* (Chicago: Aldine, 1965) and Rose Giallombardo, *Society of Women: A Study of a Women's Prison* (New York: Wiley, 1966).

6. Owen, *In the Mix,* 7.

7. Owen, *In the Mix,* 8. See also Barbara Saunders' poem, "The Grievance," in part 3 of this anthology. See Carol Burke, *Vision Narratives of Women in Prison* (Knoxville: University of Tennessee Press, 1992) for "a collection of visionary accounts of women in prison" (xi) based upon Burke's interviews with prisoners. These accounts suggest another way in which women achieve communication in prison.

8. Gresham Sykes, in his class study of men's prisons, *The Society of Captives: A Study of a Maximum Security Prison* (Princeton: Princeton University Press, 1958), describes how prison deprivations cause several "pains of imprisonment" for prisoners.

9. Other selections in this anthology relevant to the topic of psychological survival through communication and relationships include those by Bedell, Buck, Huggins, Lytton, McConnel, Metzger, Saunders, Stafford, and Wituska.

10. Stanley Cohen and Laurie Taylor, *Psychological Survival: The Experience of Long-Term Imprisonment* (New York: Pantheon, 1972), 73–74.

11. Hilde O. Bluhm, "How Did They Survive?: Mechanisms of Defense in Nazi Concentration Camps," *American Journal of Psychology* 2 (1948): 3–32, quoted in Cohen and Taylor, *Psychological Survival,* 137–38.

12. *Journey into the Whirlwind* by Ginzburg, trans. Paul Stevenson and Max Hayward (New York: Harcourt Brace Jovanovich, 1967), is an early publication of a memoir from the Stalin era. Since the 1990s several memoirs have been published, including the anthology, *Till My Tale Is Told: Women's Memoirs of the Gulag,* ed. Simeon Vilensky, (Bloomington, Ind.: Indiana University Press, 1999).

13. For discussions of wall tapping, see selections by Figner and Ginzburg in this section of this anthology and by Lytton in part 6. Additional examples can be found in

works by Constante and Samuelli, listed in the annotated bibliography. Nidia Díaz, listed in the annotated bibliography, discusses the use of hand signals for communication between prisoners.

14. Constante, *The Silent Escape*, 233–34.

15. A recent variation of solitary confinement in the United States was the small group isolation and sensory deprivation of the Lexington High Security Unit in Kentucky, used to confine female political prisoners until its closing in 1988. See Mary K. O'Melveny, "Lexington Prison High Security Unit: U.S. Political Prison," in *Criminal Injustice*, 322–33. Also see articles in *Cages of Steel: The Politics of Imprisonment in the United States*, ed. Ward Churchill and J. J. Vander Wall (Washington, D.C.: Maisonneuve Press, 1992) for a discussion of the psychological effects of confinement in High Security Units. Terry Allen Kupers, in *Prison Madness: The Mental Health Crisis behind Bars*, (Somerset, N. J.: Jossey-Bass, 1999), 58, explains that illiterate prisoners confined to solitary in a Security Housing Unit (SHU) may suffer extreme boredom from lack of mental stimulation.

16. See Rita J. Simon and Jean Landis, *The Crimes Women Commit, the Punishments They Receive* (Lexington, Mass.: Lexington Books, 1991), 77–101, and Tara Gray and G. Larry Mays, "Inmate Needs and Programming in Exclusively Women's Jails," *Prison Journal* 75, no. 2 (June 1995): 186–203, for a discussion of programs, education, and industries in women's prisons. See Jane Maher and Paul E. Dinter, "Redirection through Education," *Fortune News* (winter 2000): 20–23, for a description of a college program at Bedford Hills Correctional Facility. A recent collaborative study was done by the Graduate Center of the City University of New York and women in prison at the Bedford Hills Correctional Facility: *Changing Minds: The Impact of College in a Maximum-Security Prison* (September 2001), www.changingminds.ws. For discussion of the problems of reentry when women are released from prison, see Beth E. Richie, "Challenges Incarcerated Women Face as They Return to Their Communities: Findings from Life History Interviews," *Crime & Delinquency* 47, no. 3 (July 2001): 368–89, and Jeremy Travis and Joan Petersilia, "Reentry Reconsidered: A New Look at an Old Question," *Crime and Delinquency* 47, no. 3 (July 2001): 291–313. Marsha Norman's play, *Getting Out* (New York: Dramatists Play Service, 1979), depicts the difficulties of a recently released prisoner who must support herself but has no prospects for employment.

17. See Karlene Faith, *Unruly Women: The Politics of Confinement and Resistance* (Vancouver: Press Gang, 1993), for a discussion of the Santa Cruz program.

18. Publications from these programs include the following: The Writing Workshop at Bedford Hills Correctional Facility, *Aliens at the Border*, ed. Hettie Jones (New York: Segue Books, 1997), and *In Time: Women's Poetry from Prison*, ed. Rosanna Warren and Teresa Iverson (Boston: Boston University, 1995), which published poems from workshops at the Massachusetts Correctional Institute in Framingham.

19. Jean Trounstine, *Shakespeare behind Bars: The Power of Drama in a Women's Prison* (New York: St. Martin's, 2001), 235. A successful program using theatre with women in the San Francisco County Jail system is described by Rena Fraden in *Imagining Medea: Rhodessa Jones & Theater for Incarcerated Women* (Chapel Hill: University of North Carolina Press, 2001). Imprisoned poet Marilyn Buck (see her poems in part 6 of this anthology) states that she has participated in poet June Jordan's Poetry for the People workshop. See http://www.prisonactivist.org/pps+pows/marilynbuck. Ericka Wallach, in *Light at Midnight*, 235–36, discusses the value that the arts can hold for a prisoner.

20. Constante, 207, likewise refers to her prison's prohibition against politicals having a view of any growing things.

21. Giallombardo, *Society of Women*, 103.

22. Early discussions of social systems in women's prisons are Giallombardo, 158–89 and Lee H. Bowker, "Gender Differences in Prisoner Subcultures," *in Women and Crime in America*, ed. Lee H. Bowker (New York: Macmillan, 1981), 415. Bowker writes that kinship groups were observed as early as the late 1920s and that they are found throughout the United States and abroad. Esther Heffernan, *Making It in Prison: The Square, the Cool, and the Life* (New York: Wiley-Interscience, 1972) is an early extended discussion of social systems in women's prisons. A recent discussion is Owen, *In the Mix.*

23. Owen, *In the Mix,* 193. Marsha Norman's play, *Getting Out,* shows the importance of female friendships that sustain a woman prisoner *after* her release.

24. See Bowker, "Gender Differences in Prisoner Subcultures," 414, and Giallombardo, 141, for early discussions of lesbian relationships in prison. See Dominik Morgan, "Restricted Love," in *Breaking the Rules: Women in Prison and Feminist Therapy,* 75–84, for a more recent discussion by a prisoner of the complexity of "prison homosexuality as seen from the inside."

25. Jane Evelyn Atwood, in *Too Much Time: Women in Prison* (London: Phaidon, 2000), her photographic account of international women's prisons, notes the following: "In every prison I visited, I found ignorant women conned by men into carrying a suitcase of drugs from one country to another in exchange for money. Typically these 'mules' were mothers, desperately poor, struggling alone to support their children. They found themselves thrown into a foreign jail, tried and sentenced to eight to twelve years, unable to speak the language, therefore unable to defend themselves. Their lives were ruined because, in their own cultures, a woman who does time is abandoned by all. In some societies a man is considered a hero if he has done time; for a woman it is always a shameful thing" (13).

26. Another example of supportive relationships among female prisoners is depicted in Diane Hamill Metzger's poem "M.I.: Circa 1980," in part 3 of this anthology.

27. Norma Stafford, "[the contractions are coming harder now]". The complete poem can be found in part 6 of this anthology.

VERA FIGNER

(1852–1942)

Vera Nikolajevna Figner spent an isolated childhood, first in the home of her wealthy, strict father in Kazan, Russia, and later in a restrictive girls' boarding school. During her youth she developed a close bond with her mother. However, it was her Uncle Kuprijanov who first inspired her desire to help the uneducated masses. After marrying Alexei Filipov, a young magistrate who encouraged her interest in medicine, she began medical studies in 1870 at the University of Zurich. There, she and her sister Lydia actively studied socialism with a group of women students, the *Fritschi*, who, as revolutionaries, eventually all sacrificed their freedom and—many—their lives. As Figner's involvement in the revolutionary cause increased, she and her more conservative husband realized their differences; they later divorced.

In 1876, Figner returned to Russia to put her revolutionary theories into practice. After disillusioning attempts to educate the peasants as a peaceful preparation for reform, in 1879 she helped to found the People's Will, a revolutionary group that used terrorist methods. In 1883 she was arrested for her part in the assasssination of Tsar Alexander II and was imprisoned in St. Petersburg's Peter and Paul Prison for twenty months before her trial. Because the execution of women was frowned upon, Figner was sentenced to life imprisonment and taken to the infamous Schlüsselburg Fortress prison in 1884. There she passed twenty years in solitary confinement, of which the first five were without paper or pen. She and the only other woman prisoner, Ludmilla Wolkenstein, were kept isolated and saw each other only during their half-hour walk every other day. Her revolutionary comrades all died or went insane under the terrible prison conditions. Figner's own most "bitter grief" was her separation from her mother.

In 1904, Figner was given amnesty and exiled to Archangel in Siberia. After she was allowed to leave Russia in 1906, she lived for eight years in Paris and Switzerland, where she worked for Russian prison reform and wrote her memoirs. She returned to Russia in 1914 and two years later began working in St. Petersburg with an amnesty committee for Tsarist political prisoners. She spent her final years in Moscow, where she was greatly respected by the Russian people and by international political activists, including Emma Goldman.

Note: Background information is from Margaret Goldsmith, *Seven Women Against the World* (London: Methuen, 1935); Ethel Mannin, *Women and the Revolution* (New York: Dutton, 1939); Amy Knight, "The Fritschi: A Study of Female Radicals in the Russian Populist Movement," *Canadian-American Slavic Studies* 9, no. 1 (Spring 1975); Barbara Alpern Engel and Clifford N. Rosenthal, eds., *Five Sisters: Women Against the Tsar* (New York: Knopf, 1975); "Figner, Vera Nikolayevna," online, available: http://www.search.eb.com/bol/topic?eu=34847&sctn=1, December 13, 2001.

THE FIRST YEARS

From Memoirs of a Revolutionist, *1927.*

My own spirit was stifled and crushed during these years. And whom would Schlüsselburg not stifle and crush? What comforting thought had we, members of The Will of the People, brought with us to Schlüsselburg? The revolutionary movement had been defeated, its organisation destroyed, and the Executive Committee had perished to the very last member. The people and society had not supported us. We were alone. The noose of autocracy had been drawn more tightly, and we, passing out of the life of the world, had left no heirs to carry on the struggle which we had begun.

Schlüsselburg gave me something, however, which I had not foreseen, for which I had not prepared myself. The very last joy in my life had been my mother, and they took her away from me—the only person in the world who made life real and worth living, the only one to whom I, fallen into the depths of the abyss, could cling. Joy died within me, but, dying, left behind it a keen and bitter grief. While I was free, I had not lived with my mother, and had thought of her only occasionally. But then I had had my country to think of; my revolutionary activities occupied my mind; there were strong attachments and friendships, there were my comrades. And now there was no one, nothing. And my mother, that final loss, the loss of the very last thing dear to me, became, as it were, the symbol of all my losses, large and small, of all my deprivations, both great and petty. Never did I regret that I had chosen the path that had led me to this place. It was *my will* that had chosen that path—there could be no regret. Never once did I regret the fact that I was deprived of delicate underclothing and fine garments, wearing instead a coarse rag and a convict's gown with a brand on the back. I did not regret but I suffered. Only the thought of my mother filled my mind—her image and no other, and my overwhelming grief at being separated from her. But that grief absorbed and included all of my sufferings, all of my griefs; the grief of my crushed and wounded spirit, and the grief of my oppressed and humiliated body. And thus, symbolised in the loss of my mother, it assumed the caustic bitterness of all my losses, all my deprivations, and became vast and uncontrollable, as do all feelings which are never freely expressed but lie hidden in the dark depths of the subconscious. Destruction threatened my darkened mind.

But when one step more would have carried me to a point beyond all chance of recovery, an inner voice said, "Stop!" It was not my fear of death that spoke. Death was quite desirable; it was linked with the idea of martyrdom, which in my childhood Christian traditions had taught me to regard as sacred; while later the history of the struggle for the rights of the oppressed had strengthened this idea in me. It was the fear of insanity, that degradation of the individual, the degeneracy of his spirit and flesh, that halted me. But to stop at this point meant an effort to regain a normal outlook on life, to become again spiritually whole. My friends helped me to do this.

A dim light began to dawn in me, like the little flames of the wax candles on Palm Sunday. The dumb walls of Schlüsselburg began to speak; I was able to communicate with my friends.[1] They spoke tenderly, sent me loving messages, and Schlüsselburg's icy crust melted in the warmth of their affection. Other influences were brought to bear, stern words, lessons. Once my neighbour, a man whom I had not known before, asked me what I was doing.

"I am thinking of my mother and weeping," I replied.

My neighbour rebuked me in strong terms. He asked me if I had ever read the *Memoirs of Simon Meyer*, the Communard, and I remembered the scene on board ship, when the ship was rolling badly, and they began to shave the heads of the Communards. He put before me as an example this Simon Meyer, one of many thousands of Communards. He read me a lecture. I was startled and hurt and angry. I had read the *Memoirs of Simon Meyer*, and I remembered the scene on board ship, and many others. "Why this sermon?" thought I. "I don't need his sermons!"

But that was precisely what I did need. If my neighbour had sympathised with me, and had begun to console me tenderly, his words would have been of no avail; they would have coincided with my mood. But he censured me in no uncertain terms; he showed me plainly what my duty was, and he vexed me. And this vexation was salutary; it was in contrast with my customary frame of mind, shattered it, made it incongruous. In solitude a trifle sometimes grows to unwonted dimensions; it sticks in your consciousness, and will not be dislodged. So it was in this case. I could not get my neighbour's words out of my mind. The wall between us every day reminded me of our conversation; and each time I recalled it with an unpleasant feeling of irritation and annoyance. In this way my grief and longing were interrupted, and the annoyance served a useful purpose. . . .

I Acquire a Friend

Early in January, 1886, knowing that Ludmila Alexandrovna Volkenstein, one of my co-defendants in the Trial of 14, was also in the Fortress, I asked the inspector why they did not permit me to take my walks in company with one of the other prisoners. The inspector was silent for a moment, and then said, "We can grant you this privilege, only you mustn't . . ." He bent his forefinger and tapped on the door jamb, imitating our fashion of carrying on conversations by tapping on the wall. I replied that I did very little tapping.

The interview went no further, and I was left in solitude as before. But on January 14, when they took me out for my walk, and the door into the little enclosure which we called "the first cage," opened, I beheld an unexpected figure in a short cloth coat, with a linen handkerchief on her head, who swiftly embraced me, and I recognised with difficulty my comrade Volkenstein. Probably she also was as shocked by the change in my appearance, due to my convict garb. And so we stood, embracing one another, and not knowing whether to rejoice or to weep.

Up to this time I had seen Volkenstein only during the trial. We had not met previously, and had known each other only by hearsay. Ludmila Alexandrovna's sincerity, her simplicity and warm-heartedness at once enchanted me. It did not require much time for us to form such a friendship as was possible only under the conditions under which we were living. We were like people shipwrecked on an uninhabited island. We had nothing and no one in all the world save each other. Not only people, but nature, colors, sounds, were gone, all of them. And instead there was left a gloomy vault with a row of mysterious, walled-in cells, in which invisible captives were pining; an ominous silence, and the atmosphere of violence, madness and death. One can see plainly that in such surroundings two friendly spirits must needs find joy in each other's company, and ever afterwards treasure a most touching remembrance of the association.

Any one who has been in prison knows the influence that the sympathetic tenderness of a comrade has on one's life while in confinement. In Polivanov's memoirs of his imprisonment in the Alexey Ravelin, there is a touching picture of Kolodkevich, hobbling up to the wall on crutches to console him with a few tender words. A brief conversation through the soulless stone that separated the two captives, who were dying from scurvy and loneliness, was their only joy and support. The author of the memoirs confessed that more than once Kolodkevich's kind words saved him from acute attacks of melancholy, which were tempting him to commit suicide. And indeed, loving sympathy works veritable wonders in prison; and were it not for those light tappings on the wall, which destroy the stone barrier separating man from man, the prisoner could not preserve his life or his soul. Good reason was there for the struggle to maintain the system of tappings, the very first struggle that a captive wages with the prison officials; it is an out-and-out struggle for existence, and every one who is walled up in a cell clutches at this device as at a straw. But when those sentenced to solitary confinement are permitted to meet their co-prisoners face to face, and to replace the symbolic tapping with living speech, then the warm-heartedness and kindness expressed in the tones of the voice, in an affectionate glance, and a friendly handshake, bring joy unknown to one who has never lost his freedom.

I do not know what I gave to Ludmila Alexandrovna, but she was my comfort, my joy and happiness. My nerves and general constitution had been completely unstrung. I was physically weak, and spiritually exhausted. My general state of mind was entirely abnormal; and lo! I found a friend whom prison conditions had not affected so profoundly and painfully as they had me; and this friend was the personification of tenderness, kindness, and humaneness. All the treasures of her loving spirit she gave to me with a generous hand. No matter how gloomy my mood when we met, she always knew how to dispel it in one way or another, and how to console me. Her smile alone, and the sight of her dear face dispelled my grief, and gladdened my heart. After a walk with her I would come away reassured and transformed; my cell did not seem so gloomy to me, nor life so hard to bear. Straightway I would begin to dream of our next meeting. We saw each other every other day; prison discipline evidently found it necessary to dilute the joy of our meetings by making us pass a day in complete solitude. But perhaps this fact only made our longing to see each other more keen, and accentuated our "holiday mood," which was so pleasant to recall afterwards. . . .

The Punitive Cell

. . . [A]fter six months of separation from my friend Ludmila I came into conflict with the prison régime, which might have had tragic results.

A few days before Whitsunday, at nine o'clock in the evening, when the inspector was making his customary survey of the prison, looking through his peep-hole in every door, Popov called to me with a loud tap from his cell, which was below mine and several doors removed. I was tired. The day had been long and wearisome and empty. I wanted to lie down on my cot and go to sleep, but I did not have the heart to refuse, and I answered. But when Popov began to tap, his sentence broke off in the middle of a word. I heard a door slam, steps rang out in the direction of the exit, and everything was silent again. I understood. The inspector had taken Popov to the punitive cell.

The punitive cell was the place to which the inspector threateningly referred when he said: "I'll take you off to a place where not a living soul will hear you." Not a living soul—that was terrible to think of.

Here we prisoners were all together under the Fortress roof; all around were friends, each in his stone cell, and that was protection and defence. If you should cry out, your cry would be heard. If you should groan, they would hear it. But "off there?" There "not one living soul will hear you."

I knew that not so very long ago, Popov had been taken "off there," and that they had beaten him cruelly. The thought that he would again be put in that terrible place, that he would be alone, and that a whole pack of gendarmes would again fall upon him, an unarmed man, this thought flashed through my mind and seemed so horrible that I made my decision: I would contrive to be put there too; he should know that he was not alone, and that—if they were going to torture him, he had a witness.

I knocked on the door, and asked them to call the inspector. "What do you want?" said he, angrily, opening the little window in the door.

"It is unjust to punish one, when two were talking," said I. "Take me to the punitive cell also."

"Very well," said the inspector promptly, and unlocked the door.

Then it was that I first saw the interior of our prison as it looked lighted up at night: the little lamps along the walls of our tomb; the forty heavy, black doors standing there like coffins set on end, and behind every door, a comrade, a captive, suffering alone; dying, sick, or waiting his turn to die. Hardly had I passed along my "Bridge of Sighs," and approached the stairway, when my neighbour called out: "They're taking Vera to the punitive cell!" and scores of hands began to beat madly on the doors, and voices shouted, "Take us too!"

In the midst of the gloomy surroundings that stirred me so deeply, the sound of the familiar and unfamiliar voices of invisible people, the voices of comrades, which I had not heard for many, many years, awoke in me a certain morbid, flaming joy: we were separated and yet united; our spirits were one.

But the inspector flew into a fury. When we came out into the courtyard accompanied by three or four gendarmes, he raised his fist, which clutched convulsively the bunch of prison keys. With his face distorted from rage, and his beard quivering, he hissed at me: "Over there, just make a sound, and I'll show you!"

I was afraid of this man. I had heard of the cruel corporal punishments that the gendarmes had inflicted at his command, and the thought came to me: "If they beat me, I shall die." But I replied in a voice that sounded so calm that it seemed to belong to somebody else: "I am not going there to tap messages."

The broad wooden gate of the citadel yawned open before me, and my fear was replaced by ecstasy. For five years I had not seen the night sky and the stars. Now this sky was above me, and its stars shone down on me. The high walls of the old citadel gleamed white and the silvery radiance of the May night poured into the deep, square, well-like space enclosed by them. The whole plaza was overgrown with grass. It lay thick and fresh and cool, lightly brushing one's feet, and it had the allurement of the dewy expanse of a *free* field. From wall to wall stretched a low, white building, while in the corner a single tree loomed dark and tall. For a hundred years this splendid creature had grown there alone, without comrades, and thus solitary had spread about it, unhindered, its luxuriant crown. Keys grated, and with difficulty, as though the lock had grown rusty, they opened the outside door of the prison, which led into a dark, tiny antechamber. I smelled the musty odour of a cold, damp, uninhabited building. Before us stretched the naked stones of the broad corridor, at the far end of which glimmered a little night lamp. In the cold twilight the dim figures of the gendarmes, the indistinct outlines of the doors, the dark corners—everything looked so ominous that the thought suddenly flashed into my mind that this was a real torture dungeon, and that the inspector had spoken truly when he said that he had a place where no living soul could hear one. A moment later they opened a door on the left, and thrust in a small lighted lamp; the door slammed, and I was alone.

I was in a small, unheated cell, which had never been cleaned. The walls were dirty, and here and there crumbling from age. The floor was of asphalt; there was a small stationary wooden table with a seat, and an iron bench on which there was no mattress, nor any kind of bedding.

Silence.

In vain I waited for the gendarmes to come back and bring a mattress, and something to put over me; I had on a thin, cotton chemise, a skirt of the same material, and a prison gown, and I began to shiver from the cold. How could one sleep on the iron lattice-work of that cot, thought I. But no bedding ever arrived; I had to lie down on this Rakhmetov bed.[2] However, it was not only impossible to sleep, but even to lie for long on the metal bars of the bench. The cold wafted up from the floor, from the stone walls, and penetrated one's body in contact with the iron bars.

The next day they took even this away. They raised the cot and fastened it with a padlock for the rest of the time. At night one had to lie down on the asphalt floor, in the dust. It was impossible for me to lay my head on the floor, which was very cold, not to mention the filth that covered it. In order to save my head, I had to sacrifice my feet: I took off my rough boots and made a pillow of them. My food was black bread, old and hard. When I broke it, all the little holes within were filled with bluish mold. I could eat only a little bit of the crust. They gave me no salt, to say nothing of towels or soap.

When I went to the punitive cell, I had not planned to speak at all; I had gone there only that it might not be so terrible for Popov to be alone. But Popov had no intention of remaining silent; the very next morning he began to call me, and I was weak enough to answer. But hardly had he begun his tapping again when the gendarmes forestalled him by snatching up staves and beating furiously on our doors. A din beyond all imagination arose. One who has not spent many years in the silence of a prison, whose ear has not grown unaccustomed to sounds, cannot imagine the pain experienced by an ear grown tender through the constant stillness.

Unable to stop their furious beating, I became angry and hysterical, and began myself to beat with my fists on the door behind which the gendarmes were raging. This was beyond one's strength to endure. And yet again and again Popov attempted to send messages, and evoked torturing battles with the gendarmes through the door. At last the patience of the gendarmes was exhausted. All at once the hellish din broke off abruptly. The heavy footsteps of the inspector rang through the corridor, and some mysterious preparations and an ominous, whispered conference broke the eerie stillness.

"Now they are going to open Popov's door," thought I, "and begin to beat him. Can I possibly be a passive witness to this savage punishment? No, I can't endure it."

I began to call for the inspector.

"You want to beat Popov," said I in a strained, hard voice, as soon as he opened the little window in the cell door. "Don't beat him! You've beaten him once already—they may call even you to account!"

"We didn't beat him at all," said the inspector, quite unexpectedly beginning to justify himself. "We tied him, and he resisted, that's all there was to it."

"No, you beat him!" I retorted vehemently, feeling firm ground beneath my feet. "You beat him. There were witnesses, too. He will not do any more tapping," I continued. "I shall tell him, and he will stop."

"All right!" blurted out the inspector.

I called Popov, and told him that such a struggle was more than I could endure, and begged him to stop tapping. . . . Silence again.

The next day they brought me tea and a bed, but gave none to Popov, and I dashed the tea on the floor at the feet of the inspector, and refused to use the bed. But I broke off a piece of bread, and pointing to the mould, said to him: "You're keeping us on bread and water; just take a look then at the kind of bread you feed us."

The inspector flushed. "Give her some other bread," he ordered the gendarmes, and within five minutes they brought me a piece of fresh, soft bread.

For three more nights I lay on the asphalt in the nasty filth, in the cold, with my prison boots for a pillow. I lay there and thought, and thought. . . . What should I do next? It was evident that in the future there would be frequent occasions for collisions with the authorities. Under what circumstances, then, ought I, under what conditions would it be possible and expedient for me to resist the prison administration? By what methods should I struggle against it, how voice my protest? Must I always defend a comrade? My first impulse said, "always." But was one's comrade always right? I had lived through a test and it had been severe. I surveyed everything that had happened during the past few days; I examined my own conduct and Popov's, and asked myself: Do I wish, and have I the strength, to use Popov's methods in my struggle? He was a man with a constitution of iron, great self-control and an immense capacity for resistance, tempered in the Kara mines and the Alexey Ravelin; a cool, obstinate warrior of steel. When his jailers insulted and abused him, he repaid them in like coin. Rough treatment by the guards, noisy scuffles with the gendarmes, did not bother him at all. They bound him, and beat him; several times they beat him cruelly; and he bore it all, and took no revenge; he could still go on living. But I? I could not have done so. Plainly our ways were bound to diverge. I did not have enough strength, enough nervous energy, for the kind of warfare that he was waging; and from a moral point of view, I did not want to start a protest that I could not consistently carry out. Now was the time for me to map out my future conduct, to choose a firm position, to weigh all the conditions, both within and without, and to decide once and for all how I should act, so that there might be no opportunity for weakness or wavering. Petty daily quarrels, rough skirmishes ending in humiliation, were repellent to me, and I decided to reject such methods of warfare. I had learned the measure of my strength, and knew exactly what I could, and what I wished to do. I decided to endure everything that could be endured; but when some cause should arise worth defending with my life, I would protest in its defence, and protest to the point of death.[3]

On the fifth day of my imprisonment in the punitive cell the inspector said to me: "Prisoner Number Five has been given a bed, and a few other things."

Exhausted, and weakened as though by a wasting illness I was able at last to lie down on my bed, and it was high time; there was an incessant roaring and ringing in my ears, and I felt dazed and dull, half asleep and half awake. As I lay there in the twilight in a half-lethargic state, I suddenly heard singing. A pleasant, rather light baritone voice of unusual timber was singing, and its quality reminded me vaguely of some one or something, I did not know which. It was a plain little folk song, and its motif simple and monotonous. Who was singing? Who could be singing in this place? I wondered. Could some workman have been admitted to the building on a repair job? That was impossible. And where did the song come from? It seemed to come from the outside. Were they repairing the roof of the building?

The mystery of this unknown singer confronted me for a long time, even after I had been released from the punitive cell. It was some time after this that I suddenly recalled his name, Grachevsky, after he had passed out of this life by committing suicide. And indeed, I learned afterwards that he was in the old prison at the same time that I was there.

Two more days went by.

"Time for your walk!" said the inspector, opening my door. My term of punishment was over.

"I will not go if you are releasing only me," said I, withdrawing into the corner, and added fearfully: "You surely wouldn't drag me out by force?"

The inspector appraised my frail, bowed figure in the corner from head to foot, shrugged his shoulders, and said with a contemptuous air: "What is there to drag!" And he added: "Number Five has left already."

And so I followed.

When I came back to my old cell after my walk, I moistened the slate board, and looked at myself in its small, mirror-like surface. I saw a face that in seven days had grown ten years older: hundreds of thin little wrinkles furrowed it in all directions. These wrinkles quickly disappeared, but not the impressions of the days which had just come to a close.

NOTES

1. A reference to the system of communicating messages by tapping on the walls. —*Trans.*

2. Rakhmetov is one of the characters in Chernyshevsky's novel, *What Is To Be Done?*, who advocates and practises an extremely Spartan mode of living.—*Trans.*

3. Fifteen whole years passed before life offered me such cause.

EUGENIA SEMYONOVNA GINZBURG

(1905?–1977)

Eugenia Ginzburg's first book, *Journey into the Whirlwind*, describes the author's eighteen-year imprisonment in Stalin's prisons and Siberian labor camps. It has been compared with Solzhenitsyn's *Gulag Archipelago*. Ginzburg, who described herself as a naively dedicated and loyal Communist, was expelled from the Party, arrested in 1937 in Kazan, and charged with belonging to a terrorist organization. The former history professor and writer on the staff of the local party newspaper, *Red Tartary*, was separated from her two sons and her husband, a Communist official who was also arrested and later died during his imprisonment. One son died of starvation; her surviving son joined her in Siberia after eleven years.

In her first prison, in the "cellars at Black Lake" in Kazan, she was interrogated and kept isolated from everyone but her cell mate, Lyama. The selection below describes how Ginzburg began communicating with prisoners outside her cell when she deciphered the ancient code of wall tapping by recalling an explanation in Vera Figner's memoirs. In one of her subsequent prisons, in Yaroslavl, she endured solitary confinement by recalling great Russian poetry and mentally composing her own poems.

In 1939 Ginzburg was transferred from prison to the Siberian hard-labor camps. She discusses her experiences in the gold region of Kolyma in her second book, *Within the Whirlwind*. While working as a nurse there, she met and fell in love with the man who would become her second husband, Dr. Anton Walter. After her release she spent a period of time in exile in the Soviet Union with her son, dissident novelist Vassily Aksyonov, who learned from her of the great, forbidden Russian writers. She was finally "rehabilitated" by the Soviet government in 1955. In 1976, she traveled to Paris, where the worldwide association of writers, PEN, honored her with a reception.

Note: Background information is from "Love and Death in the Gulag," *New York Times Magazine* (June 7, 1981); Harrison E. Salisbury, review of *Within the Whirlwind*, by Eugenia Ginzburg, *New York Times Book Review* (July 12, 1981).

THE WALLS COME TO LIFE

From Journey into the Whirlwind, *1967.*

Suddenly they stopped summoning me for interrogation. The empty prison days fell into a kind of regular routine, marked by the issue of hot water in the morning, the fifteen-minute walk in the prison yard (during which we were followed by guards with rifles and fixed bayonets), the meals, the washroom. The interrogators seemed to have forgotten my existence.

"They do it on purpose," said Lyama.[1] "It's three weeks since I was last called. They hope prison life will drive you crazy, so that, in sheer desperation, you'll sign any old nonsense."

But I was so shaken by my first experience of Black Lake "justice" that I was glad of the unexpected respite.

"Well, let's make sure we don't go crazy," I said to Lyama. "Let's use our time to find out all we can about our surroundings. You said yourself that the great thing was to establish contact—and he's still tapping, isn't he?"

The prisoner in the cell to our left was still tapping on the wall, regularly, every day after dinner. But I had been too exhausted by the interrogations to listen properly to his knocking, and Lyama despaired of ever getting the hang of the prison alphabet.

One thing, however, we had noticed. On the days when our neighbor went to the washroom before us—this we could tell by the sound of the footsteps in the corridor—we always found the shelf sprinkled with tooth powder and the word "Greetings" traced in it with something very fine like a pin, and as soon as we got back to our cell, a brief message was tapped on the wall. After that, he immediately stopped. These knocks were altogether different from the long sequences our neighbor tapped after dinner, when he was trying to teach us the alphabet.

After two or three times it suddenly dawned on me:

"'Greetings'! That's what he's tapping," I told Lyama. "He writes and taps the same word. Now we know how we can work out the signs for the different letters." We counted the knocks.

"That's right!" Lyama whispered excitedly. "The tapping comes in groups with long and short intervals. And he tapped out nine letters in all: g-r-e-e-t-i-n-g-s."

During the long months and years I spent in various prisons, I was able to observe the virtuosity that human memory can develop when it is sharpened by loneliness and complete isolation from outside impressions. One remembers with amazing accuracy everything one has ever read, even quite long ago, and can repeat whole pages of books one had believed long forgotten. There is something almost mysterious about this phenomenon. That day, at any rate, after deciphering the message "Greetings" tapped on the wall, I was astounded to find a page from Vera Figner's memoirs whole and fresh in my mind. It was the page in which she gave the clue to the prison alphabet. Clutching my head, myself astounded by my own words, I recited as if talking in my sleep:

"The alphabet is divided into five rows of five letters each. Each letter is represented by two sets of knocks, one slow, the other quick. The former indicates the row, the latter the position of the letter in it."

Wild with excitement, interrupting each other and for once forgetting the guard in the corridor, we tapped out our first message. It was very short.

"W-h-o-a-r-e-y-o-u?"

Yes, it was right! Through the grim stone wall we could sense the joy of the man on the other side. At last we had understood! His endless patience had been rewarded. "Rat-tat, tat-tat-tat!" He tapped like a cheerful tune. From then on, we used these five knocks to mean "Message understood."

Now he was tapping his reply—no longer for a couple of idiots who had to have the word "greeting" repeated a hundred times, but for intelligent people to whom he could give his name:

"S-a-g-i-d-u-l-l-i-n."

"Sagidullin? Who's that?" The name meant nothing to Lyama, but it did to me. Much more boldly, I tapped:

"Himself?"

Yes, it was he—Garey Sagidullin, whose name for years past had not been mentioned in Kazan without an "ism" tacked on to it: Sagidullinism.

It was the heading of a propaganda theme. "Sagidullinism," like "Sultan-Galeyevism," stood for the heresy of Tartar "bourgeois nationalism." But he had been arrested in 1933. What on earth was he doing here now?

Through the wall my bewilderment evidently was sensed and understood. The message went on:

"I was and I remain a Leninist. I swear it by my seventh prison"—and startlingly: "Believe me, Genia."

How could he know my name? How could he, through the wall, in spite of all the strictness of our isolation, know who was next door? We looked at one another in alarm. We had no need to speak out loud. The thought was in both our minds. He might be a *provocateur.*

Once again he understood and patiently explained. It appeared that in his cell, too, there was a chink between the window boards, and for a long time he had watched us walking in the yard. Although we had never met, he had once caught a glimpse of me at the Institute of Red Professors in Moscow. He had been brought back to Kazan for re-examination on additional charges. It looked like the death sentence.

From then on, though outwardly nothing had altered, our days were full of interest. All morning I looked forward to the after-dinner hour when the guards were changed and, as they handed over their human cattle, were for a while distracted from peeping through spy holes and listening at doors.

Garey's brief messages opened a new world to me, a world of camps, deportations, prisons, tragic twists of fate—a world in which either the spirit was broken and degraded or true courage was born.

I learned from him that all those who had been arrested in 1933 and '35 had now been sent back for "re-examination." Nothing new whatever had occurred to justify this, but as the interrogators cynically put it, it was a matter of "translating all those files into the language of '37"—that is, replacing three- and five-year sentences by more radical ones.

An even more important objective was to force these "hardened" oppositionists (whose opposition in some cases had consisted in advancing untested scientific ideas, such as Vasily Slepkov's methodological research in the field of natural science) to sign the monstrous lists, concocted by the interrogators, of those whom they had "suborned." The signatures were obtained by threats, bullying, false accusations, and detention in punishment cells (the beatings began only in June or July, after the Tukhachevsky trial[2]).

Garey hated Stalin with a bitter passion, and when I asked him what he believed to be the cause of the current troubles, he replied tersely:

"Koba." (This was Stalin's Gregorian nickname.) "It's his eighteenth Brumaire. Physical extermination of all the best people in the Party, who stand or might stand in the way of his definitely establishing his dictatorship."

For the first time in my life I was faced by the problem of having to think things out for myself—of analyzing circumstances independently and deciding my own line of conduct.

"It's not as if you were in the hands of the Gestapo." Major Yelshin's[3] words rang in my mind.

How much easier and simpler if I had been! A Communist held by the Gestapo—I would have known exactly how to behave. But here? Here I had first to determine who these people were, who kept me imprisoned. Were they fascists in disguise? Or victims of some super-subtle provocation, some fantastic hoax? And how should a Communist behave "in prison in his own country," as the Major had put it?

All these anguished questions I put to Garey, ten years my senior in age and fifteen as a Party member. But his advice was not such that I could follow it, and it left me still more puzzled. To this day I cannot understand what could have prompted him, and Slepkov and many others who had been arrested in the early thirties, to act as he advised me to do now.

"Tell them straight out, you disagree with Stalin's line, and name as many others who disagree as you can. They can't arrest the whole Party, and by the time they have thousands of such cases on their hands, someone will think of calling an extraordinary Party congress and there will be a chance of overthrowing him. Believe me, he's as much hated in the Central Committee as here in prison. Of course it may mean the end for us, but it's the only way to save the Party."

No, this was something I could not do. Even though I felt obscurely, without having any proof, that Stalin was behind the nightmare events in our Party, I could not say that I disagreed with the Party line. I had honestly and fervently supported the policies of industrializing the country and collectivizing the land, and these were the basic points of the Party line.

Still less could I name others, knowing as I did that the very mention of a Communist within these walls would be enough to ruin him and orphan his children.

No; if the demagogic habits of mind I had been trained in were so deeply rooted in me that I could not now make an independent analysis of the situation in the country and the Party, then I would be guided simply by the voice of my conscience. I would speak only the truth about myself, I would sign no lies against myself or anyone else, and I would give no names. I must not be taken in by Jesuitical arguments which justified lies and fratricide. It was impossible that they could be of service to the Party I had so fervently believed in and to which I had resolved to dedicate my life.

All this—very briefly, of course—I transmitted to Garey. I had mastered the technique of tapping so thoroughly, by the end of a week, that Garey and I could recite whole poems to each other. We no longer needed to spell everything out. We had a special sign to show that we had understood, so we could use abbreviations and save time. A blow of the fist meant that a warder was about. I must confess that he used this signal much more often than I did, and I would surely have been caught if it hadn't been for him. However interesting the conversation, he never ceased to be on the alert.

I was never to set eyes on this man. He was eventually shot. I disagreed with many things he said and I never had a chance to discover exactly what his political views were. But I know one thing for certain: he endured his seventh prison, his isolation, and the prospect of being shot with unbroken courage. He was a strong man, a man in the true sense of the word.

NOTES

1. Ginzburg's cell mate at "Black Lake," her first prison in Kazan.—*Ed.*

2. Mikhail Tukhachevsky, 1893–1937, Soviet military leader who, together with Gamarnik, Yakir, Uborevich, and other members of the Soviet High Command, was executed in 1937.

3. Ginzburg's interrogator.—*Ed.*

LOLITA LEBRÓN

(1919–)

Puerto Rican Nationalist Dolores "Lolita" Lebrón was sentenced to fifty years for her part in an armed demonstration in the U.S. House of Representatives on March 1, 1954. Born in the western town of Lares, Puerto Rico, she had lived in the United States for six years and was employed in a sewing machine factory in New York City at the time of the demonstration. She led three male Nationalists who, waving a Puerto Rican flag from the visitors' gallery and crying "Viva Puerto Rico," opened fire at random onto the floor and wounded five congressmen. Lebrón, the first to fire, stated in a letter found after the incident that the violent demonstration was in support of independence for her people. She was willing to die for her country in carrying out this mission.

Lebrón was imprisoned for twenty-five years in the Federal Reformatory for Women at Alderson, West Virginia, where she actively worked to secure the rights of women prisoners. Pardoned under the Carter administration, she was released in September 1979 and returned to Puerto Rico. During her imprisonment, both her children died: her eleven-year old son, Felix, drowned and her adult daughter, Gladys, died in a fall from a moving car.

Currently Lebrón, a devoted Catholic, advocates the peaceful method of civil disobedience to achieve political objectives. She is active in the movement to protest the presence and activity of the U.S. Navy on Vieques, an island off the Puerto Rican coast.

Note: Background information is from Gloria F. Waldman, "Affirmation and Resistance: Women Poets from the Caribbean," in *Contemporary Women Authors of Latin America*, ed. Doris Meyer and Margarite Fernandez Olmos (Brooklyn, N.Y.: Brooklyn College Humanities Press, 1983); *Women Behind Bars* (Washington, D.C.: Resources for Community Change, 1975); Edward F. Ryan, "I Love My Country," *Washington Post*, March 2, 1954, quoted in Kal Wagenheim, *The Puerto Ricans: A Documentary History* (New York: Praeger, 1973); Juan Carlos Perez, "Si! to the Cause," *Philadelphia Inquirer* (August 3, 1997); David Gonzalez, "Vieques Advocate Turns from Violence of Her Past," *New York Times*, June 18, 2001.

Playing" and "I Have All the Passion of Life" are from
Poetry by and about Third World Women, 1982;
Seen You" are from Contemporary Women Authors of
w Translations, 1983.

₁ᵤ ᵤne Prisoners Playing

Those beloved voices I hear
are my own sounds,
the smoke
that in a burning echo
murmurs to the land . . .
I sing of the pain
and of the joy
of this world.

Those beloved voices! My sisters!
Confused in melodies of
upheaval, tears, and sobs,
passion and troubles,
and a spring
of complaints and misfortune.

How many times, at their simple echoes,
has my breast opened up
to pure light and reflection
through which I see their faces
like bunches of exquisite and ripe fruit.

In my heart I see all the sun
from their sad, not quite lit eyes,
sheltered within the boundaries
of the earth.

Because I know that in seeing it,
in its mistiness,
it holds all the fire
of the auguries of the splendor
of God,
in his depth and profundity.

I love them with the beating
of my black and blond plumage,
for they are my rainbow,

in my sight,
this knowing about what's hidden,
and this sensation of seeing
what is clear.

Whoever denies life its joy,
the wealth of its complexity,
its rainbow-like countenance,
its downpour and its universe
of beauty, its generous giving,
the caress, the grain
with fruit and delicacies,
the bud, the flower, pain and laughter;
those who deny life its measure
of joy
are the unseeing ones.
Nor have they drunk from
life's overflowing cup of passion.

I have all the rapture,
the savoring.
That's why they stare and ask:
"Lolita, what do you see of
any beauty?
What do you like? The sky?
These sterile and arid mountains,
these hours so full of ugliness
and injustice,
with endless sighs
and the pushing and the shoving?"

"Why do you sing and laugh, Lolita?
Is your face really lit up
with the joy of life?
Are you mad, Lolita?"

Alone

I'm quiet, like the still water
in the solitude of my cell.
I move serenely towards the sea
with my stillness and my leaping . . .
Alone. Only the voice of the rain
can console my suffering.
"The rain is Your voice." I feel
all your kisses and embraces.

the treasures yielded by
the shadows and beams of light
on these walls.

They are my wounded and bound birds,
with hollow flesh, stone-like calluses
between their terrible fists
and painted mouths gagged
in deafening confinement.

I hear them in the field on Labor Day.
What a tumult!
The tired sun reaches its zenith
as the cloud clears and the worn-out dream
erupts in the back and forth of their laughter . . .

They drag themselves through
the furrowed dust of talk
and hooch.
They are the very blood and veins
that run through the river of the world.

They are the wound
that the powerful of the earth inflict.
Yet we never see the decayed reflection
of their guns on these walls.

They are the victims of drugs
who have made millionaires of the "pure ones,"
haunting skeletons of doom
that shine like the gold and copper
stolen from us by the Yanqui colonizers.

I Have All the Passion of Life

I have all the passion of life.
I love the sun and the stars
and the seeds.
Everything fascinates me:
water, brooks, groves,
dew and cascades.

I adore looking at the
flowing streams: this clear
proof of beauty;
this joy in my marrow,

But in the prison now,
a push and a shove is more fitting.
I am a wanderer
in long ago deserts.
Only human, my wounds
ache within my heart,
For I have loved all deeply
and they have no compassion.
Alone, yes, let me be alone . . .
It's not the first time that it is so.
I have been the wanderer
forever without a home . . .

I Have Seen You

I have seen you as I searched
in the shade
of this terrifying and cold silence.
Some furniture falls to pieces . . .
and I'm left with the cell,
bereft of warmth and humor.
Everything is so alone. So disquieting.
Love has gone so far away from my eyes . . .
And there is no chirping from the birds
to make me smile away my sorrow . . .
"I am trembling, compañero,
with painful and exhausting uneasiness!"
My shoulders hurt . . . as if sinking under
the weight of tortured rock.
The hour is dark.
The day silent with a moan
hidden in its great burden.
Even prayer is wounding: in the depths of my entrails
pain tearlessly weeps.
I like forests and gardens.
The waterfalls and their tiny crabs,
their rocks,
their murmurs and bubbles,
their radiant streams,
the thought of their mysteries,
with flowers and plants surrounding them.
Their aromas.
And how I loved the washerwomen,
scrubbing upon the rocks
with a box of bluing at their side.
How they remind me of mama!

Here, jail is like a tempest,
heavy and hard-hearted . . .
A ruin that reeks of death
and unspeakable pain.
It is the white bear's domain.
Keys and blows, headcounts,
injustices and schemes.
Undisclosed tortures
from an unwritable book.
The real story of death,
unwritten, without pages.

BEATRICE SAUBIN

(1959–)

Born in France and abandoned by her mother, Beatrice Saubin was raised in a small town outside Paris by her rather strict grandmother. From her teenage years, she was exploited by men. As a young woman she worked as a secretary, but her real goal was to travel to Asian countries and leave her home behind. Her adventures took her to Penang Island, Malaysia, where twenty-year-old Saubin began an affair with a Chinese man, who arranged to meet her in Europe and marry her. As Saubin tried to leave Malaysia in January 1980, she was arrested at the Penang airport. The authorities found hidden within the lining of a suitcase given to her by her lover half a million dollars worth of heroin—enough to sentence her to death by hanging under Malaysia's harsh drug laws.

The public view in Penang as well as in France was that Saubin, who maintained her innocence, should not hang; she was the first foreigner to be sentenced to death under the law that had led to the execution of thirty drug peddlers to that time. Saubin's grandmother traveled to Malaysia to give her support, and the media publicized her case. Her death sentence was reduced to life imprisonment, but public opinion, the efforts of her supporters, and her good conduct led to her release in 1990 after ten years of incarceration.

While in prison Saubin learned Malaysian and Cantonese, worked in the prison hospital on behalf of prisoners, and formed close relationships with other women prisoners. Upon her release she returned to France and wrote two bestsellers about her prison experience: *L'Epreuve (The Ordeal)* (1991) and *Quand la Porte S'Ouvre* (1995), which has not yet been translated.

Note: Background information is from Beatrice Saubin, *The Ordeal: My Ten Years in a Malaysian Prison*, trans. Barbara Brister (New York: Arcade, 1991); Anna Norris, "Parole Interdite: La Littérature Carcérale Féminine," *The French Review* 71, no. 3 (February 1998); Colin Campbell, "Frenchwoman's Hanging Sentence Stirs Malaysia," *New York Times*, July 10, 1982; UPI, "Malaysia Relents in Narcotics Case," *New York Times*, August 26, 1982; "Frenchwoman Home After 10 Years in Malaysian Prison," *New York Times*, October 7, 1990.

Entering the Prison World

From The Ordeal, *1991.*

Prison—any prison, anywhere—means humiliation, day and night.

Embedded in the enormous portal of Penang Prison is a tiny gate through which the prisoner must pass. As I stooped to cross this threshold of shame, I had to leave my former identity outside. I was hereby annulled, nonexistent—as lowly as an animal, as a pebble on the ground. I had to bow, submit, capitulate, adapt—become the reed that bends.

I entered a vaulted area filled with benches and sealed off by an iron portcullis. Someone rattled a lock and chain and opened the grating. I walked through and found myself in a small, sun-filled prison yard. I had to go through a series of adjoining rooms. I was ordered to sit on a bench across from a long, dark wooden counter. The admitting officer had gone to lunch, so I would have to wait in silence on this bench until he returned. I began to see that waiting is the essence of the East Asian world. Nothing happens right away here.

The admitting officer arrived—a young man with glasses and a visored kepi. He joked with his colleagues. Are they joking about me, I wondered, or are they always like this? In English, he asked my name, address, and age and told me my photos and fingerprints were going to be taken the following morning. Then I waited some more. Seconds, minutes, hours—what difference did it make now? I had no watch, no point of reference. All I knew was that I was locked up. A captive.

Two female guards appeared. Same uniform as the men—a short-sleeved khaki shirt, pants, and a cap with an insignia over the visor. They didn't speak English. They motioned to me to walk ahead of them through another prison yard, walled in by beige buildings with barred windows. We were in the men's section (our itinerary was complicated because only one cellblock at Penang Prison was for women). Suddenly, inmates were clustered at the bars. They whistled, stamped their feet, made lewd noises, shouted vague obscenities.

We came to a very high pale-green wall and still another padlocked door. Had I somehow strayed behind Alice's looking glass? The woman guard rapped three times with a strange little copper knocker mounted on the door. A hatch opened halfway, and two dark eyes peered out. I imagined myself disappearing into some kind of convent of the damned. The door opened, and I climbed three steps to find myself in still another inner yard.

I was shocked to see about fifty women sitting cross-legged like silent statues baking on the cement floor. I wondered in horror if prison in this country meant vegetating under the sun all day without a word—perhaps for years. I soon learned that this was one of four daily musters, when the inmates were called together to be counted.

There was a clicking of heels, followed by men's and women's voices. Suddenly, all the prisoners stood. Confusion erupted as they rushed to and fro in little groups, raising a clamor in various languages.

The two female guards returned in the company of Zuraida, who spoke English and was going to be my interpreter. She was a beautiful Malay who seemed to be barely out of her teens. She was wearing a flowered dress. Like me, she was in custody. She explained that I had to undress and be searched. I was also supposed to bathe now, even though I had nothing to change into. She led me toward *bilik mandi*, the washroom.

Beyond a barred door and brown cloth curtain, my humiliation continued. I stood naked before a woman in uniform. She ordered me to turn around and inspected all my clothes. We were in a coarse-grained cement room with a huge, high-walled cistern in the center. Water flowed into it constantly. The tank was an ugly dirt brown, but the water was clear, and there was no bad smell.

As my clothes were being examined, I shivered in embarrassment and grief. I had to bathe standing up in front of the tank, pouring water over myself with the colored plastic bowls resting on the edge.

As soon as the guard left, the prisoners degenerated into bold-faced voyeurs. They swarmed around me and stared, jabbering away and pointing at my thighs, stomach, hips and breasts. Except for my interpreter, the women were appallingly ugly—fat and vulgar, with teeth missing. A few were walking skeletons with blue lines for veins. There was one midget who seemed swallowed up by her white pajamas, which I gathered were the prison outfit.

Zuraida gave me a set of prison whites and explained that I was going to share her cell. As I put on the ill-cut costume—drawstring waist, pants too short, top too big—the women bombarded her with questions about me. In fright, I withdrew into our cell.

The cell was cement like everything else. It was about two yards by three, with whitewashed walls and a high, small window. How many women had scrubbed this cement? How many had trod this floor? For how many years, and in what states of despondency and terror? Here too my bed was a raised slab. In the corner was our toilet: a black rubber bucket covered with a piece of cardboard.

"You're the girl from the airport," said Zuraida. "We've been expecting you."

How did she know? It hadn't even been twenty-four hours! A wild hope stirred in me: If these blabbermouths all knew about me, how could Eddy not have learned my plight? He would get me out of this.

A plastic cup and spoon now constituted my entire fortune. To see me through till I got my money back, Zuraida lent me a little plastic case holding a bar of soap, a toothbrush, and a tube of toothpaste.

The busybodies chattered nonstop, closing in around me to the point where I could hardly breathe.

"Are you married?"

"Did you really have five kilos?"

"How old are you?"

"Where are you from?"

"Do you have any kids?"

Zuraida translated as fast as they could toss the questions.

I backed up against the wall. Their rabid curiosity deformed their stump-toothed mouths and bloated their anonymous faces. How was I going to escape them?

Whew! Muster rescued me for a few minutes.

Time to be a lump on the floor, packed in with all the others. Time for a new assault on my memory, identity, dignity. Zuraida winked as if to say, "Be patient; this is only the beginning."

Four o'clock. My first dinner.

We were back in our yard, lined up in single file behind a big basket of bread and a pile of green plastic platters with the lids closed. I couldn't help thinking of boarding school at Troyes, even though it was nothing like this. After all, institutions are institutions. Boarding school, convent, psych ward, prison. We received a platter, a piece of bread, a packet of sugar, and a ladleful of tea in a plastic cup.

The guards made sure we each got our fair share.

There was no table or utensils. We sat on the ground again, to eat like dogs.

I opened my platter lid. In the main section were two fish swimming in a burned mixture of fried onions. The two smaller sections held thick, watery chunks of squash in a runny lentil sauce and a little wedge of processed cheese (concession to the Western world). For dessert, an orange.

Zuraida said, "You're lucky, Soabeen. It's the European menu, the best."

I couldn't eat and handed her my dinner. She was delighted. But before she ate it, she said, "You'll get sick if you don't eat. Keep up your strength. You're going to need it." After the meal, they locked us in our cell.

Zuraida sang softly to herself as she got ready for bed. She pulled on some shorts and twisted her soft black hair into a loose knot. She was nineteen. Her Chinese boyfriend was also in custody; the police had found heroin in the house they were renting.

She grinned. "We've been waiting to go to court for a year now."

The news staggered me. "A year! Don't you have a lawyer?"

"Yes, of course we do," she replied in her lilting voice.

I felt suddenly clammy. "They told me I'd be here a week."

Zuraida laughed. "You'll be lucky if you get out in less than three years. Some girls have been here for five. And the three communists have been awaiting trial for eight years now."

"The communists? What did they do?"

"They're communists, that's all. It's a very serious offense. They were caught with explosives. They may be executed."

"You mean women are executed here?"

"Sure, just like the men. By hanging."

And with a pretty little yawn, she turned and nestled peacefully against the wall.

Sleepless night. I couldn't think straight. No, I won't stay here three years or more. I kept telling myself. Eddy will get me out.

I couldn't stop thinking about Grandmother, hoping against hope that no one would tell her yet. How could she bear the shock, the shame? Poor Grandma! Her little girl in prison! She was so fragile, the news could kill her. She could have a heart attack, all because of me! What if these imbeciles sent her some kind of official papers without giving things time to get straightened out?

Tears were streaming down my face. Oh, Grandma! A genuine tenderness welled up in me—filial feelings I'd never known were so strong. I didn't think about how she'd unintentionally thrown me off balance, made me vulnerable, pushed me toward this trap. Tonight I forgave her for everything. Tonight I loved her. I had just one obsession: protect her from this information. Prison would be her scarlet letter of shame.

Near dawn, I began to admit to myself that Eddy was not going to resurface. He belonged to the killer breed of hard-core drug dealers. I was sure he was nowhere near Penang. Singapore, New York, Amsterdam, London? Wherever he was, he was peacefully setting more of his vile traps. Maybe another forlorn and gullible young woman was already surrendering to his calculated kisses—until she too would perish in some bottomless pit. Victim of Eddy's treachery masquerading as love.

I shuddered. Time to come to terms with all this—a lover's betrayal, but far worse than that. Eddy Tan Kim Soo had duped me, conned me, done a major number on me. I wanted the police to nab him. But in the name of the love that he took and I gave, I still could not breathe his name. What information could I give anyway? I wasn't even sure I knew his name. I'd never seen his passport or address. Being so outrageously betrayed had left my self-image in a shambles. I was nothing, nobody . . . just pain. Like the pain Grandmother would feel when she cried herself into exhaustion.

They took my mug shot and fingerprints, treating me like a dangerous criminal. They shuttled me from room to room, shone a huge lamp in my face, photographed me from all angles, turned me into a catalog entry, put me down on file.

The guard who took my fingerprints ended by pressing both my hands onto the blue dye so hard that I winced. "From now on, you are prisoner number 181-80. TMR," he declared.

The ID number felt like a ball and chain. . . .

Third week. One morning a guard hollered my number in Malay at the top of her lungs. A prisoner made me realize she was calling me: 181-80. TMR.

The police were here. My hopes soared. Maybe things were finally going to get straightened out! It was logical for the police to come. Zuraida had told me horror stories about the treatment many women got in police custody after their arrest—interrogations day and night, sleep derivation, beatings or even torture. But my experience had been nothing like that. I'd been questioned courteously in what seemed more like an administrative information-gathering session than an interrogation. I didn't think for a second that the police were here to harm me now. Surely they'd finally found some proof of my innocence. Surely they'd arrested the true culprits: Eddy and his ring.

Two officers were waiting in the front office. As we shook hands, I couldn't help blurting out the question that haunted me constantly: "Now you know who did it, don't you? I can go now?"

They laughed. In this country, laughter signaled hidden danger. Laughter made a refusal polite.

"Not so fast!" they warned. "Take it easy. We are still investigating, but don't worry. Everything's going to be all right. Don't worry. We're here to return your money to you. Your bank in Paris has confirmed that you withdrew it from your account. It will be useful to you here."

They handed the desk officer the envelope holding my thousand and some dollars. He recorded it in an account book, wrote "15 February 1980" beside it, and took my signature and fingerprints.

I was disappointed, of course, but I still had a glimmer of hope. "Don't worry," they'd said. And why return my money if I weren't going to be released soon? You don't give criminals their money back.

The money made practical matters easier. I could finally buy soap, toothpaste, a few little necessities. Pay Zuraida back, stop being dependent on her.

My period came that same day. What a relief! Eddy and I had been too swept away by the chemistry between us to take any precautions. Passion over prudence. In the royal prison of Penang, a woman's period was one more humiliation to bear. Tampons were unheard of, and sanitary pads were banned. Too many women would have thrown them down the three holes that served as our toilets, clogging the pipes. With ninety-five-degree heat day and night, the plumbing problems would have been unbearable, not to mention the cockroaches and rats.

Each month the poorest prisoners—like me, until that day—were doled out two sheets of thick paper similar to the paper used for wrapping packages. They'd rub them together for a long time to soften them. Then they'd tear them into strips and make crude diapers. Often the blood ran out and soaked their prison uniforms anyway.

One day I couldn't help gazing in disgust at a hideous woman, fat and toothless, with blood running down her legs. She read my thoughts, eyed me scornfully, and told me off in crude English. "What the fuck difference does it make? Who sees us here? Where are the men? You look down on me? White girls bleed too! When your time comes to wad paper between your legs, it's me who'll be laughing!"

Her anger upset me. I knew we had to take care of ourselves, preserve our dignity as women. Without men in our lives, our self-pride became all the more essential. Personal hygiene was one of the few sources of dignity allowed us in prison. It could help keep us sane.

I always made sure my hair and skin were clean and my clothes were spotless—never a trace of the blood that reduced us to female livestock for the guards to snicker at. They weren't basically mean, but being cooped up with us brought out the worst in them.

Now that the police had returned my money, I could buy rolls of toilet paper to tide me through the first period in prison. It was far from ideal, but it helped limit the damage to my already-shattered self-image. . . .

WOMEN FACING IMPRISONMENT TOGETHER

From The Ordeal, *1991.*

A few days before Christmas, I heard an uproar in the prison yard. Someone shouted, "*Ada orang putih baru!*" ("A new white woman!").

A tall woman had just come in wearing a flowered skirt and faded pink T-shirt. She had long, dull, tangled, light blond hair. Her pale-blue eyes were in tears. She was obviously in withdrawal—sick, frantic, in shock.

The prisoners swarmed around her. I didn't want to be one more fly buzzing around the fresh meat. I remembered too well how that felt.

The newcomer was Barbara, a thirty-three-year-old Australian. She'd just been arrested at Bayan Lepas airport with sixty grams of heroin in her underpants. She'd spent two nights in jail. The worst thing for her seemed to be the withdrawal sickness. In this respect, our traumas were quite different.

What Barbara was going through—*guian*, they called it—was extremely painful. Cramps, vomiting, diarrhea, hallucinations, slipping into a sort of coma at times. But she had to endure her agony alone. Where we were, there was no such thing as medically managed withdrawal. No intravenous hydration, no medications, no tranquilizers to ease the pain. Baba Khoo[1] just gave Barbara something for her diarrhea and vomiting. The goal was a kind of aversion therapy: make the addict feel disgusted to the point of never wanting to start again. Avoid replacing the illegal drugs with legal ones.

The Asian women somehow managed to go through withdrawal in stoic silence. It seemed harder for a Westerner.

Forced to go cold turkey behind her cell bars, Barbara raised Cain for three nights straight, rattling her cage and yelling, "I want a doctor! Filthy rotten country! An addict is a sick person! I'll die if I don't get some help!"

But people just put her off, saying, "*Nanti, nanti!*" Everyone seemed indifferent. It was a commonplace case of extreme torment.

There was nothing I could do except help spare her the shame of wallowing in her own dirt. I handed her soap, some toilet paper, a comb, cigarettes, and some candies to kill the bilious taste in her mouth. Like me in the beginning, Barbara had nothing. She didn't even have any money, since she'd used it all on drugs.

She was in pain for a week. People who have gone through that experience say they've looked death in the face, and I don't doubt it for a minute.

When she'd gone through the worst of it, she was physically and emotionally exhausted. She needed a lot of cold showers. The prisoners helped hold her, wash her, put her clothes back on, and lock her in again.

I wanted no part of that. I wanted to protect our future relationship and spare her from feeling bad when she saw me later. I didn't want her to associate my face with that period of humiliation, degradation, and temporary insanity.

The top-ranking female officer decided that sharing my cell would be good for Barbara's psychological recovery. She liked the idea of putting two white women together who had similar experiences and cultural backgrounds.

We immediately hit it off, laughing about the way we'd met. Being together broke our solitude. Barbara knew who I was from articles about my trial in an Australian newspaper. She'd done a lot of reading, and she had a rich inner world. Right away we knew we were on the same wavelength, and soon we were exchanging confidences like old friends. Even though we'd had very different childhoods, we'd both felt alone, ashamed, and misunderstood at an early age. We'd both grown up without maternal tenderness and security.

Barbara's mother was a lush. Barbara felt sorry for her, but she was disgusted too. "Once when I was fifteen, I brought a boyfriend home. My mother was on one of her binges, lying in bed with her face all bloated. Well, she got up and tried to seduce him. I thought I'd die!"

Barbara brought laughter back into my life. She'd learned to put her childhood traumas behind her, and now I was learning to laugh about episodes in Romilly that had been tragedies at the time.

Everything and everybody were fair game for our jokes. We could make fun of the guards right out loud, since they didn't understand English. The prisoners and guards would gape at us with bovine stares, obviously wondering what on earth we found so funny about being incarcerated. That made it all the funnier.

"Look at them," I said loudly to Barbara, "they think we're nuts!"

"Maybe that's because we keep laughing like crazy!"

Thanks to Barbara, I was becoming myself again. We'd stay up late talking about everything under the sun. The other women were jealous of our friendship. In prison finding a meaningful relationship with someone was the cure for boredom, the heaviest burden of all. We got along so well that it didn't even bother us to share the same latrine bucket and have no privacy. Sometimes, talking in our cell, we'd feel like characters in a Woody Allen movie. We'd describe concerts we'd been to, or talk about the books we were reading. When we came across passages we thought were especially good—or especially ridiculous—we'd read them aloud to each other. Barbara's voice broke when she talked about Australia, how she loved her country's strange beauty, its vast spaces and desert. Getting busted in Penang was the accident that stopped her short when she'd gone shopping for inexpensive drugs to feed her habit.

Aside from Nicole,[2] who came to see her right away, Barbara also had visits from the Australian High Commission. Her attorney—an Indian, like Kumar—told her she might be in prison for three years.

In February, Noor arrived.

Noor made her entrance during the last muster of the day. After scanning all the girls squatting on the ground, her gaze landed on me. Noor was svelte and androgynous. She had Malay features, short dark hair, full sensual lips, gleaming white teeth, and eyes like deep pools tapering to a slit near the temples. Her hands were slender and elegant, with long curved nails. When Noor looked me over from head to toe, it felt like an invitation. There was something Western about her boldness. Women of her race usually lowered their eyes and didn't look people in the face—especially the first time they met.

Barbara hadn't missed a thing. "Did you see the new girl?" she asked. "I think you caught her eye."

"Well, I must say she caught mine too! The pleasures of the mind are great, but it may be good to think about pleasures of the flesh once in a while, don't you think?"

We laughed. "I've had a few affairs with women myself," she said. "Nature created men and women, so why not enjoy them both?"

"You know, Barbara, it's too bad you and I aren't attracted to each other that way. Can you imagine the nights? The pillow talk we would have?"

"Who's going to score with Noor?" she kidded. "Maybe I'll compete with you! Or maybe she'll turn out to be as dumb as the rest and take up with one of those stupid little bitches. I guess time will tell!"

It turned out my first impression of Noor was right. She was nothing like the herd of mediocrity all around me. Even though she was an addict, it hadn't destroyed her exuberance. She was my age, a cabaret singer who traveled from city to city on her gigs. She had a deep, powerful, entrancing voice. She sang when she felt like singing.

At first muster the next morning, Noor sat near me. We were feeling the call of the senses, and we both knew it without saying a word.

My senses had been dormant ever since Eddy's betrayal. All my urgencies were elsewhere; all my energies were contained. At twenty-three, I wondered what needs and obsessions my body would acquire if I had to spend my whole life in prison. My playful little exchanges with Mok[3] and Baba Khoo just made things worse. I'd learned that in prison, sexuality went haywire like everything else. Intimacy was impossible, and love was reduced to animal impulses.

And now along came Noor. Troubling, unsettling Noor. It all happened very fast.

In the workshop she sat near me again. Our first physical contact came when she tucked a strand of hair back under my barrette. She lightly touched my ear and cheek. They were caresses she didn't even try to hide. I not only let her touch me, but I wished she would do it again.

Close-up, I felt drawn to the shape of her mouth, a mouth that looked gifted in the subtlest of kisses. Already I wanted to be alone with her.

It was lunchtime, but I never ate at noon. I'd have a few cigarettes and a cup of coffee in my cell and use the time to read. Barbara usually ate something out by the workshop, in the sunshine.

I was stretched out on my cement slab with my nose in a book. Suddenly I jumped. Noor was standing there beside me. "You're not eating?" she asked. Her sweeping glance over my outstretched body was eloquent and provocative. It was a defiant look that seemed to say, "Do you dare?"

She sat down next to me. She took the book gently from my hands and leaned down and kissed me. Her eyes never left mine. Her tiny kisses made me yearn to respond with kisses that had no end.

There we were, kissing feverishly on a bed as hard as a rock. It's hard to say which of us was more ardent. In a matter of seconds, we were wild about each other.

Prison constantly separated things. It was soon time for us to go back to the workshop, even though all we could think about was being in each other's arms. We had to endure the torture of brushing against each other all day without being able to consummate our desire.

Barbara laughed. I'd done a disappearing act on her. I was in love.

Love? Noor and I were obsessed with each other. My mood darkened. I hated all forms of dependence. I'd felt so happy and peaceful with Barbara! Now all of a sudden, this explosion! I even regretted that Barbara shared my cell, because otherwise it might have been Noor. In my mind I knew better. But my senses had taken over and blinded me.

Noor got her green collar.[4] She wasn't locked in at four thirty anymore. She could come join me in my cell once the workshop was over. Barbara—so generous an accomplice—would go to another cell so we could be alone.

To get some privacy and soften the harsh light, we would hang our sarongs up like curtains across the bars. Noor was an extraordinary lover. Our caresses became more and more daring. A thousand stars would sparkle beneath my skin, and my head would spin.

In prison, a lot of women had lovers. When they got out, some ended up leaving their husbands and kids to be together again. Malaysian society had religious and cultural taboos against fondling and petting; only penetration was considered acceptable. Malay and Chinese men (except in certain social classes) had no concept of foreplay. They'd just pull up a woman's sarong, enter her, and ejaculate. So a lot of women discovered pleasure with other women. It broke up many relationships that the women were pleased to be out of.

Noor's kisses . . . tender, teasing, knowing, wild, cruel.

I hadn't felt such pleasure since I'd been with Eddy.

We heard some chuckles from behind the sarong curtains, which moved now and then. Someone was watching us, envying us, intruding on us. But we couldn't have cared less. We were on top of the world, all alone in our own world.

Almost a year went by like that—sometimes heaven, sometimes hell. We expressed our passion without blushing, without holding back. We needed each other.

The whole prison knew about our affair. The women guards said to Noor, "You're not ashamed—you, a Muslim—to carry on that way with a *khafir* (infidel)?" Noor's laugh would disconcert the pontificating guards. Mok was amused. Baba Khoo shook his head and decided that this was preferable to the old Valium cures. Tuan Botak[5] looked the other way.

As for me, depression was a thing of the past! I'd embraced life with all its violence, its ecstasy, its madness, its chaos. I had no qualms about Noor and me.

But Barbara felt abandoned. "Barbara," I said, trying to console her, "I'm sorry. But there's nothing I can do. Even if Noor and I have little in common, she's the one I love. I want to be with her day and night."

"Don't feel guilty about it, Bea. Live out your passion. I understand how you need to let loose after the hell you've been through. In that sense, Noor's just what you need—even if she's not always easy to take."

Not always easy, indeed.

Noor was jealous. She hated it when I took the garbage out on the men's side with my sarong hiked up. One day I lingered a little while the guys were whistling. Noor came charging out like an angry bull. She slapped me with all her might, kicked over the smelly garbage bucket, and pulled me onto the ground with her, rolling with me and pounding on me. Watching from behind their bars, the men stamped their feet and yelled, *"Tengoh! tengoh! laki pukul bini!"* ("Look! Look! The husband is beating his wife!")

Noor raised her head in fury and hissed at them in English, "Go and eat yourself!"

We started having more and more fights, alternated with fiery reconciliations on our cement bed.

Noor had given me two tapes of her favorite Malay songs to play on my Walkman. But recently she'd been so nasty to me that I viciously unwound the tapes right in front of her and threw them on the floor. She jumped on me, hit me wherever she could, insulted me, shook me, stepped on me. For every blow she landed, she got one back. I felt like killing her. She felt the same. Our hatred was as intense as our passion.

The guards had to pull us apart.

I was beside myself. I wanted revenge. I went running to have Baba Khoo take inventory of my injuries: the bumps and bruises on my thighs, the scratch on my cheek, my bloody lip. Baba Khoo shook his head and smiled. *"Bila sayang . . . sayang . . . Bila benci benci . . ."* ("When we love we love! But my my, when we hate, how we can hate!")

Baba Khoo counted my wounds and added, at my request, a few that had nothing to do with Noor, like bruises I'd gotten scrubbing gutters. He conscientiously completed his report, which ended up on the desk of—of all people—the Muslim fundamentalist officer who detested us. Noor got a month in solitary confinement. He certainly knew how to punish me. A whole month —no ifs, ands, or buts—without Noor. He probably would have liked to see us whipped and hanged.

We'd never made love as furiously as we did when she got out.

NOTES

1. The prison's nurse, a Chinese man.—*Ed.*

2. A French nun teaching in Malaysia, who had counseled Saubin. —*Ed.*

3. The prison social worker, a young Chinese man.

4. Inmates earned privileges over time, with different colored collars denoting the level of privilege.—*Ed.*

5. The prison director, a Malaysian man.—*Ed.*

JUDEE NORTON

(1949–)

Judee Norton grew up in Arizona farming country, in an environment of "addiction, poverty, low self-esteem" (Chevigny 341). As a child she took on the responsibility of caring for her siblings. She was arrested for drugs and served a five-year sentence from the late 1980s to the early 1990s at the Arizona State Prison Complex in Phoenix and Perryville.

Norton became a writer in prison. Writing, she says, helped her to survive incarceration. She has written poetry and fiction, and has won prizes in the PEN Prison Writing Contest. Two works of fiction received first-place awards: "Summer, 1964" (1988) and "Norton #59900" (1991). She is currently working on "Slick," a larger work of fiction incorporating her award-winning pieces. Norton describes "Slick" as "an account of my experiences in prison, along with some often stark revelations about why and how I came to be there (correspondence 2001). It includes chapters drawing upon her childhood experiences as well as accounts of how she maintained her self-respect in prison and stood up to the administration on environmental and other issues.

Currently Norton lives in a small farm community at the foot of the Catalina Mountains near Tucson, Arizona. In 2001 she gave a reading of her work at the Critical Resistance East Conference on prison issues, held at Columbia University in New York City.

Note: Background information is from correspondence between Judith Scheffler and Judee Norton, 2000–2001; Bell Gale Chevigny, ed., *Doing Time: 25 Years of Prison Writing* (New York: Arcade, 1999); Rochelle Ratner, ed., *Bearing Life: Women's Writings on Childlessness* (New York: Feminist Press, 2000).

GERTA'S STORY

From "Slick," 1992–93

For if he like a madman lived, at least he like a wise one died.
—Miguel de Cervantes

One of the first people to get my attention when I am finally moved onto minimum yard is an old woman who, although it is June and temperatures are frequently in the 90s, appears to be wearing every article of clothing that the state has issued her. She has on a pair of jeans with shorts over them, two or three T-shirts, two chambray work shirts, a wool-lined denim jacket and brown high-top boots. She is so overdressed she can hardly move. Her arms stick out away from her body; her legs will barely bend;

she looks like a little kid dressed for snow by an overprotective mother. She also wears a knitted blue watchcap, pulled down low, so that a fringe of gray hair sticks out every which way from beneath it. Her startlingly blue eyes peer out from the center of the whole mess of clothing like a grand surprise. They are Crayola-blue, the color I remember from my crayon days as "cornflower." Dazzling and splendid, they seem to look everywhere and nowhere, and they are often accompanied by a Mona Lisa smile, as if she knows a sweet little secret.

My new cellie, Bam-Bam, tells me the old woman's name is Gerta, and that everyone calls her "Crazy Gert," for obvious reasons. She tells me that no one is quite sure what Gerta's doing time for, that she's been here as long as anyone can remember, and that there are as many theories about her as there are women on the yard. One story is that she caught her husband in bed with another woman and knifed them both to death. Another that she poisoned her five children in a fit of anger. Another that she killed her landlord in a dispute over the rent. And on and on and on. While Bam-Bam rambles about the myriad possible crimes Crazy Gert could have committed, I wonder briefly whether she was crazy when she committed that crime, or whether many, many years of prison have *made* her crazy. But an old lady who wears all her clothes at once can't hold my attention for long, and Crazy Gert is soon forgotten.

Several days after my move, it is late at night and I am out of my cell past lockdown, having been pulled to mop up a spilled cup of coffee in the captain's office. As my guard/escort and I pass by Gerta's "pod," I hear the most awful screams I have ever heard, wild and tormented. I look up at Brownshirt quizzically. *What's up?*

He shrugs. "Aw, that's just Gert," says he. "They're making her take a shower."

"In what?" I say. "Boiling oil?"

"Nah," he replies, running his tongue over the scraggly ends of his mustache. "She just hates it. We gotta make her take her clothes off, push her in, turn on the water, force her to clean herself. Sometimes on a bad day, we hafta scrub her ourselves. Usually the rookies." He grins. "They hate it." The grin widens, as though he is perhaps remembering a particular rookie who *really* hated it a lot.

It's a pain in the ass," he continues, talkative now with me as captive audience. "She screams bloody murder, tries to fight anyone and everyone; kicks, bites, scratches. . . . It ain't no fun, I can tell you; she's tougher than she looks. Been goin' on for, oh, long as I can remember, and I been here nine years."

"Nine YEARS?" I say, aghast. "For NINE YEARS someone has been forcibly showering her?"

"Well, ya hafta unnerstand," he responds defensively, "we got a health and hygiene code here."

Involuntarily, my eyes dart to his choppy, uneven haircut, oily and dandruff-flecked; his bulbous, greasy nose with its peppering of blackheads; his huge Dumbo-ears sprouting hairs like a summer lawn after a good rain; his ruined mouth, an odorous cavern filled with blackened and rotting stumps.

Apparently, the health and hygiene code is only for US.

Brownshirt hitches his pants up self-importantly and continues, "Hadda shower her m'self once, here 'bout three, four year ago. Quite a hell-cat, she was; like to tore me up before I was through. Ended up usin' a long-handled toilet brush on 'er."

The thought of this badly barbered brute with the big meaty arms using a toilet brush on the delicate, papery, old-lady flesh of Crazy Gert makes me stiffen in horror and my eyes go wide as I look at him in disbelief. He sees or senses my shock, but does not understand it, for he adds defensively, "It was brand new. . . ."

I begin to watch for Crazy Gert on the yard. Part of me wants to ignore her, to pretend that she is just another felon like the rest of us, that she belongs here, aberrations and all, for she has many. Another part of me wants to know her deepest secrets, to find out *why* she is the way she is, and did prison make her slightly mad? Or did her slight madness lead her to prison?

Or does one thing have nothing whatsoever to do with the other?

I watch her every chance I get, and each new episode, far from helping me "figure her out," simply leaves me with more unanswered questions, a bigger mystery.

There is a fly fan over the front door to the chow hall which blows a strong, steady current of air downward, ostensibly to discourage flies from entering. It does not deter flies one whit, but it does wreak havoc with one's hair, and creates a ceaseless and most annoying roar in one's ears. It also causes Crazy Gert no end of consternation.

Three times a day, when meals are announced, Crazy Gert stands outside the chow hall a few feet from the doorway and the offending fly fan, simply staring at it in what seems an agony of indecision. She shifts her weight from one foot to the other like an Olympic sprinter warming up for the hundred-yards. She frowns. She glares. Then, making the commitment at last, she pulls the blue knit cap even lower, lifts her jacket up over her head, and makes a mad dash through the door, her tiny wrinkled face scrunched up in anguish. Having made it through without incident, she lowers the coat and stands trembling for a moment, as though she cannot quite believe she is safe. She shakes herself then, and heads for the front of the serving line, where she simply takes her place in front of whoever happens to be there. She seems to do this not out of rudeness, but rather from a total lack of awareness that anyone else even exists. Rarely does she encounter any resistance. Mostly, these battle-hardened women who will fight anyone for any reason whatsoever, great or small, real or imagined, seem to accept that there is something seriously amiss with Gerta, something that fighting or arguing won't change, and they simply roll their eyes and let her cut in front of them.

Once Gerta has her tray of food, she heads, not for a table, but for a small corner next to the ice machine. She balances her tray on the stainless-steel ledge, and with practiced swiftness, begins dunking all her food in her water glass. She drops the food item in, gives it a quick swirl with her fingers, then scoops it out and pops it in her mouth, rapidly and methodically, like a raccoon washing clams. Everything on her tray goes into the water: peas, wieners, chunks of bun, potato chips. . . . By the time she's finished, her water glass looks like one of those globes you turn over to make it "snow," and she tips it up and drinks the whole thing at once, smacking her lips afterward and grinning foolishly.

Just as I'm starting to think that she is truly one of the oddest ducks I've ever seen, I find myself in the laundry room with her, and witness yet another of her eccentricities.

The laundry room in max yard is intended to serve an inmate population of ninety-six; it holds four washing machines and three dryers, and is only open from 8:00 A.M. until 9:00 P.M. Since standard state issue of clothing is only three pairs of jeans and four T-shirts, ninety-six women are trying to do their laundry twice a week. Some simple math will explain why the laundry room is a place rife with shouting, cursing, threats, and the occasional fistfight. Crazy Gert, marching to the beat of her own private drummer, appears to be completely unaware of the tensions in the laundry room. She comes galumphing in with an odd assortment of clothes to wash, carrying them in her arms in an untidy heap. She dances nervously from one foot to the other, which seems to be her way of showing anxiety, until a washer empties, then she crams everything in, far too much to allow for agitation. She punches the laundry down with vigor, as though it needs to be subdued before it can be washed. Always the ubiquitous jacket goes in, along with several T-shirts, a few pairs of jeans, lots of socks, two or three bras (which look *miles* too big for her), and her sheets. At the beginning of each month, she pours her entire supply of detergent in, enough for about eight loads. For the rest of the month, she will wash with water only, which seems to aggravate her no end; she tries to steal detergent from others, looks in the trash can and shakes empty soap boxes, raises her small fists up to the sky in frustration when there is none. But she never figures out how to use smaller amounts and make the detergent last.

Once the washer is running, she stands like a dutiful sentry next to it, and the instant it shuts off, she restarts it. When it finishes, she starts it yet again, and after that, again. Eventually, someone says, "Yo, Gert, man, you gotta get them clothes up outta there, I need to put mine in." Her blue eyes dart to the face of the speaker, then to her clothing, and she gathers the wet articles up in skinny arms and hugs them protectively while she determines whether there is an empty dryer in which to start them on the next leg of the journey of cleanliness. When they are safely flopping round and round in a dryer, she begins her next vigil, and her next routine of restarting again and again, which ends only when someone else says, "Yo, Gert. . . ."

It is impossible for me to feel nothing in the face of Gerta's oddness. I feel sympathy for her, and pity, and a curious sort of respect, for after all, is she not doing her time in the best of all possible ways? Lost in another, perhaps better place, unheeding of the ugliness of her surroundings? Impervious to the violence and frustration and fear that ebb and flow like a dark tide all around her?

But I am also angry with her for engendering my pity and sympathy, for those are soft and tender things, gentle feelings that cannot be displayed in prison. The soft and tender are eaten alive in here; kindness is always read as weakness. So I join ranks with my peers, pointing out Crazy Gert like an unusual landmark to the newbies, the "fish." I find myself repeating the tales told to me by Bam-Bam, the choice of story depending upon how much I want to impress or depress or horrify the listener. The only thing I know for sure is she's a lifer; anything I add to that is just trim.

Only once during all the time I know her does she truly come to *be* for me, to take on substance, a history, a past filled with the large and small business of living. Crazy Gert flashes me.

I am returning from work, trudging the length of the yard from entrance gate to my pod, and Gerta is sitting on a picnic table facing me. Usually, she stares vacantly into space, her astonishing blue eyes pinned to faraway places. Now she intently watches me approach, and when I am within ten feet of her, she suddenly grins, a gap-toothed, hayseed, Opie-Taylor-kind-of-grin that startles me with the sheer unexpectedness of it, and yanks her coat open wide. Incredibly, she is wearing nothing underneath. I have a fleeting glimpse of her fleshless chest, pale and freckled, with two tired flaps of empty skin adorned with large, brown, protruding nipples, the kind that come from having one child or another ceaselessly hanging from the breasts for most of one's childbearing years. Unbidden, an image comes to me of Crazy Gert as a mother, as a smiling young girl, tenderly cradling an azure-eyed infant, and the image infuses me with an unspeakable sense of shame, as though I am responsible, somehow, for the evolution of that radiant young mother into the thing which appears before me now.

Before I can grasp this curious swirl of guilt, Crazy Gert pulls her coat closed and leaps lightly from the table and scampers away, her skinny bowlegs pumping furiously. She disappears into her cell like a rabbit down a hole, as I blink uncomprehendingly in the bright sun.

I will not catch Crazy Gert's attention again. But she will have mine, one last time. On a cool fall morning, one that reminds me of crisp apples and woodsmoke, of scratchy wool sweaters and the smell of brand-new school books, Crazy Gert dies in this prison, giving a final and inarguable definition to the term "lifer." It is an uneventful, old person's death that claims her, a common heart attack. Butch is the first to discover her, and I the first to find them both, on the concrete walkway just outside Gerta's spartan cell.

Butch is sitting cross-legged, her blue prison-issue dress stretched tightly over her great trunk-like thighs, spread wide to make a nest for Crazy Gert's tiny, naked frailness. Butch cradles her like a baby, rocking and crooning small, comforting noises, her round, chocolate-pudding face crumpled by grief, her tears dripping onto Crazy Gert's bare head.

I have never seen Gerta without her blue cap; she is nearly bald, has only thin wisps of gray hair sticking straight up all over, scalp showing pinkly through, like a dog with a bad case of mange.

I kneel next to them, thinking wildly that I should have paid more attention in CPR class, and was it four heart-pumps then ten breaths or ten heart-pumps then four breaths or something else altogether?

"Can I help?" I whisper urgently.

And stupidly and needlessly, for Crazy Gert is clearly quite dead. I do not know how I know this, having never seen anyone dead except my granny and grandpa, prim and completely unrecognizable in their sterile, frilly coffins, but the scene before me has the unmistakable air of finality about it.

Butch shakes her head at me and grips Gerta's body fiercely, tighter. Her obsidian eyes glitter in their twin pools of tears, and stare off into some personal distance I cannot see. I simply kneel there, paralyzed by a feeling of utter helplessness and stricken by a profound sense of loss and a nameless sorrow.

If Crazy Gert looked fragile and small in life, she seems almost doll-like in death. Her matchstick legs are folded up to her sunken chest, her slight arms crossed and pulled up so that the palms of her hands nearly cup the opposite ears. And on the forearm nearest me, I see something which brings me closer. A tattoo? Yes. A tattoo, six or seven or maybe even eight digits that could be a hundred, so overwhelming are they on that puny arm with its long-fingered delicacy. The significance of this ugly mark is knocking loudly at the door of my awareness and I try to ignore it, to think wildly, in rapid-fire succession of *other* reasons there might be a number tattooed on this pitiful old woman's arm. But the knock of truth is loud and insistent, and will not be denied. The thick blue numerals marching in a clumsy row down the inside of this bony little arm are an obscene and inarguable testament to horrors I have only read about.

An awareness too large to contain suddenly springs from me, like Athena from the brow of Zeus, fully formed and perfect, irrefutable. Suddenly the *reason* for Crazy Gert's fears and phobias, her eccentricities and oddities— of showers, of air blowing down on her head, of being unprotected and vulnerable, of being contaminated, of unclean food—are as obvious and as vivid as the sun. Every bizarre behavior, every odd mannerism, each act of Crazy Gert's that I laughed at or pitied or tried to ignore or wrinkled my nose in distaste at, becomes utterly logical in this one epiphany.

Maybe everything makes sense if you wait long enough.

Maybe not.

Kneeling there beside Butch and Gerta, I become aware of the foremost sound generated by prison emergencies: the loudspeakers.

"CODE RED! CODE RED! LOCKDOWN! TO YOUR ROOMS IMMEDIATELY! THIS IS A CODE RED LOCKDOWN! CODE RED!"

I hear running feet, raised voices, slamming cell doors, electronic locks engaging, KA-THUNK, KA-THUNK, KA-THUNK. And underneath it all, I hear

Butch's raspy old dyke's voice, so often raised in threat of violence, reprisal, or lewd pronouncement, now soft and low, comforting, thick with sorrow and loss. "No mo', baby," she whispers, rocking, rocking. "No mo'."

No more what? No more prison? Pain? War?

"No mo' showers, baby, nevah no mo'. No showers in heaven baby, I swear to you. No showers. No showers." She chants it like a prayer, a litany, rocking and rocking the dead Gerta. Then she takes a deep breath and looks up, where the first stars are starting to show themselves off, preening in the deep blue Arizona summer sky, and growls fiercely, "No *showers*, you hear me? No damn motherfucker *showers*! No showers! No showers . . ." and her voice trails off and is choked silent with weeping.

I hear the heavy slap-slap of leather cop shoes approaching us on the walkway, and I know that they are coming to get us, that we are in deep trouble for being out of our cells during a code red lockdown. In the few seconds before they arrive to cuff us both, I have time to say the only thing I think can matter now.

"Butch," I whisper.

She turns to look at me with mild surprise, as though she has forgotten I was there, or perhaps never knew.

"There won't be," I say, and reach down and touch the blue numbers on Gerta's cold arm. "There won't be showers in heaven. I'm sure of it."

Then I look heavenward, just as the guards arrive, wide-eyed, panting, radios squawking, handcuffs at the ready, look straight up into God's face and say softly, "Please."

SLICK AND THE BEANSTALK

From "Slick," 1992–93

The giant vat of beans bubbles and boils beneath me, as I, standing on a small step-stool, stir the great mass with an oar-sized spatula. I have wrung every shred of pleasure possible from the repetition of the famous quotation from of Shakespeare's three witches: "Double, double toil and *trouble*!" I shriek, knowing that I can't be heard by a supervisor over the noise of the bustling kitchen. I spin around sharply to cast my rendition of an evil eye upon my nearest coworker.

"Fire, burn; and cauldron, *bubble*!" I shout, spinning the other way, waggling my eyebrows Groucho-Marx-style, for some reason, and producing what I hope is cackling laughter. I brandish the stirring paddle, but do so with cautious, nonthreatening movements that cannot be misinterpreted. I suspect that I look more like a demented fisherman than a wicked witch.

They all look at me as though I have clearly lost my mind, and I briefly wonder whether crazy people *know* they're crazy, and whether insanity happens suddenly, like a heart attack, or if it sneaks up on you, like cancer. I have never been able to remember much past the first couple of lines of the incantation, so I make up the rest: "Eye of newt and blood of TOAD, do what I say or hit the ROAD!"

Having worn out that particular form of temporary mental escape, I simply stare into the cauldron, glassy-eyed, sweaty, tired; staring as though perhaps I may see my future there, like a gypsy fortune-teller reading tea leaves. What I see, though, is beans. Beans, beans, and more beans.

I let my mind wander, trying to escape the beans, but they are powerful and inescapable; they rule my thoughts. A small seed of memory begins to germinate on this day. It is bean-related, yes, but is so very different from these hated beans before me now with their ceaseless demands for sorting, washing, rinsing, soaking, boiling, stirring, salting, tasting, and then . . . *eating*.

My memory quite clearly shows me myself at six years of age, requesting and receiving from my mother a tiny, raw pinto bean with its peculiar markings that reminded me of a tiny little cow. I see myself taking the bean and putting it gently between sheets of toilet paper, dampening the sheets carefully and lovingly, and then sitting down to watch. I remember being propelled into bed that night by dint of much shouting and pulling of hair, as I did not want to end my reverent vigil over MY BEAN. My teacher had said, "Then watch and see what happens," and, by god, it was watch I would. Perhaps this wondrous thing would not happen if I failed to watch. Perhaps it was a once-in-a-lifetime occurrence, like Halley's comet, and I would miss it forever if I were not watchful. My obsession with MY BEAN was powerful; it filled my daytime thoughts to overflowing, no room for arithmetic or spelling or playground swings and slides. It commandeered my nights, where it grew to mind-boggling heights and took on magical properties, chief among which was providing me an escape route straight up to heaven. Everything in my small world became insignificant; there was only MY BEAN.

In a very short time, which seemed an eternity in the light of my childish exuberance, my bean rewarded me with a stunning performance. Almost before my eyes, it swelled up to nearly twice its size, as though it was holding its breath as I held mine, and then split open, exhaling a tiny white tendril which groped tentatively toward the light.

So excited I could barely speak, I reported to my teacher that the incredible thing had happened, the bean had blown up. She smiled indulgently at me and instructed further: put the bean in a cup of wet dirt, not too deep, put it on a windowsill where the sun shines, keep the dirt damp, and watch for more wonders.

I followed the instructions faithfully, and again my bean delighted me with new tricks. The tiny white tendril lifted itself above the dirt gracefully, carrying the split-apart bean with it, like a lady rising from a deep curtsy in spite of the very large, cumbersome hat on her head. Soon two teensy green leaves appeared, and grew and grew and became four leaves, which became six, which became the very center of my world. My love of gardening, the pleasure I get from feeling the warm soil of Mother Earth between my fingers, my unabashed delight at the extraordinariness of the ordinary processes of green growing things, were born in that bean. To this day, a leaf can enchant me, a flower mesmerizes, a sprouting vegetable brings me to my knees in awe and gratitude to the nameless Force that engineers these small miracles.

I wipe my sweaty forehead on the back of my hand and decide, with the absolute conviction of that six-year-old, that I need, very much, the wonder of a growing bean in my life again. I look around to make sure I have no one's attention, then stroll casually to the pallet stacked with hundred-pound bags of beans. Pretending to be reading the labels, or looking for a particular bag, I use the edge of a can lid to cut a small slit in the corner of one of the bags. With another furtive look around, I slip a bean out through the opening and push it down into my sock. As I return to my post over the boiling vat of beans, with stomach rolling and limbs twitching, I offer a fervent prayer to the Great Strip-Search Goddess, that She will be taking a nap when I return from work, that the officers will simply perform the cursory pat-down of my body. If the officer in charge of transporting us back to our cells decided, on a whim, to do one of the full body-searches that we so despised, I was doomed.

For the rest of my shift, I am as nervous as a long-tailed cat in a room full of rocking chairs. The bean feels like a boulder in my shoe, and I am sure that everyone can see it, that every whispered conversation is a plot to expose me, the crazy fucking white chick, with MY BEAN. When a friend taps me on the shoulder, I nearly topple senselessly to the floor out of sheer fright. I have never been a thief and now I know why: my wild-eyed jumpiness would give me away at once.

My luck holds, and as we line up after work for readmittance to the yard, the bored CO[1] simply runs her hands swiftly over my body, makes me shake out my hair, but does *not* make me take off my shoes and socks.

Hallelujah.

At last I am safely in my cell, alone with the purloined bean. My relief quickly becomes anxiety. Where will I hide it? Will my cellie snitch? How serious an infraction is it if I am caught? *What was I thinking?!?* I turn to my P and P, *Policies and Procedures Manual.* The subsection dealing with "cultivation of plants, roots, seeds, berries, herbs and other vegetation and/or flora" is so murky and bogged down in legalese that I finally determine it does not, cannot, apply to my bean. My bean, I decide, is *food.*

Thus reassured, I repeat the steps I took 35 years ago, when I held an identical miracle in my chubby, dirty, six-year-old hands. I put it on damp sheets of toilet paper, cover it with more damp sheets, and sit down to watch it grow. I decide finally that no hiding place is truly safe. When they do room "shakedowns," nothing is sacred, and I reason that if the bean not really *hidden*, it will look better for my avowed innocence when it is discovered, as, in my heart of hearts, I am sure it will be. So I place it in the same spot as so long ago, the windowsill. My window now is only seven inches wide and its thick, yellowing glass is embedded with wire mesh. It is countersunk into ten inches of steel-reinforced block wall, and has iron bars outside it that tiger-stripe my face when I peer out. But like the earlier one, it catches the morning sun, and is protected from the wind, and will serve. I go to bed smiling.

I am almost embarrassed at the amount of joy I receive from my bean. I check it every morning before leaving for work, and sprinkle fresh water on the toilet paper. I fairly dance through my days in the dreaded kitchen, whistling or singing to myself softly while I wield my oar on the bubbling pots of beans. Even those never-ending pots of beans have taken on new meaning: there, but for the grace of me, goes my bean. I fly back to my cell in the evenings, my heart in my mouth, wondering if it has been found while I was gone, grinning foolishly when I find it safe in its niche, behind a casual arrangement of books, writing tablets, and a box of Wheat Thins.

In perfect synchronicity, the bean and the Creator repeat the miracle for me; the bean wrinkles and swells, splits in half, and sends a small pale shoot out bravely toward the light. I wash out an empty yogurt container and, under cover of darkness while pretending to tie my shoe, fill it quickly with dirt from the yard. With my pencil, I poke a perfect hole one inch deep in the damp soil, drop in the bean and whisper a fervent prayer: please-let-it-grow-oh-please—and return it to the windowsill.

Just as the saucer-eyed child of so long ago was not disappointed, so is the jaded and weary woman I have become to be enchanted by a tiny bean. It flourishes under my loving care. On a rare day off, I sit and stare at it for nearly the entire day, and am rewarded for my patience when I see the dirt clod, which sits atop the rising plant like a small brown yarmulke, actually drop off because the bean rears it little head boldly to a level that will no longer support the clump of dirt. Oh, what a sight! *It's actually growing right before my eyes!* I exult silently. That bean, it cannot be said enough, *makes me happy.*

As I have known in my heart all along that it must, the day comes when I step into my cell and find the whole place topsy-turvy, everything on the floor, my bedding stripped, my personal papers and letters confiscated, and yes—my bean plant gone. Before I can marshal my wits, I hear the hated loudspeakers: "NORTON, FIVE-NINE-NINE-ZERO-ZERO, REPORT TO THE CAPTAIN'S OFFICE IMMEDIATELY!"

Aw, shit. . . .

On my way to the captain's quarters, I rehearse my perfectly sane and logical arguments. I pull from memory everything I read in the P and P manual, and am pleased with the sound of my planned defense. By the time I arrive at the office door, I am quite composed. How hopelessly naive and foolish I am, even after nearly two years of prison.

I face my accuser unafraid, and when I respond to her question, "Do you have an explanation for *this?*" I am impressed by the calm sound of my own voice. I use a perfectly modulated, rational tone as I explain that I am sure the "cultivation clause" in Policies and Procedures is meant to halt and/or punish the growing of marijuana, or other mind-altering organic substances, for it mentions seeds and the harvesting of leaves or stems or blooms for illicit use, and blah, blah, blah. The captain nods her agreement to everything I say, then astounds me by replying, "Norton, that's all well and good, but your write-up isn't for cultivation. My officers recognized that this—" she waves her hand in the direction of my beloved bean plant, crumpled and bruised inside a plastic garbage bag, the soil torn from its roots, its once-lovely broad green leaves mashed and bleeding, "—is not marijuana. Your write-up is for altering food. That's a major."

I blink once, uncomprehending. *Altering food? Altering food?! What the fuck is* ALTERING FOOD*?!"*

"It's a class-two infraction," she continues, "section four, subsection A, paragraphs 2 and 3. Sign here." She pushes the quadruplicate form across the desk toward me. "Press hard," she says with a grin, "you're making three copies."

I pull the form toward me in a daze, my mind still scrabbling frantically with the heretofore unheard-of concept of ALTERING FOOD. Insane and unwise responses are bouncing around in my head like a pinball machine in hyper-drive: *What about when I* COOK *the damn things every day in the kitchen? That's altering food, too, right? And when I* EAT *them, they are* REALLY *altered, eh?? How about* THAT*??!? And hey, let's not forget, when I* DIGEST *them, I literally turn them to* SHIT*, don't I? Hell, I've been getting away with* MURDER *here!! I've been altering food left and right!! You'll never take me alive, bahahaha!*

When the lunatic voice in my head (which clearly does not have my best interests at heart) quiets at last, I am left with the bare facts, and they are these: I have just been issued a major write-up, the kind a disciplinary committee will "hear" before recommending suitable punishment, which can include up to ninety days in the "hole," loss of visitation privileges, room restriction, loss of recreation and inmate canteen privileges, loss of "good time" credits, and reclassification to a higher security level, for . . . altering food. For growing a bean.

Oh god.

I cannot stand it. I begin to laugh. There is a grown woman wearing a badge and a censorious frown sitting across from me, demanding my signature on a lengthy, official, press-hard-you're-making-three-copies form; there is a whole contingent of important people with earnest faces waiting to put me on trial, to hear evidence of my crime, to mete out appropriate punishment, because I GREW A BEAN. The situation appears to me at once so tragic and so hysterically funny that I garner yet another write-up before I leave the captain's office: a class-six infraction of section 2, subsection B, paragraph 1, "Refusal to obey a direct order." Her Highness, Her Royalship, O Captain! My Captain! has demanded that I stop laughing.

And I cannot, simply cannot, by all the powers that be, I cannot. Stop. Laughing.

The disciplinary committee finds me guilty even though I do not laugh once during the solemn proceedings. Instead, I look with sorrow at my bedraggled and crumpled bean plant, brown and sere now, which sits on an evidence table with a tag that proclaims it "DOC Exhibit #1." I wonder idly why my accomplices, my socks and the sharp can lid, are not displayed also. Maybe the notebooks and Wheat Thins which hid the felonious bean plant should be my codefendants, for aiding and abetting, and the yogurt cup for sheltering, the sun for contributing, God for conspiracy. . . .

My sentence is three days in the hole. I lose my coveted forty-cents-per-hour job in the kitchen for "breach of trust." They trusted me with the beans, and I stole one. I am back at the beginner's job, the one that all the "fish" get assigned to: yard crew.

Hah-Hah! The joke is on THEM! Now I'm around plants ALL DAY LONG! Granted, they do not have the style and character, the charm and grace of my bean plant, but they are green, with their roots entwined in the dark and fragrant earth, and they bring me the memory of my bean the way a song can bring the memory of a summer night. With each stroke of rake or hoe, I vow to never forget my bean, to love it always, to remember the joy it brought me.

As I pull weeds and move rocks and dig holes and sweep dirt in the hot sun for fifteen cents an hour, I make promises to myself: When I get out, I shall grow all the beans a person could ever want. I shall grow acres and acres of beautiful beans as far as the eye can see. I shall travel, like Johnny Appleseed, and sow beanseed wherever I roam. I shall end world hunger and unite the world in a Brotherhood of Beans!

I shall grow beans.

I shall grow.

I shall.

NOTE

1. Correctional officer.

PART 5

‘NO PERSON AND NO FAMILY EXISTS IN ISOLATION’:

FAMILY RELATIONSHIPS AND MOTHERHOOD IN PRISON

[I]f there are prisons, they ought to be in the neighborhood, near a subway—
not way out in distant suburbs, where families have to take cars, buses, fer-
ries, trains, and the population that considers itself innocent forgets, denies,
chooses to never know that there is a whole huge country of the bad and the
unlucky and the self-hurters, a country with a population greater than that
of many nations in our world. —Grace Paley

Then I managed to have the child allowed to stay with me in prison. And at
once I grew well again, relieved of the strain and anguish for him. And sud-
denly the prison became a palace to me, where I would rather be than any-
where. —Saint Perpetua

For an imprisoned mother, the disrupted relationship with her child is the
most powerfully destructive effect of her punishment. Individual circumstances differ. Some mothers, separated from nearly grown or adolescent
children, live in a vacuum of information about those who need the support of an adult's love. Their communication with those children all but
ends. The mother who gives birth while incarcerated endures the incom-
parable pain of almost immediate separation from a nursing infant she may
never come to know at all. In a variety of languages, from nations around
the world, imprisoned women have turned to writing to express their pain
and assuage their feelings of loss.[1] Writing offers incarcerated mothers a
means to endure a critical loss, and, for some, it is even a path to a sort of
empowerment.[2]

Although men comprise the vast majority of prisoners in American
prisons, the number of incarcerated women has been growing at a much
higher rate.[3] Important differences distinguish the trauma of incarceration
experienced by men and by women. Because three-fourths of imprisoned
women are mothers of minor children who resided with them until their
arrest,[4] these women endure a double punishment, born of the necessity to

e childcare arrangements from behind prison walls. Most children
red for by the woman's parents or relatives rather than by the father
oster parents.[5] While women prisoners face added stresses, in compar-
on with male prisoners, women's shared loss of family relationships may
lead to their mutual support.[6]

Childbirth in prison is at best a problem and at worst a scandal.
Inadequate medical care, particularly gynecological care, is a common
complaint among women in jails and prisons, and prisoners often receive
poor treatment during pregnancy and face a lonely, even frightening deliv-
ery. Women are taken to special wards of community hospitals to deliver,
since prisons do not have adequate facilities. Some prisoners claim, however, that they are not allowed to breast-feed or even to see their babies,
and that they often receive inhumane treatment under the guise of "security measures"[7] A few prisons provide facilities for incarcerated women to
keep their infants in the institution.[8]

The remote, often rural, location of women's prisons compounds the
problems of separation by making it virtually impossible for children and
other family members to visit, especially if the woman is poor and comes
from the city. Imprisoned in New York City in the 1960s for political
protest, the writer Grace Paley, who is quoted at the opening of this section, has noted the importance of a prison's proximity to the homes of the
women incarcerated there.

The atmosphere for visits in most prisons is far from ideal: the fre-
quency and duration of visits are restricted, and mothers may not always
hold their children. A few states have apartments available for conjugal
and family visits with selected prisoners, but these are by far the exception.[9] The problem continues after the sentence ends. Upon their release
from prison, most women must return to families with whom they have
lost contact but whom they need for emotional support to readjust to life
on the outside. A difficult reunion with her children consequently compounds the challenges of reentry for many women prisoners.

Some of the most deeply affecting scenes in international prison literature describe women's strained visits with their disrupted families. In her
study of what she calls the "family separation paradigm," sociologist Paula
Dressel notes the barriers to visitation in many facilities in the United
States; visits may even be used as a method of control and discipline, with
restrictions imposed for infraction of rules.[10] American political prisoner
Assata Shakur, currently living in exile in Cuba, describes in this section the
anger of four-year-old Kakuya, for whom prison rules pale beside the frustrating reality of her mother's physical absence from her life. With simple
dignity Shakur relives the intense, emotional meeting of grandmother/care-
giver, imprisoned daughter, and uncomprehending, adamant toddler. To
endure their unendurable separation, emblematic of a much broader racial
injustice, Shakur finds strength in female bonding with her own mother
and grandmother, who cautions her, "Don't you let yourself get used to it."[11]
Eritrean political prisoner Abeba Tesfagiorgis replicates Shakur's scene,

echoing the same pain and frustration with unnatural barriers to familial affection. Her scene, like Shakur's, moves from the personal to the political, from an account of one divided family to a testimony to the many families who need support and healing. With human rights as her goal, Tesfagiorgis looks forward to a time when all families will live decently and she may truly consider even her young Ethiopian guard as her "son."[12]

Concern about children and families permeates women's prison writing, causing it to differ strikingly from works written by male prisoners. An attorney for the National Women's Law Center reports, "When men get arrested, they ask for a lawyer. When women get arrested, they ask about their children."[13] Whether or not the author is a mother herself, the power inherent in maternal themes fosters creativity that is not extinguished by institutional bureaucracy. "My poetry has . . . been a way for me to express feelings of loss and shame and hope as a mother in prison, and my growing sense of remorse for the terrible losses I have caused others by my crime," says Judith Clark, a long-term political prisoner at Bedford Hills, in discussing the importance of poetry and collective writing workshops in her life. "I don't think I'm exaggerating when I say that the workshop has played a role in my reclaiming myself and my humanity."[14]

Writing serves some women prisoners as a connection with their children—a route to conversation, if only in imagination. The power of language frees the poet to transcend prison walls, address her absent child, and converse. Often the subject is their relationship itself, and the words are filled with quiet longing. "Today I cast off the lines/imprisoning my dreams/and I arrive at your golden/sun-drenched shore," writes poet Alicia Partnoy to her daughter, Ruth, in this section.[15] Partnoy, who was one of Argentina's "disappeared" political prisoners, cannot recall Ruth's face, and this simple evidence of the violated mother-daughter bond symbolizes the larger trauma of those imprisoned unjustly. Partnoy's writing, like that of the Chilean women in part 2, expresses pain on both an individual and a collective level as she testifies for tortured parents who will never return to their lost families.[16]

Those who study the effects of incarceration on women describe the grief response of imprisoned mothers and note that their coping skills are severely challenged. The very fact of imprisonment impedes a prisoner's ability to work through the grief caused by her confinement and isolation from family. The impulse to hide emotions and feign invulnerability while in prison inhibits a mother's adjustment to the separation, which is so critical to her child's own adjustment.[17] Conflicting images defining imprisoned mothers exacerbate this pain.[18] A woman's criminal activity leads to her separation from her children and defines her as soon as she enters the criminal justice system. Not only does her identity as a mother become secondary; her very fitness for motherhood is compromised.[19] "Good" mothers place their children first in their lives and do not abandon them, as women obviously do when they enter prison. They are thus considered guilty of breaking laws as well as unwritten rules regulating appropriate conduct by women.[20]

Ironically, the enforced separation of prison may deepen a mother's interest in her children's lives and increase the maturity of her parenting, particularly in cases of substance abuse.[21] Precious Bedell was imprisoned for nineteen years in Bedford Hills for the death of her toddler daughter from child abuse. Bedell, who had a history of drug use, achieved educational goals and made extraordinary contributions to her imprisoned sisters during her incarceration. In particular, she worked with prison mothers on parenting skills. Her poem "Death Train" reveals the trauma she knew and recognized in those around her. "Pieces," her play about a prison mother's desperate attempt to retain custody of her children, which is excerpted in this section, explores the complex question of fitness and parental rights, and sets the background against which readers experience the grief of one imprisoned mother.[22]

The Civil War diary of Confederate blockade-runner Catherine Virginia Baxley tells the poignant story of a woman's battle against formidable stress when she faces the permanent loss of the major relationship in her life. Readers witness the process of grief, heightened by this mother's confinement in the relentless prison heat. Baxley's story underscores the essential role of relationships and mutual support in a woman prisoner's life. Officials at the Old Capitol Prison in Washington called Baxley "the most defiant and outrageous of all the female prisoners."[23] Her unpunctuated and almost indecipherable diary reveals the inner turmoil that found release as she harassed her jailers. In a gruesome coincidence of fates, Baxley watched as her son, a wounded seventeen-year-old Confederate soldier, was carried into the prison where she was passing the sweltering spring days. Baxley swore that the young man, who had contracted typhoid, was being fed improperly, and she was so vociferous in her complaints that officials finally denied her access to the prison hospital. Baxley's son was attended by another female prisoner, Mary Surratt, who had been condemned to death and was awaiting execution for complicity in the assassination of President Lincoln.[24] Surratt ministered to wounded prisoners, including the Baxley boy, whom she held as he lay dying. Questions of guilt or innocence aside, this historical example illustrates how maternal concerns may operate on two levels for female prisoners. While separation from children distresses mothers, the support offered by their imprisoned sisters may help women in both positions to look beyond sordid and soul-destroying spaces and hope for something better, if not directly for themselves.

When they write about family, women prisoners reach the deepest and most heartfelt level, probing ethical questions that the criminal justice system rarely accepts as relevant or worthwhile. What are alternatives to the imprisonment of mothers accused of nonviolent crimes—the vast majority of imprisoned women?[25] What is the price to the public, in dollars, but more importantly, in adverse social consequences, of perpetuating the cycle of crime by separating thousands of children from their mothers? When these issues are not adequately addressed, they fuel the writing of those women prisoners inclined toward action and solidarity.

NOTES

The quotation in the title of this section is taken from Abeba Tesfagiorgis, *A Painful Season and a Stubborn Hope: The Odyssey of an Eritrean Mother* (Lawrenceville, N. J.: Red Sea Press, 1992), 114. The first epigraph to this section is taken from Grace Paley, "Six Days: Some Rememberings," in *Just as I Thought* (New York: Farrar Straus Giroux, 1998), 30. The second epigraph is taken from "Saint Perpetua's Passion," trans. Peter Dronke, *Women Writers of the Middle Ages* (Cambridge, Eng.: Cambridge University Press, 1984), 2.

1. Jane Evelyn Atwood, in her study of international women's prisons, comments, "Every woman told me that the worst thing for her about being locked up was the separation from the people she loved—especially her children." *Too Much Time: Women in Prison* (London: Phaidon, 2000), 13.

2. Other selections in this anthology that illustrate women prisoners' writing about family relationships and motherhood include writings by Roland, Perpetua, and Chilean women.

3. Allen J. Beck, *Bureau of Justice Statistics Bulletin: Prison and Jail Inmates at Midyear 1999*. Dept. of Justice, April 2000, 4. Also see Department of Justice 1995, as quoted in Susan Phillips and Nancy Harm, "Women Prisoners: A Contextual Framework," *Women & Therapy* 20: 4 (1997): 1–9.

4. Meda Chesney-Lind, *The Female Offender: Girls, Women, and Crime* (Thousand Oaks, Calif: Sage, 1997), 158.

5. See Paula Dressel et al., "Mothers behind Bars," *Corrections Today* 60, no. 7 (December 1998): 90ff.

6. See Kathy Boudin, "Lessons from a Mother's Program in Prison: A Psychosocial Approach Supports Women and Their Children," in *Breaking the Rules: Women in Prison and Feminist Therapy*, ed. Judy Harden and Marcia Hill (New York: Harrington Park Press, 1998), 103–25. See also Ellen Barry, founding director of Legal Services for Prisoners with Children in San Francisco, who explains, "Whether mothers or not, the majority of women in prison place particular emphasis on their connection to their families and communities. Women inside have a tendency to support each other—through difficult pregnancies, battles with cancer or AIDS, bad news from home, crises with children or other loved ones, or deaths in the family. Some people point out that women often "compete" with one another, frequently over men. Others contend that women in prison don't organize or come together in the way male prisoners do, that they do not resist and protest as often as men, and that they are not as 'political' as men. Even if these generalizations were true several decades ago, I would argue that these observations are largely out of date and do not accurately describe the behavior of many of the women who are incarcerated currently, or were formerly incarcerated." *Social Justice* 27, no. 3 (2000): 168–75.

7. Juanita Reedy's "Diary of a Prison Birth," *Majority Report* 5, no. 2 (31 May 1975): 1, 3, presents a graphic account of her poor medical treatment during childbirth while she was incarcerated. See also Warnice R., "Giving Birth in Prison," *Breaking Silence: Voices of Mothers in Prison* (Brooklyn, N. Y.: JusticeWorks Community, 1999) 46–47. See also Assata Shakur's account of her childbirth experience in *Assata: An Autobiography* (Chicago: Lawrence Hill, 1987).

8. Bedford Hills Nursery offers a model program for mothers to continue their involvement in their children's lives. See Elaine Lord, "A Prison Superintendent's Perspective on Women in Prison," *Prison Journal* 75, no. 2 (June 1995): 257ff, and Judith Clark, "The Impact of the Prison Environment on Mothers," *Prison Journal* 75, no. 3 (September 1995): 306ff. See also Tara Gray and G. Larry Mays, "Inmate Needs and Programming in Exclusively Women's Jails," *Prison Journal* 75, no. 2 (June 1995): 186ff.

9. Caesarina Kona Makhoere in her memoirs of her imprisonment in South Africa under apartheid, discusses a reversal of this point of view. She notes that the children of some black common-law prisoners lived with their mothers in prison and suffered from this experience: "Their future was being destroyed inside the prison walls." The children of white common-law prisoners, on the other hand, were raised outside the prison to protect them from psychological harm. *No Child's Play: In Prison Under Apartheid* (London: The Women's Press, 1988), 39.

10. See Paula Dressel et al., "Mothers behind Bars," 90ff. Judee Norton's short story, "Norton #59900," in *Bearing Life: Women's Writing on Childlessness*, ed. Rochelle Ratner (New York: Feminist Press, 2000), presents a vivid example of the use of visitation restrictions as a method of discipline in American prisons. For a discussion of visitation programs, see Zoann K. Snyder-Joy and Teresa A. Carlo, "Parenting through Prison Walls: Incarcerated Mothers and Children's Visitation Programs," in *Crime Control and Women: Feminist Implications of Criminal Justice Policy*, ed. Susan L. Miller (Thousand Oaks, Calif.: Sage, 1998), 130–50. Rini Bartlett discusses a positive program in "Helping Inmate Moms Keep in Touch—Prison Programs Encourage Ties with Children," *Corrections Today* 62, no. 7 (December 2000) 102ff.

11. Shakur, *Assata: An Autobiography*, 262.

12. Caesarina Kona Makhoere's prison memoirs describe a variation of the same scene: "My Mum came with my son; he was then six. They refused me permission to see my own son. . . . In the meantime my son was singing in the other room. My Mum asked, 'Can you hear his voice?' That small voice was so near and yet so far. I could not take it. My heart was so sore, the pain was so severe. Apartheid, how I hate you, you must be crushed once and for all." *No Child's Play*, 27.

13. E. Salholz et al. "Women in Jail: Unequal Justice," *Newsweek*, 4 June 1990, 37–8, 51, as quoted in George Kiser, "Female Inmates and Their Families," *Federal Probation* 55, no. 3, (September 1991): 6.

14. Judith Clark, "Sestina: Reflections on Writing: Bedford Hills Writing Workshop," in Bell Gale Chevigny, ed. *Doing Time: 25 Years of Prison Writing* (New York: Arcade, 1999), 114–18.

15. Alicia Partnoy, "To My Daughter (Letters from Prison) III," *Revenge of the Apple* (San Francisco: Cleis Press, 1992), 25.

16. See "Chilean Women Political Prisoners" in part 2 of this anthology for discussion of collectivity among imprisoned women in Chile.

17. For a discussion of the psychological effects upon imprisoned mothers of the loss of their children, see Phyllis Baunach, "You Can't Be a Mother and Be in Prison . . . Can You? Impacts of the Mother-Child Separation," in *The Criminal Justice System and Women*, ed. Barbara Price and Natalie Sokoloff (New York: Clark Boardman, 1982), 155–69, and Zoann K. Snyder-Joy and Teresa A. Carlo, "Parenting through Prison Walls: Incarcerated Mothers and Children's Visitation Programs." The story of Catherine Virginia Baxley's prison experience, discussed below, presents a vivid example of the psychological effects of imprisonment and separation and the prisoner's attempt to feign brashness toward the administration. Judee Norton's short story, "Norton #59900," cited above, also shows how prisoners feign invulnerability.

18. See Phyllis Baunach, "You Can't Be a Mother," 155.

19. Karlene Faith, *Unruly Women: The Politics of Confinement and Resistance* (Vancouver: Press Gang, 1993), 204.

20. Sandra Enos, "Managing Motherhood in Prison: The Impact of Race and Ethnicity on Child Placements," *Women & Therapy* 20, no. 4 (1997): 63; Enos, *Mothering from the Inside: Parenting in a Women's Prison* (Albany: State University of New York Press, 2001).

21. See Phyllis Baunach, "You Can't Be a Mother," 165. For a discussion of strategies for "turning crisis into opportunity," see Pamela C. Katz, "Supporting Families and

Children of Mothers in Jail: An Integrated Child Welfare and Criminal Justice Strategy," *Child Welfare* 77, no. 5 (September/October 1998), 495ff. See also Stephanie Bush-Baskette, "The War on Drugs and the Incarceration of Mothers," *Journal of Drug Issues* 30, no. 4 (Fall 2000): 919ff.

22. See Adela Beckerman, "Women in Prison: The Conflict between Confinement and Parental Rights," *Social Justice* 18, no. 3 (Fall 1991): 171–83, for a discussion of a mother's parental rights.

23. William E. Doster, *Lincoln and Episodes of the Civil War* (New York: Putnam's, 1915), 84.

24. Another Confederate prisoner, Virginia Lomax, gives this account in her anonymous prison memoirs, *The Old Capitol Prison and Its Inmates. By a Lady, Who Enjoyed the Hospitalities of the Government for a "Season"* (New York: Hale, 1867). Lomax notes that she has changed the names of prisoners. Her reference to "Mrs. Johnson" may be taken to mean Baxley because Lomax and Baxley were imprisoned in the Old Capitol at the same time and their accounts often coincide, particularly in Lomax's description of the death of "Johnson's" son in the same prison.

25. For a discussion of alternatives to incarceration of women, see Meda Chesney-Lind and Russ Immarigeon, "Alternatives to Women's Incarceration," in *Children of Incarcerated Parents*, ed. Katherine Gabel and Denise Johnston (New York: Lexington, 1995), 299–309; JusticeWorks Community, *Breaking Silence: Voices of Mothers in Prison* (New York: JusticeWorks, 1999) and their website: www.justiceworks.org.

CATHERINE VIRGINIA BAXLEY

(1810?–?)

Biographical information about Confederate blockade-runner Catherine Virgina Baxley is scant, but she was said to be about fifty years old during her first imprisonment in the Old Capitol Prison, Washington, D.C., from December 30, 1861, to June 2, 1862. Arrested in Baltimore on charges of "carrying information to Richmond," she was held first in the "Greenhow Prison." Rose Greenhow was a well-known Washington socialite imprisoned for spying for the Confederacy; her home at Sixteenth Street in Washington, was used as a women's political prison. Baxley was then moved to the Old Capitol Prison. There she, Greenhow, and a third Confederate spy, Augusta Morris (Mason), were at first allowed to mingle but afterward separated. All three were released and sent to Richmond on June 2, 1862, when they signed a pledge not to return north of the Potomac River during the war. In August, Jefferson Davis ordered payment of $500 to Baxley for services to the Confederacy.

Baxley did not keep her pledge long and was again imprisoned in the Old Capitol until 1865. The following selections are from her manuscript diary and notebook (February 14, 1865, to July 2, 1865), written in an interleaved copy of Tennyson's *Enoch Arden*—a gift from Post Commandant Colonel Colby. They describe her painful meeting with her son, a wounded soldier in the Old Capitol, and her struggle with intense feelings of abandonment following his death.

Note: Background information is from William E. Doster, *Lincoln and Episodes of the Civil War* (New York: Putnam's, 1915); Ishbel Ross, *Rebel Rose: Life of Rose O'Neal Greenhow, Confederate Spy* (New York: Harper & Bros., 1954); *The War of the Rebellion: A Compilation of the Official Records of the Union and Confederate Armies*, 2nd ser., vol. 2 (Washington, D.C.: Government Printing Office, 1897).

AT THE OLD CAPITOL PRISON

From Baxley's diary and notebook, February 14, 1865–July 2, 1865.

About 5 or half past five O'clock April 5—cannot sleep[1] get up and sit with my face pressed against my bars—in a little while perceive an ambulance train winding round the South East corner of the Capitol passes in front of my windows   I perceive the Gray Uniform so dear to my heart poor wounded Rebels & Prisoners God pity you I kiss my hand one, two, the third ambulance is approaching two bodies on Stretchers I see a pair of clasped hands raised toward me   a voice calls "Alls lost Our Cause is hopeless and I am badly wounded" I am too near-sighted to recognize the features, and turn from the window half broken hearted little dreaming it is my own and only child. In a couple of hours the *Asst. Supt* who is a *brute* in half human form comes in to my room and in the most brutal & unceremonious manner informs me my son is wounded and a prisoner at the Lower-or Old Capitol Prison. God help me now my only child I beg I plead implore to be taken to him. I have [not] seen my child for two years he is but a child [indecipherable]. . . .

This confinement is very tedious very *very* irksome—I have exhausted every thing which could afford a few moments relief to the mind counted over and over again the small diamond shape lozenges in the India carpet the pains [*sic*] of glass in the window—one of the panes has been struck by a stone and rays strike out from the Centre like a halo I have counted the bars in the window blinds, two up and down down and up again There is an intolerable smell of whiskey in this room which annoys me exceedingly and at last I have discovered the cause my lamp. Some new fangled Yankee oil I suppose. The guards watch my every movement but are polite and even kind—for an hour I have been watching the movements of two spiders a large and small one they have finished weaving their web or *Snare* and are trying to trap or coax the unwary flies to enter three or four have been caught but some are wiser more politic not to be trapped I moralized as I watched and will profit in the future. . . .

for 18 mos. incarcerated in Fort Delaware Exchanged only in Sept. 64—this creature Wilson is a husband and a father tis he will not take me to my wounded child. I ask permission to write it is granted but the letter *is not sent*—what Monstrous Cruelty—Col. Wm P. Wood the Supt. proper at length arrives comes immediately to my room for two days I have been waiting for you take me to my son is again the burthen of my cry and he is human—I shall never forget him I meet my son—Mr. Wood has him brought up to Carroll Prison that I may nurse him—but has to leave immediately, when Brute Wilson's tyranny again commences I am not allowed to go to my child a door only at the foot of the Stairs separates us I beg to be allowed to call through the door and ask him how he is dont grieve Ma I am better The excitement attendant upon Mr. Lincoln's death affects him seriously—they repeat carelessly in his presence the threats of the mob to tear the prison down and murder the prisoners on saturday he has a hemorrhage on the day of the procession he has a congestive chill daily he grows worse I— . . .

For behold thou hast loved know my childs days nay—his very hours are numbered—Friday night April 22 my darling my beautiful boy leaves me *all alone* a few minutes before his death he asked me "Ma" is this my birth day—again "kiss me Ma like you used to when I was a little fellow and hold my hand Ma while I sleep—a sleep from which only the trump of the arch Angel will awake him. . . .

6 O'clock June 15th I have been feverish and excited all day—feel really quite unwell if I only had something to read—They have changed my room to day from No. 25—to 23—something of an improvement—but oh how dull monotonous my brain seems on fire my very ears tingle—and to make

matters worse my glasses have fallen from the window-sill to the balcony and are broken and I cannot see across the street without them. Misfortunes come in flocks A [indecipherable] Car has toppled over just in front of the window. came men carrying the engine and tender [indecipherable] one of the employers saved himself by jumping there is quite a crowd collected trying to explore this capsized Car—such a trifling thing would have quickened my pulse sometime since now I am not at all excited I am becoming apathetic indifferent to everything—I watch the arrival of the trains hoping to see some familiar face I scan eagerly every passerby not one look of recognition am I quite forgotten? . . .

> The world too Soon exhaleth the dewy freshness
> of the hearts loving flowers—
> We water them with tears, but naught availeth,
> They wither on through all lifes later hours.

> Liberty. In dungeons brightest thou art
> Madame Roland . . .

12 O'clock at night later perhaps for the chickens are crowing. Sultry snoring outside my door but I cannot sleep Oh! God how utterly desolate and lonely I feel have been reading my darling boys diary. Oh! how much have I lost my child my child I saw you murdered deliberately murdered before my eyes by cruel unrelenting and base men and your wretched mother powerless and impotent to aid you. . . .

June 17th. Still a prisoner I watched the day dawning from the window of my pent-up room tis dull and gloomy—Oh! I begin to feel as if bereft of all hope a few poor homeless Gray jackets are washing themselves at the pump beneath my window and wiping upon the remnants of what were once pocket handkerchiefs poor fellows *perhaps* some wife or Mother is watching hoping praying for their return I am *all alone* no one to watch for None to watch wait and hope for me—tis sad tis bitter bitter bitter— Oh! that God would give us hearts of flesh bowels of Compassion—

NOTE

1. Baxley uses very little punctuation in her diary.—*Ed.*

ABEBA TESFAGIORGIS

In 1975 Abeba Tesfagiorgis, her husband, Mesfun, and their four daughters were living a comfortable life in Asmara, the capital of Eritrea. Both Tesfagiorgis and her husband were professionals active in efforts to improve the life of Eritreans. In 1965 she had been a founder of the Asmara YWCA, which afterward established the Relief and Rehabilitation Association for Eritrea. She and her husband supported the cause of the Eritrean Liberation Front (ELF) and the Eritrean People's Liberation Front (EPLF) in their resistance to the occupation of Eritrea by the Ethiopean military.

Tesfagiorgis was suddenly arrested in September 1975 as she worked at her office at Ethiopean Airlines. She was taken to a cell at the Palace Prison in Asmara, where she was interrogated about her activities in Eritrean relief efforts. As her own physical condition deteriorated, Tesfagiorgis witnessed the imprisonment of her husband and her father. She formed a close bond with her cellmates, whose stories she tells in *A Painful Season & a Stubborn Hope*. After her transfer to Haz Haz Prison for Women and her trial, she was released in March 1976 and exiled to Addis Ababa, Ethiopia, where she was reunited with her family.

Tesfagiorgis writes of her difficulty in accepting the decision of her two elder daughters to join the EPLF. Her daughters Tamar and Ruth, adamant in their dedication to the Eritrean cause, cut their long hair and remained in Eritrea to fight. Together with her younger daughters and her husband, Tesfagiorgis began her travels in exile, eventually moving to the United States. She has continued her human rights activities on behalf of Eritreans, supporting drought relief efforts in the 1980s and speaking out on behalf of Eritrean women victimized by the Ethio-Eritrean war.

Note: Background information is from Abeba Tesfagiorgis, *A Painful Season & a Stubborn Hope* (Lawrenceville, N. J.: Red Sea Press, 1992); Tesfagiorgis, "The Plight of Eritrean Women Rape Victims," online, available: http://allafrica.com/stories/200008210459.html, August 21, 2000.

RECONCILIATION THROUGH 'FAMILY' BONDS

From A Painful Season & a Stubborn Hope, *1992.*

I had such a hideous night that the next day I developed a headache early in the morning, which grew worse with each passing hour. It felt like someone was banging on my head with a hammer. My eyes were stinging. My ears hurt. My tongue was dry. My stomach was burning. My whole body ached. It was unbearable; death would be a relief, I thought. My cellmates were asking me how I felt, but I was too weak and in too much pain to reply.

Semhar banged on the door and cried out for help. It may have been around three or four in the afternoon when a snarling guard came.

"What the hell is going on here, you idiotic rebels?" he fumed. "Who gave you permission to bang on the door like that?"

Ribka told him that I was fearfully sick, that he should report it to the head of the prison. The guard spitefully slammed the door with a bang that made my head hurt more than ever.

Then who should show up but the Major himself, threatening to punish my cellmates for their behavior. I heard him say: "She is such a fool. If only she had confessed by now she would be home with her children."

The Major left the door to the cell open and I could hear him grumbling as he stomped off down the corridor. The pain did not ease much throughout the night. In the morning, the Major came to check on me but I cannot remember what he said.

Toward the end of the third day after the terrible headache had begun, I perspired profusely; and as the beads of sweat ran from my forehead so did the migraine; the aches in my joints, the burning in my stomach, the pain throughout my whole body dwindled away, leaving me weaker than before but much more comfortable.

Three days later, at about ten in the morning, the door was opened slowly, unlike other days, and the guard asked me to come out. With my *netsela* (shawl) wrapped tightly around my waist to help me to walk straight, I followed him down the corridor and outside into the courtyard to a jeep that was parked near the office.

As we passed through the huge black iron gates of the Palace Prison, and saw Cinema Roma and the blue sky with its soft clouds and the people walking in the streets, I was euphoric. As we passed my parents' house, which was on the way to the army hospital, Selassamestegna, I grew nostalgic. I somehow expected to see my mother coming through the gate. Then I was gripped by fear. The horrors of the Expo Prison came to mind, and I imagined my brothers, Dawit and Michael, just twenty and eighteen years old, in the hands of the enemy. Oh God, please protect them, I implored. As we approached the gate of the hospital, I saw two lines of women and children, and others sitting on the lawn. The weather was perfect for lazily sitting about anywhere, but especially on beautiful grass with flowers scattered here and there. As I stepped out of the jeep and dragged myself slowly toward the entrance, I heard a murmur from the women sitting on the lawn: "*esregna . . . esregna*"—prisoner . . . prisoner.

One of my guards made his way inside. The other stood beside me in front of the door while the women in line fell away to let us pass. The doctor must have instructed us to wait. Leading me to a bench just inside the entrance, my guard gestured for me to sit. The driver and the other guard left us, saying they would check back before noon.

The women, Ethiopian armed forces wives, were staring at me, and I was marvelling at the brilliant reds, blues, yellows, and greens of their *shashes*—the scarves that Ethiopian women wind around their heads.

Half an hour passed with my young guard hovering over me. I decided to speak to him:

"You've been standing much too long. The rifle must be very heavy—why don't you sit here beside me and hold it in your lap?"

He looked at me wide-eyed.

"You can see that I'm too weak to even consider escaping," I continued. "Anyway, I have four daughters and all I want is to be legally free and to be with them."

"You are the mother of four children?"

"Yes, I am."

"How old are they?"

"The eldest is sixteen and the youngest five."

"And they are all girls? You mean you have no boys at all?"

"No, I don't. But I love my girls. I wouldn't trade anyone of them for anything."

The guard slowly removed the gun from his shoulder and sat on the bench with me. "I want to ask you something," he said. "Why do you want to sell your beautiful country to the Arabs? Asmara is the loveliest place I have ever been."

I just smiled wearily and asked him a question: "Where were you, and what did you do, before you came to Asmara?"

"I was in Debreberhan. In school. Seventh grade."

"Seventh grade!" I exclaimed. "The best time of my life was in school—particularly junior high."

"You went to school . . . and you were a seventh-grader once! This is so interesting."

He forgot for a moment that he was a uniformed guard and became his real self. I went on and told him what my favorite subjects were when I was in the seventh and eighth grade, how much I enjoyed school and all the fun that went with it.

The guard seemed fascinated. Then he sank into deep thought.

"You seem perturbed. Are you not feeling well?" I asked.

"No. No, I'm all right. I was just thinking about my mother, my poor mother."

"What about your mother?"

"Well. . . . It was a Saturday morning and we were standing near our neighbourhood playground in Debreberhan listening to a portable radio. A truck with soldiers stopped near us. The soldiers got out and forced us—my friends and I—to board the truck. We yelled and shouted, but it did no good. They also took two other groups of men and boys on the way. Finally, we arrived in Addis Ababa. After we had basic military training for three months, several of us were assigned to Eritrea. They told us how easy it would be to capture the bandits and take whatever we wanted from the people, but I knew it was a lie. I have not participated in any combat so far, but if I do I'll never make it—I've heard enough from the ones who have been there. I'm sure my mother thinks I'm dead by now. The people who saw us must have told her I was carted away to fight."

"And what about your father?" I asked.

"My father was in the military service and he died seven years ago. My mother raised my two younger sisters and me on her own."

My young guard tried to hide his face so that I would not see the tears welling up in his eyes.

"The situation we are all in now will come to an end." I said, "When you go back home, study hard—with an education you will be able to do whatever you want. If you become an educated, God-fearing, honest person, it will be a great tribute to your mother." I avoided his eyes for fear of embarrassing him.

I felt like hugging my guard and calling him "son," for he was only seventeen years old.

At that moment, I heard my name being called. I looked at my guard. Lifting his gun onto his shoulder again, he helped me up. I appreciated the support since I was already tired, and he held my arm until I had stepped into the doctor's office.

"*Selam*"—Hello, I said, bowing my head a little in a gesture of courtesy; but the short, dark-skinned doctor in his white gown had no intention of being friendly and merely motioned for me to sit. I suppose that just because I was outside the prison compound I had expected normal treatment! The guard went to the waiting room.

Sitting on a comfortable chair before a modest desk was a treat for me. I breathed deeply and tried to relax.

"What is your problem?" the doctor asked rudely.

What is my problem! This was not the approach I expected from a doctor.

"I am not feeling well."

I told him about my headaches and about the stomach ache that still persisted. I had lost my appetite and could not keep much down, I added, and I had a continual headache although it had become milder.

"How did this start?

"I have dormant gastritis that flares up whenever I eat too much spicy food, but it has never been this bad. The constant headache is something new."

"When did all this happen?"

"Four days after my imprisonment."

"Exactly when?"

"The fourth of October."

He took my blood pressure and felt my pulse, handling me as though I were a piece of furniture. What happened to the oath that doctors and nurses take to treat every human being equally, friend and foe alike? I wondered. To put him at ease, I asked:

"Is my heart still beating? And how low is my blood pressure?"

The doctor tried to hide his smile. "You will survive, but I have to make blood and urine tests." He asked me all sorts of questions regarding my medical history. I had never had a serious problem, only appendicitis years earlier.

As I came out of the office my guard saw me and jumped up. "*Itiye* Abeba," he said. *Itiye* is a name given to an older sister in Amharic. "What did the doctor say, and what can I do for you?"

"I have to go to the other room for a specimen. You just make don't escape," I joked.

He smiled a genuine, broad smile, and replied, "*Eshi*"—Okay.

As I sat on a bench in the corridor waiting for the test results, the doctor passed by and I asked if I could talk to him a moment. He nodded.

"Ever since I was arrested I have had no appetite," I said. "Now all of a sudden I feel hungry. I have no money with me, but I would be glad to give you some when I'm released. Could you please buy me something to eat?"

"We have a small cafeteria here but it is already closed. I could bring you bread and tea. Would that help?"

"Of course. Anything would do."

Suddenly he said: "Woman, why did you get involved with those so-called freedom fighters? You should have just minded your own business and led a peaceful life."

When you do not know what to answer, it is best to keep quiet. I'm sure the doctor didn't expect a reply, at any rate, because he went on about his business. The hall was full of women with babies, many of them crying, and there were only two doctors and two nurses. When my doctor passed by again I reminded him, and after a while he returned with the bread, but no tea. I shared it with my new-found son.

The tests revealed that I had anaemia and an acute gastrointestinal disorder requiring bed rest and intravenous feeding. The doctor called the Major and told him that I should be hospitalized.

"We cannot afford a twenty-four hour guard. Send her back here with her medication," said the voice at the other end.

"*Eshi, eshi,*"—ok, ok—replied the doctor.

I could tell from the doctor's voice that the news was not good. He gave me various medications, including sleeping tablets, for I had told him I was not sleeping well. Just as I was about to leave, he made sure nobody was listening and said:

"Woman, your blood pressure is very low and your red cell count is way below normal. You are susceptible to any minor or serious disease. So be careful. Those damn rebels are the cause of all this. Unless they are totally wiped out Ethiopia will never have peace."

Our *tegadelti* are the cause of all this! What a joke, I thought. But all I said was, "Thank you, doctor."

As I turned to make my way to where Tadesse, my guard, was waiting—now joined by the other guard and the driver—I could tell by his face that the sweet, memorable mother-son relationship was over. We had become total foes again. . . .

...alled one of the guards.

...myself. I was told there would be no interrogation at ...u, am I not through with it!

... guard saw my apprehension and told me there were visitors to ...e me.

Relief!

It was only when she went to the Palace Prison to deliver my lunch that my mother discovered I had been transferred. Two hours after my arrival at Haz Haz Prison there she was, along with Mesfun and my father.

Slowly I walked through the long corridor to the door; I couldn't believe my eyes when I saw my parents and my husband, from a distance, behind barbed wire. I wanted to embrace them, but we were not permitted to get that close.

Mother wept openly. Mesfun and *Abboi* acted brave and tried to make me feel comfortable. After some time I was ordered back inside, and it was only when the three of them turned to leave that I, too, felt the emotion welling up inside me. All three of them came again the next day, with food, pillows, a mattress, and a Bible. We felt a little more relaxed this time, and my mother and I were able to talk.

In the hope that my release was imminent, Mesfun and I thought it would be better if the children waited until I got home rather than see me behind bars. But after three weeks of waiting and waiting, we decided they should come to the prison.

It was therefore arranged that on the third Saturday after my transfer, the four of them would visit me in Haz Haz. On the morning of the big day, I woke up disoriented but happy. I had dreamt that I was holding my daughters close and telling them we would never again be separated. When my mind cleared and I realized it was a dream, I panicked. I was afraid I would break down in front of my children, that I would be unable to hold back my tears.

Even though my stomach was in knots, I made myself as presentable as possible. Since mirrors were not permitted, I had to rely on the judgment of my cellmates. They all assured me that I looked fine, yet somehow their faces told me they could clearly see the anxiety that I was trying so desperately to conceal.

I was the first prisoner called to see her visitors that Saturday. With my chin up, and with a forced smile, I walked down the corridor and came to a stop one foot away from the door.

There, standing face to face with me, behind barbed wire, were my four children.

Ruth had never worn a *netsela* before, but I noticed that she had one on now, and she looked very graceful in it. Tamar's long hair was cut short and she wore a short skirt. Muzit and Senait had on cute dresses and wore their hair in their usual pony tails.

I tried to comment on how wonderful they looked—but my speech was incoherent. The fact that I could not get closer and embrace them made it all the more painful, and I had to battle with myself to keep calm. When my husband saw me struggling, he went to the office of the chief guard to ask if the girls could come inside with me for a brief reunion. The chief guard came to survey the situation. When he saw the children weeping and me standing there motionless, he said that my two younger daughters would be allowed to come inside.

After some moments of total silence, I opened my mouth to speak: "Please let my other children come in too," I pleaded.

"For security reasons, I cannot let your grown-up daughters in. Proceed to the office and you will meet the younger two," he ordered.

I avoided the eyes of Ruth and Tamar and was led to the office, about twenty-five yards away, where a woman motioned for me to take a seat on one of the four chairs.

I had barely sat down when in walked another guard with Muzit and Senait. I stood immediately and they threw themselves at me, their tears brushing my face. Stroking their hair gently and kissing them all over their faces and hands, I felt that at least half of my world was secure. Then I tried to be cheerful and act as though everything was completely normal.

"Mommy, how long are you going to stay here?" Muzit asked.

"I don't know yet—not too long, I hope."

"Can we see your room, where you sleep?" Senait joined in.

"The prison rules don't allow for visitors to go into the bedrooms, even children like you. But we all have good beds and nice bedside tables and everything. We live very well here." I could see from their faces that their suspicions had not been allayed.

Although I had managed to keep the tears from flowing up to that point, the emotional upheaval was bound to manifest itself in some way, and now my legs shook so violently that I had to take the children off my lap. I saw that one of the guards was weeping, while the other three were simply looking down at the floor.

The guard told me with tears in her eyes that it was time for Muzit and Senait to go and for me to return to my cell. With some degree of outward calm, I told my babies that we would be seeing each other more often from then on, and that I had some great stories from my cellmates to tell them when I was released. Again, they demanded to know when I was coming home.

"I don't know; it may not be too long. Just keep on hoping and praying," I said.

Muzit told me that her teacher at the Comboni School was praying for me, and then with a final big hug we parted.

It was becoming impossible to hold back the tears, so I dared not even look at my family beyond the fence on the way back to the cell. Again, I avoided looking Ruth and Tamar in the eye.

Ignoring my cellmates, who were so anxious to hear about the reunion, I let all my anguish explode. I wiped away the tears and felt a great sense of relief. The ordeal of facing my children after twelve weeks in detention was over, and something inside me assured me that things were going to be better from then on.

The children kept coming every Sunday, and their second visit was not as painful as the first. The authorities never again allowed Muzit and Senait to come inside, though. Seeing them over the fence, nonetheless, well dressed and looking pretty, telling me about their school and about the stream of visitors who kept bringing them treats—it was my greatest source of comfort during those trying weeks at Haz Haz Prison.

The night after my daughters' second visit, Berekti read us some verses from the Bible and we all said good night. The lights were never turned out at Haz Haz Prison.

I could not sleep that particular night, not even a wink. I felt hot and my palms were sweaty. It was a good time to reflect. Since there was far less tension at Haz Haz Prison than there had been at the wretched Palace, one could think about things other than merely surviving the torture and the interrogation. My mind wandered far and wide.

The EPLF—once it has succeeded in liberating the country, what does it stand for, and what does it mean to me personally and to my family? I posed the question to myself. I thought of the principles laid down by the EPLF. Thanks to my parents, I had had a fairly good education. Thanks to Mesfun, our children went to the best school, even though we sometimes worried that they would end up alienated from their own culture. With all these privileges, why was I not happy and at peace?

No person and no family exists in isolation. No conscious, aware person could be content living in our country as it was. I was affected by the sight of Eritrean children in tatters, eating scraps of rotting fruit in the market. The heartbreaking stories of my *ghebi* and Haz Haz cellmates were, in fact, perfect examples of the sorry, unjust lot of most Eritreans.

The EPLF's values seemed to offer the changes that I craved: pride in being Eritrean and African; free education for all children—urban and rural alike—up to the twelfth grade, combining theory with practice; the creation of job opportunities; women's rights, including equal pay for work of equal value; economic development; and freedom of speech and assembly, freedom from fear and want, freedom to breathe the beautiful and healthy air of Eritrea.

Critics in the West called the EPLF Marxists or socialists. Marxist or not, their statement of principles appealed to me, and in the deepest recesses of my heart I hoped that in their ambitious push towards economic prosperity they would not make the mistake of losing touch with individuals, families, and humanity; that they would understand that development follows only when minds and hearts are free; that love and honesty are far more powerful than fear and corruption.

Toward dawn I was worn out from turning these thoughts over and over in my mind all night long, and I wanted to doze off. But I was afraid I would miss Mesfun's visit in the morning. Throughout my stay at Haz Haz, he came every single morning between a quarter to eight and a quarter past eight, and Mother came between one and two o'clock every afternoon.

In my state of exhaustion I hated the idea of seeing Mesfun through the barbed wire. I wanted to be in his bosom. I saw him in the flesh every day, right in front of me, yet I could not touch him.

I hated prison.

ALICIA PARTNOY

(1955–)

In 1977 Argentinean political activist and university student Alicia Partnoy was kidnapped from her home by military forces of Argentina's dictatorship and separated from her husband and eighteen-month-old daughter. She was "disappeared" for months of imprisonment and torture in a secret concentration camp called "The Little School." In October 1977 Partnoy was transferred to a Buenos Aires political prison; her three-year imprisonment ended with her exile to the United States, where she now lives with her husband and daughters.

During her imprisonment, Partnoy endured abuse, the constant use of blindfolds, and the painful knowledge that many of her friends, also "disappeared," were murdered. She wrote poetry to maintain her strength and courage. Her writings as a political prisoner were smuggled out to human rights journals that published them anonymously. Since her release and exile, Partnoy has published her writings, lectured extensively, and worked as a bilingual receptionist and translator. In 1984 she returned to Argentina to testify about abuses under the military dictatorship. Her testimony on human rights violations has been presented to the United Nations and to the Organization of American States. She is currently assistant professor of Spanish at Loyola Marymount University in Los Angeles, and a member of Amnesty International's board of directors. The vocal group Sweet Honey in the Rock has set her poems to music. In the following selections, Partnoy describes her separation from her own family and also bears witness to the torture of Graciela, a young "disappeared" woman who gave birth at the Little School.

Note: Backgroundl information is from Alicia Partnoy, *The Little School: Tales of Disappearance and Survival* (San Francisco: Cleis Press, 1986); *Revenge of the Apple* (San Francisco: Cleis Press, 1992); *You Can't Drown the Fire: Latin American Women in Exile* (San Francisco: Cleis Press, 1988).

THREE POEMS

"[Outside it's April, it's nighttime]" is from The Little School, *1986; "To My Daughter" and "Visit" are from* Revenge of the Apple, *1992.*

[Outside it's April, it's nighttime]

Outside it's April, it's nighttime.
Two fierce shadows in a fight.
Life: the power of childbirth,
Death: the sound of firearms.
Two unmeasurable shadows

are fighting inside your womb.
Life: the child is pushing out.
Death: the fear is taking over.
Do you think both these shadows cou
          win this hard battle?
"Yes, they could," the echo answers,
echo of bullets just waiting
to ravage the mother's womb
as soon as the new life is born.
Outside it's April, it's nighttime.
Two fierce shadows in a fight.

To My Daughter
(Letters from Prison)

I.

Listen:
My throat befriends the winds
To reach you
Dear gentle heart, new eyes.
Listen:
place your ear to a sea shell,
or to this infamous prison phone,
and listen.

The reason is so simple,
so pure,
like a drop of water
or a seed
that fits in the palm of your hand.
The reason is so very simple:
I could not
keep from fighting for the happiness
of those who are our brothers our sisters.

II.

To write you,
my sun caramel, my *chiquita*,
I would have to . . .
I would have to gather so much tenderness . . .
And your mother, my love,
your mother has hardened,
her soul is made of stone,

st never cries . . .
when she writes to you,
sun caramel,
my moon crystal.

III.

Today I cast off the lines
imprisoning my dreams
and I arrive at your golden
sun-drenched shore.
My dear daughter, I am a sailor
on a ship of hopeful dreams
with one port of call:
your soft face and your voice.
To buckle your shoes,
to let loose your laughter,
to walk by your side
through a better world . . .
For these tasks
I know what is needed:
my hands and my tenderness,
my freedom and my voice.
To let loose your laughter,
to buckle your shoes,
to tear down the walls
that block out the sun . . .
It is for these tasks
I am preparing
my word, my life,
my fist and my
song.

Visit

On Fridays Mama breaks through
the locks and gates
to play ring-around-the-rosy with you,
counting the minutes.
Papa, from far away
in his walled-in day,
dreams of your warm skin
and your numbered minutes.
If I could, dear child,
explain to you the reason
for all the locks,

for all the gates,
for all the bars,
for the high walls,
for all . . . all
the numbered minutes . . .
My child, if I could
devour space
and play ring-around-the-rosy
far from every prison . . .
oh we'd be playing free
and my hands
would lose all track of time . . .

A PUZZLE

From The Little School, *1986*

For a while now I've been trying to recall how Ruth's face looks. I can
remember her big eyes, her almost nonexistent little nose, the shape of her
mouth. I recall the texture of her hair, the warmth of her skin. When I try
to put it all together, something goes wrong. I just can't remember my
daughter's face. It has been two months since I've seen her. I want to
believe that she's safe.

"Vasca! Do you remember my daughter's face?" I whisper.

"What?"

"I said, do you remember my daughter's face? I can't. . . ."

"Of course I do, she's so pretty."

I think I'll turn in my bed; that will help me reorder my thoughts. . . . No,
it doesn't work. It's funny, 'cause I can recall the things we did together,
even when I'm not thinking about them all the time. Rather, I've tried not
to remember too much, to avoid crying . . . but right now, I want to imagine her face, to put together the pieces of this puzzle. . . .

The other day, after the big rain, the guard brought a puppy into our
room. He allowed me to keep it on my bed for awhile. It was playful and
sweet, like my baby. I felt so good that afternoon that I wanted to laugh.
It was not like the urge to laugh that I experience when I'm nervous or
when I use black humor to shield myself. It was a feeling almost close to
happiness. While caressing the puppy, I thought of Ruth. Then, I didn't
worry about trying to remember her face; I just wanted to reminisce about
being close to her, to recall that warm tingling in my blood.

Perhaps if I tried to bring to mind some scenes when we were together. . . .
For example, that day while coming back from my parents: I was pushing
her stroller along the street, when suddenly she looked up at the roof of a
house. An immense dog was impatiently stalking back and forth. Ruth

pointed to the dog with her little finger. "Meow," she said, since she was only used to watching cats climb up high. Thrilled, I kissed her; that kiss was a prize I awarded myself for such a display of wisdom by my child. I stopped the stroller to kiss her . . . but how did her face look? I can only remember her small triumphant smile.

Night is coming; somebody stepped into the room to turn on the lights. We were told that we could take a shower today, but it looks like we're out of luck. It makes me so angry. I shouldn't believe the guards' promises.

The radio is on, not very loud this time . . . playing Roberto Carlos' song again. When the newscast starts, they turn the radio off.

One morning while on the bus I heard on the radio:

"Fellow citizens, if you notice family groups traveling at odd hours of the day or night, report them to the military authorities. The number to call is. . . . "

I was one of a few passengers on that early bus. It was 6:30 A.M. and I was traveling to a suburban neighborhood with my baby and two bags. For a short while I thought the driver was going to stop the vehicle and run to the nearest phone to alert the army. He just glared at my reflection in the rear view mirror. The night before some friends of mine had been kidnapped. Since they knew where I lived, I thought of moving out for a few days just to be safe. . . . But I can't remember my daughter's face on that bus. I know that she was wearing the pink jacket, that I had the bag with stripes, the same one my mom used to take to the beach. I have perfect recall of every item in the bag . . . but I try so hard and I still can't remember my daughter's face. I could describe her toys, her clothes. . . . If only I had her picture. But again, maybe it's better this way. If I could look at a picture of her face, I would surely cry . . . and if I cry, I crumble.

GRACIELA: AROUND THE TABLE

From The Little School, *1986*

Fifteen days ago this business of walking around the table began. At least it's something different to do every afternoon. I've already walked around the table eight times today. Two more steps to the edge. . . . I feel a little dizzy. . . . Now in the opposite direction: *one, two, three, four, five, six . . . one, two, three, four . . . one, two. . . .*

"What name did you choose, ma'am?"

What a question! As if they cared. I must admit that now they feel some sort of compassion; they no longer beat or molest me. In fact, I've just realized that for the past few days they haven't screamed at me either. Well, with this huge belly! But they weren't worried about my belly when they arrested me. The trip from Cutral-Co to Neuquén was pure hell. . . . They knew I was pregnant. It hadn't occurred to me that they could torture me while we were traveling. They did it during the whole trip: the electric prod on my abdomen because they knew about the pregnancy. . . . *One, two, three, four.* . . . Each shock brought that terrible fear of miscarriage . . . and that pain, my pain, my baby's pain. I think it hurt more because I knew he was being hurt, because they were trying to kill him. . . . Sometimes I think it would have been better if I had lost him.

Twelve rounds already. I wonder whether this "exercise program" is just one more sham or if they'll let me live until my child is born. And what after that? Better not to think for a while. . . . The thirteenth time around the table. The "doctor" prescribed thirty. He may not even be a doctor. How could a doctor be an accomplice? That was a stupid thought. There can be assassins in any field.

Adrianita. I swear I won't think about her, at least until I reach the twentieth round; if I make it to the twentieth perhaps I'll be able to make it to the twenty-fifth, the thirtieth. . . . Afterwards I'll request to be taken to the bathroom. If they take me I could even wash my hands. They've been allowing me to use their bathroom for the past month. I couldn't keep my balance at the latrine because of my weakness. When I get back I'm going to eat that little piece of bread I saved from my lunch. . . . I'm going to make it last, as always. Maybe that will keep me busy for a while so I won't think of Adrianita: I spent all day yesterday thinking of her. . . . I cried all day long. My little girl, where are you? If only my parents were taking care of her!

The twentieth time around this table. Somebody is asking for water. It's María Elena's voice. María Elena, so little and so strong, so determined to fight injustice: "We must do something, sister," she said. I guess she was repeating what she'd heard from Raul and me. I thought I was going to lose my mind when they brought her to the Little School. When I noticed that they suspected she was involved, I imagined a thousand ways of warning her, all of them impossible, there was no escape. . . . That's why when they brought in Alicia, the first thing I thought was to ask her if she still had any communication with the outside world. . . . In Hell there probably isn't any communication with the outside world either. Now the guilt feelings . . . one more chain, the blindfold around my eyes, the gauze around my hands. . . . At times I would like to disappear—to truly disappear—to fly away with the wind that blows through the window, to vanish from the world. Such a heavy burden. . . . If only Raul was here! Where have they taken him? That day, while the guard was changing my blindfold, I asked him—Viejo—if he knew anything. He said, "To the South, to another concentration camp." Vaca didn't want to talk about it. It's funny, I wanted to divorce him before they caught us. Now I'm short of breath because he's not with me. Well, at least I don't hear them torturing him. . . . However, the gag of anguish loosened when I heard him whisper, "I'm okay, honey, don't worry." He was okay, lying on a wooden floor, getting kicked and punched day and night, he was okay. . . . "Be strong, Graciela. Take heart. Do it for Adrianita . . . for the baby. . . ."

The baby walks around this table with me, within me. . . . Four more rounds to go. I'm already exhausted from walking, no breath left . . . I know this table by heart, I'd pick it out from all the tables of the world, even if I could never see it well. Thirty rounds, fifteen days . . . four hundred and fifty rounds. . . . Today my blindfold is very tight and I can't even see my feet or the dress with the flowered pattern. Who was the owner of this dress? The child is moving . . . my love, to protect you, my dear child? Me?. . . so unprotected myself. If only your father were here. Perhaps you could hear his whispers, "Be strong my child, take heart. . . . The future is yours." Your future, my child . . . we gave up sunshine on our skin for your future. . . . The thirtieth round of this living death. Don't forgive them, my child. Don't forgive this table, either.

NATIVITY

From The Little School, *1986*

"Sir, when's the doctor coming?"

The labor pains and contractions are almost constant, very close together. This child wants to get out. What will they do to me after it's born? They've said they'll transfer me to a regular prison where I'll be able to take care of the baby. I'm scared. . . .

"Don't worry, ma'am, everything is going to be alright."
"Don't I have reason to worry, being in your hands?"

Today I was sitting in the backyard; it was a sunny day. My eyes without blindfold, looking at the garage door. Out there, just sixty feet away, freedom. How does it feel to be free? I can't even remember. And the doctor isn't coming. . . . The sunshine, the trees, everything seemed to be so good in the backyard this morning. . . . For a second I thought I was on the other side of the door. . . . The contractions are coming more frequently. . . . The child is going to be born.

Problems, problems again. First we run out of wine, and now this fucking child. It might be 11:00 P.M. Water was put on to boil; now the big square bowl, the one we use for salad, should be washed, as well as other pans for more water. Someone has gone to get Rosa so she can wash the pans for us. It's better if I put on my hood right now. Some days ago I went into the kitchen without noticing that she was there. She saw my face. I don't like it at all that she's seen my face. I don't know whether this one will come out alive or not. Afterward, I asked her, "If you run into me once you are released, you'll surely shoot me, won't you?"

"No," she answered, "I'll buy you coffee," and she laughed. I don't believe what these characters say. On top of all this I've got a headache. I guess I had too much wine again. Well! I'd been controlling myself for almost two days, because my boss was coming to visit.

"He isn't there."

"How come he isn't there?"

"He isn't. We went to look for him, but he isn't there."

"Now what?"

"Who knows? Do you know anything about delivering babies?"

"No, but Zorzal does; he says he's helped to deliver animals in the country."

"Okay. Tell him to get ready."

"Yes, sir."

"Where's the doctor?"

"He'll probably be late, but don't worry, I know enough about these matters."

Jesús! He's pushing. . . . Don't take him away. . . . If only I could keep my baby inside. . . . Ugh. . . . Now I have to push, if I don't it hurts more. If we could survive, my child. . . . If we survive. . . .

A new cry makes its way through the shadows fighting above the trailer. Graciela has just given birth. A prisoner child has been born. While the killers' hands welcome him into the world, the shadow of life leaves the scene, half a winner, half a loser: on her shoulders she wears a poncho of injustice. Who knows how many children are born every day at the Little School?

FROM CASES OF THE DISAPPEARED AT THE LITTLE SCHOOL

From The Little School, *1986*

January–April 1977

The case of Graciela Alicia Romero de Metz and Raul Eugenio Metz:

Graciela was arrested on December 16, 1976 in Cutral Co (Neuquén) along with her husband, Raul Eugenio Metz. Heavily armed individuals broke into their home, also threatening the neighbors. Both were 24 years old at the time of their detention. They had one daughter, Adrianita, who was two or three years old; once detained, they received no news of her fate. Graciela was five months pregnant at the time, and during the transfer by truck to Neuquén she was tortured with electric shocks to her stomach and hit brutally.

Later they were both transferred to the Little School, and were already there at the time of my arrival on January 12th. Raul was forced to remain prone on the floor, hands tied behind his back. Towards the end of January he was taken, according to the guards, to Neuquén. A writ of habeas corpus was requested. His name is registered in Amnesty International's list of disappeared people.

Graciela stayed at the Little School, forced to remain prone, blindfolded and handcuffed like the rest. In the last month of her pregnancy she was permitted "exercise"—blindfolded walks around a table, holding on to the edge. A few days before giving birth they took her to a trailer on the patio. On April 17 she had a son—normally, but without medical assistance. I persistently asked the guards to let me help her or keep her company, but they didn't allow me. She was helped by the guards. On April 23 she was removed from the Little School and I never heard of her again. She is on Amnesty International's list of disappeared people. Her son, according to the guards, was given to one of the interrogators.

ASSATA SHAKUR

(1947–)

Assata Shakur, formerly known as JoAnne Chesimard, grew up in Wilmington, North Carolina. As a student she became involved in revolutionary activity and joined the Black Panther Party. On the FBI's Most Wanted List, she was charged with a number of crimes in the early 1970s—bank robbery, attempted murder, and kidnapping. She was never convicted of any of these charges; some were dismissed and she was acquitted of others.

In May 1973 Assata Shakur and two male companions were stopped by state police on the New Jersey Turnpike. A shootout followed that severely wounded her and killed one of her companions and a white trooper. Shakur and Sundiata Acoli, the other man who had been with her, were both arrested. Shakur was imprisoned in the Middlesex County, New Jersey, jail and afterward at Riker's Island Correctional Institution for Women in New York City. Shakur's daughter Kakuya was conceived during her trial and born in prison. Shakur adamantly maintained her innocence, amid considerable negative media publicity of the case. Despite her insistence that the trial was not just, she was convicted in 1977 as accomplice to the murder of a white state trooper and sentenced to life in prison.

In 1978 Shakur was transferred to the federal prison for women at Alderson, West Virginia, where she met Puerto Rican nationalist Lolita Lebrón (see Lebrón's selection in this anthology). She was again transferred to the Clinton Correctional Institution for Women in New Jersey. In November 1979 Shakur escaped from that prison with the help of her supporters. Since 1984 she has lived in exile in Cuba, where she was visited in 1985 by her daughter, who had been raised by Shakur's mother in New York. Despite attempts to extradite her, Shakur currently remains in Cuba. A documentary film about Assata Shakur, "Eyes of the Rainbow," written and directed by Gloria Rolando, an AfroCuban filmmaker, appeared in 1997.

Note: Background information is from Assata Shakur, *Assata: An Autobiography* (Chicago: Lawrence Hill Books, 1987); Evelyn Williams, *Inadmissible Evidence: The Story of the African-American Trial Lawyer Who Defended the Black Liberation Army* (Brooklyn, N.Y.: Lawrence Hill Books, 1993); "AfroCubaWeb: Assata Shakur," online, available: http://afrocubaweb.com/assata.htm, December 6, 2001.

SISTERS IN PRISON

From Assata, *1987.*

I was transferred on April 8, 1978 to the maximum security prison for women in alderson, west virginia, the federal facility designed to hold "the most dangerous women in the country." I had been convicted of no federal crime, but under the interstate compact agreement any prisoner can be shipped, like cargo, to any jail in u.s. territory, including the virgin islands, miles away from family, friends, and lawyers. Through the device of this agreement, Sundiata had been transferred to marion prison in illinois, the federal prison that was the most brutal concentration camp in the country.

Alderson was in the middle of the west virginia mountains, and it seemed as if the mountains formed an impenetrable barrier between the prison and the rest of the world. It had no airport, and to reach it, days of travel were necessary. The trip to alderson was so expensive and difficult that most of the women received family visits only once or twice a year.

I was housed in the maximum security unit (msu) called davis hall. It was surrounded by an electronic fence topped by barbed wire, which in turn was covered by concertina wire (a razor-sharp type of wire that had been outlawed by the Geneva Convention). It was a prison within a prison. This place had a stillness to it like some kind of bizarre death row. Everything was sterile and dead.

There were three major groups in msu: the nazis, the "niggah lovers," and me. I was the only Black woman in the unit, with the exception of one other who left almost immediately after i arrived. The nazis had been sent to alderson from a prison in California, where they had been accused of setting inmates on fire. They were members of the aryan sisterhood, the female wing of the aryan brotherhood—a white racist group that operates in California prisons and is well-known for its attacks on Black prisoners.

Hooked up with the nazis were the manson family women, sandra good and linda "squeaky" froame. Sandra had been sentenced to fifteen years for threatening the lives of business executives and government officials, and froame was serving a life sentence for attempting to kill president gerald ford. They were like the Bobbsey twins and clear out of their minds.

They called themselves "red" and "blue." Everyday "red" wore red from head to toe and "blue" wore blue. They were so fanatic in their devotion to charles manson that they wrote to him everyday, informing him about everything that happened at msu. They waited for his "orders," and you can be sure that if he told them to kill someone they would die trying to do it. Also hooked up with the nazis were the hillbilly prisoners: an obese sow who never bathed and walked around barefoot and a tobacco-chewing butch who acted like she was in the confederate army. There was one "independent" nazi who had fallen out with the others. She sported a huge swastika embroidered on her jeans.

Luckily, Rita Brown, a white revolutionary from the George Jackson Brigade,[1] a group based on the West Coast, was among the four or five "niggah lovers." She was a feminist and a lesbian, and helped me to better understand many issues in the white women's liberation movement. Unlike Jane Alpert,[2] whom i had met in the federal prison in New York, and whom i couldn't stand either personally or politically, Rita did not separate the oppression of women from the racism and classism of u.s. society. We agreed that sexism, like racism, was generated by capitalis. governments, and that women would never be liberated as lo institutions that controlled our lives existed. I respected Rita becau. really practiced sisterhood, and wasn't just one of those big mouths who on and on about men.

I'm sure that a lot of prison officials thought i'd never leave the place alive. It was the perfect setup for a setup, and i dealt with the situation seriously. I didn't look for trouble, but i let the nazis know that i was ready to defend myself at any time, and that if they wanted ass (like they say in prison) they would have to bring ass. I made it clear to them that i hated them as much as they hated me, and that if anybody's mother had to cry it would be theirs, not Ms. Johnson. After a few run-ins, the nazis stayed out of my way.

After i had been at alderson for a while, we learned that the msu would be closed down because it had been declared unconstitutional. A phase-out stratification program was implemented that enabled those in msu to leave it during the day and to participate in the same activities permitted those in the general population. I got a job working on the general mechanic's crew, was allowed recreation, attended classes, and was able to eat and visit with the other women in general population.

Many of the sisters were Black and poor and from D.C., where every crime is a violation of a federal statute. They were beautiful sisters, serving outrageous sentences for minor offenses. Similar to the situation that existed at the federal prison in New York, some women could not afford to buy cigarettes without forgoing necessities, while others had money, contacts, wore fur coats, and lived as if they were in a different prison. That small group of women had been convicted of drug trafficking. Rumor had it that they performed the same services in prison as they had on the street, only now they worked for the guards.

One day, as i was returning to davis hall, a middle-aged woman with "salt-and-pepper" hair caught my eye. She had a dignified, schoolteacher look. Something drew me towards her. As i searched her face, i could see that she was also searching mine. Our eyes locked in a questioning gaze. "Lolita?" I ventured. "Assata?" she responded. And there, in the middle of those alderson prison grounds, we hugged and kissed each other.

For me, this was one of the greatest honors of my life. Lolita Lebrón was one of the most respected political prisoners in the world. Ever since i had first learned about her courageous struggle for the independence of Puerto Rico, i had read everything i could find that had been written about her. She had spent a quarter of a century behind bars and had refused parole unless her comrades were also freed. After all those years she had remained strong, unbent and unbroken, still dedicated to the independence of Puerto Rico and the liberation of her people. She deserved more respect than anyone could possibly give her, and i could not do enough to demonstrate my respect.

In our subsequent meetings i must have been quite a pain in her neck, falling all over myself to carry her tray, to get a chair for her, or to do whatever i could for her. Lolita had been through hell in prison, yet she was

d extremely kind. She had suffered years of isolation in
on to years of political and personal isolation. Until the
vement for Puerto Rican independence in the late 60s,
ery little support. Years had gone by without a visit. For
n cut off from her country, her culture, her family, and
to speak her own language. Her only daughter had died
prison.

olita a hundred percent, but there was one thing about
which we did not agree. At the time we met, Lolita was somewhat anticommunist and antisocialist. She was extremely religious and, i think, believed that religion and socialism were two opposing forces, that socialists and communists were completely opposed to religion and religious freedom.

After the resurgence of the Puerto Rican independence movement, Lolita was visited by all kinds of people. Some were psuedo-revolutionary robots who attacked her for her religious beliefs, telling her that to be a revolutionary she had to give up her belief in God. It apparently had never occurred to those fools that Lolita was more revolutionary than they could ever be, and that her religion had helped her to remain strong and committed all those years. I was infuriated by their crass, misguided arrogance.

I had become close friends with a Catholic nun, Mary Alice, while at alderson, who introduced me to liberation theology. I had read some articles by Camillo Torres, the revolutionary priest, and i knew that there were a lot of revolutionary priests and nuns in Latin America. But i didn't know too much about liberation theology. I did know that Jesus had driven the money changers out of the temples and said that the meek would inherit the earth, and a lot of other things that were directly opposed to capitalism. He had told the rich to give away their wealth and said that "It is easier for a camel to go through the eye of a needle than for a rich man to enter into the Kingdom of God" (Matthew 19:24). I knew a little bit, but i had too much respect for Lolita to open my mouth carelessly. I decided to study liberation theology so that i could have an intelligent conversation with her.

I never got around to it, though. The maximum security unit closed, and i was shipped back to new jersey. Lolita is free now, and she is no longer isolated from what is going on in her part of the world or in her church. I know that wherever she is, she is praying and struggling for her people.

MOTHER AND DAUGHTER

From Assata, *1987.*

My mother brings my daughter to see me at the clinton correctional facility for women in new jersey, where i had been sent from alderson. I am delirious. She looks so tall. I run up to kiss her. She barely responds. She is distant and standoffish. Pangs of guilt and sorrow fill my chest. I can see that my child is suffering. It is stupid to ask what is wrong. She is four years old, and except for these pitiful little visits—although my mother has brought her to see me every week, wherever i am, with the exception of the time i was in alderson—she has never been with her mother. I can feel something welling up in my baby. I look at my mother, my face a question mark. My mother is suffering too. I try to play. I make my arms into an elephant's trunk stalking around the visiting room jungle. It does not work. My daughter refuses to play baby elephant, or tiger, or anything. She looks at me like i am the buffoon i must look like. I try the choo-choo train routine and the la, la, la song, but she is not amused. I try talking to her, but she is puffed up and sullen.

I go over and try to hug her. In a hot second she is all over me. All i can feel are these little four-year-old fists banging away at me. Every bit of her force is in those punches, they really hurt. I let her hit me until she is tired. "It's all right," i tell her. "Let it all out." She is standing in front of me, her face contorted with anger, looking spent. She backs away and leans against the wall. "It's okay," i tell her. "Mommy understands." "You're not my mother," she screams, the tears rolling down her face. "You're not my mother and i hate you." I feel like crying too. I know she is confused about who i am. She calls me Mommy Assata and she calls my mother Mommy.

I try to pick her up. She knocks my hand away. "You can get out of here, if you want to," she screams. "You just don't want to." "No, i can't," i say, weakly. "Yes you can." She accuses. "You just don't want to."

I look helplessly at my mother. Her face is choked with pain. "Tell her to try to open the bars," she says in a whisper.

"I can't open the door," i tell my daughter. "I can't get through the bars. You try and open the bars."

My daughter goes over to the barred door that leads to the visiting room. She pulls and she pushes. She yanks and she hits and she kicks the bars until she falls on the floor, a heap of exhaustion. I go over and pick her up. I hold and rock and kiss her. There is a look of resignation on her face that i can't stand. We spend the rest of the visit talking and playing quietly on the floor. When the guard says the visit is over, i cling to her for dear life. She holds her head high, and her back straight as she walks out of the prison. She waves good-bye to me, her face clouded and worried, looking like a little adult. I go back to my cage and cry until i vomit. I decide that it is time to leave.

To My Daughter Kakuya

i have shabby dreams for you
of some vague freedom
i have never known.

Baby,
i don't want you hungry or thirsty
or out in the cold.

And i don't want the frost
to kill your fruit
before it ripens.

i can see a sunny place—
Life exploding green.
i can see your bright, bronze skin
at ease with all the flowers
and the centipedes.

i can hear laughter,
not grown from ridicule.
And words, not prompted
by ego or greed or jealousy.

i see a world where hatred
has been replaced by love.
and ME replaced by WE.

And i can see a world
where you,
building and exploring,
strong and fulfilled,
will understand.
And go beyond
my little shabby dreams.

'YOU'RE COMING HOME'

From Assata, *1987*

My grandmother came all the way from North Carolina. She came to tell me about her dream. My grandmother had been dreaming all of her life, and the dreams have come true. My grandmother dreams of people passing and babies being born and people being free, but it is never specific. Redbirds sitting on fences, rainbows at sunset, conversations with people long gone. My grandmother's dreams have always come when they were needed and have always meant what we needed them to mean. She dreamed my mother would be a schoolteacher, my aunt would go to law school, and, during the hard times, she dreamed the good times were coming. She told us what we needed to be told and made us believe it like nobody else could have. She did her part. The rest was up to us. We had to make it real. Dreams and reality are opposites. Action synthesizes them.

I was extremely pleased that she had come. Her air was confident and victorious. The rest of the family prompted her to tell me her dream.

"You're coming home soon," my grandmother told me, catching my eyes and staring down into them. "I don't know when it will be, but you're coming home. You're getting out of here. It won't be too long, though. It will be much less time than you've already been here."

Excited, i asked her to tell me about her dream. We were all talking, i noticed in a conspiratorial tone.

"I dreamed we were in our old house in Jamaica. I don't know if you remember that house or not."

I assured her that i did.

"I dreamed that i was dressing you," she said, "putting your clothes on."

"Dressing me?" i repeated.

"Yes. Dressing you."

Fear ran up and down my back. "Was i little or grown?"

"You were grown up in my dream."

I felt slightly sick. Maybe my grandmother dreamt about my death. Maybe she dreamt that I was killed while trying to escape. Why else would she be dressing me, if i wasn't dead? My grandmother caught my drift of thought.

"No, you're all right. You're alive. It's just as plain as the nose on your face. You're coming home. I know what I'm talking about. Don't ask me to explain it anymore, because I can't. I just know you're going to come home and that you're going to be all right."

I drilled her for more details. Some she gave and some she didn't. Finally, after i had asked a thousand questions, my grandmother let all the authority show in her voice. "I know it will happen, because I dreamt it. You're getting out of this place, and I know it. That's all there is to it." My grandmother sat looking at me. There was a kind of smile on her face i can't describe. I knew she was serious. My grandmother's dreams were notorious: her dreams came true. All her life her uncanny senses have been like radar, picking up and identifying all kinds of things that we don't even see. My family and i just sat there vibing on each other. Talking and laughing, bringing up old memories and telling funny stories. Calmness rolled down my body like thick honey.

When i got back to my cell i thought about it all. No amount of scientific, rational thinking could diminish the high that i felt. A tingly, giddy excitement had caught hold of me. I had gotten drunk on my family's arrogant, carefree optimism. I literally danced in my cell, singing, "Feet don't fail me now." I sang the "feet" part real low, so i guess the guards must have thought i was bugging out, stomping around my cage singing "feet," "feet."

"You can't win a race just by running," my mother told me when i was little. "You have to talk to yourself."

"Huh?" i had asked.

"You have to talk to yourself when you are running and tell yourself you can win."

It had become a habit of sorts. Anytime i am faced with something difficult or almost impossible, i chant. Over the years i have developed different kinds of chants, but I always fall back on the old one "i can, i can, yes, i can."

I called my grandparents a day or two before i escaped. I wanted to hear their voices one last time before i went. I was feeling kind of mush and, so as not to sound suspicious, I told them I wanted to hear some more about the family's history, tracing the ties back to slavery. All too soon it was time to hang up. "Your grandmother wants to say something else to you," my grandfather told me.

"I love you," my grandmother said. "We don't want you to get used to that place, do you hear? Don't you let yourself get used to it."

"No, grandmommy, i won't."

Every day out in the street now, i remind myself that Black people in amerika are oppressed. It's necessary that I do that. People get used to anything. The less you think about your oppression, the more your tolerance for it grows. After a while, people just think oppression is the normal state of things. But to become free, you have to be acutely aware of being a slave.

NOTES

1. George Jackson was an African American revolutionary prisoner who was killed by guards at San Quentin Prison in 1971.—*Ed.*

2. Alpert was active in radical antiwar causes, and her book is listed in the annotated bibliography in this anthology.—*Ed.*

PRECIOUS BEDELL

(1954–)

Precious Bedell's many achievements are the more remarkable because she accomplished most of them while incarcerated at Bedford Hills Correctional Facility, the New York State women's prison. She was released in November 1999, after almost twenty years' imprisonment. Her release resulted from the committed efforts of her supporters, including the district attorney from the county office that had originally prosecuted her: "This is not a routine case where the woman has done the ordinary or even the extraordinary," he stated. "This is . . . far, far beyond that" (*New York Law Journal*).

In November 1979, Bedell was a twenty-five-year-old single mother of three, with no prior history of child abuse. She was accused of beating her two-year-old daughter Lashonda in the restroom of the Syracuse steakhouse where they were dining. When the child later died of head injuries, Bedell, who had a drug abuse problem, was convicted of second-degree murder and sentenced to a maximum of twenty-five years to life. Appeals to the New York State governor for clemency had failed several times, but review of her trial record revealed legal errors that opened the way to Bedell's release.

A high-school drop-out, Bedell earned her high-school equivalency (GED), a bachelor's degree with honors from Mercy College, and a master's degree in psychology from Norwich University during her imprisonment. Her support of other women prisoners was exemplary: she worked at the Bedford Hills Children's Center, developing programs such as Parents as Reading Partners; served as chairperson of the Inmate Foster Care Committee; and co-authored a handbook for imprisoned mothers to explain the foster care system. Together with a Columbia University law professor, she developed prison classes in family law.

During her imprisonment, Bedell developed a close relationship with her own children, who supported efforts for her release. Bedell's goals upon release were to develop child abuse prevention programs to help women on the outside.

Note: Background information is from Precious Bedell, letter to Judith Scheffler, August 17, 2001; "Court Decisions," *New York Law Journal*, January 6, 1995; William Kates, "Inspiring inmate has life to get back on track," The Associated Press State & Local Wire, November 23, 1999; "Columbia Law School in the News," online, available: http:// www.law.columbia.edu/news/facnewsarchives, Fall 1999; Jennifer Gonnerman, "Campaigning for Clemency," http://villagevoice.com/features/9851/gonnerman.shtml, May 17, 2001.

PIECES

From Prison Life, *1995*.

Act III

Scene ii. *The visiting area of a prison, a large room with low tables and chairs. Adjacent is a spacious toy-filled room and in big lettering "The Children's Center" is painted over the entrance. The acrylic windows enclosing this room have pictures of children leaving school buses. A few prisoners and a civilian staff person are putting scenes on a bulletin board. Prisoners in the main visiting room sitting with visitors are talking in low hushed tones. Prisoners enter this area from behind a closed door, and must pass a long iron rail and an officer's desk. Milagros enters. Milagros Gonzalez is a prisoner in this women's maximum security prison. Recently arrested, she explains, "The parole office violated me for a dirty urine. I just don't know how this happened." She has been in prison before and knows some of the women there. She has gone through the process of arranging care for her children before and is greatly anxious about the possibility of losing them. The officer at the desk, a male, hands her a sheet of paper and pencil. Milagros signs hurriedly and starts toward the visiting room area. The officer looks at the sheet and calls Milagros back. Sandy, who appears toward the end of the scene, is a prisoner who works in the Children's Center, helps prison mothers arrange care for their children on the outside, and teaches foster care and parenting education. Sandy has also created many parenting programs, in particular one called Breaking the Cycle, which Milagros mentions at the end of this act. Abri is also a prisoner.*

OFFICER: Hey Gonzalez! Get back here and sign your State I.D. number. You know the rules. This ain't your first visit, or your first bid.

MILAGROS [*coming back*]: Sorry, Mr. Browneville. I'm so excited 'bout seeing my kids I forgot. [*adds a number on paper and goes into visiting room to a table where Mr. Waltzman, the caseworker, is sitting. He is a white man, pudgy and bald, wearing a seersucker suit. Milagros speaking to Mr. Waltzman, looking around for the children*] Where is my kids?

MR. WALTZMAN: Hello, and how are you too, Ms. Gonzalez.

MILAGROS: Hey Mr. Waltzman. I haven't seen my kids since I was arrested. Are they in The Children's Place?

MR. WALTZMAN: Ms. Gonzalez, there has been a change in plans since we last spoke. That's why I came alone to speak with you. The children are having some problems.

MILAGROS [*angry and hurt*]: What's wrong with my kids? You're damn right, they havin' some problems. They ain't seen their mother.

MR. WALTZMAN: Don't get so excited. I'll bring the children next week. You and I need to talk.

MILAGROS [*extremely agitated, goes on as if she doesn't hear her caseworker*]: How can you do this to me? Have me thinkin' for the past month you was gonna bring my kids. How they doin'? Do they ask for me? I know they miss me cause I sho' do miss them.

MR. WALTZMAN [*shifting uncomfortably in his seat*]: Yes, they do miss you but your daughter, Angela, is angry at you and really didn't want to come to see you but will come if your son, Petey, does. He wants to come very badly.

MILAGROS [*defensively*]: Of course he wants to see me! And so does Angela. [*sadly*] She's just mad at me right now. But I'll make it up to her as soon as I get outta here and take her and Petey home again.

MR. WALTZMAN [*looks down to the floor and takes a deep breath and looks back at Milagros*]: It may not be that easy this time. I came to discuss the papers the agency sent to you on Riker's.

MILAGROS [*pouting*]: I don't wanna discuss no papers.

MR. WALTZMAN: Ms. Gonzalez, please stop pouting. What I'm going to say is difficult. I'm very sorry indeed that it has come to this point.

MILAGROS [*angry but also afraid*]: Don't be so damn sorry. Just say what you gotta say.

MR. WALTZMAN: I wish there was another option but there isn't and we have to think about the best interest of the children. I'm asking you to consider giving the children up for adoption.

MILAGROS [*incredulously*]: You must be crazy if you think I'm gonna give my kids away.

MR. WALTZMAN: This is not the first time your children have been in care for prolonged stays. I know you have a drug problem but foster care is only a temporary placement.

MILAGROS: You're damn straight it's temporary. I'm gettin' my kids outta there. I'm not havin' no adoption. I'm not havin' it.

MR. WALTZMAN [*a bit sternly*]: It's no longer up to you to have or not have. If there is a family member willing to take the children the agency will consider them because family has the first priority.

MILAGROS: If I had family to keep my kids, they wouldn't be in foster care and you know that. My kids know I'm their mother and you'll hurt them if you take them away from me.

MR. WALTZMAN: I'm sorry, Ms. Gonzalez. The foster care agency and I have no choice other than to recommend adoption for these children. You must think about what is best for them.

MILAGROS: What's best for them is to be with me. I'm their mother and I'll go to court and tell the judge.

MR. WALTZMAN: If you go to court and contest this, which is your right, you don't have a very good chance of winning.

MILAGROS: You and nobody ain't taking mine without a fight. Win or lose, I'm gonna go to court. Those my children and they know me.

MR. WALTZMAN: Since the children do know you we can look into "Open Adoption" so you can have some contact with the children. If you want our lawyer will explain this agreement to you.

MILAGROS [*thinking fast*]: If you're so sho' 'bout me losin' in court, then why did you drive all the way up here to try to con me into signin' my kids away. And why does your lawyer have to explain anythin' to me? I supposed to have my own lawyer. I know my rights!

MR. WALTZMAN [*embarrassed a bit*]: Oh, ah, yes. You're entitled to a lawyer.

MILAGROS [*puts her face in her hands and begins to cry, no sound, just shoulders heaving. Looks up at caseworker with tears rolling down her cheeks*]: Please don't take my kids. They're all I have. I know I've messed up but give me just one more chance. Please.

MR. WALTZMAN [*softening*]: Ms. Gonzalez, it's not up to me. The Administration for Children's Services and the agency have already filed the petition to terminate your parental rights. The children were returned to you but you placed them back and you didn't visit regular.

MILAGROS: Can't you see I love my kids if I placed them back in foster care? I couldn't take care of them while I was smokin' Crack. That ain't no kind of life for them. But I'm gonna go to a drug program while I'm in here.

MR. WALTZMAN [*shaking his head sadly*]: I'm not saying that you don't love your children but I cannot in good conscience give you a favorable recommendation since you have had more than one chance and you're still not able to provide a home for your children.

MILAGROS: You're new to my case. You have no right to recommend anything without givin' me at least one shot at doing the right thing.

MR. WALTZMAN [*agitated*]: That's the point I'm trying to make. You've had more than enough chances. I read your file and I have been the caseworker for more than a year.

MILAGROS: What chances have I had? You don't know nothin' bout my life. Those so-called files you read and judge me by don't tell the whole truth.

MR. WALTZMAN: Ms. Gonzalez, in the time that I have had this case you haven't shown me any reason why these children shouldn't be adopted. You can't keep using your drug addiction as an excuse for not being a mother to your children. I'm really not that new to this case. I was your caseworker for sometime prior to your incarceration but you missed all of the appointments I scheduled.

MILAGROS [*angrily*]: That's right I missed them cause all that stupid ass agency did for me was nothin'. Not Jack-shit, okay. When I left here I needed all the help I could get but the caseworker was always too busy or out in the field and not in the office and she was supposed to help me. The old caseworker hated me and she never returned my calls and she ain't shit either. That agency is no good and you know it.

MR. WALTZMAN: I can't speak for what the agency did or didn't do for you but you must understand we can't help you if you don't want to be helped.

MILAGROS: Like I said, nobody did nothin' for me or my kids. No help with housin' or a drug program to help me stay straight.

MR. WALTZMAN: We can only suggest services like I'm doing now with the "Open Adoption" option but you have to want the help. It's up to you in the long run.

MILAGROS: That's right it's up to me and I ain't signin' no fuckin' papers.

MR. WALTZMAN: Again, I'm sorry but I'm not changing my position in this case. I'll bring the children next week. Please give this matter careful consideration.

MILAGROS [*losing control completely*]: What the fuck you sorry for, you bald headed mutherfucker? You don't know shit. You come up here so damn proper and shit. You don't know how hard it was for me. That's one of the reasons why I started to use drugs again.

MR. WALTZMAN [*indignantly*]: Look, I understand you're upset. But you have no right to insult me. Stop making me the bad guy. I know you love your children and that's why I recommended that you have some contact. I'm sorry it has to be this way.

MILAGROS [*hysterical*]: You have no right to come here without my children and with this fuckin' bullshit. [*screaming*] Get out you cold lyin' bastard. This visit is over. I'm outta here. [*to officer*] I'm leavin'. [*starts to cry again*] I'm not gonna give you my babies and I'll die before I sign any stinkin' ass adoption papers. Open or fuckin' closed adoption, they won't be my kids no more and, oh God, help me. . . . [*Milagros falls in a heap on the visiting room floor. The caseworker starts toward her but the correction officer waves him out and goes over to Milagros. He helps Milagros into a chair but she doesn't sit down. Instead she goes out of the visiting room by the same route she entered.*]

Scene ii. *Milagros has left the visiting room and is alone in a 6'x 9'cell. There is a toilet with sink over it and a mirror above the sink. A cot or twin bed is center stage without any bedding only a mattress. Her belongings are still in the plastic bags and the cell is rather bare. There is a window without a curtain and a small cabinet is near it. Milagros walks to the sink and stares into the mirror glaring at the toilet, then walks to the cot and sits down. Walking to the window she looks out and takes a letter from the top of the cabinet. As she reads it tears are rolling down her face and she throws it to the floor. She turns the mattress over, panics, searches frantically until she finds a small hole removing a crumpled piece of what appears to be tissue paper, then turns the mattress again and sits for a short time staring at the wad of paper in her hand. Opening it carefully she examines its contents as if unwrapping the blanket of a newborn child, then empties twenty or so orange colored pills from the paper into her hand. She stretches out on the bed and starts to cry again but this time the sobs rack her body. This look is of someone who has lost touch with reality. She curls into a fetal position and is sucking her thumb. She walks over to the mirror and stares at herself intently then faces audience.*

MILAGROS [*in a crazed voice*]: I'm so stupid. All my fault. I should'a knew this was comin', but no, I'm so stupid. Dumb mutherfuckin' Mr. Waltzman askin' me can someone in my family take my kids. HA! My family . . . what family? [*starts to talk to her mother*] Hey Mommie, remember how many times you called me stupid? Well, I am and crazy to believe somebody could ever love me cause you sure never did. You left me with Abuela in Puerto Rico until I was big enough to help you with your other kids. Si, si, that's the only reason why you came back to get me and to have another kid to add to your welfare budget. And I was stupid enough to think you came back cause I used to wish so hard that you would come and just hug me so I could smell your pretty perfume.

And then you finally did. I can't forget Abuela's warnin' me not to leave with you cause she knew you was gonna mess up my life like you did your own. I can't even depend on you to go get my kids even if I don't really want them with you, I don't want them with no strangers so I can't never see them no more. It's my fault you say that I'm here again. [*screaming*] Yeah right! Just like it's my fault one of your drunken boyfriends raped me when I was nine. You didn't believe me not even when you saw the blood in my panties and blood on my face from him bustin' open my lip from sayin' no to him. You slapped me right on the same lip, called me puta, yellin' it was all my fault. [*goes over to the bag and takes out a picture of the children with their father*] Oh mis pobres ninos, lo lamento mucho, los amo, siempre los amare. Now I'm doin' the same thin' to you. [*crying*] Always leavin' you to get high, thinkin' you don't know what's goin' on.

Tryin' to protect you and me from Chino's fierce ass whippin' [*talking to the children's father*] And you fuckin' bastardo, hijo de puta, tu maldita madre, Chino. Telling me in that stupid ass letter you gonna kill me if I let the state adopt our kids. What the fuck did you ever do for me but take me away from Mommie when I was fourteen and fuck me morning, noon, and night and give me drugs? [*looks at the picture and rubs the faces of her children saying to them*] Now I'm gonna lose you cause of the drugs and cause I'm just no damn good, like my mother. [*speaking to Sandy*] Break the cycle, how Sandy? I don't blame you for bein' mad at me. I did you wrong, so fucked up, so wrong. I can't do this time without my kids, Sandy. [*the music of "Fairy Tales" by Anita Baker is playing in the background*] That must be Abri's music. That girl sho' loves that song. She has a good family but they still couldn't save her from that cocaine. But her family tried and stick by her and that's more than anyone ever done for me or you Sandy. [*starts to take the pills, some of them spill to the floor, and goes and lies on the bed and starts to cry very softly*] Oh, my babies. Please forgive me but maybe you'll have a better life than what I had. Angela, maybe you'll break the cycle. Those foster people better be good to you. I'm so tired of all of it. I couldn't live in this world knowin' I can't ever see you or Petey again. [*closes her eyes and the lights fade out*]

"I Couldn't Have Told You Then," "Death Train," and "Mirror Images" are from Aliens at the Border, *1997.*

Jazz Moon

Too many nights I've found myself like this
Thoughts of freedom flashing
Hearing the train whistle moan low and seductive
Imagining the steel kiss the tracks
Melting together coupled like lovers perfect in union

Moonlight flickers eerily
Shadowing barred windows
My mind spins like the Ferris wheel
And the wild Jack Rabbit ride in the Seabreeze Amusement Park
My little girl self lost in the Spook House

My thoughts travel to Main Street
The bus stop in front of Lerner's Department Store
The clothes on racks
Waiting in line for the dressing room
My first taste of lipstick to boast orange pedal pushers

Too many nights like this I fight to sleep to not think
My other long ago lost life
I sink to my knees—drift and feel the chill and isolation
The dark pathway of loneliness arching deep in my back

Facing my naked reality with sheer helplessness
Past depression into a void that only the barred prison cell claims
My mouth clammy and dry gulps down welcomed air
Try to bring myself back to prayer

Prayer for redemption and peace
Peace to combat stale bile that threatens to erupt
My little children playing in a grassy backyard
Young adults now kissing me goodbye ending the prison visit

In a mind sweltering with memories
I can't decide which ones to claim
They come fast, evaporate or linger like an unwanted passion.
I fight my way out of the dark abyss
To the calmness of the 23rd Psalm

The train whistle moans
I rise from my knees
The moonlight illuminates my warrior stance
And I travel with the train
Transforming the low note
Of its whistle to a jazz sax
            And I dance!

I Couldn't Have Told You Then

Then you were too young. Now
you are twenty-one,
breathing life into your own child.
I couldn't have told you then
that you were the sin of my youth
and we both laugh as we do now
I couldn't cry to you and have you hold me
couldn't tell you about men—
couldn't share the swell of love
for you in my breast, frozen in my heart
when I look at you. Years have only made me
love you more than I could ever have told you then!

Death Train

Thinking of the tears she cried to me
Tears for the loss of her children, loss of her childhood
I feel tears hot on my own cheeks.
My rage bubbles up and erupts like an angry volcano
Spilling over and smelling like the death train that rides so slowly
Capturing our youth in their prime, disguised as the
Treacherous and tricky white powder guaranteed to make you feel better
And destined to ride still and cold in the back of its wagon.
Yesterday it was King Heroin and the elegant White Lady.
Today it's Madam Queen Crack much like the crack in the sidewalk
Splitting up mothers and children, leaving gaps
Where nothing lives but anger and pain that grows moldy and festers
How painful it is to watch my sisters of so many colors lose themselves to
    you, Madam Queen Crack!
Even more when they lose children they can never hold again, and that this
    can happen without an aye or nay from their lips.
Reality slowly sinks into her face and the pain is so sharp that her features
    are transformed in front of my eyes.
She vows to get her children back somehow, someway.
"These white folks ain't gonna take mine. Those my kids, my babies, mine,
    mine."

I can smell the death train waiting for her, pushing and nudging her
   urgently

I can see her resistance but she is weak from all the pain of her recent loss
   and yesterday's too.
Don't go, I cry, struggling to wrestle her to the ground
Waking up sweating holding my pillow amid tangled sheets, feeling so
   lost.

Mirror Images

Images reflect from her nervous movements
her badly broken English that compels
      me irritably to correct her
her eagerness to learn
her willingness to share all the pain that is
      too much for me
                  to bear

   Anger floods me
   I check it with amazing and deliberate
               control
   trying hard to understand
   that the strained distance between us
         is caused by my not wanting to see

            those mirror images.

For she is so much me
   that I see
            another time and place
               a little brown girl
            dragged down too early from full womanhood
            knowing too much but never enough
               of the right stuff.

   She collects herself
   states her needs
   gets what she came for
   thanks me aloofly
   turns with the grace of a queen

      God, I can hardly bear it for she is so much me
            transforming into another for another life

She turns back to me
offers a shy smile
bridges the distance to hug me

I hug her back
        too tightly—
           thinking sisterhood,
       thinking kinship.

PART 6

SOLIDARITY WITH OTHER WOMEN

We your sisters
also mothers
also daughters
bathed in tears and our own fears
rocking, rocking, holding you.

A child's death
stops
our breath

—Kathy Boudin

Something happened to the prisoners' rights movement from 1975 to the 1990s. Women happened.   —Ellen M. Barry

Empathy is the defining component of solidarity in women's prison literature. Boldly stated political protests as well as personal celebrations of women's friendships announce the solidarity of imprisoned women. It is a solidarity endorsed by empathy and made genuine and honest through acknowledgment of a shared pain that transcends the particulars of individual experience: an audacious solidarity, which risks uniting women inside and outside through their common challenges. As suggested by imprisoned author Kathy Boudin and prisoners' rights activist Ellen M. Barry above, the pain may arise from social rejection, personal bereavement, or even impending capital punishment. Whatever the source, the writing of women prisoners proclaims a humanity capable of empathizing with their sisters' pain and motivated to act.

Although some earlier writers, such as Madame Roland, disdain other female prisoners and desire to set themselves apart from the general population, authors from the twentieth century on more typically announce support for the female society of a women's prison.[1] In spite of differing backgrounds and circumstances, these writers unite to advocate women's causes. The writers included in the following selections acknowledge the same need for communication and relationships expressed in the writings in part 4, but they carry that concern one step further. Starting at the personal level of recognized individual need and vulnerability, they move to statements of collective strength. The selections in this section declare pride in unity and especially in female solidarity.

The prison memoirs of British suffragette[2] Lady Constance Lytton present an especially fascinating early narrative of this spirit of sisterhood. In her late thirties, this upper-class, unmarried, and childless woman developed a profound interest in prison reform, which she explained as an emotional substitute for "what maternity there lurks in me."[3] Enraged that she had been given preferential treatment when imprisoned with other suffragettes, she posed as a working-class suffragette during her imprisonment in 1910, and, at great expense to her fragile health, exposed the class injustices of British prisons. Her love for the women she met in prison is evident in her memoirs' "Dedication to Prisoners":

> Lay hold of your inward self and keep tight hold. Reverence yourself. Be just, kind and forgiving to yourself.
>
> In my ignorance and impudence I went into prison hoping to help prisoners. So far as I know, I was unable to do anything for them. But the prisoners helped me. They seemed at times the direct channels between me and God Himself, imbued with the most friendly and powerful goodness that I have ever met.[4]

Lytton did, indeed, help her sister prisoners, contrary to her modest self-assessment. After Lytton's death, Mrs. Coombe Tennant, one of the first women appointed to the position of visiting justice in the prisons, stated that Lytton "was denied an active life in the tussle of things," but "her thoughts lived, and were worked out by others. . . . [S]he had a share in altering the world and shaping thought among women."[5] The writings of female political prisoners have long served as the voice of those sisters silenced by repression, lack of education, or institution-bred apathy and despair. Testimonial literature of women imprisoned under repressive regimes dramatically serves this function today.[6]

American journalist Agnes Smedley, imprisoned in the New York City Tombs[7] during World War I, voiced the plight of the women she met there. Her prison sketches, "Cell Mates," depict the courage of her sister political prisoners, birth-control activist Kitty Marion and Russian revolutionary Mollie Steimer; equally memorable are her sketches of a prostitute and a forger who, although uneducated, boast colorful personalities and stories of their own. Through her writing, Smedley gave individuality and dignity to nameless criminals behind the walls of the Tombs.

Social protest in the American labor and civil rights movements has led to the imprisonment of women from varied racial and ethnic backgrounds.

Several have written of their experiences in works that promote women's causes. Ericka Huggins, Angela Davis, and Emma Goldman, for example, strikingly illustrate the power of women's prison literature to articulate the continuity of the personal and the political, as they link their individual stories of imprisonment to wider struggles. Elissa D. Gelfand has written that French women prisoners are twice criminal, because their crimes violate the law as well as social codes of acceptable behavior for women.[8] Taking her point one step further, many imprisoned American women are thrice criminal, since from birth they have borne the burden of classism and racism as well as sexism. For them, writing and art may offer a means to resist oppression.[9]

In contemporary American prisons, writing workshops, organized by outside universities and prison associations or by the prisoners themselves, have promoted solidarity among women writers. But programs tend to come and go and are not available at all facilities. Workshops such as the Santa Cruz Women's Prison Project at the California Institution for Women, led by Karlene Faith in the 1970s, the Free Space Writing Program, led by Carol Muske and Gail Rosenblum at Riker's Island also in the 1970s, and more recently the Writing Workshop at Bedford Hills Correctional Facility, led by Hettie Jones, and the Massachusetts Correctional Institute in Framingham poetry workshop led by Rosanna Warren, have offered much more than avenues to individual creativity and literacy. These programs have fostered a communal spirit to counter the negativity of the community outside the walls. They, too, provide women the hope of resistance through writing.

The creative work of these groups displays the collective aesthetic that H. Bruce Franklin, in his now classic analysis of men's prison writing, has linked to the heritage of black American literature.[10] Published in workshop anthologies, prison newsletters, journals, or websites, these writings not only bear the names of individual authors, but also carry the force of voices united in protest. They demonstrate that women prisoners' intention to reclaim self-respect and undermine the system's power negates stereotypes of passive, "fallen women." The preface of *Songs from a Free Space: Writings by Women in Prison* from Riker's Island, for example, boldly announces its authors' collective purpose:

> [T]his anthology is a crime. A crime of conspiracy, an informed, fully-consenting adult decision to commit poetry, an invention of the imagination that will never tear down the bars or break the system's back, but has ripped off some room for people to "breathe together" (another definition of "conspiracy") and pulled off a heist of institutional supermind, liberated the space as a continuum. This anthology is about possibilities. It is nothing flashy—not an act of realpolitik—just a homey little crime among friends.[11]

In *Aliens at the Border*, a collection of poems from Bedford Hills, the voices of fourteen writers blend to describe the lifestyles that brought them to prison: "Parole board is approaching/ No home to go to!") and the lives they lead in prison ("No letters! No packages! Phone disconnected!")[12] Although poems from workshops like this one have a powerful effect when read separately, as products of individual poets, anthologies offer readers a richer experience through the collective impact of the groups' poems. These are collective, communal creations, generated through the mutual support of the group. They are "choral" or "plural," to borrow a term from Carole Boyce Davies' description of women's collective oral histories.[13] In the choral voices of prison workshop anthologies, form and content reinforce each other's message of solidarity.[14] The ultimate expression of this form is a collaboratively written poem. For example, in "Tetrina," written by collective members of the Writing Workshop at Bedford Hills, "Six women argue with their lives/ as they write among their dreams. . . ." Writing, to them, signifies freedom and power; in poetry dreams become "words to change our lives. . . ."[15] The potential for art to transform reality may have limits, however. Former U.S. political prisoner Susan Rosenberg, currently a prison rights activist, offers a relevant caveat in her discussion of theater projects in women's prisons: "[A]rt can liberate and transform self-conceptions and creating theatre can give women alternative visions of their own lives, but these cannot last without changes in the long-term underlying conditions that the majority of incarcerated women face."[16]

The concerns voiced in the collaborative works of prison writing workshops are reinforced in writing by individual women prisoners who, in their own ways, seek connection with sisters outside prison. Contemporary women's prison literature affirms solidarity in its definition of the word "prisoner," as illustrated by Ericka Huggins's poetry in this section. Although some women prison writers of the past have defended themselves by proclaiming their *differences* from other women prisoners, Huggins destroys barriers in a spirit of camaraderie that opposes racism, sexism, and classism. Her breadth of vision regards women's prison experience as paradigmatic of women's position in society. While imprisoned in Connecticut in 1970–71 during her trial as a Black Panther, Huggins used her poems as a medium to make a revolutionary statement: women inside and outside bars face the same oppression and must not be divided by an adversarial relationship imposed by society. In poems that share the assertive energy of black women poets like Sonia Sanchez, Huggins calls all women to embrace solidarity. Traditional male prison literature, with its metaphors of romantic transcendence, is subverted in bold metaphors linking prison with poverty, degradation, and power imbalances. Huggins's poems likewise reject the self-justification of prison writings like Madame Roland's memoirs; rather than defending herself by insisting that she differs from her sister prisoners, Huggins proclaims that *all* women are prisoners.

Norma Stafford, a working-class woman and a lesbian, discovered the liberating power of her writing talent at the Santa Cruz Women's Prison Project in the 1970s. She writes poetry that resonates with an honest yearning for emotional and physical contact to combat prison's sensory deprivation. Celebrating the magical healing power of love in its many forms, Stafford's poems are both intimate messages to beloved individuals and a glorification of female spiritual and physical energy. Her poems explore the possibilities of compassion and sisterhood, a paradox for those "locked together, bound together/ in this small hated space," where institutionalization undermines positive feelings. As she proclaims the power of the "sweet sweet woman soldier," Stafford's poems confront the complexity of imprisoned women's solidarity. They transcend binary distinctions of gender to affirm women's desire for relationship and need to name "the unspeakable."[17]

Marilyn Buck's poems in this section echo the desire of Norma Stafford's art. The "unspeakable" is made eloquent in Buck's lines that extol female beauty, yet speak poignantly of loss, because walls and restrictions frustrate desire and intentionally divide and fragment women's relationships. An American political prisoner with an eighty-year sentence, Buck writes sensual love poems that complement her more political and theoretical discussions in other poems.[18] These more private poems, however, carry their own social message in images of relationships that never happen, lovers who never meet, humans unnaturally separated as they live out "another khaki clad day." One of Buck's most moving poems, "Prison Chant," is a theatrical piece depicting a moment when connection is made, although that connection ironically is one-sided, unseen, and anonymous. The poet witnesses the anguished phone call of prison mother Cassandra and testifies that the institution has destroyed a family. Cassandra mourns her distant children, yet never knows that her pain has truly touched her sister poet and, through her, the reader.

Writer and editor Patricia McConnel shatters readers' complacency with her short fiction. Stories like "Sing Soft, Sing Loud," based upon McConnel's experiences in American prisons, expose inhumane policies and acts of institutionalized brutality that abuse lawful power. Each woman, affirms McConnel, has the right to be treated with dignity, whatever her crime. Her stories about women's survival originated in her personal struggle and her observations of others, and they deal candidly with her own pain and outrage. Decades after her imprisonment, McConnel has achieved a distance and perspective that she feels are best conveyed through fiction. Even when they are in pain, her imprisoned characters sing—for singing, throughout her stories, symbolizes "the indestructibility of the spirit." She writes:

> An extremely important element in my motivation to write these stories is to give the reader some sense of the reality of this form of societal madness—that these are real human beings being destroyed by a machine designed and run by madmen, for the most part. In spite of this dark theme, most of the stories are life-affirming in some way. I am impressed, all these years afterwards, at the resiliency of the spirits of the women I knew.

My stories are about women struggling to preserve their wills, their self-respect in a system intent on destroying them.[19]

McConnel tells the reader that if women prisoners unite, even if only in spirit, they can mitigate the cruelties of the system and find a measure of freedom. Her comments echo and update Lytton's "Dedication" to the prisoners she loved, reinforcing the links between texts written by women prisoners. Both works are more than their authors' personal accounts of the pains of imprisonment, written for an intimate family audience or the public. They are messages of love and encouragement, written for the women they knew and respected in prison and forwarded in solidarity and hope to all imprisoned sisters.

NOTES

The quotation in the title of this section is taken from Ericka Huggins, "I wake in middle-of-night terror," *Off Our Backs: A Women's News Journal* 1, no. 17 (February 1971). The first epigraph to this section is taken from Kathy Boudin, "For M.," in *Breaking Silence: Voices of Mothers in Prison,* compiled by JusticeWorks Community (Brooklyn, N.Y.: JusticeWorks Community, 1999). The second epigraph is taken from Ellen M. Barry, "Women Prisoners on the Cutting Edge: Development of the Activist Women's Prisoners' Rights Movement," *Social Justice* 27, no. 3 (2000): 168–75 (168).

1. Other relevant selections in this anthology include the writings by Bedell, Chilean Women, Lebrón, Makhoere, Metzger, Norton, Partnoy, Saadawi, Shakur, and Women of the ACE Program.

2. Throughout this book *suffragette*, rather than *suffragist*, is used to refer to the women who worked in the militant arm of the British woman suffrage movement. Suffragist was a more general term used for supporters of woman suffrage. See Caroline J. Howlett, "Writing on the Body? Representation and Resistance in British Suffragette Accounts of Forcible Feeding," *Genders*, issue 23 (1996): 3–41, note 5, p. 37.

3. Lady Constance Lytton to her mother, 24 February 1909, in *Prisons and Prisoners* (London: Heinemann, and East Ardsley, Yorkshire: EP Publishing, 1914), 33.

4. Lytton, *Prisons and Prisoners,* x.

5. Mrs. Coombe Tennant, J.P., to Lytton family, quoted in *Letters of Constance Lytton,* ed. Betty Balfour (London: Heinemann, 1925), 265–66. See Caroline J. Howlett, "Writing on the Body?" for a discussion of the resistance of suffragettes, particularly of Lytton.

6. See John Beverly, "The Margin at the Center: *On Testimonio* (Testimonial Narrative)," in *De/Colonizing the Subject: The Politics of Gender in Women's Autobiography,* ed. Sidonie Smith and Julia Watson (Minneapolis: University of Minnesota Press, 1992), 91–114.

7. The Tombs was the name given to the Halls of Justice, a New York City prison opened in 1838. Its massive Egyptian style architecture inspired the name of the Tombs. Museum of the City of New York. Online, available: www.mcny.org.

8. Elissa D. Gelfand, "Women Prison Authors in France: Twice Criminal," *Modern Language Studies* II, no. 1 (Winter 1980–1981): 57–63.

9. For a discussion of the resistance of women prisoners and women prison activist movements, see Ellen M. Barry, "Women Prisoners on the Cutting Edge: Development of the Activist Women's Prisoners' Rights Movement," *Social Justice* 27, no. 3 (2000) 168–75. See also Karlene Faith, "Reflections on Inside/Out Organizing," *Social Justice* 27, no. 3 (2000); "The Politics of Confinement and Resistance: The Imprisonment of Women," in *Criminal*

Injustice: Confronting the Prison Crisis, ed. Elihu Rosenblatt (Boston: South End Press, 1996), 165–83; and *Unruly Women: The Politics of Confinement and Resistance* (Vancouver: Press Gang, 1993). Interesting parallels can be drawn between women's resistance expressed in prison writing and the use of writing as an expression of resistance by female victims of the Holocaust. See Rachel Feldhay Brenner, *Writing as Resistance: Four Women Confronting the Holocaust* (University Park: Pennsylvania State University Press, 1997). See Juanita Díaz-Cotto, *Gender, Ethnicity, and the State: Latina and Latino Prison Politics* (Albany: State University of New York Press, 1996) for a discussion of Latina prisoners' politicization. See Kum-Kum Bhavnani and Angela Davis, "Fighting for Her Future: Reflections on Human Rights and Women's Prisons in the Netherlands," *Social Identities*, 3, no.1 (Feb. 1997): 7ff, for a discussion of the progressive attitude toward human rights in Dutch prisons.

10. H. Bruce Franklin, *The Victim as Criminal and Artist: Literature from the American Prison* (New York: Oxford University Press, 1978), 250–51.

11. Carol Muske and Gail Rosenblum, eds., *Songs from a Free Space: Writings by Women in Prison* (New York: New York City Correctional Institution for Women, Free Space Writing Program, n.d.). See the annotated bibliography in this anthology for information on contemporary anthologies and newsletters from women's prisons. For further information on prison publications, see Russell N. Baird, *The Penal Press* (Evanston, Ill.: Northwestern University Press, 1967).

12. Joy Wosu, "Worrywart," *Aliens at the Border*. The Writing Workshop, Bedford Hills Correctional Facility. Ed. Hettie Jones (New York: Segue, 1997), 29.

13. Carole Boyce Davies, "Collaboration and the Ordering Imperative in Life Story Production," in *De/Colonizing the Subject: The Politics of Gender in Women's Autobiography*, ed. Sidonie Smith and Julia Watson (Minneapolis: University of Minnesota Press, 1992), 3–19. See also Caren Kaplan, "Resisting Autobiography: Out-Law Genres and Transnational Feminist Subjects," in *Women, Autobiography, Theory: A Reader*, ed. Sidonie Smith and Julia Watson (Madison: University of Wisconsin Press, 1998), 208–16.

14. Similarly, Rhodessa Jones's Medea Project in the San Francisco County Jail and Jean Trounstine's Shakespeare theatre program at Framingham Women's Prison in Massachusetts provide incarcerated women with a means for collective expression and solidarity through theater. See Rena Fraden, *Imagining Medea: Rhodessa Jones and Theater for Incarcerated Women* (Chapel Hill: University of North Carolina Press, 2001) and Jean Trounstine, *Shakespeare behind Bars: The Power of Drama in a Women's Prison* (New York: St. Martin's Press, 2001).

15. Workshop Collaboration 1996, "Tetrina," *Aliens at the Border*. The Writing Workshop, Bedford Hills Correctional Facility. Ed. Hettie Jones. (New York: Segue, 1997), 3.

16. Susan Rosenberg, "Escape Routes," review of *Imagining Medea: Rhodessa Jones and Theater for Incarcerated Women*, by Rena Fraden, and *Shakespeare behind Bars: The Power of Drama in a Women's Prison*, by Jean Trounstine, *The Women's Review of Books*, 19, no. 7 (April 2002): 15–16.

17. See Julia Watson, "Unspeakable Differences: The Politics of Gender in Lesbian and Heterosexual Women's Autobiographies," in *De/Colonizing the Subject: The Politics of Gender in Women's Autobiography*, ed. Sidonie Smith and Julia Watson (Minneapolis: University of Minnesota Press, 1992), 139–68, for a discussion of the use of the term "unspeakable" with reference to lesbian autobiography. See Dominik Morgan, "Restricted Love," in *Breaking the Rules: Women in Prison and Feminist Therapy*, ed. Judy Harden and Marcia Hill (New York: Harrington Park Press, 1998), 75–84, for a prisoner's perspective on lesbian relationships in prison.

18. For her prose discussion of the position of female political prisoners, see Marilyn Buck, "On Self-Censorship," Parentheses Writing Series (Berkeley, Calif.: Small Press Distribution, 1995).

19. Patricia McConnel to Judith Scheffler, 1 April 1983; 6 July 1983; 2 March 1985.

LADY CONSTANCE LYTTON

(1869–1923)

Constance Georgina Lytton was a daughter of British diplomat Edward Robert Bulwer-Lytton, first earl of Lytton and viceroy of India. She was born in Vienna, raised in India, and spent much of her childhood abroad with her family. Educated at home, where she was not encouraged to pursue a career in one of her interests, which included music and journalism, Lytton led an uneventful life of service to her family. After her father's death she remained unmarried and devoted herself to her mother, her friends, and domestic interests, especially flower arranging.

The turning point of Lytton's life came in 1906, when she inherited £1,000 from Lady Bloomfield, her godmother and great-aunt. Seeking a public cause to support, she became interested in the revival of British folk-dancing and -singing, and through it coincidentally met British suffragettes in 1908. Her interest in prisons drew her to their work, since many of them were being imprisoned. Gradually she came to accept the suffragettes' militant tactics. She served as a movement lecturer and agitator for four years, despite her delicate health and her distaste for public life. She was imprisoned a total of four times: twice in Holloway Prison outside London, in Newcastle, and in Walton Jail, Liverpool. As Lady Constance, she received preferential treatment and, unlike other suffragette prisoners, was not forcibly fed when a test of her heart revealed its weakness. Outraged at this injustice, Lytton disguised herself as working-class suffragette Jane Warton, was arrested during a demonstration in Liverpool in 1910, and was imprisoned in Walton Jail, where she was forcibly fed without examination. Though she successfully exposed the class injustices of prison treatment, she suffered impaired health for the rest of her life. After a stroke of paralysis in 1912, Lytton spent her last eleven years as an invalid, cared for by her mother and admired by other suffragettes. During the first two years of that period she wrote *Prisons and Prisoners*, her account of her imprisonment, with her left hand.

As Mary Gordon, a psychologist and the first British woman prison inspector, described Lytton and the women's suffrage movement: "Such spiritual upheavals are always irrational, and irrational human types are swept into them as high priests. Con was seized and used. She was both flame and burnt offering."

Note: Background information is from Betty Balfour, ed., *Letters of Constance Lytton* (London: Heinemann, 1925); E. Sylvia Pankhurst, *The Suffragette Movement: An Intimate Account of Persons and Ideals* (London: Longmans, Green, 1931); Emmeline Pethick-Lawrence, *My Part in a Changing World* (London: Gollancz, 1938); *The Europa Biographical Dictionary of British Women*, 1983, s.v. "Lytton, Lady Constance"; *The American Heritage Dictionary of the English Language*, 4th ed., Lytton, First Earl of."

DISGUISED AS JANE WARTON

From Prisons and Prisoners, *1914.*

Under a Government which imprisons any unjustly, the true place for a just man (or woman) is also a prison.   [—Henry David Thoreau]

I was sent to Liverpool and Manchester to join in working an Anti-Government campaign during a General Election in January, 1910. Just before I went, there came the news of the barbarous ill-treatment of Miss Selina Martin and Miss Leslie Hall, while on remand in Walton Gaol. They had been refused bail, and, while awaiting their trial, their friends were not allowed to communicate with them. This is contrary to law and precedent for prisoners on remand. As a protest they had started a hunger-strike. They were led by force, in answer to which they broke the windows of their cells. They were put in irons for days and nights together, and one of them was frog-marched in the most brutal fashion to and from the room where the forcible feeding was performed. These facts they made known to their friends at the police court on the day of their trial.

I heard, too, of another prisoner in Liverpool, Miss Bertha Brewster, who had been re-arrested after her release from prison, and charged with breaking the windows of her prison cell, which she had done as a protest against being fed by force. She had been punished for this offence while in prison. She did not respond to the summons, and when arrested on a warrant, three and a half months later, she was sentenced to six weeks' hard labour for this offence.

I felt a great wish to be in Liverpool, if possible, to get public opinion in that town to protest against such treatment of women political prisoners. If I failed in this, I determined myself to share the fate of these women.

When I was in Manchester, Mary Gawthorpe was ill with the internal complaint which has since obliged her to give up work. She saw me in her room one day. We had been distressed beyond words to hear of the sufferings of Selina Martin and Leslie Hall. Mary Gawthorpe said, with tears in her eyes, as she threw her arms round me: "Oh, and these are women quite unknown—nobody knows or cares about them except their own friends. They go to prison again and again to be treated like this, until it kills them!" That was enough. My mind was made up. The altogether shameless way I had been preferred against the others at Newcastle, except Mrs. Brailsford who shared with me the special treatment, made me determine to try whether they would recognise my need for exceptional favours without my name. . . .

I joined the W.S.P.U.[1] again, filling up the membership card as Miss Jane Warton. The choice of a name had been easy. When I came out of Holloway Prison, a distant relative, by name Mr. F. Warburton, wrote me an appreciative letter, thanking me for having been a prisoner in this cause.

I determined that if it were necessary to go to prison under another name, I should take the name of Warburton. When I went to Newcastle, my family raised no objection. Now nobody was to know of my disguise, but Warburton was too distinguished a name; that would at once attract attention. I must leave out the "bur" and make it "Warton." "Jane" was the name of Joan of Arc (for Jeanne is more often translated into "Jane" than "Joan") and would bring me comfort in distress. A family sympathetic to our cause, who lived in the suburb near Walton Gaol, were informed that a keen member, Miss Warton, would call at their house in the afternoon before the protest meeting to investigate the outside of the gaol and the Governor's house by daylight, and that she was ready to be arrested if she could not obtain the release of the prisoners. . . .

[Lytton, masquerading as Jane Warton, was arrested during a demonstration in Liverpool and imprisoned in Walton Jail.—*Ed.*]

At last the longed-for moment had arrived, and I was taken off to my cell. To my joy there was a window which opened a little bit; at night it was lit by a gas jet that was set in the depth of the wall behind the door, the passage side, and covered in by a thick glass. I was ever so tired—I laid down and slept.

The next day was Sunday (January 16), but they did not ask us to go to chapel. For several days I did not wear my cap and apron in my cell, but did not in other ways continue my protest against the clothes. The cold seemed to me intense, and I wore the skirt of my dress fastened round my neck for warmth. The Governor, accompanied by the Matron, came to see me, but he was in a temper about our having broken his windows, so I said nothing. He was in a fury at the way I had fastened my skirt. I answered that it was for warmth and that I would gladly put on more clothes and warmer ones if he gave them to me. Later on the Senior Medical Officer came in. He was a short, fat, little man, with a long waxed moustache. I should have said he disliked being unkind; he liked to chaff over things; but as I looked at him I thought I would rather be forcibly fed by anyone in the world than by him, the coarse doctors at Newcastle and the cross little doctor I had seen the night before. I said I had not asked to see him, but he made no examination and asked no questions.

I lay in my bed most of the day, for they did not disturb me, and I tried to keep warm, as I felt the cold fearfully. They brought me all my meals the same as usual, porridge in the morning at 7, meat and potatoes mid-day at 12, porridge at 4.30. When they were hot I fed on the smell of them, which seemed quite delicious; I said "I don't want any, thank you," to each meal, as they brought it in. I had made up my mind that this time I would not drink any water, and would only rinse out my mouth morning and evening without swallowing any. I wrote on the walls of my cell with my slate pencil and soap mixed with the dirt of the floor for ink, "Votes for Women," and the saying from Thoreau's *Duty of Civil Disobedience*—"Under a Government which imprisons any unjustly, the true place for a just man (or woman) is also a prison"; on the wall opposite my bed I wrote the text from

Joshua, "Only be thou strong and very courageous." That night I dreamt of fruits, melons, peaches and nectarines, and of a moonlit balcony that was hung with sweetest smelling flowers, honeysuckle and jessamine, apple-blossom and sweet scented verbena; there was only the sound of night birds throbbing over the hills that ranged themselves below the balcony. On it there slept my sister-in-law, and on the balustrade, but making no noise, was a figure awake and alert, which was my brother. My dream was of a land which was seen by my father in his poem of "King Poppy," where the princess and the shepherd boy are the types etherealised. I woke suddenly. I could sleep a little in detached moments, but this dream had made the prison cell beautiful to me; it had a way out.

The strain was great of having to put on my shoes, which were too small, every time I was taken out of my cell to empty slops or to see the Governor. The Matron was shocked that I did not put the right heel in at all and every day I was given another pair, but they were all alike in being too small for my right foot.

The next day, Monday (January 17), the wardress took my bed and bedding away because I would not make it up, but lay on it in the daytime. I told her if she wished she must roll me off, but that I did not intend voluntarily to give it up. She was quite amiable, but rolled me towards the wall and took the bed and bedding from underneath me. There was a little table in my cell which was not fastened to the wall. I turned it upside down and was able to sit in it with my body resting against one of the legs. It was very uncomfortable, but I felt too ill to sit up in the chair, and the concrete floor was much too cold without the bed. Every now and then I got up and walked backwards and forwards in the cell to get a little warmth into me. The Chaplain came in for a moment. He was a tall, good-looking man, of the burly, healthy sort. It seemed to me, from his talk, that he would be very well suited to be a cricket match or football parson, if there were such a thing, but he was totally unsuited to be the Chaplain of a prison, or anyhow of a woman's prison. He thought it wise to speak to me as a "Suffragette." Look here, it's no good your thinking that there's anything to be done with the women here—the men sometimes are not such bad fellows, and there are many who write to me after they've left here, but the women, they're all as bad as bad can be, there's absolutely no good in them." I did not answer, but I felt inclined to say "Then good-bye to you, since you say you can do no good with the women here."

Presently an officer came and led me out. The manner of nearly all the officers was severe; one or two were friends but most of them treated me like dirt. I was shown along the gangway of the ward, which seemed to me very large, much larger than the D X at Holloway, and went in various directions like a star. I was shown into the Governor's room, which lay at the end of the gangway. It was warm, there were hot pipes against which I was made to stand with my back to the wall, and for a moment, as I put my feet to rest on the pipes, I could think of nothing else but the delight of their heat. The Governor was very cross. I had decided not to do the needlework which constituted the hard labour, for this he gave me three days on bread and water. He would not let me speak to him at all and I was led out, but, before I had got to my cell, I was called back into his presence. "I hear you are refusing to take your food, so it's three days in a special cell." I was taken out and down a staircase till we reached the ground floor. I think my cell was two stories above, but I am not sure; then down again and into a short passage that looked as if it was underground, with a window at the top seemingly only just level with the ground. The door of a cell was opened, I was put inside and the door locked. It was larger than the cell upstairs, and the jug, basin, etc., were all made of black guttapercha, not of tin, placed on the floor. This would have been bad for the ordinary prisoner, as it was quite impossible to tell whether the eating things were clean or not and, in any case, it smelt fairly strong of guttapercha; but as the rule for me was neither to eat nor drink, I was able to put up with it well. The bed was wider than an ordinary plank bed and nailed to the ground, so that I was able to lie on it without being disturbed. Best of all was the fact that it was nearer to the heating apparatus and so seemed quite warm when I was led in. I did not notice at first that the window did not open, but when I had been there six or seven hours it became wonderfully airless. I only left my cell for minutes at a time, when I was allowed to draw water, and the air of the corridor then seemed fresh as mountain air by comparison. I had an idea that Elsie Howey or some of the others would have been put into a punishment cell too. I called, but in vain, my voice had grown weak and my tongue and throat felt thick as a carpet, probably from not drinking anything. I tried signalling with raps on the wall, "No surrender—no surrender," Mrs. Leigh's favourite motto, but I was never sure of corresponding raps, though sometimes I thought I heard them. I could not sleep for more than about an hour at a time, my legs drew up into a cramped position whenever I went off and the choking thickness in my mouth woke me.

Tuesday, January 18, I was visited again by the Senior Medical Officer, who asked me how long I had been without food. I said I had eaten a buttered scone and a banana sent in by friends to the police station on Friday at about midnight. He said, "Oh, then, this is the fourth day; that is too long, I shall have to feed you, I must feed you at once," but he went out and nothing happened till about 6 o'clock in the evening, when he returned with, I think, five wardresses and the feeding apparatus. He urged me to take food voluntarily. I told him that was absolutely out of the question, that when our legislators ceased to resist enfranchising women then I should cease to resist taking food in prison. He did not examine my heart nor feel my pulse; he did not ask to do so, nor did I say anything which could possibly induce him to think I would refuse to be examined. I offered no resistance to being placed in position, but lay down voluntarily on the plank bed. Two of the wardresses took hold of my arms, one held my head and one my feet. One wardress helped to pour the food. The doctor leant on my knees as he stooped over my chest to get at my mouth. I shut my mouth and clenched my teeth. I had looked forward to this moment with so much anxiety lest my identity should be discovered beforehand, that I felt positively glad when the time had come. The sense of being overpowered by more force than I could possibly resist was complete, but I resisted nothing except with my mouth. The doctor offered me the choice of a wooden or steel gag; he explained elaborately, as he did on most subsequent occasions, that the steel gag would hurt and the wooden one not, and he urged me not to force him to use the steel gag. But I did not speak nor open my mouth, so that after playing about for a moment or two with the wooden one he finally had recourse to the steel. He seemed annoyed at my resistance and he broke into a temper as he plied my teeth with the steel implement. He found that on either side at the back I had false teeth mounted on a bridge which [he] did not take out. The superintending wardress asked if I had any false teeth, if so, that they must be taken out; I made no answer and the process went on. He dug his instrument down on to the sham tooth, it pressed fearfully on the gum. He said if I resisted so much with my teeth, he would have to feed me through the nose. The pain of it was intense and at last I must have given way for he got the gag between my teeth, when he proceeded to turn it much more than necessary until my jaws were fastened wide apart, far more than they could go naturally. Then he put down my throat a tube which seemed to me much too wide and was something like four feet in length. The irritation of the tube was excessive. I choked the moment it touched my throat until it had got down. Then the food was poured in quickly; it made me sick a few seconds after it was down and the action of the sickness made my body and legs double up, but the wardresses instantly pressed back my head and the doctor leant on my knees. The horror of it was more than I can describe. I was sick over the doctor and wardresses, and it seemed a long time before they took the tube out. As the doctor left he gave me a slap on the cheek, not violently, but, as it were, to express his contemptuous disapproval and he seemed to take for granted that my distress was assumed. At first it seemed such an utterly contemptible thing to have done that I could only laugh in my mind. Then suddenly I saw Jane Warton lying before me, and it seemed as if I were outside of her. She was the most despised, ignorant and helpless prisoner that I had seen. When she had served her time and was out of the prison, no one would believe anything she said, and the doctor when he had fed her by force and tortured her body, struck her on the cheek to show how he despised her! That was Jane Warton, and I had come to help her.

When the doctor had gone out of the cell, I lay quite helpless. The wardresses were kind and knelt round to comfort me, but there was nothing to be done, I could not move, and remained there in what, under different conditions, would have been an intolerable mess. I had been sick over my hair, which, though short, hung on either side of my face, all over the wall near my bed, and my clothes seemed saturated with it, but the wardresses told me they could not get me a change that night as it was too late, the office was shut. I lay quite motionless, it seemed paradise to be without the suffocating tube, without the liquid food going in and out of my body and without the gag between my teeth. Presently the wardresses all left me, they had orders to go, which were carried out with the usual promptness. Before long I heard the sounds of the forced feeding in the cell next to mine. It was almost more than I could bear, it was Elsie Howey, I was sure. When the ghastly process was over and all quiet, I tapped on the wall and called out at the top of my voice, which wasn't much just then, "No surrender," and there came the answer past any doubt in Elsie's voice, "No surrender." After this I fell back and lay as I fell. It was not very long before the wardress came and announced that I was to go back upstairs as, because of the feeding, my time in the punishment cell was over. I was taken into the same cell which I had before; the long hours till morning were a nightmare of agonised dread for a repetition of the process.

The next day, Wednesday, January 19, they brought me clean clothes. When the wardresses were away at breakfast I determined to break the thick glass of my gas jet to show what I thought of the forcible feeding, it seemed the last time I should have the strength required. I took one of my shoes, which always lay at my side except when I moved from my cell, let it get a good swing by holding it at the back of my shoulder and then hurled it against the glass with all the strength that I had. The glass broke in pieces with a great smashing sound. The two wardresses, who were in charge of the whole ward while the others were away, came into my cell together; I was already back in my bed. They were young, new to the work, and looked rather frightened. I told them I had done it with a shoe, and why. "But that is enough," I said, "I am not going to do any more now." This reassured them and they both laughed. They took away the shoes as "dangerous," and brought me the slippers instead, and, to my intense relief, I never saw them again. As the morning wore on, one after the other of the officials proclaimed that I had done a shameful thing. On being changed to the cell next door, one of the head wardresses—I never made out exactly who she was—was in a great temper. I had told her, as I did every one of the officials, why I had broken my gas jet. "Broken it, yes, I should just think you had, indeed. And all that writing scribbled over your cell; can't keep the place decent." "I'm so sorry," I said; "I assure you there was nothing indecent in what I wrote on the wall." "No, not indecent, but—" she hesitated and, as the words would not come to her assistance, the remark remained unfinished.

I had not been long in the other cell before the doctor and four or five wardresses appeared. He was apparently angry because I had broken the jet glass; he seized one of the tin vessels and began waiving it about. "I suppose you want to smash me with one of these?" he exclaimed. I said to him, so that all the wardresses with him could hear, "Unless you consider it part of your duty, would you please not strike me when you have finished your odious job" (or I may have said "slap me," I do not remember). He did not answer, but, after a little pause, he signed to me to lie down on the bed. Again the choice of the wooden or steel implement, again the force, which after a time I could not withstand, in the same place as yesterday where the gum was sore and aching. Then the feeling of the suffocating tube thrust down and the gate of life seemed shut. The tube was pressed down much too far, it seemed to me, causing me at times great pain in my side. The sickness was worse than the time before. As the tube was removed I was unavoidably sick over the doctor. He flew away from me and out of the cell, exclaiming angrily, "If you do that again next time I shall feed you twice." I had removed my serge jacket and taken several precautions for my bed, but I am afraid one or two of the officers and the floor and wall were drenched. I shut my eyes and lay back quite helpless for a while. They presently brought in fresh clothes, and a woman, another prisoner, came and washed the floor. It seemed terrible that another prisoner should do this, it was altogether a revolting business. Two wardresses came and overlooked her work, one of them said, in a voice of displeased authority: "Look at her! Just look at her! The *way* she's doing it!" The woman washed on and took no notice; her face was intensely sad. I roused myself and said, "Well at any rate, she's doing what I should be doing myself and I am very grateful to her." The wardresses looked surprised at me but they said nothing. . . .

That day I thought I would clean my window. . . . Though the day was generally spent in loneliness, I knew that I might be visited at any hour, so I put off till about 3.30, when the ward was generally quiet for a time. All the furniture in the cell was movable, so I placed the table in front of the window and the chair on the top, then I climbed up. Through the small part of the window that opened I looked down, and in a beautiful red glow of the sinking sun I saw a sight that filled my very soul with joy. In the gloaming light—it was an exercise ground that I looked down upon—I saw walking round, all alone, a woman in her prisoner's dress, and in her arms she carried another little prisoner, a baby done up in a blanket. I was too high up to hear her, but I could see distinctly that she cooed and laughed to her little companion, and perhaps she sang to it too. I never saw maternal love more naturally displayed. The words of the Chaplain came back to my mind—"The women, they're all as bad as bad can be, there's absolutely no good in them." No good in them! and yet amongst them there was this little woman who, at least, loved her child and played with it as only a motherheart can!

I got down and put the table and chair in their place; I felt amazed, having seen a sight as beautiful as the most beautiful picture in the world.

NOTE

1. Women's Social and Political Union.—*Ed.*

AGNES SMEDLEY

(1892–1950)

As a young woman, Agnes Smedley, who was born in northern Missouri and raised in poverty, regarded marriage as economic slavery. She was determined to escape the life of hard work and childbearing that had killed her mother before age forty. Although she had little formal education, Smedley trained as a stenographer through the assistance of an aunt who earned her own living by prostitution. Her quest to advance herself took her to a normal school in Arizona, where she met and married a Swedish-American civil engineer. After a few years their marriage ended in divorce and Smedley moved to New York City, where she studied at New York University, began to work in journalism, and became actively involved in socialist politics and in Margaret Sanger's birth-control work.

In New York during World War I, Smedley studied with Lala Laipat Rai, an exiled Indian professor, and met with young Indian Nationalists who sought independence from Britain. She was arrested in March 1918 and held in the Tombs, a New York City jail used mainly for detention, for six months, principally on the charge that she had violated the Federal Espionage Act by acting unlawfully as an agent for the Indian Nationalist Party; she learned only later that her Indian associates had German connections that had precipitated her arrest. An additional charge was her violation of an anti-birth-control law, as a few copies of Margaret Sanger's pamphlet, *Family Limitation* had been found in her possession. John Haynes Holmes, Unitarian minister and supporter of Sanger's work, raised Smedley's $10,000 bail. She was released from jail after the World War I Armistice but never tried, and the charges against her were dropped in 1923.

The experience of imprisonment, much of it spent in solitary confinement, influenced Smedley's later writing. She could articulate the thoughts and feelings of her silent sister prisoners because she shared their background of poverty. In her autobiographical novel, *Daughter of Earth* (1929), she describes her imprisonment through the experiences of the heroine, Marie Rogers. A more direct description is in "Cell Mates," an intriguing series of character sketches that appeared in 1920 in the Sunday magazine section of the socialist daily, the *New York Call*.

Margaret Sanger held a small reception in her New York apartment for Smedley following her release on bail. After working on the staff of the *Call* and with Sanger's group, Smedley sailed to Germany and began her career as a foreign correspondent. She is best known for her firsthand reports of the Chinese Revolution. Smedley's close association with the Chinese Communists caused political trouble for her in the United States during the cold war era and is largely responsible for the eclipse of her work until recently. She died in England from complications following an operation, and was buried with honors in Beijing.

Note: Background information is from Jan MacKinnon and Stephen MacKinnon, "Agnes Smedley: A Working Introduction," *Bulletin of Concerned Asian Scholars* 7

(January–March 1975); MacKinnon and MacKinnon, "Agnes Smedley's 'Cell Mates,'" *Signs* 3 (Winter 1977); MacKinnon and MacKinnon, introduction to *Portraits of Chinese Women in Revolution*, by Agnes Smedley (New York: Feminist Press, 1994); Margaret Sanger, *An Autobiography* (1938; reprint, Elmsford, N.Y.: Maxwell, 1970).

CELL MATES

From the Call Magazine, *Sunday supplement to the* New York Call, *1920.*

Nellie

My first impression of Nellie was gained when I looked up from my luke-warm breakfast coffee to listen to an avalanche of profanity in an Irish brogue. Nellie was swearing at the food, and was showering blessings of wrath upon the wardens and matrons of the Tombs prison, who she swore by all the angels and the Blessed Virgin, had built the jail and ran it for their own pleasure and profit.

The matron spoke: "Shut your mouth, Nellie, or I'll lock you in your cell."

Nellie looked up, took up the matron's words, and set them to music. She sang hilariously and, finishing her coffee, two-stepped down past the matron and looked her in the eye, still singing. She two-stepped down the corridor and around behind the iron gate into the "run," in which the old offenders are locked during the day.

Nellie was short, blocky, square in build. Fifty-three summers had come and gone without leaving their touches in her hair. She had grown ugly and scarred, knotted, twisted and gnarled like an old oak. But her vitality had never waned. Her figure had been permitted to develop, unhampered by corsets—and it had developed, particularly her stomach and hips. The expression on her square, scarred Irish face was good-natured and happy-go-lucky, with a touch of sadness which gripped your heart at times.

From the North of Ireland, Nellie had come to America while still a girl under 20. And, being pretty and very ignorant, with no means of support, she had, in due course of time, become a prostitute. Since that time she had served innumerable short terms in all the jails in Jersey and New York City. Her offenses generally consisted of intoxication, fighting, or "hustling."

In her day, according to her story, she had been much sought after by "gentlemen," and her "clients" included pillars of the law—all the local judges and such. She told me that once she had been brought by a police-man before one of these estimable personages, and after he had rebuked her and sentenced her to pay a nominal fine, she had made some interesting disclosures in the court room and insisted upon his paying the fine for her.

Nellie had never lost her Irish brogue in all these years, and she greeted those whom she liked with "Top o' the mornin' to ye," and those whom she disliked with a "Well, damn ye, ye're able to git up this mornin' and raise hell, ain't ye?"

The girls at the long bare breakfast table had laughed as Nellie gaily responded to the matron's rebuke. From back of the iron gates Nellie's voice came like a fog-horn from a distance. She was feeling fine this morning, and the girls finished breakfast quickly.

"Come on, give us a jig, Nellie," one called.

She pulled her old dirty blue skirt half way to her knees, exposing [illegible] white stockings, and started to jig. It was an Irish jig, and her old run-down shoes made a sound like fire-crackers on the cement floor. She sang as she danced—Irish songs and songs indigenous to the soil of America and to Nellie's peculiar mode of life. Some of them are unprintable. One of them began:

> Oh-h-h-h!
> Did you ever have a fight
> In the middle of the night
> With the gur-r-rl you love?

And so throughout the day Nellie kept the girls at attention, vile in talk, always profane, dipping snuff and brow-beating the matrons. When visitors appeared at the gate and gazed back with round eyes at the strange creatures in the cage, Nellie would call "Oh-h-h! Where did you get that hat!" or "Top o' the mornin' to yet [*sic*], lady; are ye plannin' to break in?"

No one could be depressed for long, with Nellie present. One morning I came in from my gray cell into the dull gray corridor. Life seemed quite as dull and gray as my surroundings. Nellie was sitting on a bench near my door, baking her feet against the radiator. She looked up, and her voice scattered the gloom into a thousand fragments:

> Oh-h-h!
> Good mornin', O Missus O'Grady,
> Why are you so blue today?"

I sat down by her.

"Ye're a nice thing," she said; "and why are ye in this place?"

"I don't think you'd understand if I told you, Nellie," I replied.

Nellie fixed her eyes on space for a few moments. That expression of sadness crept about her mouth.

"I guess ye're right," she said. "I mighta once. I was a purty gir-rl once"—

I felt that I had inadvertently recalled long-dead summers of a tragic life. But before I had time to rebuke myself, she kicked the radiator and brightly asked:

"And how do ye like this hotel?"

I asked why she was there. She reflected for a moment.

"By the holy mother uv Jesus," she started, "I'm as innicent as a baby."

"What is the charge?"

"Hittin' a man on the head with a hammer," she replied.

"I didn't do it," she reiterated, to my back.

"Why didn't you?" I asked.

"She chuckled and took some snuff.

"Jest ye wait till I git out."

Then she told me how it happened. It took a long time, and she went into the family history and her personal relations with all the neighbors. She had been out all night, it seems, and in the early morning had gone home. She stopped at a saloon beneath her flat and reinforced herself with liquor before facing her husband, Mike.

Tim, the bartender, had warned her.

"Nellie," he cautioned, "ye'd better not go home now. Ye'll sure git in a tussel with Mike if ye do."

But Nellie, according to her own statement, was "feelin' like a bur-r-d"; so she "ups and flits up the stairs jist as airy as ye please."

Mike was indignant, as husbands sometimes are. He questioned his erring and reinforced wife. The forewarned struggle ensued. The kitchen suffered somewhat, and Mike retreated down the stairs to the first landing. There a friend opened the door, grasped his predicament, and came to his assistance. Somewhat pressed, Nellie picked up a hammer which was lying on a trunk and laid low the intruder.

When Mike's would-be-assistant came to consciousness he got a bandage and a policeman, the former for himself and the latter for Nellie.

Nellie concluded her tale. "They arristed me—an', would ye believe me, it wuz Holy Thursday!"

She had been in the Tombs for a number of months. Once Mike came to see her, and she had asked him for a dollar to buy a little extra food. What he replied I don't know, but when she returned to us she sat down in a corner and cried piteously.

The next morning she came in as usual, to see if I wished to get up for breakfast. I asked her to order some extra food from the restaurant.

"And, Nellie," I said, "order yourself a good breakfast."

She grinned and thanked me. And about an hour later her breakfast bill was sent in to me. Nellie had done as I asked, and had ordered a *good* breakfast! It included, among a dozen other things, four or five pieces of pie. It seems she had stocked up for the winter. And I paid the bill gladly.

When I saw Nellie last she came around to the iron gate to tell us goodby. She had on a clean white waist, and her hair was combed. She was being released, without going to trial.

"What are you going to do now?" I asked.

Her old face assumed that peculiar expression of goodness and sadness— and of helplessness. I knew she didn't know, and that it didn't matter much what she did. She was turned loose on the streets again. No one met her; no one was waiting to welcome her. She turned and left us, a little stooped, and I heard her old shoes click as she went down the cement corridor.

May

May sat near the barred gate smoking a cigarette and resting her fat hands on her fatter knees. If convicted of forgery this time it meant eight fingerprints—one for each year she had been in the business. She was no amateur; one isn't an amateur at 45, after passing from the factory and the stage into private business.

May's complaint wasn't so much that she had been caught, but that she had been caught on such a trifle. She had sent cigars to a fictitious son in Camp Upton and given a check to the cigar store, receiving only $10 in change.

Her bail was $500, but her man, Vic, was too cowardly to furnish it. It meant trouble for him if he did. He had managed to keep out of the law's grip for eight years, just as she had managed to keep in it; but as years went by the danger seemed to creep closer. Even when May had been arrested this time he had been with her. But she had explained to the detective that he was a strange man who had kindly offered to carry her packages. So he had escaped the law again.

Of course, she realized that Vic couldn't risk arrest; but it seemed unfair at times; she had always shouldered the blame, and always served time, often for him. Even now he wrote letters declaring that had it not been for rheumatism he would have been down to leave money for her personal expenses; but it never occurred to him to send money by mail. Yet again she would forgive him, as women often do. She had his picture in her purse; it was dim and worn from much handling, and she looked at it with mingled anger and compassion. When any one agreed with her that Vic was a worthless scoundrel, she launched into a long defense which would have wrung tears from any jury who didn't happen to know the facts.

"How you worry about a $500 bail!" I exclaimed. "Mine is $10,000."

"Well," May retorted, "*I* didn't try to swing the world by the tail. All I wanted was a little change."

"Tell me," I asked her, "why did you stop working in a factory?"

"Go work in a factory and find out," was her reply.

"Well, why did you leave the stage?"

"Look at me," she challenged sarcastically, "and look at my figger!" I looked. It *was* rather discouraging; about five feet high and five feet wide, yellow hair and an accordion pleated chin. Eight years ago she had been thirty-seven. One can't be a successful chorus girl at thirty-seven, after your renowed [*sic*] cuteness becomes buried beneath a bed of fat.

"Couldn't you do something else besides—this?" I inquired, hesitatingly.

"Yes," she grimly retorted. "I could scrub floors or take in washin', or 'hustle,' or do a few little things like that."

May warned me that a "stool pigeon" would undoubtedly be put in to watch me and try to get information from me, that perhaps one was there already; that maybe she, herself, was one. She was scornful of my "greenness."

"Gawd!" she exclaimed once, "I guess if some bull came in here dressed up like a priest, you'd believe him. Now, listen to me, never trust a man dressed like a priest."

May constituted herself my guardian and carefully kept the other girls out of my cell. "Get out, you hussey, you low-down thief," she yelled at them when they wandered into my cell. And if they didn't get out, she would put them out.

"Don't give them any money," she cautioned me time and again. But when she left, she carried some of my money with her. My "greenness" was very profound.

When taken to court, she wore a hat over which flowed a long black veil.

"Some veil," she laughed. "It ought to be a mask!" But even her jokes were told in a tremulous voice, as if she were telling them to keep from thinking of other things.

When the women returned from court, they told me that a very ugly man had appeared against May and that she, when asked if what he said were true, had replied that "any man with a face like that ought to have a check passed on him." She and the other women had been compelled to walk between the long row of masked detectives, veils thrown back; two of the detectives recognized May. She was given the "Indefinite," which means anything from three months to three years in the penitentiary.

Mollie

For circulating leaflets opposing intervention in Russia, Mollie Steimer, with three men comrades, had been sentenced to 15 years in prison, a $500 fine and deportation to Russia. A good start for a little Russian girl less than five feet in height who had not yet reached the age of 21.

Mollie had come from the Ukraine five years before, and since that time had worked in a waist factory for $10 a week. A few months preceding her arrest she had received $15. She was the eldest of five children. A sister, aged 17, and a brother, aged 14, as well as her father, were all factory workers.

Mollie was sitting in her cell writing when I was put into jail. Her greeting was characteristic of her cast of mind.

"I am glad to see you here!" she said. "I wish the prisons to be filled with the workers. They soon will be. Then we will wake up."

Before her, pasted on the wall, were newspaper photographs of Karl Liebknecht, Eugene V. Debs and John Reed, and, printed in red letters high up on the stone wall, were the words, "Long live the Social Revolution!"

Mollie wore a red Russian smock. Her short hair was glossy black and curled up at the ends. Her face belonged to Russia, and the expression of seriousness and silent determination had first been cast in that country many years ago. Her carefully chosen words were expressed with a slight foreign accent. Seldom did she speak of anything save Russia, the revolution in Germany and Austria and the future of the workers in America. She was always looking toward that world which she had described on the witness stand to a judge from Alabama:

"It will be a new social order," she had said, "of which no group of people shall be in the power of any other group. Every person shall have an equal opportunity to develop himself. None shall live by the product of another. Every one shall produce what he can and enjoy what he needs. He shall have time to gain knowledge and culture. At present humanity is divided into groups called nations. We workers of the world will unite in one human brotherhood. To bring about this I have pledged myself to work all my life."

"Is there any such place as you tell about?" the prosecuting attorney had sneered. Mollie replied:

"I believe those who represent Russia have been elected by the workers only. The parasites are not represented in the Bolshevik administration."

The girls in prison loved Mollie. She talked with them at great length, disagreeing with them and frankly criticizing them if she thought best. At night she would talk gently to some girl who was trying to smother her sobs in the rough prison blankets. After the cell doors clanged behind us in the late afternoon, Mollie would stand grasping the steel bars. In simple, slow words she would talk to the girls. She used English which the most humble could understand, and as she spoke the three tiers would become silent and only an occasional question would interrupt her talk.

Mollie's philosophy of life had not been gleaned from books. A child of the soil, the finely-worded sentiments of the *intelligencia* did not impress her as being sincere. The *intelligencia* had deserted the workers of Russia when the great crisis came, when the workers of that country had challenged. "Peace to the huts, war to the palaces, hail to the Third International!"

With her own hands Mollie had labored for many years, had longed for, but never enjoyed, the beautiful things of life, and little, save the most sordid, bare necessities. Even the possibility of school had been closed to her. About her in the factory she had seen thousands like herself, pouring out their lives for crumbs, suffering, and then dying, poor and wretched. The class struggle to her became a grim reality.

Mollie championed the cause of the prisoners—the one with venereal disease, the mother with diseased babies, the prostitute, the feeble-minded, the burglar, the murderer. To her they were but products of a diseased social system. She did not complain that even the most vicious of them were sentenced to no more than five or seven years, while she herself was facing 15 years in prison. She asked that the girl with venereal disease be taken to a hospital; the prison physician accused her of believing in free love and in Bolshevism. She asked that the vermin be cleaned from the cells of one of the girls; the matron ordered her to attend to her own affairs—that it was not *her* cell. To quiet her they would lock her in her cell. "Lock me in," she replied to the matron; "I have nothing to lose but my chains."

Then the news of the German revolution and of the armistice came. Outside the whistles shrieked and people yelled. In the prison yard outside some of the men prisoners were herded together as a special favor to join in the rejoicing. The keepers moved about among them, waving their arms and telling the men to be glad. The men stood with limp arms and dull faces, looking into the sky and at each other. A few endeavored to show signs of happiness when the warden came their way.

"Peace has come," Mollie said, standing at my side, "but not for us. Our struggle will be all the more bitter now."

The time came when Mollie's old mother, arising from the sick bed, came with a bandaged ear to the prison to tell her of the death of her father and of her 14-year-old brother. Mollie did not cry. She returned to the cell and quietly sat down on the bed beside me. But once I felt the convulsive trembling of her body. Her words came slowly at last:

"You should have seen my father," she said, "so thin, so worked out! Since he was but 10 years old he had worked 14 to 15 hours each day. He was so worked out, so thin! I knew he did not have the strength to live if he ever became ill."

Then, later: "Our dreams," she said; "how fragile! I have dreamed for years—oh, such dreams! Of my brother and sister in school, of studying, of a new order of society. In one minute my dreams are shattered!"

Through the bars of the cell door, through the dirty windows across the corridor could be seen the tops of unbeautiful, dingy buildings. Outside the windows the great stone wall surrounding the prison obstructed all view of the street. The roar of the elevated train, the rattle of drays on cobblestone pavement, and the shouts of men, disturbed but slightly the misery of the jail. From the tiers below came the shouts and the curses of the old offenders.

"Our dreams—how fragile!" mingled with the curses of the women, and before long it seemed that the women, too, were saying, "Our dreams— how fragile; our dreams—how fragile." At times they laughed it, and at times they cursed and sneered as they said it.

Yet the thought: Can that which is so fragile endure so much? And the doors of the past swung back and revealed dreams which have endured for thousands of years, suffering defeat only to rise again; braving prisons, torture, death, and at last wrecking empires.

Mollie was released under $10,000 bail to await her appeal to the Supreme Court. I watched her pass through the prison yard. A marshal walked beside her, talking out of the corner of his mouth. He did not offer to carry her suitcase, heavy with books. His neck bulged with fat, his chest was high and his shoulders primitive. Mollie did not listen to him. Her eyes were looking straight ahead into the distance.

Weeks passed, and in the world outside I met Mollie once more. She was on strike with the 40,000 clothing workers and was among the many pickets arrested. A few weeks afterward she came to see me. Her shoulders had grown sharp and thin and she cynical. She had been arrested a number of times upon suspicion; secret service men seemed to follow her and arrest her as a matter of general principle. At last she was arrested for alleged distribution of radical leaflets and held at Ellis Island for deportation. There she went on hunger strike to protest segregation from her fellow political prisoners. A friend, holding her thin, cold hand, asked if she thought it worth while. Mollie replied:

"Every protest against the present system is worth while. Some one must start."

Mollie did not object to deportation—provided it was done at once, and to Soviet Russia instead of to the region under Czarist generals. The city authorities evidently conferred with Federal agents, and decided to try her in the city courts instead. She was sentenced to serve six months in Blackwells Island jail, a place notorious for its filth and barbarity.

A short time has now elapsed since the Supreme Court upheld the decision of the lower court on the first indictment against Mollie. And she, frail, childlike, with the spirit which made the Russian revolution possible, will be taken after her jail term is finished to Jefferson City prison, where she is sentenced to spend 15 years of her life at hard labor.

Mollie's reasoning is something like this: Under the Czar we knew there was no hope; we did not delude ourselves into believing that he would release those who worked against the system which he represented and upheld. In America we have been carefully taught that we live in a democracy, and we are still waiting for some one to feed us democracy. While waiting, we starve to death or are sent to prison, where we get free food for 15 or 20 years.

Kitty

Kitty Marion[1] was serving thirty days for giving a pamphlet on birth control to a Mr. Bamberg, who had come to her office and told her with much feeling of his large family, his low salary and the fear of adding more children to his household. Bamberg turned out to be a "stool pigeon" for the notorious Association for the Suppression of Vice. He justified his existence by making people break the law and then having them arrested. Kitty Marion was one of his victims.

Kitty came clattering down the stone corridors every morning with her scrub pail in her hand. "Three cheers for birth control," she greeted the prisoners and matrons. And, "Three cheers for birth control," the prisoners answered back.

Her marked English accent recalled to mind that she had been one of Mrs. Pankhurst's[2] militants in London, had been imprisoned time without number and had had her throat ruined by forcible feeding. She holds the record; she was forcibly fed 233 times in Halloway prison.[3]

"Dirty work," I remarked one morning, as she came in to scrub the Tombs corridors.

"Not half so dirty as cleaning up the man-made laws in this country," she replied. Then we continued our discussion of peace and change.

The prison physician came in to examine two infants.

"Three cheers for birth control," Kitty called to him from her kneeling position. She held her mop rag in mid air. He turned, and she, scrubbing away, remarked:

"Some way or other every time I see a man the more I believe in birth control."

When visitors or keepers came into the prison Kitty was always heard cheering for birth control. When peace was declared she expressed the hope, in a voice that those who run might hear, that now America would apply a little freedom to her own people and grant women the right of personal liberty. So taken up by the injustice of her imprisonment was she that when her room was infested by vermin she remarked that they reminded her of a mass-meeting of Bamber[*sic*]'s vice society; and when she had been forced to put on a striped dress of the convicted women, she looked at it and remarked, "Ah! blue and white stripes! Now, if there were only a few red stripes and some white stars!"

The matrons were glad when her term was finished. When she left she announced that she had come in a spark but was going out a living flame.

NOTES

1. British singer, actress, and suffragette.—*Ed.*
2. Emmeline Pankhurst, leader of British militant suffragettes.—*Ed.*
3. Holloway Prison, London, where Lady Constance Lytton and other suffragettes were held (see Lady Constance Lytton's writings in this section).—*Ed.*

ERICKA HUGGINS

(1948–)

Born in Washington, D.C., to a family she describes as "relatively poor," Ericka Huggins studied to become a teacher and in 1968 joined the Black Panther Party in Los Angeles. As an organizer among Panthers there and in Connecticut, she suffered the loss of her husband, John, who was killed by the FBI in 1969. Shortly afterward, Huggins, the mother of an infant daughter, was herself charged with kidnapping and conspiracy to commit murder, in the death of Panther Alex Rackley. She was imprisoned in Niantic State Prison for Women in Connecticut during her controversial New Haven trial that ended in a hung jury. All charges against her and Panther Bobby Seale were dismissed in May 1971 because the enormous amount of publicity had made a fair trial impossible.

In the courtroom during the trial, Huggins wrote poetry that expressed her pain and her faith in humankind and belied the prosecution's insistence that she was a ruthless murderer. The poems and her diary made prison officials particularly nervous; they objected not only to the political statements, but also to Huggins's frank expressions of tenderness and unity with her fellow prisoners. Matrons feared these were love letters or "kites" addressed to other imprisoned women. It was in prison that Huggins began to practice meditation. Confiscation of Huggins's writings led her to join Seale in a suit for their rights as prisoners.

After her release, Huggins continued her social activism and her meditation practice; in 1972 she was elected to membership in the Berkeley, California, Community Development Council, an antipoverty agency. She served also as director of the Oakland Community School, a progressive model elementary school in East Oakland, California. In her capacity as the first African American member of the Alameda County Board of Education, Huggins worked to improve conditions and educational programs in county juvenile and special education institutions. She has also lobbied the California legislature for the National Action Against Rape, a victim rights organization. Presently she works with Siddha Yoga Dahm of America Foundation (SYDA), a worldwide organization dedicated to teaching meditation in its ashrams and meditation centers as well as in community organizations, prisons, schools, and agencies. She is also a consultant to public, charter, and private schools to develop programs in teacher and student resiliency based on relaxation, mindfulness, and esteem-building.

Note: Background information is from Ericka Huggins, letters to Judith Scheffler, 18 July 1985, 17 December 2001; Donald Freed, *Agony in New Haven* (New York: Simon & Schuster, 1973); Angela Davis, *If They Come in the Morning* (New York: Third Press, 1971); *New York Times*, 7 January–31 May 1971, 20 August 1972; *Black Panther* 11 (February 1974), 20 (February 1980); *Life* 7, no. 13 (December 1984); Pomona College (California) Events Calendar, April 2001.

Three Poems

"Morning Drifts In" and "The Oldness of New Things" are from Insights &
1975; *"I wake in middle-of-night terror" is from* Off Our Backs, *1971.*

[Morning drifts in]

I. Morning drifts in
    bringing pots
      teeth
      arms
      soap
      feet dragging to the
bathroom. Another prison camp,
damp Sunday morning—"ladies
if you're going to church please
bring your coats down with you.

                   —ladies,

     please come . . . 'lord Jesus
     be our guest' . . .
             —ladies, come
   with me, your dresses are too short
            —ladies, girls
children, robots, degenerates—come
with me."
morning drifts in
bringing misery
    loneliness
    depression

II. Endless music/sound that covers/disguises
   reality. They sit shift groan squirm
   yell scream moan pretend
              to be
    happy. They know they are
   not. I know they are not.
   Within these walls it is
   loneliness that keeps us going,
    hoping for freedom—
      any second
      minute
      day
   in the corner a woman sits,

ddles. Maybe crying on the in-
e for her children,
er life.

ke in middle-of-night terror]

in middle-of-night terror
the warm sleeping body of my lover
ne in the conviction that I am in a prison cell
snut away, suddenly, from all that makes my life.
I sense the great weight of the prison
pressing down on the little box of room I lie in
   alone.   forgotten.
How often do women awake
in the prison of marriage,
of solitary motherhood
   alone and forgotten
of exhaustion from meaningless work,
of self-despising learned early,
of advancing age
   alone and forgotten.
How many women lie awake at this moment
   struggling as I do against despair,
   knowing the morning will crush us once again
   under the futility of our lives.
And how short a step it is
   —for us—to the more obvious imprisonment
   of bars and concrete
   where our sisters lie
   alone   forgotten.
See now, in this middle-of-the-night emptiness
   how little it matters
   whether we wear a convicts' ill-made cotton dress
   or a velvet pantsuit—
We are possessions to be bought and sold,
We are children to be curbed and patronized,
We are bodies to be coveted, seized, and rejected
   when our breasts begin to sag,
We are dummies to be laughed at.

   I sense the great weight of the society
   pressing down on the little box of room I lie in
   alone   forgotten
   like my sisters in prison.
If you hear me
   consider
   how the bomb of human dignity

Poems,

could be planted outside your cell
how its explosion could shake
the foundations of our jail
and might burst open the door that separates you
how we might struggle together to be free.

[The oldness of new things]

The oldness of new things
  fascinates me;
  like a new feeling about love,
      about people,
        snow,
  highways that sparkle at night; talk,
  laughter . . .
  that old longing for freedom that this
             place renews— —
it all makes me know that humankind
has longed to be free ever forever
since its break from the whole

  maybe the longing for freedom
  will soon make others homesick
    for our natural state
    not dead
    but living;
    not asking for freedom—but free.

NORMA STAFFORD

(1932–   )

Norma Stafford was the youngest of ten children in a poor farming family of the Tennessee hill country. As a young woman she experienced hardships as a result of classism and sexism. Although she was able to begin nursing school in Alabama, she was aware of her socioeconomic differences with the staff. Her training ended when the school learned of her lesbianism and forced her resignation. After a brief marriage failed, Stafford began a ten-year relationship with a woman. During this time Stafford began writing bad checks and running from the law. She describes her amusement that police consistently ignored her homosexual relationship and insisted that she reveal the identity of the man for whom she broke the law. Once, during a relentless interrogation, she was forced to fabricate a story about a lover and his car in order to get some sleep.

During five-and-a-half years, Stafford was imprisoned in several county jails and in Alabama and California state prisons. In 1972, during her incarceration at the California Institution for Women, she participated in the beginning of the Santa Cruz Women's Prison Project. Through the project, a large volunteer staff brought college-level classes to the women, who received credit from the University of California at Santa Cruz. In this supportive setting, Stafford began to write prose and poetry and to recognize her gift as a writer.

After her parole in 1973, Stafford gave public readings of her poetry and worked to support the Santa Cruz Women's Prison Project. Stafford is a rancher in California and she has completed an autobiography.

Note: Background information is from Karlene Faith and Jeanne Gallick, introduction to *Dear Somebody: The Prison Poetry of Norma Stafford*, by Norma Stafford (Seaside, Calif.: Academy of Arts and Humanities, 1975); "Writings of Norma Stafford," *Crime and Social Justice*, no. 2 (Fall–Winter 1974); Stafford, letter to Judith Scheffler, 10 August 2001.

SEVEN POEMS

From Dear Somebody: The Prison Poetry of Norma Stafford, *1975.*

[may i touch you?]

may i touch you?
that is what I have missed
more than anything else
a warm human touch.

i will not touch you hard.

[i am smiling]

i am smiling
for no particular reason
i do this at times
like now when I am alone
silence all around me
where many people
have suddenly shut their mouths
in sleep behind locked doors.

In Santa Cruz

Sitting warming her back in the spring sun
that dared to force its way through the cafe blinds
an ivory-handled walking cane leaned against her thigh.
The beauty of all her ages was upon her.
Seven face lines bore a hard east to west direction,
made a sharp right turn at her ear
then disappeared into the north.

Nibbling toast past her old woman's black whiskers,
hands lined like two roadmaps
gave a delicate tremble, then
lifted her cup of Sanka
and sent it chasing after the toast.
I said to her, "My sister, the growth rings of a tree
know many secrets of this life,
but the tree does not speak.
These lines that you wear
are your growth rings, hiding the
knowledge you have gained while
traveling this life for almost a century.
Tell me what you know."

She carefully wiped her almost invisible lips,
took her cane and walked away from me
leaving on her empty seat
bits of bark and one oak leaf.

for barbara whitaker

in private shadows of slumber
animated by mysteries of moonlight
arose a woman
the photographer's dream

would cause agonized envy
in the master of canvas
renowned wielder of
the magic brush

edges of fantasy
stroking reality
    you
turning in slow-motioned
movements of my mind
revealing all beauty
and true essence of woman
witnessed alone
by this sleeper's eyes.
in the private shadows of slumber.

sensuous lady soft sweet sister
sharing a moment
in the millenniums of time
curled together
in mysteries of moonlight
  warming my life healing my mind
    private
      in the shadows of slumber.

Woman Soldier

Sweet sweet woman soldier
swift sure female warrior
gentle hands warm eyes tending your child
determined hands deadly eyes aiming your weapon
soft lips smooth skin beauty
long lashes veiling the knowledge pride
and self-worth blazing in your eyes of all colors
laughter at party time dancing with your lover
death at battle time for your unbelieving enemy

Entering into battle heavy with child
expensive coiffure wearing levis Arpege
laces boots sneakers barefoot with uncombed hair
giving off the healthy body odor
of determined female sweat.

Comrade in arms my sister
battling daily we were like two bees

stinging the Power in many places
dodging his armies we were alert and cunning

he was confused swatting wildly
slapping places he could not see
looking everywhere trying to pin down
to eliminate the source of his discomfort
a false god perched on his tower
we made him turn move run
screaming curses at his soldiers
ordering them to "seek out and destroy."

You and I my comrade beloved friend soldier woman
survived many years in this battle
before our instinct tuned to his danger
became clouded with fatigue and slept
letting us wake up here
among the other prisoners of war.
I see you smile in here
when that same confused angry power
curses and swears at our resistance
we still cause him pain
never allowing his overstuffed body
to know the luxury of total relaxation.

Lying in your captive labor bed
womb straining sweat pouring
you deliver your child
within these concrete walls and steel bars
because your infant is born of you/in here
she is labeled numbered and her mug-shot is taken
before she has breathed before the cord is cut
she has a number and she is called criminal
but you and I know you have delivered to us
another awesome female warrior.

I hear your deep woman's laughter
ring out through every cell block
and my heart is strengthened
my courage renewed because you are here
just as you are everywhere noble warrior
goddess of Death to the Power
giver of life sweet sweet woman soldier.

This Is Not The End

notes of the score

you say that i am fixed in my black and white state
watch the smoothness of my runs
see my blackness blur
in the taut acrobatics of the violin strings
never am i fixed
neither in black, white, or gold or brown
hear me sing in the heat of the sun
whose rays change me to the golden hue
        that is light
to reach the darkest depths of your life
like ginger i penetrate the air.

the black bars that try to encase me
are only my soft resting place
smell the sweet air of freedom that i bring
weep as i touch the red blood of your heart
laugh as i rub the softness of your feet
never again say that i am fixed.

for bobbie and terry

we sit together, you and i,
bound by our mutual suffering
at the hands of our keepers
we make jokes that force
our minds to leave here
and follow the hard path of laughter
we laugh at our condition
both the physical and the mental.
tears are pushed forward
by the onslaught of anger
we strike out at each other
hard furious blows that bruise
and sometimes draw blood
then we fall sobbing into
the arms of each other
the tender hands of each
ministering to the wounds of the other
such gentleness, such hate, such love
we feel one for the other
locked together, bound together
in this small hated space.

[tonight loneliness is n

tonight loneliness is my bed p.
he has been every night for five
as steel bars wrapped in blackne
                take over my life
when the guard turns out my ligh

[the contractions are coming har

the contractions are coming harder now
all my efforts are more concentrated
i feel the wall thinning
more endeavor goes into my efforts
the pushing the straining the pain
bearing down from everywhere
will end
blessed relief the emergence of me
when I finally walk out those gates.

MARILYN BUCK

(1947–)

Texan Marilyn Buck has been imprisoned since 1985 for politically motivated actions, including the liberation of Assata Shakur (see her selection in this anthology) in 1980. She states that she "is an internationalist who continues to participate in the struggle for social and economic justice and for liberation and equality among all human beings." She describes herself as "a lifelong women's liberationist," who "refuses to be silenced" and that this has led to her "becoming a writer from behind the walls." Her intent, she says, "is to bear witness to the oppression of women as prisoners, colonized subjects and workers, and to advocate for women as subjects of our own histories" (letter to Judith Scheffler).

Buck began her political activism as a teenager in antiwar and antiracism movements. She was imprisoned at the Federal Prison for Women at Alderson, West Virginia, in 1973 on weapons charges. During a furlough of her ten-year sentence, she went underground. Since her 1985 recapture and conviction for conspiracy, she has been held at the Federal Correctional Institution for Women in Dublin, California. Her sentence totals eighty years. Her activities within prison include completion of work for a bachelor's degree in psychology and support for Spanish-speaking women prisoners as a translator.

Buck works to convey her political message from within prison through writing and ceramic sculpture. A winner of PEN prison writing awards for poetry and nonfiction, she is a participant in June Jordan's Poetry for the People workshop and, with Linda Evans, she writes "Notes from the Unrepenitentiary," a quarterly column appearing in *Prison Legal News*.

Note: Background information is from Marilyn Buck, letter to Judith Scheffler, August 2001; "Marilyn Buck," online, available: http:www.prisonactivist.org/pps+pows/marilynbuck, December 5, 2001; Bell Gale Chevigny, ed., *Doing Time: 25 Years of Prison Writing* (New York: Arcade, 1999).

SIX POEMS

"My Sister Lives Across the Line" is from Self-Censorship, *n.d. "[This rainy day]" and "The Waiting" are from* Concrete Garden, *1994.*

Backlit

the telephone rings
I await connection
my eyes travel the tier
stop at Lupe's door
she stands back lit

as is unseen except herself
before the mirror

her arms sail upward
poise electric bronze in the light
her hands flow serpentine
over black cherry-bright tresses
down her neck
they linger on sequestered breasts
deprived of lover's lips
languorous she sighs
wraps her shoulders
in solaced embrace
lashed eyes close
into some other orb
her hands drop empty bereft

she turns into the dark
I turn to the *hello* in my ear
I look up
as Lupe steps out pressed
into another khaki clad day

Prison Chant

Cassandra is on the phone
her screams bounce off walls
staccato chant
> *Jesusfathergod*
> *Jesusfathergod*
> *Maurice listen to me*
> *Stop listen to me*
> *listen*
> *listen*
> *you must be responsible*
> *I'm not there*
> *take care of your sister*
> *help her*
> *I don't care*
> *she's young*
> *you're grown*
> *20 is grown*
> *I'm sorry you must*
> *be responsible*
> *I'm not there*
> *Let me talk to her*

LISA   LISA
Jesusfathergod
Stop
listen to me
listen to your brother
TIME OUT
what's going on
Stop   STOP   STOP
Jesusfathergod
I'm sorry

no the phone has cut me off
I need more time
please let me call again
I know you're next
please
please Jesusfathergod
I must call back
I'm going to call again
I know it's your turn
you have to wait

    Maurice I'm sorry
    I'm not there
    what can I do
    I know your brother's
dead
    yes I told
    I had to
    to come home
    yes I'm still here
    you're there
    you're alive
    you must be responsible
    I'm not there
    I'm still not there
    jesusfathergod
    jesusfathergod

Bird Watchers

Francine, glistening headwrapped
firm on young cinnamon legs
consults with Nancy,
frayed blonde rope of a woman
bleached on the back of Harleys

and crystal meth
two keen bird watchers
they feed purloined bread
delectable to Canadian geese and ducks
who refuse to leave
until days sizzle hot or blow too cold

once the geese go
Francine and Nancy
do not notice each other

[My sister lives across a line]

My sister lives across a line
I know she's there
My heart lifts to hear her
in brief encounters through
                    the wall
a whispering space
for stolen words.
She lives there through the glass
I glimpse her days
she glimpses mine
but we cannot meet.

The Waiting

I watched waited wanted you
til one day
I whispered these words
wrapped in a gentle wind
through the flowering of my lips
languidly cool with spring rain
saturated by want.

Your eyes flirt
then flee
alarmed at my lack of artifice.
Do I frighten you?
I cry laughing.

How fast you run
feet tripping on a hot steaming sidewalk
dancing and dodging your dangers
till at last your running becomes seeking

etly
rapped in a cool breeze
med indifference
g
you.

his rainy day]

his rainy day
estless in its cloak of gray
envelops the slow bitter-sweet hours.
Intimate in its coolness
it captures me in a warmth
peculiar to the falling sky.

The radio plays quiet blue jazzy notes
that dance between the raindrops
in crescendos that flirt with my flesh
and caress my dreams.

Blue sighs rise to the surface
to escape in rainbowed crystal
I pace this tiny space
the swish of my robe
joins in a concert of desire
calling for you
to step out of the golding gray
to place your kiss upon my thigh.

PATRICIA MCCONNEL

(1931–)

When she was in her early twenties, Patricia McConnel spent time in six jails and in the Federal Reformatory for Women at Alderson, West Virginia. It took almost thirty years for her to recover from her prison experiences; she began writing in her mid-thirties in order "to purge the prison horrors" (letter to Scheffler, 1985). "Sing Soft, Sing Loud" is the title story of her collection of short fiction about women in jails and prisons. Grants in literature from the National Endow-ment for the Arts (1983, 1988) supported her work.

McConnel explains that her stories are "extremely autobiographical," with authentic incidents and narrators that either are invented or are composites of her-self and the women she knew in prison. "Sing Soft, Sing Loud," based upon an actual incident in the San Diego City Jail, "is about a woman who would not sur-render her will" (letter to Scheffler, 6 July 1983) and the consequences of her action. In all McConnel's stories, singing symbolizes "the indestructibility of the spirit" (letter to Scheffler, 1985).

McConnel now lives in southeastern Utah. She gives readings of her work and teaches workshops in prisons and at writers' conferences. She works at home as an editor, page designer, typesetter, and programmer. One of her favorite places for writing is in the back of her pickup truck, parked in the mountains or desert.

Note: Background information is from "About the Author," in Patricia McConnel, *Sing Soft, Sing Loud* (Flagstaff, Ariz.: Logoría, 1995); McConnel to Judith Scheffler, 1 April 1983, 6 July 1983, 2 March 1985; "Amazon.com Author Interview," online, available: http://www.amazon.com/exec/obidos/show-interview/m-p-cconnelatricia/ref=pm_dp_ln_b_8/102-2648996-0524953, July 25, 2001.

SING SOFT, SING LOUD

From Sing Soft, Sing Loud, *1995.*

You gotta understand what it's like in here at night. We can start with black. In here, when they say "Lights out!" they mean lights fuckin' *out*. They don't leave *nothin'* on. There's no windows, so light can't even filter in from the street, and when they throw that switch, you're just lost in a black hole. The first guy who said "You can't see your hand in front of your face" was talking about this here jail. That's why when they come in here in the middle of the night and throw the lights on, you're so blinded you can't see nothin' for a couple of minutes, and you feel like somebody threw a spotlight on you.

The reason all this is going on is this is the receiving tank where I'm at, cuz I ain't been to trial yet and I can't get out on bail cuz Arnie's holding all the money and he won't go my bail cuz it's a felony this time. I'm gonna do some real time behind this one and he figures I'm just a lost cause, even though I got busted on accounta him, holding his shit, me that never yet stuck a needle in my arm. So here you are trying to sleep and a bunch of things happen all at once: you hear the creak and groan of this giant metal door opening, blinding lights go on in your eyes, some woman is screaming all kinds of bad shit cuz she's drunk and they're dragging her in here, and the metal door gets slammed shut hard cuz the screw is pissed off with the drunk giving her a bad time, and if you happen to be deep asleep when all this goes off you wake up thinking the world blowed up in your face.

But that ain't all. When they bring the drunks in they're hollering and cussing, mad to be busted if they even know what the hell is going on. But more than likely they got busted cuz they been wrecking some joint or beating up on their ol' man or their kids, and they was mad to begin with. So they raise hell for about a half a hour before they conk out. Then along towards three in the morning some of 'em start with the throwing up and the d.t.'s. Them that's sober enough to think of it tries to find the toilet to throw up in, but it's so dark they can never find it, and in the morning you wouldn't believe the smell and the mess. Some of them has fell down and bruised themselves. Anyway, when they start with the throwing up and the d.t.'s you'd be glad to go back to the lights and the cussing. These women are snake-pit crazy. They think someone's trying to kill 'em, or they think they're eating poison food, or someone's coming at 'em with a knife, or they're being thrown in a pit of fire, or there's rats and snakes coming out of the walls—that last one's a favorite around here. Weekends are the worst of course. When five or six of 'em get to going at once it's like being in a insane asylum in hell.

One night all this stuff is going on and I'm just layin' there trying to be cool and stay sane through the night, and I hear this one woman with a strong clear voice and she ain't seeing rats or nothin', what she's seeing is flying saucers full of enemy aliens, and they're landing in her backyard and eating up her children, and she's taking charge of everything and she's telling someone to put on his radiation-proof suit and get the ray gun. And then I guess they're going out there to save the kids, cuz she's shouting, "Watch out for that radioactive puddle!" and shit like that.

There's something about that voice that gets to me. I feel like crying, I feel like I know that person, and after a while I realize I *do* know that person. That's Millie's voice. I sit straight up on my bunk and listen hard. Maybe it's somebody sounds like Millie, but it's not, it's Millie; she's got just this certain combination of small-town Western accent and cigarette husky in her voice that ain't like nobody else's.

Jeezuz god on a fuckin' bicycle, I never been here when Millie come in before. I never knew she got that crazy drunk. After I'm sure who it is, I can't even lie down again I'm so freaked out and miserable. First I try not to listen and then I *have* to listen; this is *Millie* talking crazy here. I feel embarrassed, like I'm someplace I ain't supposed to be, like I walked in on somebody masturbating or something, but worse. But I can't help listening, this is *Millie* for chrissake, like I never knowed her. Fuckin' bonkers, jeezuz.

So I'm sitting bolt upright on my bunk, staring out into the black, when the lights go on again and the tank door whocks open. In a few seconds I hear the screws stomping up the steel stairs to the upper ramp. They must be full up on the first tier. And in another few seconds they go by my cell with a black chick who looks like she can't hardly walk, like her legs are gonna buckle under her any second, and there's two screws with her instead of one like usually, and they're holding her up and pushing her along by her arms. I only see her for a couple of seconds, but you know how it is when something's knocked you for a loop. All your circuits is blowed wide open and it don't take you long to take in a whole lot, and that's how I am when they go by with this chick. I get a good look at her face, and in the condition I'm in, all upset about Millie, this chick's face hits me hard. She's got a look people only get when they been down and out a long time, usually they been in and out of jails a lot, and so that's why I call this look *jailface*.

Partly, jailface just happens when you been under everybody's heel too long, but after a while you learn to do it on purpose so you never let on that you're scared or feeling pain or worry or sickness. What you do is, you freeze your face so nothin' moves. Your eyebrows don't scrunch together in a frown, your mouth don't twitch or smile or sneer. Freeze ain't exactly the right word cuz it makes it sound like the face goes hard, when actually it goes limp and you don't let it tighten up over nothin' at all, ever. The real mark of jailface, though, is the eyes. They don't never look straight at nobody and they don't even focus half the time. You can't look into the eyes of somebody with jailface cuz your look bounces off a glassy surface of eyeball that's so hard it would bounce bullets.

Jailface ain't necessarily a bad thing to have, cuz the minute a certain kind of screw knows you're scared or weak she's got the upper hand, and she jumps on you with both feet and don't let up 'til she's had her satisfaction, which in most cases is to see your spirit dead. But if you're walking around with jailface she can't tell if something is still stirring in there or not. Most likely she thinks by your look that you're already dead, so there's no challenge, nothin' in there to kill, see. But people ain't really dead 'til they're really dead, if you know what I mean. Maybe you've given up, maybe you're a fuckin' zombie, but just about anybody got a little life left in 'em that can spark up the minute they latch on to a little piece of hope, and if you got jailface you can keep that hid from the screws so they can't stomp it out of you.

Well, anyway, in this second or two while this chick is passing my cell I decide she's a junkie, cuz a junkie going to jail is about the most given-up person you ever seen, and cuz she's black, cuz funny thing is, black chicks don't get jailface as a general rule. I mean they can, but not usually. I get in trouble saying stuff like this cuz you ain't supposed to say Black is like this and White is like that, but I can't help it, it's the truth. Black women just seem to do their time different. They sing more, goof around more. They don't zombie out like the rest of us. They even get mad more, fight more, and when they turn funny in here, they fall in love harder. I figure the singing and the goofing around is how black chicks cover up, something they use instead of jailface. I don't know for sure—I never been black. But all I know is, when a black chick has jailface it's gotta be something very very bad that's going on, like being a sick hype.

When the screws put her in the cell next to mine I think, Oh great, now I'm gonna have a sick junkie screaming right next door, on top of everything else. As the screws leave, ol' Blodgett sees me sitting up on my bunk and she says, with this nasty grin on what she has the nerve to call a face, "What's the matter, Iva, can't you sleep?"

"Ha ha ha," I says, but they already gone by.

There's a lull in the alkie olympics downstairs. Maybe they was shocked silent by the lights. I'm glad I can't hear Millie no more. But in the quiet I can hear the chick next door moaning, "Oh sweet Jesus, I'm sick, I'm sick."

"Don't you start too," I says. "It's bad enough around here. I don't need nobody moaning and groaning right next door." She don't answer and I don't hear another peep outa her. Millie seems to be quiet now too. In fact, they all quieted down now, finally wore out and passed out, I guess. But I'm too shook up about Millie to go to sleep. I just sit there staring into the dark for a while, and then I start hearing the junkie next door breathing. She's breathing funny, not regular like you're supposed to, catching her breath and trying not to cry or something. I start to feel bad about yelling at her. "You want a cigarette?" I says.

She says, "Girl, I'm too sick to smoke."

So I just sit there staring in the dark, and I wonder what Millie's gonna be like in the morning, and then I don't want to think about it so I don't think about nothin'. I just sit there staring. It's about twenty minutes later when the junkie begins to sing. Real soft, real tender her voice is, and I like listening to a sweet voice singing soft like that. She sings sad dreamy songs, like "Me and My Shadow" and "Down in the Valley." She's gonna sing herself to sleep and me with her. It don't feel so much like being buried alive in the dark with her singing sweet like that. What a relief from all that screaming and crying.

But in a while her songs start getting more upbeat, 'til finally she's singing stuff like "I Can't Get No Satisfaction," and some Aretha Franklin and Tina Turner and Janis Joplin—jeez, I didn't think nobody even remembered ol' Janis no more. She's singing a whole lot of stuff I'm really into, and I just can't help singing with her. When she hears me chiming in she starts clapping her hands, and so I clap too, and when the pace wears us out we go back to old funkies like "Frankie and Johnny" and "Bye Bye Blackbird." Finally somebody hollers, "For chrissake shut up!"

We stop singing and I ask her, "How you feeling?"

"I think I better sing some more. It helps to sing."

"Don't they give you nothin' to help you through it?"

"Girl, they don't know I'm sick. I got busted for soliciting and they never checked me for no marks. If I can keep them from finding out I'm sick, maybe I'll get thirty days for soliciting 'stead of having to take the cure. What's your name?"

"Iva. What's yours?"

"Angora. What you in for?"

I do some fast thinking. I don't want to tell her I'm here for possession for sale, her being a junkie and all. It don't matter that the stuff wasn't even mine—everybody says that. So I says, "Same as you—soliciting."

"And you don't got a habit?"

"No."

"Good for you, girl. Does your old man treat you good?"

"He's all right."

"Uh-huh. I hear you ain't saying he treat you real fine. Listen, don't let him give you no habit. They like you to get hooked so they can control you. You stay clean. There ain't nothin' worth this misery."

"I managed so far. Listen, you said you want to sing some more. Do you know the slow version of 'Cocaine Blues'?"

"How do it go?"

I sing,

> Early one morning while a-making the rounds
> Took a shot of cocaine and I shot my woman down
> Shot her down cuz she made me sore
> I thought I was her daddy but she had five more.

"Naw, I don't know that one. I never heard it."

So I teach her all the words I can remember, then she says, "Do you know the peaches song?"

"No."

She sings,

> If you don't like my peaches
> Why do you shake my tree?
> If you don't like my peaches
> Why do you shake my tree?
> Get out of my orchard
> And leave my fruit tree be.
>
> Let me be your little dog
> 'Til the big dog come.
> Let me be your little dog
> 'Til your big dog come.
> When the big dog come
> Just tell him what the little dog done.

We giggle over that one, and then I think of "C. C. Rider," and she knows it too, so we sing it together, and then she asks me if I know "Gloomy Sunday," and I says, "Yeah. You know, when that song first come out thousands of people committed suicide all over the country, and they tried to outlaw the song."

"Yeah, I heard that too."

So we sing "Gloomy Sunday" and "I Shall Be Released." These are all songs you learn if you spend a lot of time sitting around in jails, and she's pretty impressed that I know all that stuff. We're having a real party considering the circumstances. Then we hear the tank door clang open and heels clunking on the concrete floor. That can only be Blodgett. She's built like a buffalo and wears size thirty shoes with lead in the heels. The footsteps stop somewhere under us and Blodgett yells, "Cut out that singing up there or I'll throw you in flatbottom." Then she stomps out and I tell Angora, "A screw can't stand to think there's ever ten minutes you ain't doing real hard time. If we was crying or moaning with pain or screaming with the d.t.'s she wouldn'ta said nothin'."

"I need a cigarette now."

We have to grope in the dark for each other's hands and when her hand touches mine it's ice cold and she's shaking. I pass her a book of matches and when she's lit up she says, "What's flatbottom?"

"It ain't a nice place. Ain't you been in jail before?"

"Not this one."

"I thought all jails had flatbottoms. Some places they call 'em strip cells. Anyway, it's a cell on the first tier with nothin' in it. No toilet, no cot, no water, no nothin'. If you piss, you piss on the floor. If you shit, you shit on the floor. Then you sleep in it 'til they let you out to clean it up. They ain't supposed to leave you in there more than twenty-four hours but they keep you there long as they want. It ain't supposed to be for punishment but that's what they use it for."

"What's it spose to be for, then?

"Protective custody, they call it. Somebody's crazy, trying to commit suicide or something, they put 'em in there 'til they cool off. Sort of like a padded cell without the padding."

"I don't see what good it do to make a person shit on the floor."

"I seen people try to stuff their heads down the toilet. Anyway, the screws use it mostly to keep people in line, and it works pretty good that way. So we better not sing no more."

But Angora says, "Girl, if I don't sing, I'll scream. Now I don't mind if I have to go to flatbottom, but I don't want to start screaming cuz once I start I won't be able to stop." And so she starts off again. At first I keep quiet, but after a while I think, Oh, what the hell, I strung along with her this far, I can go to the end. So I sing with her, but softly now. And pretty soon the screw comes back and this time the lights all go on and she comes upstairs and marches straight to Angora's cell. I hear the cell door open and then shut, and then she pushes Angora past my cell and Angora is singing "Won't You Come Home Bill Bailey" and she's doing a little dance step as the screw drags her along the ramp to the stairs. This time I notice how skinny she is. Like a anorexic or somethin'.

I hear the door to flatbottom open and then slam shut. Even though I know I was singing too soft for Blodgett to hear me this time, I wait for the sound of her boots coming back up the stairs to get me. Instead, the lights go out and the tank door clongs shut and it's deep pit black again.

At first I feel relieved, but in a few minutes I feel bad. I know this chick is really hurting now, and lying on a cold cement floor. So I start singing a Dinah Washington song, and in a couple of minutes Angora chimes in and away we go again. But when we sing a couple of songs she calls up to me, "You better cool it, girl, or you gonna be down here with me."

"Hell, I don't care. I got a lotta time ahead of me anyway. I might as well do something."

"You ain't gonna do a lot of time for soliciting."

I forgot I tole her that. I think fast. "I been busted a bunch of times before. They're gonna give me a habitual this time."

"That's too bad, and maybe you don't care 'bout coming down here, but I do. Think how it gonna smell in here in the morning with two of us in here."

"You got a point there."

I don't sing no more, but she keeps right on. I never knew one person could know so many songs. Blodgett pokes her head back in once to tell her to shut up, but the kid is already in flatbottom, what more can they do to her? So she don't pay no attention and keeps right on singing. I lie down at last and I'm almost sung to sleep when I hear the tank door open again. This time the lights don't go on. Angora keeps on singing like she don't even hear the screw coming, but over the song I can hear the heels clunk-clunking and they don't stop 'til it sounds like she's all the way to the back of the tank. I sit up on my bunk and listen close cuz I can't figure out what she could be doing in the dark. Then the faucet goes on and I can hear water filling up a bucket and I think, Oh shit, she's gonna douse her, and then I think, Christ, she's gonna have to sit in water all night and her sick as a dog already. I'm gonna call out to tell her to shut up but what's the use? She's gonna get it now anyway, and right then I hear the splash.

Angora screams like someone knifed her in the gut, a awful wail that bounces off the walls and breaks over me from all sides and I think for a second that she's shattered the walls and the jail is gonna cave in on us. I'm so scared I can't move, and then the scream dies away and it's quiet except for the women whimpering, scared out of their gourds, and I can hear Margarita praying. Then I hear the clunk-clunks working their way back to the door and the clang and the click that mean we're locked up tight again.

From flatbottom I hear Angora moaning and crying, and the whole damn thing is finally too much for me, Arnie and Millie and Angora and this fuckin' snake pit, and I scream, OH JESUS LET ME OUT OF HERE! and I cry loud enough for myself to drown out the sobs of the sick hype in flatbottom and the chorus of women crying and praying and after a while I just give out and go to sleep.

In the morning I wake up when they bring the breakfast cart in, but I don't want to get up. I must not've slept more than a hour or so, but mainly

I don't want to go down and see Angora. I don't want to see Millie. But we don't get enough to eat around here and if I skip breakfast I'm gonna be awful hungry the rest of the day, and besides, I remember that I got floor-scrubbing detail after breakfast. I got to get up anyway. So I go down and look in flatbottom but Angora ain't there, just a puddle of water. She ain't in any of the other cells either, but Millie's asleep in number 8. She smells awful and she looks sick. And old. Millie's about forty, but today she looks sixty. Just smelling her makes me feel sick too, and I think of all the mornings Millie and me has moved our card game upstairs to avoid the stinking alkies and I wonder, Don't Millie know she smells like that when she comes in? I wonder should I wake her up for breakfast but I decide she's not gonna feel like eating, just the smell of food will prolly make her sicker, so I leave her there sleeping.

I ask Elsie, the trusty[1] who comes with the breakfast cart, if she knows what happened to the chick in flatbottom. "They moved her to the other tank," she says. "What happened, anyway? Her face and arms are all blistered, like she got burned."

"They throwed a bucket of water on her."

"It musta been boiling, then. They brought her over there at five in the morning, and it woke me up, is how I happened to see her."

"I never knowed tap water could be hot enough to blister you."

"Well, I guess it must be."

I'm depressed and ain't had enough sleep and all I feel like doing is hiding in my bunk, but if I don't do my floor I'll get hassled by the screws and maybe go to flatbottom myself, so I figure I better get to it. After I eat I go to fill my bucket and I can't find the box of lye we use for scrubbing the cement, there was a full box here just yesterday, and it only takes a second for it to hit me what become of it. Oh jeezuz. I sit down on the floor against the wall and hold my knees and put my head down on my arms and cry, but when I hear the tank door open for the screw to let Elsie out with the cart I jump to my feet and start working.

All morning I keep checking Millie's cell, waiting for her to wake up, but she's totally zonked. I want to talk to her, even though I know when she wakes up she ain't gonna be in no shape to talk to. But I want to talk to her anyway. I never been so depressed in here like I am today.

When the lunch wagon comes, Elsie hands me a kite.[2] She says, "The spade chick you were asking about give it to me." I stick the kite in my pocket 'til the screw that comes with the food cart is gone and the tank is shut up tight. Then I go to my bunk and read it:

Dear Barbera Strysand,
They took me out of flatbottom cause they was afraid I'd catch cold and give there nice hotel a bad name. I got some frends gonna come bring me some loot today and i'll send you the cigs I owe you. Hang in there, girl. I'll sing loud enuf tonight so you can hear me over there.

Very truly yours,
Angora

I feel a whole lot better after I read this, and I write her a note back saying I hope she's feeling better and she better not sing if she knows what's good for her, and maybe I'll see her after I been to court and get transferred out of the holding tank. I gotta hold the kite til supper time and give it to a trusty, so I stick it in my pocket and go on downstairs.

Millie is up at last, sitting on a bench just staring, and I see now she has a big black eye and bruises on her arms. But when I walk up to her she busts into this big happy grin, and I see right away why she looks so old. She got no teeth in her mouth. She looks so pitiful I just about cry to look at her, but she says, "Iva! Fancy meeting you here!" And she laughs.

"Millie, if I wasn't so sorry to see you all beat up I'd be glad to see you. What happened to you?"

"Oh well. I fell down, I guess." Millie looks down at her feet, cuz she's lying, of course. I shouldn'ta asked. I know perfectly well that her ol' man beats up on her when they get to drinking. Jeezuz. What the hell else is gonna happen around here? But I know he didn't knock every one of her teeth out. She musta had false ones. So I says, "What happened to your teeth?"

Millie puts her hand over her mouth, all embarrassed, like she just now realized she don't have 'em. She says, "Well, to tell the truth, I don't know. I mighta lost 'em somewhere along the line, but sometimes when I come in they take 'em away from me so's I won't break 'em or something. If they got 'em, I'll get 'em back later. You got a cigarette?"

I hand Millie a cig and when I go to light it her hand is shaking so bad I can hardly connect. The stench coming off her is sickening, and I'm having trouble with the fact that my friend Millie looks and smells just like all them alkie hags I bitch to her about all the time.

Millie says, "What day is this?"

"Sunday."

"Well, we don't go to court 'til tomorrow then."

"I got no trial date yet, Millie."

"What do you mean?"

I sit down and tell Millie what happened, about holding for Arnie, about not having no bail money, about for sure I'm gonna go to the joint since I got all these priors for hustling. She listens to all this just sitting there shaking her head and looking real sad. I want to talk to her about Angora too, about how I lied to Angora about being busted for possession for sale, like somehow it was my fault she's a junkie, and about everything that happened last night, but somehow I just can't get myself to say nothin'. Millie says, "It's a little late to say this, Iva, but I don't think you should have anything to do with that Arnie when you get out. I shoulda said that to you a long time ago maybe."

"Millie, you don't always have a choice about who you got to do with."

"Yeah, I'm a fine one to talk, huh? Me with my Merv. Listen, I gotta take me a nap."

"You want me to wake you up for supper?"

"Naw. I won't be able to keep anything down 'til tomorrow prolly. "

I figure I got a nap coming myself, and so I go upstairs to my cell and zonk out.

I don't know the trusty that comes with the dinner cart, and you gotta be careful about trusties around here since half the time they only get to be trusties cuz they're the screws' little stoolies, so I hang on to my kite and wait 'til the next morning to ask Elsie about Angora.

"Christ, she's a mess," she says. "They won't let her go on sick call cuz of the way it happened, and she's got a fever and stuff running out of her ear."

Like a dope I ask, "Is she singing?"

"Singing? Have you flipped out? What's she got to be singing about? She don't even sit up or eat."

At lunch time Elsie tells me they let Angora loose, just like that. Just turned her loose. No court, no bail, no nothin'.

I try not to think about her after that, and I got plenty of my own miseries to keep me busy for a while. But after I go to the state joint, sometimes I sit up at the window after lights out and sometimes someone is singing out a window across the mall in one of the other dormitories and my heart gets a catch in it and I think for a second it's Angora. Or sometimes there's not even any singing and she just comes into my mind and I start singing for her again, only this time I sing as loud as I can. But I never keep it up very long cuz I know it don't matter how much I sing, I can never sing loud enough or long enough to change what happened to her back there. It was singing that got her in that fix in the first place, anyway. I just wish I had sang louder at the time, that's all, even though it wouldn'ta done no good then either. Or maybe I coulda got all the women in the tank to sing with us. Just suppose I coulda got 'em to do it. Feature this: all them alkies and junkies and hookers and boosters raising the jailhouse roof with song, and Angora singing lead. Wouldn't that be something? What could the screws do—throw scalding lye on all of us? Of course I know not even all of us singing at the top of our lungs woulda changed a goddam thing in that goddam jail, but it tickles me to think of it. Them screws—it woulda blown their friggin' minds.

NOTES

1. A trusty is a trusted inmate who has been given privileges and responsibilities by the prison administration.—*Ed.*

2. A kite is a note from one inmate to another.—*Ed.*

CONNECTIONS AMONG WOMEN PRISON WRITERS

A survey of the collective wealth of women's prison literature reveals that it indeed constitutes a literary tradition. Many women prisoners knew and refer to each other in their writings. Some note the sustaining power of reading each other's work. The lists below may aid the reader in exploring connections among women prison writers. The first list, in roughly chronological order, includes writers who make direct references to other women prisoners, whether or not they actually knew these women. Some of these references are to the woman herself and some are to her writing. The second list, also in roughly chronological order, includes women prisoners who were contemporaries, acquaintances, or comrades in the same movement. Many entries in the two lists overlap. Boldface type denotes a writer for whom a selection is included in this anthology; most references are included in the annotated bibliography.

These two lists may help the reader begin to investigate the many linkages among women prison writers. The reader will surely discover many more connections to reward further research.

WOMEN PRISON WRITERS WHO REFER DIRECTLY TO OTHER WOMEN PRISONERS

Queen Elizabeth I corresponded with Mary, Queen of Scots.

Katherine Evans refers to Sarah Cheevers.

Catherine Virginia Baxley quotes **Madame Roland.**

Rose Greenhow refers disparagingly to **Catherine Virginia Baxley.**

Virginia Lomax refers admiringly to **Catherine Virginia Baxley** (using the pseudonym "Mrs. Johnson" for Baxley).

May Churchill Sharpe writes that she knew Countess Markievicz in prison.

Eugenia Ginzburg writes that she learned the wall tapping code from the memoirs of **Vera Figner.**

Vera Buch Weisbord writes that she was encouraged by the memoirs of **Vera Figner.**

Edith Bone writes that she was encouraged by the memoirs of **Vera Figner.**

Ekaterina Constantinovna Breshko-Breshkovskaya writes fondly of **Vera Figner.**

Emma Goldman refers to Margaret Sanger, **Vera Figner,** and Louise Michel; states that she read the prison letters of Ekaterina Constantinovna Breshko-Breshkovskaya; refers to Kate Richards O'Hare in her autobiography; writes admiringly of Maria Alexandrovna Spiridonova and **Agnes Smedley**; regretted the death of Rosa Luxemburg.

Agnes Smedley wrote a letter from prison to Margaret Sanger; describes Kitty Marion as she knew her in prison.

Lady Constance Lytton corresponded with Kitty Marion regarding an appeal to Madeleine Doty for assistance; refers to Emmeline Pethick-Lawrence.

Emmeline Pethick-Lawrence writes admiringly of **Lady Constance Lytton**, with whom she was imprisoned.

E. Sylvia Pankhurst writes of **Lady Constance Lytton** and Helen Gordon [Liddle].

Ada Flatman writes fondly of **Lady Constance Lytton.**

Ethel Rosenberg refers to Joan of Arc in her letters.

Elizabeth Gurley Flynn refers admiringly to Ethel Rosenberg.

Dolores Ibarruri refers to meeting Elizabeth Gurley Flynn.

Ericka Huggins refers to Ethel Rosenberg.

Elaine Brown refers to **Ericka Huggins.**

Angela Davis wrote a review of poetry by **Ericka Huggins.**

Jane Buxton and Margaret Turner collaborated on a prison book.

Lindy Chamberlain refers to Mary Durand (French Protestant prisoner).

Mary Tyler wrote an introduction to the prison diary of Akhtar Baluch.

Joan Baez Sr. writes that she was imprisoned with Kay Boyle.

Alice Panaiodor and Nicole Valâery refer to Sabina Wurmbrand.

Alicia Partnoy refers to Latin American women prisoners.

Assata Shakur writes admiringly of **Lolita Lebrón**; refers to Jane Alpert.

Evelyn Williams refers to **Assata Shakur.**

Marilyn Buck refers to **Lolita Lebrón, Assata Shakur,** and Susan Rosenberg; refers admiringly to **Nawal El Saadawi**.

Jean Harris refers to Kathy Boudin, **Precious Bedell**, and Judith Clark.

CONTEMPORARIES/ ACQUAINTANCES/COMRADES

Queen Elizabeth I ordered the execution of Mary, Queen of Scots.

Katherine Evans and Sarah Cheevers traveled together in the Quaker ministry.

Charlotte Corday occupied a cell previously used by **Madame Roland.**

Helen Maria Williams was friendly with **Madame Roland.**

Louise H., Duchesse de Duras was the sister-in-law of Louise Noailles; knew Madame Latour.

Rose Greenhow, **Catherine Virginia Baxley**, Virginia Lomax, and Eugenia Levy Phillips were contemporaries; Greenhow and Lomax knew Baxley

Eugenia Levy Phillips was initially imprisoned in the home of Rose Greenhow, which was used as a prison for Confederate women during the Civil War.

Ekaterina Constantinovna Breshko-Breshkovskaya knew **Vera Figner.**

May Churchill Sharpe knew Countess Markievicz in prison.

Dolores Ibarruri met Elizabeth Gurley Flynn.

Emma Goldman knew Kate Richards O'Hare; met Maria Alexandrovna Spiridonova.

Mollie Steimer (described in **Agnes Smedley**'s "Cell Mates") was imprisoned at Jefferson City when Kate Richards O'Hare was there.

Agnes Smedley knew Margaret Sanger, Haru Matsui, and Kitty Marion.

Lady Constance Lytton was imprisoned with Kitty Marion and Emmeline Pethick-Lawrence.

Myra Sadd Brown, Elsie Duval, Ada Flatman, Annie Kenney, Helen Gordon [Liddle], **Lady Constance Lytton,** Kitty Marion, Hanna Maria Webster Mitchell, Christabel Pankhurst, Emmeline Pankhurst, E. Sylvia Pankhurst, Emmeline Pethick-Lawrence, Mary R. Richardson, Evelyn Sharp, Mary Ellen Taylor, Jane Terrero, and Olive Wharry all worked in the British woman suffrage movement.

Jane Buxton and Margaret Turner were imprisoned together.

Ericka Huggins knew Angela Davis.

Elaine Brown knew **Ericka Huggins.**

Joan Baez Sr. is the mother of Joan Baez the folksinger; knew Kay Boyle

Dai Qing was imprisoned in a cell once occupied by imprisoned writer Ding Ling.

Assata Shakur was imprisoned in the same facility as **Lolita Lebrón.**

Kathy Boudin, Judith Clark, Jean Harris, and **Precious Bedell** were imprisoned at the same time in Bedford Hills Correctional Facility.

Marilyn Buck, Susan Rosenberg, Susan Saxe, **Assata Shakur**, and Laura Whitehorn were imprisoned in the United States for political activism.

An Annotated Bibliography of Writings by Women Prisoners

Compiling this bibliography has been a continuing and fascinating part of the research for this book. Although the bibliography is intended to be as comprehensive as possible, there are doubtless many sources remaining to be identified by the serendipitous route that led to so many of the entries in the following pages. In particular, prison newsletters, prison writing workshop anthologies, and chapbooks of prison poetry are difficult to locate and may well have been inadvertently omitted. The updated bibliography in this revised edition includes about 100 new entries. In compiling these additions, I have had the advantage of the Internet as a research tool, and I owe many of the new entries to its use. Researching online, however, has made me even more aware of the potential for bypassing available material. In particular, new English translations of prison literature written in other languages are a continuing source of bibliography entries. A truly comprehensive bibliography must of necessity be a collaborative and ongoing project. I would certainly welcome word of any additional titles.

The purpose of this bibliography is to guide the reader who would like to find primary material in English or in English translation by women prisoners. No such bibliography now exists. Even the excellent bibliographies of prison writing compiled by H. Bruce Franklin and Daniel Suvak reveal relatively few works by women. Many works by women prisoners are still rare, out of print, in unpublished manuscript form, or available only in obscure journals. Sources are often elusive because they are not readily identified as prison-related through titles or authors' names.

In order to make this bibliography specific and manageable, I have restricted entries to works written during the author's imprisonment or, later, about her experience. All genres have been included. I have endeavored to include all foreign works translated into English. Concentration camp writings, wartime camp internment writings, works written while in hiding, captivity narratives, and testimonies are excluded because they constitute large bodies of literature in their own right that would broaden the scope of this bibliography and make the research unmanageable. Readers are encouraged to consult reference sources relevant to these genres. The authors of these works certainly share fundamental concerns with prison authors listed in the following bibliography, and such correspondences offer potential for fascinating research and discoveries. Several prisoners have written autobiographical works in collaboration with a professional author. While these collaborative writings reveal many insights about prison experience, I have included only works that, to my knowledge, were written entirely by the woman prisoner herself or by a group of women prisoners. Finally, I have excluded works written in prison but about other subjects, without reference to the prison experience. Examples of such writing would be political tracts that do not discuss the woman's imprisonment.

The following bibliographies and reference works have been useful in assembling this bibliography. I am particularly indebted to the work of H. Bruce Franklin, Daniel Suvak, and, for the updated bibliography, Bell Gale Chevigny and Barbara Harlow. Chevigny's anthology of PEN American Center prison–writing prizewinners includes many excellent entries by female authors. Harlow's work on women writers and political detention includes a useful bibliography of those authors.

Agosín, Marjorie, ed. *A Map of Hope: Women's Writing on Human Rights—An International Anthology.* New Brunswick, N. J.: Rutgers University Press, 1999.

Barrow, Margaret. *Women 1870–1928: A Select Guide to Printed and Archival Sources in the United Kingdom.* London: Mansell, 1981.

Begos, Jane. *An Annotated Bibliography of Published Women's Diaries.* Pound Ridge, N.Y.: 1977.

Chevigny, Bell Gale. *Doing Time: 25 Years of Prison Writing—A PEN American Center Prize Anthology.* New York: Arcade, 1999.

Dutton, Helen. "Prison Writings of Women." In *Women and Law* microfilm series, section v: Special Films—Rape/Prison/Prostitution. Berkeley, Calif.: Women's History Research Center, 1972.

Engelbarts, Rudolf. *Books in Stir: A Bibliographic Essay about Prison Libraries and about Books Written by Prisoners and Prison Employees.* Metuchen, N.J.: Scarecrow, 1972.

Franklin, H. Bruce. *The Victim as Criminal and Artist: Literature from the American Prison.* New York: Oxford University Press, 1978; 2d ed., 2 vols. Vol. 2, *American Prisoners and Ex-Prisoners: Their Writings: An Annotated Bibliography of Published Works, 1798–1981.* Westport, Conn.: Lawrence Hill, 1982.

Harlow, Barbara. *Barred: Women, Writing, and Political Detention.* Hanover, New Hampshire: University Press of New England, 1992.

Hinding, Andrea. *Women's History Sources: A Guide to Archives and Manuscript Collections in the United States.* 2 vols. New York: Bowker, 1979.

Kuhlman, Augustus F. *Bibliography of Crime and Criminal Justice, 1927–1931.* New York: Wilson, 1934; rev. ed. by Dorothy C. Culver. Montclair, N.J.: Patterson Smith, 1969.

———.*Bibliography of Crime and Criminal Justice, 1932–1937.* New York: Wilson, 1939; rev. ed. by Dorothy C. Culver. Montclair; N.J.: Patterson Smith, 1969.

———. *A Guide to Material on Crime and Criminal Justice.* New York: Wilson, 1929; rev. ed. by Dorothy Campbell Culver. Montclair, N.J.: Patterson Smith, 1969.

McDade, Thomas M. *The Annals of Murder: A Bibliography of Books and Pamphlets on American Murders from Colonial Times to 1900.* Norman, Okla.: University of Oklahoma Press, 1961.

Philip, Cynthia Owen, ed. *Prison Communications: 1776 to Attica.* New York: Harper & Row, 1973.

Prison Activist Resource Center (PARC). Oakland, California. Online: http://prison-activist.org.

Rubin, Rhea Joyce. *Barred Visions: A Bibliography of Materials by Prisoners and Ex-offenders.* Chicago: Chicago Public Library, 1974; rev. ed. 1975.

Suvak, Daniel. *Memoirs of American Prisons: An Annotated Bibliography.* Metuchen, N.J.: Scarecrow, 1979.

Women Offenders: A Selected Bibliography. Olympia, Wash.: Institutional Library Services, Washington State Library, 1970. Educational Resources Information Center (ERIC) document.

Note: An asterisk denotes a writer whose work was included in the first edition of *Wall Tappings* (Boston: Northeastern University Press, 1986), but not the second edition.

Aguilar, Mila D. *A Comrade Is as Precious as a Rice Seedling.* Latham, N.Y.: Kitchen Table/Women of Color Press, 1987. A teacher and journalist who went underground in 1972, Aguilar writes of dissent by Filipino youth in the early 1970s. She was imprisoned from 1984 to 1986.

————. *Journey: An Autobiography in Verse (1964–1995).* Quezon City: University of the Philippines Press, 1996. Included in this collection are poems written during the period of Aguilar's imprisonment.

Alpert, Jane. *Growing Up Underground.* New York: William Morrow, 1981. Alpert, active in radical antiwar causes, describes her stay in 1969 in the Women's House of Detention, New York City, as she awaited trial on charges of conspiracy to destroy government property. There is a brief discussion of her incarceration in the State Correctional Institute at Muncy, Pennsylvania, 1975–77.

Alvarez de Toledo y Maura, Isabel, Duchess of Medina Sidonia. "Eight Months in Franco's Jail." *Nation,* 6 April 1970, 396–99. A brief account of her imprisonment (*see* next entry).

————. *My Prison.* Translated by Herma Briffault. New York: Harper & Row, 1972. The Duchess of Medina Sidonia's account of her imprisonment in 1969 in the women's prison at Alcalá, thirty miles west of Madrid. She was given a one-year sentence by Franco's court for publicly demonstrating in support of Spanish peasants in Palomares. They sought redress for environmental damage done to their village in the crash of an American B-52 bomber there in 1966.

"The American Microcosm." *Greenfield Review* 7, nos. 1/2 (Fall 1978). This special double issue, edited by Michael Hogan and Joseph Bruchac, includes poems by prison writers and features work by the 1976 and 1977 PEN winners. A few female poets are represented, but most works are by men.

Angoulême, Marie Thérèse Charlotte, Duchesse d'. "The Narrative of Marie Thérèse de France, Duchesse D' Angoulême." In *The Life and Letters of Madame Élisabeth de France followed by The Journal of the Temple, by Cléry, and The Narrative of Marie Thérèse de France, Duchesse D'Angoulême,* translated by Katharine Prescott Wormeley, 209–92. Boston: Hardy, Pratt, 1902. Marie Thérèse, Madame Royale de France, describes events during 1789–95. The only surviving child of Louis XVI and Marie Antoinette, Marie Thérèse began writing her narrative in 1795 while she was imprisoned in the Tower of the Temple, and completed it in 1799 while exiled in Vienna. During her imprisonment with the royal family, beginning in 1792 when she was thirteen years old, she survived her father, mother, aunt, and brother. She was released in December 1795.

Arrowsmith, Pat. *Jericho*. London: Cresset Press, 1965. A novel about persons demonstrating nonviolently against nuclear weapons and the personal consequences of their actions. Arrowsmith wrote this book during a six-month term in Holloway Prison. This was one of her six prison terms for work with the British Campaign for Nuclear Disarmament, the Direct Action Committee against Nuclear War, and the Committee of 100. The book describes the problems peace workers face when they encounter violence or when they disagree among themselves.

Arrowsmith, Pat, ed. *To Asia in Peace: The Story of a Non-Violent Action Mission to Indochina*. London: Sidgwick & Jackson, 1972. "The first draft of the book was written by Pat Arrowsmith in 1969 while serving a six-month prison sentence for organising action in this country [England] against the Vietnam war" (from the jacket). She is also co-author of one selection:

> Arrowsmith, Pat, and Rachel Blake. "Thailand," pp. 127–56. This essay describes the 1968 peace mission of twenty-six persons who traveled from London to Indochina to protest the Vietnam War. Among them were Arrowsmith, a thirty-seven-year-old British peace worker from London, and Rachel Blake, a forty-three-year-old British teacher and painter from London. Both women were arrested by the Thai police and imprisoned in the "monkey house" (police station lock-up) at Udon, Thailand, following an attempted nonviolent demonstration at the U.S. base in Udon. They were subsequently transferred to the monkey house prison section at the immigration office in Bangkok, where they were held for two weeks.

Askew, Anne. *The Examinations of Anne Askew*. Edited by Elaine V. Beilin. New York: Oxford University Press, 1996. Anne Askew, a young Lincolnshire gentlewoman who subscribed to Reformed beliefs, was twice imprisoned in London for heresy. She was arrested in March 1545 and imprisoned in the Counter, a prison of the City of London, and later in Newgate. She was tortured on the rack in the Tower of London, and burned for heresy on July 16, 1546, at the age of about 25. In her two "Examinacyons," she describes her interrogations and imprisonments, affirming her Reformed beliefs, particularly concerning the Eucharist. Her accounts reveal her courageous determination and the particular challenges she faced as a young woman opposing church authority.

Baez, Joan, Sr. *Inside Santa Rita: The Prison Memoir of a War Protester*. Santa Barbara: John Daniel, 1994. Baez, the mother of singer Joan Baez (*see* next entry), describes her jailing in 1967 for her nonviolent protest against the Vietnam War. Baez and her daughters, Joan and Mimi, were part of a group of men and women arrested at the Oakland (California) Induction Center and held in the Oakland Jail. She describes meeting author Kay Boyle (*see* entry below) in prison.

Baez, Joan. *Daybreak*. New York: Dial Press, 1968. In these reminiscences and meditations on her life, singer/songwriter Baez recalls her imprisonment for nonviolent resistance to the Vietnam War. She and her mother were held for civil disobedience at the Oakland (California) Induction Center and were imprisoned together twice in the Santa Rita Prison, California. The book describes their warm relationships with fellow prisoners—drug addicts, drug pushers, and prostitutes—and Baez's resistance to prison authority.

Baluch, Akhtar. "Preface to Akhtar Baluch's Prison Diary." *Race & Class* 18, no. 4 (Spring 1977): 389–95. Baluch's diary begins on July 25, 1970, when she entered the Central Prison in Hyderabad, Pakistan, and began a hunger strike. An eighteen-year-old Sindhi college student, she was charged with supporting Sindhi nationalist leaders. Her diary includes letters of support from her family. When moved to the Central Jail in Sukkur in August, she expressed solidarity with fellow prisoners convicted of murder. She was freed on December 18, 1970.

———. " 'Sister, Are You Still Here?': The Diary of a Sindhi Woman Prisoner." With an introduction and notes by Mary Tyler (*see* entry below). *Race & Class* 18, no. 3 (Winter 1977): 219–45.

Barnacle, Helen. "Ali's Visit." In *Harsh Punishment: International Experiences of Women's Imprisonment*, edited by Sandy Cook and Susanne Davies, 47–49, Boston: Northeastern University Press, 1999. Barnacle was imprisoned for nearly eight years as a result of her heroin addiction. She now works as a drug program director in Melbourne, Australia. Her autobiography, *Don't Let Her See Me Cry* (Sydney, New South Wales: Transworld), is forthcoming.

Barrows, Isabel C. "The Massachusetts Reformatory Prison for Women." In *The Reformatory System in The United States*, edited by Samuel J. Barrows, 101–28. Washington, D.C.: Government Printing Office, 1900. Included in this article are excerpts from anonymous writings by ex-prisoners of the Massachusetts Reformatory Prison for Women in Sherborn. Letters declare that the writers are doing well in their lives on the outside and express gratitude to the prison for its educational and vocational programs and constructive moral atmosphere. One educated ex-prisoner compares her relatively negative first impressions about the prison environment and her fellow prisoners with her later appreciation for the orderly prison management and the humanity of the other imprisoned women.

Battle, Hellen. *Every Wall Shall Fall*. Old Tappan, N.J.: Hewitt House, 1969. In 1962 Battle, a young American woman, traveled to Germany to work as an English teacher and to study in West Berlin. In 1965 she was arrested in East Berlin for attempting to help an East Berlin soldier escape. She was imprisoned in East Berlin and in Neustrelitz in the north of East Germany. After being sentenced to four years of hard labor, she was transferred to Hohenschoenhausen prison and Bautzen penitentiary. She writes of her fellow prisoners and her deepening Christian faith. She was released in 1967, and the soldier she had aided was also released to West Germany.

Baxley, Catherine Virginia. Diary and Notebook, 14 February–2 July 1865. Rare Books and Manuscripts Division, New York Public Library. Baxley, a Baltimore woman working for the Confederacy, was arrested as a blockade-runner and imprisoned at the Old Capitol Prison, Washington, D.C. There she met her own son, who was dying in the prison.

———. Letters to William H. Seward, Secretary of State, Edwin M. Stanton, Secretary of War, and others, January–April 1862, written from the Old Capitol Prison concerning her imprisonment. In *The War of the Rebellion: A Compilation of the Official Records of the Union and Confederate Armies*, 2d ser., vol. 2, 1316–21. Washington, D.C.: Government Printing Office, 1897.

Baxter, Carolyn. *Prison Solitary and Other Free Government Services: Poems by Carolyn Baxter*. Greenfield Review Chapbook, no. 41. Greenfield Center, N.Y.: Greenfield Review Press, 1979. Poems of social protest and keen observation of women's pre-trial, courtroom, and prison experiences. Baxter's works are also included in *Songs

From *A Free Space: Writings by Women in Prison*, an anthology compiled by the New York City Correctional Institution for Women (*see* entry below*).*

Bedell, Precious. Poems in *Aliens at the Border*. The Writing Workshop/Bedford Hills Correctional Facility. Edited with an introduction by Hettie Jones. New York: Segue Books, 1997. Bedell was sentenced to twenty-five years to life for the 1979 murder of her toddler daughter. After she had served nineteen years of her sentence at the Bedford Hills Correctional Facility in New York, her case was reviewed and she was released in 1999. While in prison she was active on behalf of incarcerated mothers.

Belfrage, Sally. "Jail." Chap. 9 in *Freedom Summer*. New York: Viking, 1965. Belfrage, a student volunteer in the 1964 Mississippi Summer Project with the Student Nonviolent Coordinating Committee (SNCC), describes her arrest and imprisonment in Greenwood, Mississippi, for supporting African Americans' attempt to register to vote.

Bickston, Diana. *Street Birth . . . or The Little Brown Eyed Girl*. COSMEP Prison Project. Greenfield Center, N.Y.: Greenfield Review Press, 1982. A collection of poems by Bickston, who began writing in 1979 in a workshop at the Arizona Prison for Women. She was also incarcerated at the California Institution for Women, Frontera.

Blake, Allison. Poems in *Doing Time: 25 Years of Prison Writing—A PEN American Center Prize Anthology*, edited by Bell Gale Chevigny. New York: Arcade, 1999. Poems in *Concrete Garden* 4 (1994), "Women and the Criminal Justice System Issue," published by the Buffalo Group on Justice in Democracy at SUNY/Buffalo.

Blaugdone, Barbara. *An Account of the Travels, Sufferings & Persecutions of Barbara Blaugdone. Given forth as a Testimony to the Lord's Power, and for the Encouragement of Friends*. Printed, and sold by T. S. at the Crooked-Billet in Holywell-Lane, Shoreditch, 1691. An early Quaker, Blaugdone was persecuted for her religion throughout her travels. She describes her cruel whipping at Exeter Prison and her attempt to minister to a Catholic while they were imprisoned in Dublin.

Bone, Edith. *Seven Years Solitary*. London: Hamish Hamilton, 1957. The account of the seven-year, one-month (1949–56) imprisonment of the author in Communist Hungary, where she was sentenced to prison as an "English spy." Born in Budapest in 1889, Bone was a physician, translator, and former Communist Party member who had resided in England since 1933. She was held in the Conti Street Prison in Budapest until 1954, when she was transferred to a prison in Vác. Her early years in solitary confinement were made easier through her recollection of the examples of prison literature she had read by Silvio Pellico and Vera Figner (*see* entry below*).* She describes her delight in teaching herself to read Greek, writing a diary, and studying mathematics; she had won the right to these intellectual pursuits through a "language strike," during which she refused to speak Hungarian to her jailers.

Bonfield, Lynn A. *Jailed for Survival: The Diary of an Anti-Nuclear Activist*. San Francisco: Mother Courage Affinity Group, 1984. Bonfield describes her imprisonment in the Santa Rita Jail from June 20 to July 4, 1983, for her part in blockading the highway around California's Lawrence Livermore Laboratory for nuclear weapons. Her book describes jail conditions and how the women with her maintained a positive spirit. (Information from Jennifer P. McLean's review in *Women's Diaries: A Quarterly Newsletter* 2, no. 4 [Winter 1984]: 6.)

Boudin, Kathy. Poems in *Doing Time: 25 Years of Prison Writing—A PEN American Center Prize Anthology*, edited by Bell Gale Chevigny. New York: Arcade, 1999. Poems in *Concrete Garden* 4 (1994), "Women and the Criminal Justice System

Issue," published by the Buffalo Group on Justice in Democracy at SUNY/Buffalo. Poems in *Breaking Silence: Voices of Mothers in Prison*, compiled by JusticeWorks Community. Brooklyn, N.Y.: JusticeWorks Community, 1999. Poems in *The Writing Workshop/Bedford Hills Correctional Facility. Aliens at the Border*, edited with an introduction by Hettie Jones. New York: Segue Books, 1997. Writings in *Breaking the Walls of Silence: AIDS and Women in a New York State Maximum-Security Prison*. The Members of the AIDS Counseling and Education (ACE) Program of the Bedford Hills Correctional Facility, New York. Woodstock, N.Y.: Overlook Press, 1998. Boudin has been serving a twenty years-to-life sentence at the Bedford Hills Correctional Facility for participating in the robbery of a Brinks truck in Rockland County, New York. She was affiliated with the Weathermen. While at Bedford Hills, she has been active in programs for imprisoned mothers and their children and for AIDS awareness education.

Boyd, Belle. *Belle Boyd in Camp and Prison*. Edited by Curtis Carroll Davis. New York: Thomas Yoseloff, 1968. Originally published in London by Saunders, Otley, 1865. Arrested as a Confederate spy, Boyd was imprisoned in Baltimore in 1862, in Washington's Old Capitol Prison in 1862 and 1863, and in Boston in 1864. She became an actress after the war and, in 1886, toured the country to lecture about her war experiences.

Boyle, Kay. "Report from Lock-Up." In *Words That Must Somehow Be Said: Selected Essays of Kay Boyle*, edited by Elizabeth S. Bell. San Francisco: North Point Press, 1985. Noted American writer Kay Boyle's 1977 essay stating her views on America's prison system and her account of political prisoners in American history. In 1968 she was jailed for thirty-one days for demonstrating against the Vietnam War at the Oakland Induction Center in California.

———. *The Underground Woman*. Garden City, New York: Doubleday, 1975. Novel describing the jail experience of a forty-two year old woman arrested for an antiwar demonstration at a California induction center.

Break de Chains of Legalized U.S. Slavery. Durham, N.C.: Triangle Area Lesbian Feminists Prison Book Project, 1976. A collection of poetry, letters, essays, and artwork by prisoners of the North Carolina Correctional Center for Women. Works express solidarity and describe the struggle for justice in prison.

Breaking Silence: Voices of Mothers in Prison. Compiled by JusticeWorks Community. Brooklyn, N.Y.: JusticeWorks Community, 1999. National anthology of writings by imprisoned women about the experience of women and mothers in prison. Included among writers represented are Kathy Boudin, Judith Clark, Delores Hornick, and Katherine Alice Power (*see* entries below).

Breaking the Walls of Silence: AIDS and Women in a New York State Maximum-Security Prison. The Members of the AIDS Counseling and Education (ACE) Program of the Bedford Hills Correctional Facility, New York. Woodstock, N.Y.: Overlook Press, 1998. Written collectively by members of the ACE Program, this book describes the history of the program and includes an extensive section on its curriculum.

Breshko-Breshkovskaya, Ekaterina Constantinovna (Katerina Breshkovskaia). *Hidden Springs of the Russian Revolution: Personal Memoirs of Katerina Breshkovskaia*. Edited by Lincoln Hutchinson. Stanford, Calif.: Stanford University Press, 1931. This volume contains memoirs begun by Russian revolutionary Breshkovskaia in 1917, when the Russian Revolution made it possible for her to begin to write the experiences that she could not write while in prison. She continued the work during 1921 and 1922 in

Prague. The translation was done by several persons over a period of years. Beginning in 1874 Breshkovskaia was held in several prisons, including those in Bratzlav, Kiev, the Sushtchev police station, the House of Preliminary Detention at Petersburg, Litovski Castle, Petrograd, and Irkutsk. She was also exiled to Siberia. She writes fondly of fellow women revolutionaries, including Vera Figner (*see* entry below*)*.

————. (Catherine Breshkovsky). *The Little Grandmother of the Russian Revolution: Reminiscences and Letters of Catherine Breshkovsky.* Edited by Alice Stone Blackwell. Boston: Little, Brown, 1918. Breshkovsky, as she wrote her name in the United States, was a Russian revolutionary. Editor Blackwell notes that this biographical edition combines a translation of a Yiddish account of Breshkovsky's early life with an account of her later life that she dictated through an interpreter to Ernest Poole of the *Outlook.* This volume includes her own writing also, in the form of a translation of her letters to her son from prison in 1909 and to her son and others from Siberia. Emma Goldman recalls having read this book by and about "Babushka" while she was in the Missouri State Penitentiary, 1917–19 (Goldman, *Living My Life*, 2: 661) (*see* entry below*)*.

Brown, Elaine. *A Taste of Power: A Black Woman's Story.* New York: Pantheon, 1992. Brown's memoirs of her experiences with the Black Panthers includes a brief description (pp. 169–74) of her arrest with Ericka Huggins (*see* entry below) and their brief incarceration in the Sybil Brand Institute women's county jail in Los Angeles in 1969.

Brown, Joyce Ann. *Joyce Ann Brown: Justice Denied.* Chicago: The Noble Press, 1990. In 1989 Brown was released after spending ten years unjustly imprisoned in Gainesville, Texas, for an armed robbery in which a man was killed. She was found to be innocent and her conviction was overturned. She is the founder of Mothers (Fathers) for the Advancement of Social Systems Inc. (MASS), a nonprofit organization that supports prisoners and those unjustly imprisoned.

Brown, Myra Sadd. Papers. Suffragette Fellowship Collection, Museum of London (50.82/1136). Autograph letter, to "Sir." Letter to the press, dated 7 May 1912. British suffragette Brown gives an "account of my experience of forcible feeding." Imprisoned in Holloway in 1912, she was forcibly fed despite the fact she had once had a broken nose and had undergone throat and nose surgery .
Autograph letter, to "Sir." Letter to the press, dated 21 May 1912. Brown thanks the press for printing part of her previous letter, but regrets that all was not printed. She gives her motives for her actions leading to her arrest and for her hunger strike.
A declaration regarding forcible feeding, November 1913. Brown gives her reasons for her hunger strike, her previous medical condition, and the effects of her forcible feeding. She made this declaration before a commissioner for oaths.

Browne, Martha Griffith. *Autobiography of a Female Slave.* New York: Redfield, 1857. Reprint, New York: Negro Universities Press, 1969. This work includes Browne's account of her imprisonment in Kentucky for attacking the man instructed by her master to whip her. The man had attempted to rape her, and she had attacked him in self-defense.

Bryan, Helen. *Inside.* Boston: Houghton Mifflin, 1953. Prison memoirs of Bryan, who was sentenced for contempt of Congress and imprisoned in the Federal Reformatory for Women at Alderson, West Virginia, from November 1950 to January 1951. In 1940 she had served as executive secretary of the Joint Anti-Fascist Refugee Committee, an organization that sent aid to Spanish-Republican refugees. She was convicted for her refusal in 1945 to submit her agency's books and lists of contributors and recipients of funds to the House Committee on Un-American Activities. Her account of her imprisonment focuses on the life stories, as she heard them, of socially disadvantaged women serving sentences for federal crimes.

Buber, Margarete (Margarete Buber-Neumann). *Under Two Dictators*. Translated by Edward Fitzgerald from the original 1949 German edition. London: Gollancz, 1949. Buber and her husband, Heinz Neumann, were German Communists on assignment as translators in Moscow from 1935 until Neumann's arrest by the Soviet secret police in 1937 and Buber's arrest in 1938. She was imprisoned in Moscow's Lubyanka and Butyrka prisons and then sent to the Siberian labor camp Karaganda as a "socially dangerous element." In 1940 she was transferred to Ravensbrück, the Nazi concentration camp, where she spent five years. She never saw her husband again.

Buck, Marilyn. Poems in *Doing Time: 25 Years of Prison Writing—A PEN American Center Prize Anthology*, edited by Bell Gale Chevigny. New York: Arcade, 1999. Essay and poems in *Concrete Garden* 4 (1994), "Women and the Criminal Justice System Issue," published by the Buffalo Group on Justice in Democracy at SUNY/Buffalo. Buck is a political prisoner incarcerated at the Federal Correctional Institution for women in Dublin, California. She has an eighty-year sentence for political activities including the freeing of Assata Shakur (*see* entry below*)*, the bombing of U.S. property, and an armored-car robbery.

———. *Rescue the Word: New Poems*. San Francisco: Friends of Marilyn Buck, 2001. Eleven poems by PEN prizewinner Buck. Included are drawings by Buck and others. (Not examined).

Budiardjo, Carmel. *Surviving Indonesia's Gulag*. London: Cassell, 1996. Budiardjo was an Englishwoman married to an Indonesian who was arrested after Suharto's military coup. Carmel Budiardjo herself was arrested in 1968, held in detention, and then imprisoned until 1971 on charges that she was a communist. During part of this period she was held in Bukit Duri Prison in Jakarta. Following her release, she worked actively in support of human rights for Indonesian prisoners.

Bunney, Marcia. "One Life in Prison: Perception, Reflection, and Empowerment." In *Harsh Punishment: International Experiences of Women's Imprisonment*, edited by Sandy Cook and Susanne Davies, 16–31. Boston: Northeastern University Press, 1999. Bunney, a prisoner at the California Institution for Women, has published in the *San Jose Mercury News*, the *Sonoma County Free Press*, the *Calfornia Prisoner*, the National Lawyers Guild/Prison Law Project *Legal Journal*, and *Frontiers of Justice, Vol. 2: Coddling or Common Sense?* (Brunswick, Me.: Biddle Publishing, 1998).

Buxton, Jane, and Margaret Turner. *Gate Fever*. London: Cresset Press, 1962. Buxton and Turner were imprisoned in Holloway Prison from April to October 1960 following a civil disobedience demonstration for the Campaign for Nuclear Disarmament. Their book takes the form of letters written from prison to a friend outside, but the authors note that these letters were in fact written after their release, because their frank descriptions of prison conditions would have been censored by prison authorities.

The Captive Voice/An Glor Gafa. Quarterly magazine written by Irish Republican political prisoners held in Ireland, England, Europe, and the United States. Published by Sinn Fein's POW Department.

Cassidy, Sheila. *Audacity to Believe*. Cleveland, Oh.: Collins-World, 1977. Cassidy, a British physician and a Catholic, was thirty-four years old when she traveled to Chile in 1971 to gain further practical experience in surgery. In 1975 she was arrested, tortured, and imprisoned in the Casa Grimaldi, Tres Alamos, and Cuatro

Alamos prisons in Santiago for treating a wounded revolutionary. She was expelled from Chile in December 1975 after spending several months in prison.

———. "Tortured in Chile." *Index on Censorship* 5, no. 2 (Summer 1976): 67–73. The main part of Cassidy's testimony on January 19, 1976, in Geneva before the United Nations Ad Hoc Working Group of the Commission on Human Rights. She spoke about her arrest, torture, and imprisonment in Chile.

Cellier, Elizabeth. *Malice Defeated and the Matchless Rogue.* Introduction by Anne Barbeau Gardiner. The Augustan Reprint Society. Publication Numbers 249–50. University of California: William Andrews Clark Memorial Library, 1988. Cellier, a convert to Catholicism, was a well-to-do London midwife who was falsely accused of involvement in a Catholic conspiracy and arrested in 1679. Defending herself at her trial, she was acquitted, and *Malice Defeated: Or a Brief Relation of the Accusation and Deliverance of Elizabeth Cellier* (1680) is her account of the events. That same year she was arrested a second time and charged with libel, for which she was found guilty, fined, and sentenced to stand in the pillory.

Celmina, Helene. *Women in Soviet Prisons.* New York: Paragon House, 1985. Latvian-born Celmina was a translator who was arrested by the KGB for "anti-Soviet agitation" and "spying" and held for six months in the Riga Cheka (KGB prison) before her sentencing to four years (1962–66) in a labor camp.

Chamberlain, Lindy. *Through My Eyes: An Autobiography.* Melbourne, Australia: William Heinemann, 1990. Chamberlain, an Australian homemaker, was accused of murdering her infant daughter in 1980 when the baby was missing from the family's campsite in the Australian Northern Territory. Despite her insistence that a dingo had stolen the child, Chamberlain was convicted in 1982 and imprisoned until her conviction was overturned in 1988. Chamberlain's story was a cause célèbre in Australia of the 1980s and was the basis for the major motion picture, *A Cry in the Dark,* starring Meryl Streep (1988).

Chevers, Sarah, and Katharine Evans. "Isle of Malta, Anno 1661." Chap. 13 in *A Collection of the Sufferings of the People Called Quakers,* edited by Joseph Besse, vol. 2, 399–420. London: Luke Hinde, 1753. A narrative written by Evans, and letters from Chevers and Evans to their inquisitors and to their families and other Quakers in England. These two English Quaker women were imprisoned by the Inquisition at Malta while they were on their way to Alexandria in 1661. They were held for three years.

Clark, Judith. "The Impact of the Prison Environment on Mothers." *Prison Journal* 75, no. 3 (September 1995): 306. Clark is a political prisoner who began serving her seventy-five-years-to-life sentence at Bedford Hills Correctional Facility in New York in 1983 for the 1981 killing of three people in the attempted robbery of a Brinks truck. This article presents the results of her ethnographic research study of the experience of mothers with long sentences. Clark's research was done for her master's thesis in psychology.

———. Poems in *Doing Time: 25 Years of Prison Writing—A PEN American Center Prize Anthology,* edited by Bell Gale Chevigny. New York: Arcade, 1999. Poems in *Concrete Garden* 4 (1994), "Women and the Criminal Justice System Issue," published by the Buffalo Group on Justice in Democracy at SUNY/Buffalo. Poems in *Breaking Silence: Voices of Mothers in Prison.* Compiled by JusticeWorks Community. Brooklyn, N.Y.: JusticeWorks Community, 1999. Poems in *Aliens at the Border.* The Writing Workshop/Bedford Hills Correctional Facility. Edited with an introduction by Hettie Jones. New York: Segue Books, 1997.

Clitherow, Saint Margaret. "Life of Margaret Clitherow." By her Confessor John Mush. In *The Troubles of Our Catholic Forefathers: Related by Themselves*, edited by John Morris, 333–440. 3d ser. London: Bums & Oates, 1877. This account of Roman Catholic martyr Margaret Clitherow's life, written by her confessor, "a distinguished secular priest," includes quotations from Clitherow. She was martyred at the age of thirty in 1586 for her adherence to conscience in harboring Catholic priests in her home in York during the Protestant persecution of Roman Catholics in England. A convert from Protestantism, she was imprisoned several times, "sometimes by the space of two years together," during the twelve years that she was a practicing Catholic. She was executed by being pressed to death in the York tollbooth on March 25, 1586. She was beatified in 1920 and canonized in 1970.

Concrete Garden. "Literary Issue," 3 (1994), published by the Buffalo Group on Justice in Democracy at SUNY/Buffalo. Includes poems and essays by incarcerated women.

———. "Women and the Criminal Justice System Issue," 4 (1994), published by the Buffalo Group on Justice in Democracy at SUNY/Buffalo. Includes poems and essays by incarcerated women.

Constante, Lena. *The Silent Escape: Three Thousand Days in Romanian Prisons.* Translated by Franklin Philip. Berkeley: University of California Press, 1995. Originally published in French in 1990. Constante, a Romanian artist, was a victim of the Stalin "show trials" and accused of espionage. She was imprisoned in 1950 and spent eight years in solitary confinement, during which time she learned the code of wall tapping. She was released in 1961 and exonerated.

Contemporary Prison Writings: 1980. Edited by Jitu Tambuzi and Jeff Elzinga. New Paltz, N.Y.: Tambuzi Publications, n.d. Included in this collection of writing by prisoners, community supporters and others involved in the prison system are works by Assata Shakur (*see* entry below). (Not examined; source: *COSMEP Prison Project Newsletter*, Fall 1980.)

Corday, Charlotte. "Letters from Prison." Reprinted in Michel Corday, *Charlotte Corday*, translated by E. F. Buckley, 12, 134–35, 208–14. New York: Dutton, 1931. Also reprinted in Marie Cher, *Charlotte Corday and Certain Men of the Revolutionary Torment*, 83–4, 128–130, 132. New York: D. Appleton, 1929. Prison letters of the French revolutionary woman who assassinated Marat and was executed by the guillotine in Paris at the Place de la Révolution in 1793. During her brief incarceration in the prisons of the Abbaye and the Conciergerie, where she occupied a cell previously used by Madame Roland (*see* entry below) she wrote a letter to her father and a long letter to the Girondist Barbaroux, telling him of her actions and motives.

Crane, Margaret. "Five Vignettes from the Tennessee Prison for Women." *Prison Writing Review* 8, no. 2 (Winter–Spring 1985): 10–22. Sketches of Crane's prison experiences at the Tennessee Prison for Women, where she was sentenced to one to two years for concealing allegedly stolen goods worth $75. Crane maintained her innocence and held that she was being prosecuted in order to drive her and her mother "out of the county" because of their social activism. Her sketches describe prison conditions and her attempt to provide fellow prisoners with legal counseling. She narrates several cases of the women she counseled.

Crime and Punishment: Inside Views. Edited by Robert Johnson and Hans Toch. Los Angeles: Roxbury Publishing, 2000. Anthology of essays by female and male prisoners about crime and the prison experience. Women writers represented include Rita Biggs, Jennifer Howard, Blanca Chavez, Janelle Cole, Diane Hamill Metzger (*see* entry below), Kim Redifer, and Christina Nankervis.

Crisp, Dorothy. *A Light In the Night*. London: Holborn Publishing, 1960. Prison memoirs by English author and political writer Dorothy Crisp, a regular contributor to the London *Sunday Dispatch* during World War II. In 1958 she was sentenced to Holloway Prison for one year for misdemeanors under the Bankruptcy Act. Her prison memoirs describe conditions in Holloway in order to call attention to the need for prison reform.

Cuevas, Tomasa. *Prison of Women: Testimonies of War and Resistance in Spain, 1939–1975*. Translated and edited by Mary E. Giles. Albany: State University of New York Press, 1998. Writing in 1975 Cuevas, a former Spanish political prisoner, describes her own imprisonment and records the oral testimonies of women imprisoned in 1939 after the Spanish Civil War ended.

D'Arcy, Margaretta. *Tell Them Everything: A Sojourn in the Prison of Her Majesty Queen Elizabeth II at Ard Macha (Armagh)*. London: Pluto Press, 1981. Irish playwright D'Arcy has been involved in antinuclear and Irish Republican activities, which have influenced the plays she writes with coauthor John Arden. She was imprisoned several times, beginning in 1969. In this book she discusses her stay in Armagh Prison in Northern Ireland. She was imprisoned for refusing to pay a fine for her protest against Armagh prison conditions on International Women's Day in 1979. During her sentence, she joined thirty Republican prisoners for three months in 1980 in their "no-wash protest" in Armagh. She wrote her book at the request of these women to "tell them everything."

Darel, Sylva. *A Sparrow in the Snow*. Translated from the Russian by Barbara Norman. New York: Stein & Day, 1973. The memoirs of Darel, a Russian Jew, include an account of her arrest at the age of nineteen, and her imprisonment in Leningrad and a series of transit prisons on her journey "home" to Siberia. She had been arrested in 1953 for "escaping" to Leningrad from Siberia, where for over ten years her family had been living in exile as "socially dangerous elements." She wrote this account while in exile in 1953.

Davis, Angela Yvonne. "Angela Introduces Ericka's New Book." *Black Panther* 8, no. 9 (20 May 1972): 2, 7–8. Writing from Santa Clara County Jail, California, in December 1971, Davis reviews and praises Ericka Huggins's (*see* entry below) forthcoming book of poetry, in which Huggins presents the struggle of African American women.

———. *The Angela Y. Davis Reader*. Blackwell Readers. Edited by Joy James and Angela Y. Davis. Oxford: Blackwell, 1998. Anthology of three decades of writing by Davis, including several selections dealing with prisons and prisoners.

———. *If They Come in the Morning: Voices of Resistance*. New York: Third Press, 1971. In *An Autobiography*, Davis describes the work that she did while in prison on this anthology of writings about the black liberation movement. She contributed several selections, and there are prison interviews with her.

———. "The Soledad Brothers." *Black Scholar* 2 (April–May 1971): 2–7. From her own prison cell in the Marin County Jail, San Rafael, California, Davis writes a defense of the three Soledad Brothers, including George Jackson. The essay is of interest to those researching Davis's own case, because prosecutors claimed that her uncontrolled love for Jackson motivated her to support a plot by African American prisoners to free him.

———. "To Mexican Political Prisoners." *Transcontinental* 6, no. 66 (September 1971): 5. Davis writes from Marin County Jail, San Rafael, California, on June 14, 1971. Her letter expresses support for Mexicans imprisoned following a demonstration in Mexico City on June 10, 1971.

———. "Walls." In *An Autobiography*. New York: Random House, 1974. A former UCLA professor active in black revolutionary causes, Davis describes her imprisonment in Marin County Jail and Santa Clara Jail, California, in 1970–71, on charges of murder, kidnapping, and criminal conspiracy. While imprisoned, she fought to take an active part in her own legal defense.

Day, Dorothy. *The Eleventh Virgin*. New York: Albert and Charles Boni, 1924. Pages 180–218 of part 2, chapter 3, of this autobiographical novel describe the prison experience of June Henreddy (Dorothy Day), a young radical journalist who is arrested in Washington, D.C., with a group of suffragists demonstrating for the rights of political prisoners. She spends sixteen days in a workhouse outside Washington, where the suffragists stage a hunger strike.

———. *From Union Square to Rome*. Silver Spring, Md.: Preservation of the Faith Press, 1938; reprint, New York: Arno, 1978. At the age of forty, Day recalls her past life and conversion to Catholicism in this book addressed to her brother. She gives details of her stay in Occoquan Workhouse and the Washington city jail in 1917 for suffrage activity (pp. 81–87). There is also a description of her imprisonment, about 1920, for several days in the West Chicago Avenue Police Station, Chicago. She was mistakenly charged with prostitution, and she writes of the kindness of the prostitutes jailed with her (pp. 98–107).

———. "Jail." In *The Long Loneliness*. New York: Harper &. Row, 1952. Day describes her experience in a Washington workhouse and jail after her arrest for picketing in front of the White House in support of suffragists' rights in prison. Sentenced to thirty days' imprisonment, she went on a hunger strike for ten days.

———. "Thoughts After Prison." *Liberation: An Independent Monthly* 2, no. 6 (September 1957): 5–7. Day writes of family disintegration, materialism, and war from her perspective as an ex-prisoner who is especially sensitive and powerless. She describes the poor with whom she was imprisoned in the 151st Street Police Station in New York City on July 12, 1957. She had been arrested for disobeying the Civil Defense Act, when she picketed instead of taking shelter during an announced air-raid drill in New York City. She and others of the Catholic Workers movement were sentenced to thirty days.

De Beausobre, Iulia. *The Woman Who Could Not Die*. London: Gollancz, 1948. In February 1932, De Beausobre was arrested by the GPU, the Soviet police, for complicity in the alleged treason of her husband, Nicolay. She was held in the Inner Prison of the GPU and in Boutyrki Prison, and then sentenced to five years' hard labor in the GPU penal camps. Upon her release she learned that Nicolay had been shot. De Beausobre feared living in Russia any longer and was able to immigrate to England because an old friend agreed to sponsor her. Her prison memoirs describe her fellow prisoners.

Deming, Barbara. "In the Birmingham Jail." *Nation*, 25 May 1963, 436–37. Deming describes events leading to her imprisonment in the women's ward of the Birmingham City Jail for peacefully demonstrating for racial equality. She relates how the poor white female prisoners initially resented her actions but later came to listen to her beliefs on nonviolence and equality. She also describes the jailing of children who were demonstrating.

* ———. *Prison Notes*. New York: Grossman, 1966. A description of Deming's 1964 imprisonment in the city jail of Albany, Georgia, for participation in a civil rights demonstration. There is a discussion of the theory of nonviolent protest, in the form of a letter to a friend who had urged Deming to give up her efforts.

————. *We Are All Part of One Another: A Barbara Deming Reader*. Edited by Jane Meyerding, with a foreword by Barbara Smith. Philadelphia: New Society, 1984. This collection includes "In the Birmingham Jail" and selections from *Prison Notes*.

Dergan, Bridget. *The Life And Confession Of Bridget Dergan, Who Murdered Mrs. Ellen Coriell, The Lovely Wife Of Dr. Coriell, of New Market N.J. to which is added Her Full Confession, and an Account of her Execution at New Brunswick*. Philadelphia: Barclay, 1867. Bridget Dergan (Deignan) immigrated to America from Ireland (about 1864) as a young woman, and was employed by the Coriells as a servant. This volume contains a letter written to her brother in Ireland from the Middlesex County Jail, New Brunswick, and Dergan's confessions, dictated because she was illiterate. She claims to have murdered Mrs. Coriell so that she "might take her place." The case aroused great public interest, and tickets were issued to five hundred persons to witness her execution in August 1867.

Diaz, Gladys. "Roles and Contradictions of Chilean Women in the Resistance and in Exile: Collective Reflections of a Group of Militant Prisoners." Presented at the Plenary Session of the International Conference on Exile and Solidarity in Latin America During the 1970s. New York: Women's International Resource Exchange (WIRE), 1979. Chilean resistance worker Diaz presents the collective testimony of her sisters who had been imprisoned and exiled for their work in the Chilean Resistance. Diaz herself had been arrested, tortured, imprisoned in Villa Grimaldi and Tres Alamos, and finally released into exile as the result of an international campaign on her behalf.

Diaz, Nidia. *I Was Never Alone: A Prison Diary from El Salvador*. Melbourne, Australia: Ocean Press, 1992. Diaz, otherwise known as Maria Marta Valladares, was a leader in the Farabundo Martí National Liberation Front (FMLN). She was wounded, captured, and imprisoned in solitary confinement in 1985. After six months she was released and she continued her work in the leadership of the FMLN.

Doing Time: 25 Years of Prison Writing—A PEN American Center Prize Anthology. Edited by Bell Gale Chevigny. New York: Arcade, 1999. Includes poems by Allison Blake, Kathy Boudin, Marilyn Buck, Judith Clark, Lori Lynn McLuckie, Diane Hamill Metzger, Vera Montgomery, Judee Norton, Susan Rosenberg, and Barbara Saunders (*see* entries in this bibliography). Also includes poems by the Bedford Hills Writing Workshop and Vera Montgomery.

Dole, Dorcas. "Once More a Warning to Thee O England: But More Particularly to the Inhabitants of the City of Bristol. From Newgate Prison in Bristol, 1683." Wing D 1834, Reel 814, pp. 11–12. Reprinted in *English Women's Voices 1540–1700*, edited by Charlotte F. Otten, 79–80, Miami: Florida International University Press, 1992. Quaker visionary Dole describes her sufferings while imprisoned for her prophecies against Bristol, England.

Doty, Madeleine Zabriskie. *Society's Misfits*. New York: 1916. Doty, a young lawyer, voluntarily entered the New York State Prison for Women at Auburn in 1913. Dedicated to prison reform, she posed as "Maggie Martin," a convicted forger, in order to investigate and report on prison conditions for women.

Duras, Duchesse de (Louise H.), née Noailles. "Prison Life During the French Revolution. Written in 1801, the Year IX. of the Republic." In *Prison Journals during the French Revolution*, translated by Mrs. M. Carey, 6–157. New York: Dodd, Mead, 1891. To fulfill her son's request, the Duchesse de Duras wrote her memoirs upon her release from prison. She was imprisoned in the old convent at Saint-Francois à

Beauvais on October 6, 1793, and transferred to the prison at Chantilly on October 20, 1793. She was again transferred, to the Collège du Plessis at Paris, on April 5, 1794, and released on October 19, 1794. The memoirs are dated "Paris, February 11, 1804," and signed "Noailles de Durfort-Duras." This section of the volume also includes prison writings of her sister- in-law Louise Noailles (*see* entry below).

Duval, Elsie. Papers. Fawcett Library, City of London Polytechnic, London. Included are prison diaries from 1911 to 1912 and 1913, and personal correspondence from 1913, 1914, and 1918. Duval, a British suffragette, was forcibly fed in prison. (Not examined; source: Margaret Barrow, *Women 1870– 1928: A Select Guide to Printed and Archival Sources in the United Kingdom* [London: Mansell, 1981].)

Dyer, Mary. Letters. In Chap. 5, "New England," in *A Collection of the Sufferings of the People Called Quakers*, edited by Joseph Besse, vol. 2, 196–207. London: Luke Hinde, 1753.

————. Letters. In Appendix 2 of *Mary Dyer of Rhode Island: The Quaker Martyr that Was Hanged on Boston Common June 1, 1660*, by Horatio Rogers, 84–93. Providence, R.I.: Preston & Rounds, 1896. Dyer's letters to the Massachusetts General Court in 1659, after she had received the death sentence for disobeying an order of banishment from Puritan Massachusetts Bay Colony, and after she was at first reprieved.

Elizabeth I. *Collected Works*. Edited by Leah S. Marcus et al. Chicago: University of Chicago Press, 2000. Includes letter and poems written from her imprisonment at Woodstock (1554–55). The twenty-one-year-old Protestant princess, herself in line for the English throne, was imprisoned when her Catholic half-sister Mary Tudor became queen.

Elliott, Grace Dalrymple. *Journal of My Life During the French Revolution*. London: Richard Bentley, 1859. King George III of England requested Mrs. Elliott, who was known for her beauty and grace in court society, to write this journal. It includes a description of her incarceration in the prison of St. Pelagie, in the Prison of the Recollets, at Versailles, and in the Carmes prison in Paris. Held under suspicion of espionage against the Republic, she describes her acquaintance with prisoners about to be executed.

Empire! The Creative Writing Journal of New York State Inmates. Edited by Paul Gordon. New York State Dept. of Correctional Services, 1984. An annual literary arts magazine for prisoners of New York State Correctional facilities. The first issue, Fall 1984, contains poems by Althea Sellers and Elly Kessler.

Evans, Katharine. *See* Chevers, Sarah, and Katharine Evans.

Figner, Vera. "When the Clock of Life Stopped." In *Memoirs of a Revolutionist*, translated by Camilla Chapin Daniels et al., Book 2, 179–318. New York: International, 1927; reprint, Westport, Conn.: Greenwood Press, 1968; Northern Illinois University Press, 1991. A description of Figner's imprisonment in the Schlüsselburg Fortress, from 1884 to 1904, for revolutionary terrorist activity in Russia. She spent much of this period in solitary confinement, communicating through coded wall tappings.

First, Ruth. *117 Days*. New York: Stein &. Day, 1965; Penguin, 1982. South African journalist who was first imprisoned without trial under the ninety-day detention law in 1963. She was held in solitary confinement in the women's cells of the Marshall Square Police Station, Johannesburg, and in the Women's Central Prison, Pretoria. Books were not allowed and she was forbidden to write. She was imprisoned longer than any white woman in South Africa before her. Even before her imprisonment she had been served banning orders that forbade her to write and thus ended her fifteen-year career in journalism. Her activist lawyer husband, Joe Slovo, had previously fled the country, and after her release she joined him in exile in England. In 1978 she became director of the Centre for African Studies in Maputo, Mozambique. She was killed by a letter bomb in her office in 1982.

Fitzgerald, Tamsin. *Tamsin*. Edited by Richard A. Condon. New York: Dial, 1973. Editor Richard A. Condon explains that the book is based mostly upon Tamsin's correspondence from prison. A number of brief poems are included. Eighteen-year-old Tamsin was incarcerated from May 1969 to December 1970 at the Federal Reformatory for Women at Alderson, West Virginia. She and her boyfriend, Michael, also imprisoned, were convicted of attempting to hijack an airplane from New York to Havana in order for Michael to avoid the draft.

Flatman, Ada. "Reminiscences of a Suffragette," typescript. Suffragette Fellowship Collection, Museum of London (Group C, vol. 2: 58.87/67). British suffragette Flatman was imprisoned in Holloway in 1908. She writes fondly of Constance Lytton (*see* entry below).

Fleming, Amalia. *A Piece of Truth*. London: Jonathan Cape, 1972. A Greek woman who had been active in the Greek Resistance during World War II, Lady Fleming married an Englishman, Sir Alexander Fleming, in 1953, but returned to Athens in 1962. She was arrested by the military police in 1971 for her opposition to its repression. Her memoirs describe her pretrial experience and her sentence of sixteen months in Korydallos Prison, between Athens and Perama. Her sentence was suspended because she was ill, but upon her return home she was expelled to England.

Fletcher, Susan Willis. *Twelve Months in an English Prison*. Boston: Lee and Shepard, 1884. American Spiritualist Susan Willis Fletcher was arrested in 1880 and imprisoned in Her Majesty's Prison, Westminster, a women's prison in London, until 1882. Although she maintained her innocence, she was convicted of fraud and receiving jewels and valuable clothing under false pretenses. Her supporters contended that she had been unjustly "tried" in newspaper reports of the scandal, and that Spiritualism, not Fletcher, was really on trial. Fletcher's account of her year's imprisonment is unique in her detailed description of the spirits who visited her prison cell.

Flynn, Elizabeth Gurley. *The Alderson Story: My Life as a Political Prisoner*. New York: International, 1963. Flynn, a labor organizer in the Industrial Workers of the World (IWW), a founder of the ACLU, and later a communist, was arrested in 1951 under the Smith Act and charged with "teaching and advocating the violent overthrow of the government." She spent the years 1955 to 1957 in the Federal Reformatory for Women at Alderson, West Virginia.

Forest, Eva (Genoveva). *From A Spanish Prison*. Translated by Rosemary Sheed. New York: Moon Books/Random House, 1976. Journal and letters written in 1974 and 1975 from Yeserías Prison, Madrid, where Forest, a psychiatrist by profession and a communist, was imprisoned on charges of terrorist activity against Franco's government. Recipients of letters included her husband, also imprisoned, and their children.

Fortune News. Bimonthly. Edited by David Rothenberg. A newspaper of the Fortune Society, a nonprofit service and advocacy program for prisoners and ex-prisoners. Issues include prisoners' writings and winning works from the PEN prison writing contest. The April 1979 issue focuses on women.

Fox, Margaret. *The Life of Margaret Fox. Wife of George Fox. Compiled from her own narrative, and other Sources; with a Selection from her Epistles, Etc.* Philadelphia:

Association of Friends, "for the Diffusion of Religious and Useful Knowledge," 1859. A biographical account of the "Mother of Quakerism"—her life, convincement, various imprisonments, and excerpts from letters written during her four-year imprisonment in Lancaster Castle, 1664–68.

From Women in Prison Here to Women of Vietnam: We Are Sisters. San Francisco: Peoples Press, 1975. A collection of letters written by women from the California Institution for Women (Frontera) to women political prisoners in South Vietnam. The letters express solidarity and warm wishes in their struggle.

Frontiers of Justice. Brunswick, Me.: Biddle Publishing, 1997–2000. Anthology series edited by Claudia Whitman and Julie Zimmerman. It contains writings about prisons, by prisoners, and by prisoners' advocates.

Fumiko, Kaneko. "Women and Treason in Pre-war Japan: The Prison Poetry of Kanno Sugo and Kaneko Fumiko." Article and translation of poems by Helene Bowen. In *Lilith: A Feminist History Journal* 5 (1998): 9–251. Fumiko, a Japanese anarchist, was condemned to death for conspiracy to assassinate the emperor. She wrote poems while she awaited sentencing. Although her death sentence was commuted to a life sentence, Fumiko committed suicide in 1926 by hanging herself in her cell.

Gaines, Patrice. *Laughing in the Dark: From Colored Girl to Woman of Color—A Journey from Prison to Power.* New York: Crown, 1994. Gaines, a *Washington Post* journalist, writes of her life's struggle against racism, abusive relationships, and drug abuse. She describes her experience in a North Carolina jail. When she was twenty-one she had been arrested on a drug charge, for which she received probation.

Gannett, Betty. Papers, 1929–1970. Madison, Wis.: State Historical Society of Wiscon-sin. Gannett was active in the Communist Party in America from 1923 until her death in 1970. She was a writer, editor, Marxist theoretician, and teacher. Her papers at the State Historical Society of Wisconsin include papers relating to her 1955–57 imprisonment in the Federal Reformatory for Women in Alderson, West Virginia. She and other party leaders were charged under the Smith Act with conspiracy against the government. (Not examined; source: *The Papers of Betty Gannett: Guide to a Microfilm Edition*, 1976.)

Ginzburg, Eugenia. *Journey into the Whirlwind.* Translated by Paul Stevenson and Max Hayward. New York: Harcourt Brace Jovanovich, 1967. Ginzburg, a dedicated Communist and a history professor, was arrested in 1937 during Stalin's purges, and imprisoned for eighteen years in Kazan, Moscow, and Yaroslavl prisons, followed by penal camps in Siberia. In this volume, the first of her two books, she describes the prisons and her transfer to the Kolyma camps. Her second book, *Within the Whirlwind*, translated by Ian Boland, with an introduction by Heinrich Böll (New York: Harcourt Brace Jovanovich, 1981), deals with Siberian camp experiences.

"Girl Delinquent, Age Sixteen: An Undecorated Autobiography." *Harper's* 164 (June 1932): 551–59. An anonymous autobiographical article by a Chicago teenager, writing from a state penal institution. It deals mostly with the problems faced by the author as a girl growing up on the streets of a slum neighborhood, and how this background led her to prison.

Goldman, Emma. "Letters from Prison." *Little Review* 3, no. 3 (May 1916): 17–18. Reprinted in The *Little Review Anthology*, edited by Margaret Anderson, 62–63. New York: Horizon Press, 1953. Included are excerpts from letters written by Goldman from Queens County Jail, Long Island City, New York, during her fifteen-day imprisonment in April 1916. She had been arrested in New York in February

1916 for lecturing on birth control. Advocates of birth control enthusiastically supported her in this case, which served the purpose of boosting the birth control movement.

————. *Living My Life*. 2 vols. New York: Knopf, 1931; reprint, Dover, 1970. Vol. I: chap. 12; vol. 2: chaps. 45–49. A description of Goldman's imprisonment in 1893 in Blackwell's Island Penitentiary, New York, for inciting to riot, and from 1917 to 1919 in the Missouri State Penitentiary, for conspiracy against the draft. Includes reference to her friendship with her fellow prisoner Kate O'Hare (*see* entry below).

Gorbanevskaya, Natalya. "Fourteen Poems." *Index on Censorship* I, no. 1 (Spring 1972): 107–15. Poems written from 1964 to 1970, excerpted from *Selected Poems by Natalya Gorbanevskaya*, with a transcript of her trial and papers relating to her detention in a prison psychiatric hospital, edited and translated by Daniel Weissbort. Oxford: Carcanet Press, 1972.

————. *Selected Poems by Natalya Gorbanevskaya, with a transcript of her trial and papers relating to her detention in a prison psychiatric hospital.* Edited and translated by Daniel Weissbort. Oxford: Carcanet Press, 1972. A translator and poet, Gorbanevskaya was confined in mental hospitals because she was a leading dissident intellectual in Moscow. In 1968, during a problem pregnancy, she was transferred, under KGB direction, from her maternity hospital to the Kashchenko mental hospital. She was released, she claimed, because of her pregnancy. She was later diagnosed as schizophrenic and taken to the hospital section of Moscow's Butyrka Prison in 1970 and transferred to a psychiatric hospital in Kazan in 1971. This book includes a poem from Butyrka Prison, letters to her mother and son from Butyrka Prison, and "Free Health Service," a series of notes recording her experience in the maternity hospital and the Kashchenko mental hospital.

Gordon, Helen (Helen Gordon Liddle). *The Prisoner: A Sketch. An Experience of Forcible Feeding by a Suffragette.* Letchworth, Eng.: Garden City Press, 1912. Gordon writes of her imprisonment for one month (October–November 1907) in Strangeways Prison, Manchester. She was arrested for a suffrage protest in which she broke a post office window. While in prison she was forcibly fed when she demanded to be treated as a political prisoner and protested against prison regulations and food. Her aim in the book is to describe the prison atmosphere and its effect on the prisoner, in order to awaken the public to the situation.

Gratz, Simon. Autograph Collection. "Criminals and their Victims." Case 13, Box 39. Philadelphia: Historical Society of Pennsylvania. This collection includes writings by two women imprisoned in nineteenth-century America: Ann Carson, autograph letter, signed, to Hon. Chief Justice Tilghman from prison, 14 February 1822. She writes to request that her bail be lowered. Carson, a Philadelphia belle, was imprisoned several times during her brief life. In 1816 she had been imprisoned in Philadelphia, Harrisburg, and Lancaster prisons pending trial for a series of charges including accessory to the murder of her husband, conspiracy to abduct the governor of Pennsylvania, and bigamy. In 1820 she was convicted and sentenced to two years in the Philadelphia Penitentiary as accessory after a robbery was committed. Released before the expiration of her sentence, she engaged Mrs. M. Clarke to write her "autobiography," so that Carson could earn money for living expenses. She was later imprisoned again in Philadelphia, where she died at the age of thirty-eight, probably from injuries inflicted by other prisoners. *The Memoirs of the Celebrated and Beautiful Mrs. Ann Carson* was enlarged and published in its second edition by Mrs. Clarke in 1838. Mary Mors (Morris), confession, n.d., written in another hand signed by her "mark." She confesses to arson, as "Accessary and the instrument of the late dredfull fire in Boston."

Graves, Sheila. *Marriage to Murder: My Story*. Edinburgh: W. & R. Chambers, 1980. Graves describes events leading to her sensational trial in Scotland for the murder of her husband. She was convicted in 1968 and sentenced to life in prison, although she claimed to be innocent. She was paroled in 1978.

*Greenhow, Rose. *My Imprisonment and the First Year of Abolition Rule at Washington*. London: Richard Bentley, 1863. The electronic edition is available through the University of North Carolina at Chapel Hill Libraries Documenting the American South project: http://docsouth.unc.edu/greenhow/menu.html. Many of Greenhow's other papers are available in the Rose O'Neal Greenhow Papers: An On-line Archival Collection of the Special Collections Library, Duke University: http://scriptorium.lib.duke.edu/greenhow. Arrested as a Confederate spy, whose home was a center of espionage activity, and whose information had helped the Confederate victory at Bull Run, this popular Washington hostess and her small daughter were imprisoned in the Old Capitol Prison, Washington, D.C., in 1862. She continued her espionage from prison and openly defied Union authorities.

Grey, Lady Jane (Lady Jane Dudley). *Memoirs and Literary Remains*. Edited by Sir Harris Nicolas. London: Henry Colbum, 1832. Lady Jane Grey (1537–54) reigned briefly as Queen of England after the death of King Edward VI, but Queen Mary's claim to the throne was successful and Jane and her husband, Guildford Dudley, were charged with high treason. This collection includes writings of Lady Jane from the Tower of London, where she was imprisoned in July 1553 and executed in February 1554. There are letters to her father and sister Katherine, and a prayer.

Guernsey, Isabel Russell. *Free Trip to Berlin*. Toronto: Macmillan, 1943. Wartime memoirs of Guernsey, a Canadian civilian who was traveling to South Africa when her ship was captured by the Germans. A prison ship took her and other passengers with British passports to Germany, where she was held in a series of jails during her journey to the Liebenau Women's Internment Camp. After three months there, she was allowed to live in relative freedom in Berlin until, over a year later, she was released to the United States.

Guyon, Jeanne Marie Bouvier. *Autobiography of Madame Guyon. Complete in two parts*. New York: Edward Jones, 1880. This is the English translation of the French original, dated 1709. Madame Guyon, a French writer on spiritual subjects, was criticized by the Catholic Church for her quietist doctrines and her lifestyle. In 1688 she was arrested and imprisoned in the Convent of the Visitation of St. Mary, near St. Antoine. As the result of a controversy over the quietist doctrines she shared with Abbé Fénelon, she was again imprisoned in 1695 at Vincennes and later in the Bastille, from which she was released in 1703. Her autobiography, she states, was written at the command of her spiritual director.

Harris, Emily. "On the Open Road." *Fortune News*, 23 June 1981, 4. Harris, imprisoned in the California Institution for Women, Frontera, describes what she feels when she jogs around the prison yard and remembers how she and her husband, Bill, were arrested by the FBI while jogging in San Francisco in 1975. Members of the terrorist Symbionese Liberation Army (SLA), they had been hunted by the FBI for one and a half years for their part in the case of Patricia Hearst, a newspaper heiress abducted by the SLA in 1974. The Harrises were tried in 1976 for robbery, kidnapping, and assault. This piece received third place for nonfiction in the 1981 PEN prison writing awards.

Harris, Jean. "Finding the Gift in It." *Parabola* 17, no. 1 (Spring 1992): 22. Essay on the ways in which women prisoners experience solitude, originally conceived by Quaker prison reformers as a means of rehabilitation. Harris discusses the AIDS Counseling and Education (ACE) Program at Bedford Hills Correctional Facility, New York. Harris, former headmistress of the Madeira School in McLean, Virginia, was imprisoned in Bedford Hills in 1981 following her conviction in the shooting death of Dr. Herman Tarnower. She was granted clemency by New York governor Mario Cuomo in 1992 and released.

———. Lecture in *Concrete Garden* 4 (1994), "Women and the Criminal Justice System Issue," published by the Buffalo Group on Justice in Democracy at SUNY/Buffalo.

———. *Marking Time: Letters from Jean Harris to Shana Alexander.* New York: Zebra Books, 1991. This book is a collection of Harris's correspondence with journalist Shana Alexander, in which she describes the women imprisoned at Bedford Hills and her own perceptions of the prison system.

———. *They Always Call Us Ladies: Stories from Prison.* New York: Zebra Books, 1988. Harris describes prison life at Bedford Hills and the women she knew there. She draws upon her extensive reading about education and corrections in her discussion.

———. *Stranger in Two Worlds.* New York: Macmillan, 1986. Harris's autobiography, describing her relationship with Dr. Herman Tarnower, her trial, and her responses to imprisonment.

Heller, Tzila Amidror. *Behind Prison Walls: A Jewish Woman Freedom Fighter for Israel's Independence.* With a foreword by Menachem Begin. Translated by Elizabeth Maor. Hoboken, N.J.: KTAV Publishing House, 1961; 1999. Heller was a member of the Irgun (National Military Organization) that resisted British occupation and fought for the creation of the State of Israel. She writes of her own imprisonment by the British and describes her cellmates in the women's prison at Bethlehem.

Henry, Joan. *Women in Prison.* New York: Doubleday, 1952. Published in London by Gollancz under the title *Who Lie in Gaol* (1952). Henry, a British author, was imprisoned in 1951 for passing bad checks. She writes of life in two English prisons for women: Holloway and Askham Grange, York.

———. *Yield to the Night.* London: Gollancz, 1954. A novel written in the first person about a murderess's last days in an English prison.

Hooton, Elizabeth. Letter to Noah Bullock, Derby, England, 1650/51. Swarthmore Manuscripts, Friends House, London; a fair copy made by George Fox is at the Historical Society of Pennsylvania, Philadelphia. Reprinted in Hugh Barbour and Arthur O. Roberts, eds. *Early Quaker Writings, 1650–1700,* 381–83. Grand Rapids, Mich.: Eerdmans, 1973. Hooton, believed to be the first follower of Quaker leader George Fox, was jailed several times in England and persecuted in Massachusetts for her beliefs. She was imprisoned in Derby jail, England, sometime during Fox's own imprisonment there in 1650–51. Her offense was reproving a priest. She wrote her letter to Noah Bullock, magistrate or mayor of Derby, admonishing him for jailing her unjustly and warning him to follow God's teachings. This letter and Fox's Derby writings are believed to be the oldest surviving Quaker writings, according to Barbour and Roberts.

Hornick, Delores. Poems in *Trapped under Ice: A Death Row Anthology,* edited by Julie Zimmerman. Brunswick, Me.: Biddle Publishing, 1995. Poems in *Breaking Silence: Voices of Mothers in Prison,* compiled by JusticeWorks Community. Brooklyn, NY: JusticeWorks Community, 1999 Hornick is imprisoned in Danbury, Connecticut.

Hsieh Pingying. *Girl Rebel: The Autobiography of Hsieh Pingying*. With extracts from her *New War Diaries*. Translated by Adet Lin and Anor Lin. New York: John Day, 1940. London: Pandora, 1986. As a twenty-year-old student, Hsieh Pingying left her Chinese village of Hsiehtushan in 1927 to join the Chinese Revolution and to escape her family's plans for her marriage. Her *Autobiography* (1936) tells of her adventures with the army and the publication in a Chinese newspaper of her letters describing the war. In 1927, when young revolutionaries, particularly bobbed-haired females, were persecuted as Communists, Hsieh Pingying was imprisoned and escaped sentencing only because the judge knew her father. *The New War Diaries* (1938) tell of her imprisonment in Japan during the 1930s, but the section about this imprisonment has not yet been translated and is not included in the extracts in *Girl Rebel*.

Huggins, Ericka. "before a woman becomes grown." *Crime and Social Justice*, no. 1 (Spring–Summer 1974): 50. A poem from Niantic Prison, 1970, about injustices faced by poor African American women.

———. "Excerpts from a Letter from Ericka." *Black Panther* 6, no. 3 (13 February 1971): 6.

———. "A Letter from Sister Ericka Huggins." *Movement* 5, no. 8 (September 1969): 7. In her letter dated 8 July 1969, Huggins supports political prisoners in their fight against government repression.

———. Letter to "don," 18 November 1970. In Donald Freed, *Agony in New Haven*. New York: Simon & Schuster, 1973, p. 63. Huggins refers to Ethel Rosenberg: "i know how ethel r. must have felt. . . ."

———. Poems. In *Off Our Backs: A Woman's News Journal* 1, no. 17 (February 1971); 2, no. 8 (April 1972.). Poems describing Huggins's prison experiences, her identification with women prisoners, and her feminist consciousness.

———. Poems and a message from Niantic Prison. In *If They Come in the Morning: Voices of Resistance*, edited by Angela Davis. New York: Third Press, 1971.

———. "Revolution in Our Lifetime." *Black Panther* 5, no. 28 (9 January 1971): 5.

Huggins, Ericka, and Huey Newton. *Insights and Poems*. San Francisco: City Lights Books, 1975. The collection includes poems written in 1970 and 1971, when Huggins, a Black Panther, was imprisoned at Niantic State Farm for Women in Connecticut.

Hunt, Antonia. *Little Resistance: A Teenage English Girl's Adventures in Occupied France*. London: Leo Cooper, Secker & Warburg, 1982. Born Antonia Lyon-Smith, the author was an English teenager living in France from 1940 to 1944, during the German occupation. She spent four months in the barracks of a wartime internment camp in Besançon and was later imprisoned by the Gestapo in Gestapo headquarters, Rue des Saussaies, Paris. She was held five months in solitary confinement because the Germans believed she had contacts in the French Resistance. She tells of her illness in prison and the complications she faced when a Gestapo translator saved her life and proposed marriage.

Huré, Anne. *In Prison*. Translated by Emma Craufurd. London: MacDonald, 1965. Originally published in France as *En Prison* (1963).

———. *The Two Nuns*. Translated by Emma Craufurd. London: MacDonald, 1964. Originally published in France as *Les Deux Moniales* (1962).

———. *The Word Made Flesh*. Translated by Emma Craufurd. London: MacDonald, 1967. Originally published in France as *Le Péché Sans Merci* (1964). Huré, an upper-class

French woman, became a Benedictine nun and later left the convent to acquire a doctorate in theology. She was imprisoned numerous times in la Roquette and Haguenau prisons between 1962 and 1971 for robberies, writing bad checks, fraud, and nonpayment of bills. She has written several novels that draw upon her prison experience and use imagery from life in the prison and the convent. The autobiographical novel *In Prison* is the most directly about prison. *The Two Nuns*, which was very successful in France, is set in a Benedictine abbey for women, and *The Word Made Flesh* is set in a religious school for girls. The novels are abstract and philosophical. (Information from Elissa Gelfand, *Imagination in Confinement: Women's Writings from French Prisons* [Ithaca, N.Y.: Cornell University Press, 1983].)

I Am Waiting to Be Free. Santa Fe, N.M.: Koyemsi Press, 1981. An anthology of writing from the Women's Penitentiary of New Mexico. It includes poems by Lorri Martinez (*see* entry below).

Ibarruri, Dolores. *They Shall Not Pass: The Autobiography of La Pasionaria*. Translated from the 1962 Spanish edition. New York: International, 1966. Ibarruri, a Spanish Communist, explains that this book is not her memoirs, but a "testimony to the traditions of struggle of the Spanish people." In 1931, while working as editor of a Communist newspaper in Madrid, Ibarruri was arrested for helping a fugitive and was held in the Women's Prison of Madrid and Larrínaga Prison in Bilbao until January 1932. She was rearrested shortly afterward in Madrid and released in 1933. She describes her imprisonment with thieves and prostitutes and her attempts to instruct them in Communism. Her difficulty as an imprisoned revolutionary and mother who could not properly care for her children is discussed. She met with Elizabeth Gurley Flynn (*see* entry above) in Moscow in 1960.

In Time: Women's Poetry from Prison. Edited by Rosanna Warren and Teresa Iverson. Boston: Boston University Prison Education Program, 1995. Poems from writing workshops conducted by Rosanna Warren and Teresa Iverson at the Massachusetts Correctional Institute in Framingham, 1994–95. Poets represented include Deborah Conaghan, Jacqueline Dash, Kathleen Gamache, Katherine Jamie Papa, Katherine Alice Power (*see* entry below), and Rebekah Sanford.

Inside/Out: Poetry and Prose from America's Prisons. A quarterly newsletter. The Summer 1982 issue (vol. 3, no. 1) includes a special women's supplement, with artwork and photographs. Also included are poetry, fiction, and drama by Rae S. Stewart, Diane Hamill Metzger (*see* entry below), La'Shawn Marcella Russell, Diana Bickston (*see* entry above), and Michele Roberts.

Inside: Prison American Style. Edited by Robert J. Minton, Jr. New York: Random House, 1971. Most selections in this anthology are written by prisoners themselves, but almost all are by men. It does include two short pieces by Nellie Sloan, who was imprisoned in Corona, a correctional facility for women in southern California. Her husband was a prisoner whose work is also included in the book. Nellie Sloan describes the prison intake process and the prison psychiatric unit.

Invincible Spirit: Art and Poetry of Ukrainian Women Political Prisoners in the U.S.S.R. Translated by Bodhan Yasen. Baltimore: Smoloskyp Publishers, 1977. Text in English and Ukrainian. This volume contains poetry, letters, and color photographs of symbolic embroidered designs created by Ukrainian women prisoners who have been incarcerated in Soviet labor camps for defending human rights and Ukrainian national rights. The written and embroidered works emphasize the women's religious and cultural heritage. The poets are Iryna Senyk, Iryna Stasiv-Kalynets, and Stefaniya Shabatura. Their works were also published in the Ukrainian underground press.

Irving, Addie. Unpublished letters from Sing Sing, 1866. Manuscript Collection, New York Historical Society, New York City. As quoted in Cynthia Owen Philip, *Imprisoned in America: Prison Communications 1776 to Attica*, 79–83. New York: Harper & Row, 1973. Irving was a thief and a recidivist because it was not easy for women alone, particularly ex-convicts, to earn a living in 1866. While in Sing Sing Prison, she wrote letters to Mrs. E. C. Buchanan, a charitable New York woman who visited and wrote to her. Irving had previously been imprisoned on Blackwell's Island, where, she states, female prisoners were sexually abused and faced temptations that prevented their rehabilitation.

Joffe, Maria. *One Long Night: A Tale of Truth*. Translated by Vera Dixon from the original Russian (1977). Clapham: New Park, 1978. Born in the United States and raised in Russia, the author married Adolphe Joffe in 1918. Both she and her husband, who was at one time Russian ambassador to Germany, opposed Stalin. Adolphe Joffe committed suicide, but Maria, editor at the U.S.S.R. State Publishing House, continued to protest Stalin's practices. From 1929 to 1957 she endured imprisonment, exile, and incarceration in penal labor camps. Her memoirs, dated Moscow 1958, describe experiences in the camps, in solitary confinement, and in Lefortovo Prison. Only after her rehabilitation in 1957 did she learn of the "liquidation" of her seventeen-year-old son during her imprisonment.

Joffe, Nadezhda A. *Back in Time: My Life, My Fate, My Epoch*. Translated by Frederick S. Choate. Oak Park, Mich.: Labor Publications, 1995. Joffe was the daughter of Adolf Joffe, a Bolshevik leader and friend of Trotsky. She had actively opposed Stalin, and was arrested in 1936 and held in Lubyanka and Butyrki prisons. She was sentenced to five years in Kolyma corrective labor camp in Siberia and released in 1941.

Jones, Mary H. *Autobiography of Mother Jones*. Edited by Mary Field Parton. Chicago: Charles H. Kerr, 1925; reprinted by Chas. H. Kerr, for the Illinois Labor Historical Society, 1972. Born in Ireland and raised in America, Mother Jones was a major force in the American labor movement from 1880 and was particularly active with striking miners and railroad workers. She describes her several arrests and imprisonments. She was jailed in Parkersburg, West Virginia, in 1902 for speaking in support of the bituminous miners' strike in Clarksburg. In 1913 she was placed under military arrest in Pratt, West Virginia. She was again held under military arrest in 1914 in the Mount San Rafael Hospital, Trinidad, Colorado, and later in Walsenburg Jail, Colorado, for her support of striking miners.

Journal of Prisoners on Prisons. Published by the School of Criminology, Simon Fraser University, Burnaby, British Columbia, Canada. Published annually by Canadian Scholars' Press, the *Journal*'s "purpose is to encourage research on a wide range of issues related to crime, justice, and punishment by prisoners and former prisoners." Volume 5, no. 2 (Summer 1994) focuses on women in prison.

Kanturková, Eva. *My Companions in the Bleak House*. Woodstock, N.Y.: The Overlook Press, 1987. Kanturková, a Czech author and human rights activist, was accused of sedition and detained for one year in Ruzyne Prison near Prague in the early 1980s. In this book she describes, chapter by chapter, the women she met in prison.

Karsov, Nina, and Szymon Szechter. *In the Name of Tomorrow: Life Underground in Poland*. Translated from the Polish. London: Hodder &. Stoughton, 1970; New York: Schocken, 1971. Karsov, a Polish Jew, was an intellectual arrested by the Communists in Poland in 1966 and sentenced to three years' imprisonment for preparing and distributing dissident literature. Her description of her arrest and imprisonment in Mokotow and in the prison hospital at Grudziadz is interwoven, in dialogue format, with that of Szechter, a Polish Jew and intellectual who married Karsov while she was in prison. She was released in 1968 and their marriage was annulled in London.

Kennedy, Jane. "Detroit Jail Abuse." *Health Rights News* 4, no. 3 (May–June 1971): 10–11. Kennedy describes conditions in the Detroit House of Correction. As a member of Beaver 55, a radical group opposed to the Vietnam War, she was sentenced to one to four years for a raid and destruction of computer tapes at the Dow Chemical Research Center, Midland, Michigan.

———. "Letter from Prison." *Womankind* 1, no. 1 (May 1971): 16. Kennedy describes the feeling of powerlessness of women prisoners and the effort of women at the Detroit House of Correction to assert their power by changing visiting policies.

———. "Letters from Prison." *Health Rights News* 4, no. 1 (January 1971): 14. Kennedy describes conditions in the Marion County Jail, Indianapolis, where she spent twenty-four days in July 1970. She was awaiting trial for an alleged raid on an Indianapolis draft board. Her article emphasizes the inadequacy of health care in the jail.

———. "Women in Prison." *Women's Rights Law Reporter* (July–August 1972): 55–7. Kennedy describes conditions in the Detroit House of Correction. She emphasizes inadequate medical treatment and inhumane punishments.

Kenney, Annie. *Memoirs of a Militant*. London: Edward Arnold, 1924. Kenney, a British suffragette from a working-class background, describes her series of imprisonments, beginning in Strangeways Gaol (1905) and Holloway Prison (1906). She was a close associate of Christabel (*see* entry below) and Emmeline Pankhurst (*see* entry below).

Kinney, Hannah (Hanson). *A Review of the Principal Events of the Last Ten Years in the Life of Mrs. Hannah Kinney: Together with Some Comments upon the Late Trial. Written by Herself.* Boston: J. N. Bradley, 1841. Kinney's work includes a brief description of how she spent her imprisonment in Boston Jail for about five months in 1840. Most of the work is devoted to a narrative of the events leading to her imprisonment on the charges of poisoning her third husband, G. T. Kinney. Mrs. Kinney was acquitted of murder charges and went to live with her sister's family.

Kites. Edited by Laverne Hanners. Pine Bluff, Ark.: Women's Unit, Arkansas Dept. of Corrections, 1978. A collection of poems written by about thirty women in the Poetry/Creative Writing Workshop conducted by poet Hanners.

Kowalska, Anka. "Poems from an Internment Camp." Translated by Adam Czerniawski. *Index on Censorship* 12, no. 2 (April 1983): 16–18. Polish poet Kowalska was held in Goldap and Darlowek detention centers from the beginning of martial law in Poland in December 1981 until May 1982. Included here are translations of three poems she wrote in March and April 1982.

Kozameh, Alicia. *Steps under Water: A Novel*. Translated by David E. Davis. Berkeley: University of California Press, 1996. Originally published in Spanish in 1987. Kozameh was imprisoned in Rosario and Buenos Aires, Argentina, from 1975 to 1978, when she was released to "freedom under surveillance" until 1980. She went into exile, returned to Argentina, and finally left in 1988 for Los Angeles. *Steps under Water* is an autobiographical novel about her prison experiences.

Kulkielko, Renya. *Escape from the Pit*. With a foreword by Ludwig Lewisohn. New York: Sharon Books, 1947. Originally published in Hebrew. Memoirs of the war years by a twenty-two-year-old Jewish woman, writing from a kibbutz in Israel in 1946. She gives an account of her courageous attempts to survive in Nazi-occupied

Poland until her arrest in 1943, when her forged passport was detected. She was imprisoned in Katowice by the Gestapo and then transferred to a prison in Myslowice. She describes the conditions of her fellow women prisoners. Aided by her sister Sarah, she escaped and in 1944 arrived in Palestine.

Lafarge, Marie Cappelle. *Memoirs of Madame Lafarge; Written by Herself.* Translated from the French. Complete in 1 volume. Philadelphia: Carey &. Hart, 1841. Memoirs of her life, written in 1841, during her incarceration in the Prison of Tulle, for the poisoning of her husband.

Lai Ying. *The Thirty-Sixth Way: A Personal Account of Imprisonment and Escape from Red China.* Translated, adapted, and edited by Edward Behr and Sydney Liu. Garden City, N.Y.: Doubleday, 1969. This book must be read as Lai Ying's own work with some reservations, because it is unclear to what extent *Newsweek* correspondents Behr and Liu have "adapted and edited" the account that they asked Lai Ying to write. Born into a "bourgeois" family, she was arrested as a Catholic counterrevolutionary in Canton in 1958. She was sentenced to prison for five years and held in Canton's Tsang Pien Jail, Niu Tou K'eng Reform Camp, and New Life United Enterprises, a prison camp where she worked as an artist and member of a theatrical troupe. She was released in 1963 and escaped to Macao in 1966.

Larina, Anna. *This I Cannot Forget: The Memoirs of Nikolai Bukharin's Widow.* New York: Norton, 1993. The widow of Bukharin, a Bolshevik leader executed by Stalin, Anna Larina was herself arrested in 1937, separated from her infant son, and imprisoned in Lubyanka and exiled to Siberia. She was exonerated and left Siberia in 1959.

Last Letters: Prisons and Prisoners of the French Revolution, 1793–1794. Olivier Blanc. Translated from the French by Alan Sheridan. London: André Deutsch, 1987. This volume includes a collection of letters written by French women and men prisoners before their execution during the French Revolution. Most were aristocrats. Blanc discusses the historical context of the revolution and the culture of the prisons. Several of the translated letters are by French women, including Olympe de Gouges and Marie Antoinette.

Latour, Madame. "Memoir: Containing an Account of the Life in the Prison of the Luxembourg, where she was Imprisoned During the Years 1793 and 1794, in Company with Madame La Maréchale Duchesse de Mouchy ." In *Prison Journals during the French Revolution,* translated by Mrs. M. Carey, 159–97. New York: Dodd, Mead, 1891. Madame Latour wrote her memoirs after her release from prison. She describes her close association in prison with the Duchesse de Mouchy, mother of the Duchesse de Duras (*see* entry above).

Lebrón, Lolita. Poems. Translated by Gloria Waldman. Reprinted in *Voices of Women; Poetry by and About Third World Women.* New York: Women's International Resource Exchange (WIRE), 1982. Also reprinted in Doris Meyer and Margarite Fernandez Olmos, *Contemporary Women Authors of Latin America, New Translations.* Brooklyn College Humanities Series. Brooklyn, N.Y.: Brooklyn College Press, 1983. Originally published as *Sandalo en la celda* (Sandlewood in the cell) Catano, Puerto Rico: Editorial Betances, 1974. Poems by Puerto Rican Nationalist Lebrón, who was imprisoned for twenty-five years in the Federal Reformatory for Women at Alderson, West Virginia, for her part in a 1954 armed demonstration in the U.S. House of Representatives. Released in 1979, she returned to Puerto Rico.

Lee, Soon Ok. *Eyes of the Tailless Animals: Prison Memoirs of a North Korean Woman.* Translated by Rev. Bahn-Suk Lee. Bartlesville, Okla.: Living Sacrifice Book Co., 1999. In 1986 Soon Ok Lee was a Communist Party member with a responsible job and a family when she was arrested in an attempt to cover up an official's corruption. She was imprisoned, tortured, given a sham trial, and held for six years.

Lemmé, Janet E. *Conviction*. New York: Norton, 1970. Lemmé, an American married to an East German immigrant, was arrested with her husband as they attempted to help his sister and brother-in-law escape through Hungary in 1966. They were imprisoned in the Marko Prison in Budapest. Lemmé was sentenced to six months' imprisonment and released in 1967, while her husband was sentenced to eight months. Her account of her experience gives details on prison conditions, her relationship with fellow prisoners, and her treatment by Communist officials.

Lermolo, Elizabeth. *Face of a Victim*. Translated from the Russian by I. D. W. Talmadge, with a foreword by Alexandra Tolstoy. New York: Harper & Brothers, 1955. Lermolo, a Russian woman and wife of an alleged counterrevolutionary, had been living in exile in the town of Pudozh when she was arrested in 1934 for complicity in the assassination of a top Communist official. Stalin himself aided in her cross-examination. She was imprisoned for eight years, at first in the Leningrad jail of the secret police and then in the Political Isolator of the secret police in the town of Chelyabinsk.

Letters, dated 1846, from Ohio Penitentiary. In *Memorials of Prison Life*, by James Bradley Finley, 185–86; 188–89. Cincinnati: L. Swormstedt & A. Poe, 1855; reprint, New York: Arno, 1974. Two anonymous letters, dated 1846, written by female prisoners of the Ohio Penitentiary. Addressed to "Beloved Husband" and "Dear Mother," they are heavily moralistic and penitent in tone. Rev. Finley, chaplain of the prison, quotes them in his account of the prison as he knew it.

Lewis, Primila. *Reason Wounded: An Experience of India's Emergency*. New Delhi: Vikas Publishing House, 1978. Lewis gives an account of her imprisonment in 1975 during the Emergency declared by Mrs. Gandhi's government. Lewis was arrested and held for eighteen months because of her support of a union for poor agricultural workers south of Delhi.

The Light from Another Country: Poetry from American Prisons. Edited by Joseph Bruchac. Greenfield Center, N.Y.: Greenfield Review Press, 1984. This anthology of writing by male and female American prisoners includes poems by Carolyn Baxter (*see* entry above), Diana Bickston (*see* entry above), Lorri Martinez (*see* entry below), Michelle Roberts, Jessica Scarbrough, and Terri Meyette Wilkins.

Lipper, Elinor. *Eleven Years in Soviet Prison Camps*. Translated from the 1950 German original by Richard Winston and Clara Winston. Chicago: Henry Regnery, 1951. Lipper, a Dutch Socialist working for a Moscow publisher of foreign literature, was imprisoned in 1937 in Moscow's Lubyanka and Butyrka prisons. She spent a total of eleven years (1937–48) in ten of Stalin's Soviet prisons. She was convicted of counterrevolutionary activity and support of a foreign state against the Soviet Union. As a child she had lived in Holland and Switzerland and she had studied in Germany and Italy. At the time of her incarceration she knew no Russian.

Little, Joanne. Letter. *Off Our Backs: A Women's News Journal* 5, no. 1 (January 1975): 5. A letter to Madeleine Janover of the *Off Our Backs* staff. Little expresses gratitude for the journal's support and describes her prison routine in solitary confinement, her feelings about her self-defense killing of her jailer, and her growing self-awareness.

———. Poems. *Crime and Social Justice*, no. 3 (Summer 1975): 44. Two poems written about Little's prison experience.

[Lomax, Virginia]. *The Old Capitol and its Inmates. By a Lady, Who Enjoyed the Hospitalities of the Government for a "Season."* New York: Hale, 1867. An anonymous description of the 1865 imprisonment in the Carroll and Old Capitol prisons, Washington, D.C., of Baltimore resident Lomax on suspicion of disloyalty to the Union. She describes prison conditions and her fellow prisoners, including Mrs. Surratt, who was later hung as a conspirator in Lincoln's assassination. All other names are changed, including her own (she refers to herself as Maria Miller). Lomax states her admiration for the boldness of Catherine Virginia Baxley (*see* entry above) whom she calls "Mrs. Johnson."

Look for Me in the Whirlwind: The Collective Autobiography of the New York 21. With an introduction by Haywood Burns. New York: Random House, 1971. Defendants in the New York trial of the Black Panther 21 tell their individual life stories, interwoven in this "collective autobiography" written in prison. The Panthers had originally been arrested in April 1969 on a number of charges, but the trial was delayed until September 1970. In May 1971 all were acquitted. Writings by two women, Joan Bird and Afeni Shakur (*see* entry below) are included. Bird describes the Women's House of Detention in New York City in 1971.

Luxemburg, Rosa. "Letters from Prison." Translated from the German by Eleanor Clark. *Partisan Review* 5, no. 1 (June 1938): 3–23; "Letters from Prison." Translated from the German by Ralph Mannheim. *Partisan Review* 10, no. 4 (July–August 1943): 362–71. Letters written by Luxemburg during her imprisonment in Wronke and Breslau prisons, 1917–18. Recipients were Sonia Liebknecht and Hans Diefenbach.

* ———. *The Letters of Rosa Luxemburg.* Edited by Stephen E. Bronner. Boulder, Colo.: Westview Press, 1978. This collection includes letters written between 1916 and 1918, during her imprisonment in Wronke and Breslau. "Red Rosa," a leading intellectual in the German Social Democratic Party, was imprisoned during most of World War I. Recipients of letters include Hans Diefenbach, her last love, and Sonia Liebknecht, her dear friend and the wife of her imprisoned comrade, Karl Liebknecht.

Lytton, Constance. Papers. Suffragette Fellowship Collection, Museum of London (50.82/119). Correspondence. Typed copy of a letter to her mother, 24 February 1909, written from King's Cross Station, London, to be sent upon her imprisonment in Holloway.
Autographed letter, signed, to her mother, Edith Villiers, from Lytton's cell in Bow Street, February 24, 1909.
Autograph letter, signed, to her sister, Lady Betty Balfour, October 11, 1909, from Central Police Court cell, Newcastle.
Autograph letter, signed, to Kitty Marion (*see* entry below), October 11, 1915 and autograph letter, signed, to Kitty Marion, October 15, 1915. Marion had been seeking the name of an American to write to for assistance and Lytton suggested Madeleine Doty (*see* entry above). Lytton notes that Mrs. Pethick-Lawrence (*see* entry below) agreed that Doty was the right person to help Marion.
Notes on her weights while in prison and list of clothes, 1910.
Typed copies of her statements with reference to medical reports, April 1910.
Typed "Detailed Statement of Prison Experiences by Jane Warton (Constance Lytton) Jan. 1910."
Diary of arrest and imprisonment at Walton Jail, 1910.
Statement of Constance Lytton on treatment of Jane Warton.

———. *Prisons and Prisoners.* London: Heinemann, and East Ardsley, Yorkshire: E. P. Publishing, 1914; reprint, Boston: Charles River Books, 1977. This title is currently under construction in the "Build-A-Book project of "A Celebration of Women

Writers" at: http://digital.library.upenn.edu/. Imprisoned for suffrage activity in England, Lytton posed as Jane Warton, a homely working-class suffragette, in order to expose the inequality of treatment by social class in British prisons. She was incarcerated in Holloway Prison, New Castle Prison, and Walton Jail, Liverpool, where she endured brutal forcible feedings.

Makhoere, Caesarina Kona. "Gender and the Truth and Reconciliation Commission," prepared by Beth Goldblatt and Shiela Meintjes, May 1996. A submission to the Truth and Reconciliation Commission (South Africa). Contains information gleaned from interview with Makhoere (though not a transcript). Available at http://www.truth.org.za/submit/gender.htm.

————. *No Child's Play: In Prison under Apartheid*. London: The Women's Press, 1988. Makhoere was a student involved in anti-apartheid activity when she was arrested in 1976 and imprisoned in Pretoria. Convicted under the Terrorism Act, she was not released until 1982.

————. Oral history interview with Makhoere by Hilda Bernstein, held in Mazimbu, Tanzania. Vol. 19, p. 13, MCA7-1567. University of the Western Cape–Robben Island Mayibuye Archives, Robben Island Museum, Cape Town, South Africa. Part of Bernstein's series of interviews with South African exiles, between 1989 and 1991.

Marion, Kitty. Papers. Suffragette Fellowship Collection. Museum of London (50.82/1120.1121). Autograph letter, signed, to Edith (?), 10 December 1938, from New York City. Marion, a British singer, actress, and suffragette, refers to the enclosed manuscript on her prison experiences, which she wishes to have published in England. She states that she is looking for a ghostwriter.
Typescript autobiography referred to above. It gives an account of her activities with the suffragettes and refers to her series of imprisonments in Holloway Prison in 1909, 1912, and 1914.
Typescript account of Marion's experiences in Newcastle Prison, dated November 14, 1909 (Group C, vol. 3). Marion was imprisoned there with Constance Lytton (*see* entry above). She writes of forcible feeding.

Markievicz, Countess Constance de. *Prison Letters of Countess Markievicz*. London: Longmans, Green, 1934; reprint, Millwood, N.Y.: Kraus, 1970. This collection includes letters written between 1916 and 1921, during de Markievicz's imprisonment at Aylesbury, Holloway, Cork, and Mountjoy prisons for Irish revolutionary activity. The recipient of most letters is her sister, poet Eva Gore-Booth.

Martinez, Lorri. *Where Eagles Fall*. Brunswick, Me.: Blackberry, 1982. A collection of poems by Martinez, a Chicana prisoner at the Women's Penitentiary of New Mexico. She writes of the pain of separation from loved ones.

Mary, Queen of Scots. *Letters of Mary, Queen of Scots, and Documents Connected with her Personal History*. Edited by Agnes Strickland. New York: J. Winchester, 1842. Letters written by Mary to her supporters and to Queen Elizabeth during her extended imprisonment by Elizabeth in England, beginning in 1568 and ending with her execution in 1587 in Fotheringay Castle, where she was last imprisoned.

————. *The Letters and Official Documents of Mary Stuart, Queen of Scotland*. Translated by William Turnbull. Edited by Prince Alexander Labanoff. London: Charles Dolman, 1845. These letters do not duplicate those in the Strickland collection.

Matsui, Haru. *Restless Wave: An Autobiography*. New York: Modern Age, 1940. Matsui (pseudonym of Ayako Ishigaki) was a wealthy, young Japanese feminist and activist with the Farmer-Labor Party in the 1920s. Her memoirs include a description of her three-day imprisonment in a detention center. Unwelcome in Japan because of her activism, Matsui spent twenty-five years in the United States and became a close friend of Agnes Smedley (*see* entry below).

Maybrick, Florence Elizabeth. *Mrs. Maybrick's Own Story: My Fifteen Lost Years.* New York: Funk & Wagnall's, 1905. Maybrick, an American living near Liverpool, England, was convicted in 1889 of murdering her husband by poisoning. She spent fifteen years in Walton Jail, Woking Prison, and Aylesbury Prison, England, during which time she continued to declare her innocence and receive support from American and British political figures. Unlike many nineteenth-century works by convicted murderers, Maybrick's is an analysis of prison conditions rather than confessions or a moralistic treatise. A recently discovered diary identified as belonging to Florence Maybrick's husband, James Maybrick, has given rise to speculation that he may have been the serial killer Jack the Ripper.

McConnel, Patricia. *Eye of the Beholder.* Chapbook. Flagstaff, Ariz.: Logoria, 1994. (Not examined.)

———. *Guidebook for Artists Working in Prisons.* Utah Arts Council, 1994.(Not examined).

———. "Holy Night, Silent Night." *13th Moon* (Fall 1983). A short story drawn from McConnel's prison experience. In her early twenties McConnel spent time in the Federal Reformatory for Women at Alderson, West Virginia, and in six jails.

———. *Sing Soft, Sing Loud.* New York: Atheneum, 1989; Flagstaff, Ariz.: Logoria, 1995. Short fiction, based closely on autobiography, about McConnel's prison experiences.

———. "The Tourist." *Day Tonight, Night Today* (Summer 1983). A short story drawn from McConnel's prison experience.

McConnel, Patricia, ed. *Women's Voices Within: An Anthology of Writings from the Women's Correctional Facility, Draper, Utah.* Utah Arts Council, 1993. (Not examined).

McShane, Yolande. *Daughter of Evil.* London: Star/W. H. Allen, 1980. McShane, a sixty-one-year-old Englishwoman, was imprisoned in Holloway and Styal prisons and Moor Court Open Prison, England, from January 1977 to February 1978. She was charged with aiding a suicide by giving sleeping pills to her ill and aged mother, but in fact her mother never had committed suicide. She writes of prison routine and conditions and of the need for prison reform.

Metzger, Diane Hamill. *Coralline Ornaments.* Sedona, Ariz.: Weed Patch Press, 1980. A collection of poems by Metzger, who entered Pennsylvania's Prison for Women at Muncy in 1975, and who has also published poems in *Eagles Way, Gravida, Grit*, and *Inside/Out.* Her poetry and fiction have won awards in the Philadelphia Writers' Conference (1969), Writers' Digest Creative Writing Contest (1978), and PEN Writing Awards for Prisoners (1978, 1981, and 1985).

———. "Only Beginning." *Inside/Out* 3, no. 1 (Summer 1982.): 2, 7–8. Special women's supplement. A short story describing the flight and arrest of a woman and her husband, who were accused of killing his ex-wife.

———. Poems in *Doing Time: 25 Years of Prison Writing—A PEN American Center Prize Anthology*, edited by Bell Gale Chevigny. New York: Arcade, 1999. Essay and interview in *Concrete Garden* 4 (1994). "Women and the Criminal Justice System Issue," published by the Buffalo Group on Justice in Democracy at SUNY/Buffalo.

Meyrick, Kate. *Secrets of the 43: Reminiscences by Mrs. Meyrick.* London: John Long, 1933. Meyrick describes her career as an owner of nightclubs in London and Paris in the 1920s. With the responsibilities of supporting her children, Meyrick notes, "I went into night-clubs simply because I discovered that men will pay anything to be amused." She served several relatively brief terms in Holloway Prison when her clubs were raided.

Michel, Louise. *The Red Virgin: Memoirs of Louise Michel.* Edited and translated from the French by Bullitt Lowry and Elizabeth Ellington Guntel. University, Ala.: University of Alabama Press, 1981. Heroine of the Paris Commune of 1871, Michel published her memoirs in 1886, at the age of fifty-six. They were begun during her third imprisonment, in 1883. She describes her incarceration at the prison of Chantiels and the reformatory at Versailles in 1871, and the Auberive prison in 1872–73, before she was finally exiled to New Caledonia. She traveled there by prison ship in 1873 and remained in the prison colony for six years, until her pardon in 1880. Again in 1882, she spent two weeks in jail for disturbing the peace. For leading a Paris crowd in an anarchist demonstration in 1883, she was sentenced to six years' solitary confinement. She was sent to the Centrale Prison at Clermont and to Saint-Lazare Prison and pardoned after three years. Writing from prison, she showed particular sensitivity to the plight of poor women prisoners.

Middleton, Jean. Testimony of her imprisonment in Barberton, South Africa, in 1968. In *South Africa: The Imprisoned Society*, edited by Allen Cook, 71–72. London: International Defence and Aid Fund, 1974; reprinted from *Anti-Apartheid News*, June 1973. Middleton, a white political prisoner, describes conditions in the Women's Prison in Balberton, where she was held from 1965 to 1968.

Mikolajska, Halina. Letter from prison. *Index on Censorship* 12, no. 2. (April 1983): 15–16. A letter from renowned Polish actress Mikolajska, from the Darlowek women's internment center in April 1982. She writes to the director of the Polish Theatre in Warsaw, Kazimierz Dejmek, to thank him for his efforts for her release and to explain her position of conscience that she cannot sign a loyalty oath to satisfy the authorities. She describes the human rights violations experienced by women refusing the oath.

Mitchell, Hanna Maria Webster. *The Hard Way Up: The Autobiography of Hannah Mitchell, Suffragette and Rebel.* Edited by Geoffrey Mitchell, with a preface by George Ewart Evans. London: Faber & Faber, 1968. Hannah Mitchell, born in Derbyshire, England, into a poor family, received virtually no formal education. At the age of fourteen she ran away from her family's farm to work in the town's shops. Self-educated, with a lifelong desire to write, she became active in the woman suffrage movement and the Independent Labour Party. She differed from most suffragettes in coming from the working class rather than the middle class. In 1906 Mitchell was arrested with other suffragettes at a Liberal Party rally and charged with obstruction. She was sentenced to three days in Strangeways Prison, Manchester. After one night in prison, she was released when her husband paid her fine. In 1926 she was appointed a magistrate for the city of Manchester, administering the law and trying to correct injustices she had experienced. Her grandson has edited her manuscript, which has not been substantially altered.

———. Typed autobiographical account of Hannah Mitchell (n.d.). Suffragette Fellowship Collection, Museum of London (Group C, vol. 2: 60.15/ 21).

Morgan, Dominik. "Restricted Love." In *Breaking the Rules: Women in Prison and Feminist Therapy*, edited by Judy Harden and Marcia Hill 75–84. New York:

Harrington Park Press, 1998). Serving a nineteen-year sentence in Seattle, Washington, Morgan writes an essay that "explores the myriad lesbian relationships in prison," from a prisoner's point of view.

Morgan, Elizabeth. "The Violence of Women's Imprisonment: A View from the Inside." In *Harsh Punishment: International Experiences of Women's Imprisonment*, edited by Sandy Cook and Susanne Davies, 32–46. Boston: Northeastern University Press, 1999. A Washington, D.C. plastic surgeon, Morgan was incarcerated for civil disobedience in the District of Columbia Department of Corrections Detention Center three times during the period from 1986 to 1989. She refused to send her toddler daughter on unsupervised visits with her father, whom Morgan accused of child sexual abuse. In 1997 she gained safe custody of her daughter.

Nation, Carry. *The Use and Need of the Life of Carry A. Nation. Written by Herself.* Topeka: F. M. Steves & Sons, 1904. In this autobiography, Carry Nation gives an account of her numerous jailings for destroying taverns in order to protest the sale of alcohol. She was first imprisoned in 1900 in Wichita Jail for "malicious mischief"; she describes in detail the harsh conditions there. She became a public lecturer on temperance, and she helped to pay expenses by selling souvenir hatchets, often from her cell window. Her imprisonments included Wichita (3), Topeka (7), Kansas City (1), Coney Island (1), Los Angeles (1), San Francisco (1), Scranton, Pennsylvania (2), Bayonne, New Jersey (1), and Pittsburgh (3). Her final imprisonment was in 1904 in Philadelphia, where she opened a saloon door and "a two legged beer keg in the form of a policeman grabbed me."

Nelson, Belle Harris. 1863 Prison Journal. Historical Department, Church of Jesus Christ of Latter-Day Saints, Salt Lake City, Utah. Belle Harris Nelson, a Mormon, was imprisoned with her infant son in the Salt Lake Penitentiary from May 18, 1883, to August 31, 1883, for contempt of court when she was called before a grand jury and refused to testify against her former husband, Clarence Merrill. She had been a plural wife and had divorced Merrill in 1862 because of his neglect. When Merrill was charged with polygamy in 1883, she refused to give information about their marriage. The journal contains Belle Nelson's letter to the *Deseret News*, 26 June 1883, and describes prison conditions and her visits with Mormon women.

Nevinson, Evelyn Sharp. Papers. Bodleian Library, Oxford University. The collection includes letters (1892–1955), notebooks and scrapbooks (1907–27), manuscript drafts, and press-cuttings (1909–46) of British journalist and suffragette Nevinson, who went on a hunger strike in prison. (Not examined; source: Margaret Barrow, *Women 1870–1928: A Select Guide to Printed and Archival Sources in the United Kingdom* [London: Mansell, 1981].)

Nguyen, thi Hong [pseud.]. "A Prison Memoir." *Indochina Chronicle*, no. 40 (April 1975): 3–5. A working-class woman imprisoned in Tan Hiep, South Vietnam, on suspicion of being a Communist, describes the spirited protest of women prisoners who demanded better conditions.

Noailles, Louise. Letters to Monsieur Grelet, her children's tutor; her husband, Louis, Vicomte de Noailles; and Alexis, her eldest son; and extract from her last will and testament. In "Addenda" to the Duchesse de Duras's memoirs (*see* entry above) in *Prison Journals during the French Revolution*, translated by Mrs. M. Carey, 139–57. New York: Dodd, Mead, 1891. Louise Noailles writes from the Prison of the Luxembourg, Paris, before her execution on July 22, 1794. She was the sister-in-law of the Duchesse de Duras.

No More Cages: Women's Prison Newsletter. Bimonthly. Women Free Women in Prison Collective, Brooklyn, N.Y. A newsletter containing letters, poetry, and articles by and about women in American prisons and psychiatric institutions.

Norroy, Muriel. *I Robbed the Lords and Ladies Gay.* London: Methuen, 1939. Norroy describes her life of crime and the time she served in English prisons, mostly in Holloway. Born to a French mother and an English father, she had a privileged childhood and was raised in a French convent. She was first arrested for bicycle theft in her early twenties, and later became a jewel thief. She wrote her book while on probation in an attempt to earn money honestly.

Norton, Judee. Autobiographical essay in *Doing Time: 25 Years of Prison Writing—A PEN American Center Prize Anthology,* edited by Bell Gale Chevigny. New York: Arcade, 1999. Norton served a sentence in Arizona State Prison for drugs. She now lives in Tucson and writes stories about her prison experience.

No Title at All Is Better than a Title like That! 1, no. 1. (1974), published by Santa Cruz Women's Prison Project, Santa Cruz, Calif. A collection of poems and essays by prisoners of the California Institution for Women at Frontera. Writing workshops were conducted by the Santa Cruz Women's Prison Project.

O'Brien, Edna V. *So I Went to Prison.* New York: Frederick A. Stokes, 1938. In 1933, O'Brien, a New York stockbroker, was arrested and imprisoned in the House of Detention on charges of grand larceny. After her conviction, she was imprisoned in the State Reformatory for Women at Bedford, New York, in 1935, for fifteen months. She was released in 1936.

Off Our Backs: A Women's News Journal 8, no. 2 (February 1978): 9–11. This issue explores the violation of women prisoners' rights at the Bedford Hills Correctional Facility for Women, New York State. Included are articles by prisoners Carol Crooks, Laura Carey, Sheila Liles, Alberta James, Lydia Navarette, Delores Smith, and Irma Jean Mitchelle.

O'Hare, Kate Richards (née Cunningham). "Human Ostriches." *Nation* 120, no. 3118 (8 April 1925): 377–78. O'Hare describes deplorable prison conditions and exploitation of prison labor that she observed during her imprisonment at the Missouri State Penitentiary at Jefferson City in 1919.

———. *In Prison.* New York: Knopf, 1923; reprint, American Library, no. 30. Seattle: University of Washington Press, 1976. Imprisoned in Missouri State Penitentiary from 1919 to 1920 for her protests against American involvement in World War I, Socialist O'Hare planned to do a sociological study of conditions while incarcerated. Her book explains her theories on the role of political prisoners in prison reform, and gives a picture of prison life, based upon her study of fellow prisoners.

———. *In Prison, being a report by Kate Richards O'Hare to the President of the United States as to the conditions under which women federal prisoners are confined in the Missouri State Penitentiary, under the authority of the United States Department of Justice and the United States Superintendent of Prisons. Based on the author's experience as a federal prisoner from April 14, 1919, to May 30, 1920.* St. Louis, Mo.: F. P. O'Hare, [ca. 1920].

———. *Kate O'Hare's Prison Letters.* Modern Series no. 1. Girard, Kan.: Appeal to Reason, 1919. This volume contains sixteen letters from O'Hare to her family. They were written from April 1919 to September 1919, during her imprisonment in the penitentiary in Jefferson City, Missouri. Her letters describe prison conditions, her observations of fellow prisoners, including Mollie Steimer (*see* the Agnes Smedley selection in this anthology) and her personal responses to imprisonment.

————. Letters from prison. Mimeographed copies of O'Hare's prison letters to her family are available in several collections, including New York Public Library; Missouri Historical Society, St. Louis; Schlesinger Library, Radcliffe College, Cambridge, Mass.; The Sophia Smith Collection, Smith College, Northampton, Mass.; Swarthmore College Peace Collection, Swarthmore, Penna.; University of Missouri Library, State Historical Society of Missouri, Columbia, Mo.; University of Oregon Library, Special Collections, Eugene, Ore.

* ————. *Selected Writings and Speeches*. Edited by Philip S. Foner and Sally M. Miller. Baton Rouge: Louisiana State University Press, 1982. This book includes letters written to O'Hare's family and other party workers, from the Missouri State Penitentiary (1919–20). Also included are selections from *In Prison*.

O'Leary, Fran. "Fran O'Leary Reflects on Past Life." *Fortune News* "Women in Prison Issue" (May 1979): 6. O'Leary, president of the Fortune Society (*see Fortune News*, above) writes about what led her to prison. As a young, jobless woman, she became a prostitute and was imprisoned in New York City's Women's House of Detention, which served as a school of crime. From there she went on to robbery and served time in the Los Angeles County Jail. As a parolee living in New Jersey, she could not find work, but the Fortune Society and her work counseling teenagers helped to keep her from returning to prison.

Out of the Night: Writings from Death Row. Edited by Marie Mulvey Roberts. Cheltenham, England: New Clarion Press, 1994. Includes a brief essay by Donna S. Cox, Death Row, North Carolina. Most pieces by women are by those on the outside, working against the death penalty.

Paley, Grace. "Six Days: Some Rememberings," in *Just as I Thought*. New York: Farrar, Straus and Giroux, 1998. Noted author and activist Paley describes her six days' imprisonment in the 1960s in the Women's House of Detention, at that time in Greenwich Village, New York. She had been arrested for her involvement in a protest against the war in Vietnam. Women she met in the prison told her that the indignities of the intake examination process were less severe because "some months earlier" feminist Andrea Dworkin had fought the examinations during her own imprisonment. Dworkin had been arrested for an antiwar protest at the U.S. Mission to the United Nations.

Panaiodor, Alice. *Walk through Flames*. London: Pickering & Inglis, 1979. Translated from the French. Panaiodor describes her imprisonment in Communist Romania in 1959. A follower of Pastor Richard Wurmbrand and his wife Sabina (*see* entry below) she was imprisoned for her Christian beliefs. She was released in 1964 after five years in prison.

Pankhurst, Dame Christabel. *Unshackled: The Story of How We Won the Vote*. Edited by Lord Frederick Pethick-Lawrence. London: Hutchinson, 1959. After Christabel Pankhurst's death in 1958, her executrix found a typescript of these memoirs, which were then edited by Lord Pethick-Lawrence, husband of suffragette Emmeline Pethick-Lawrence (*see* entry below) and a committed supporter of woman suffrage. Christabel Pankhurst had worked with her mother, Emmeline Pankhurst (*see* entry below) in the British militant suffrage movement. She writes of her imprisonment in 1905 for protesting at the Liberal Party's rally in the Manchester Free Trade Hall, and in 1907 for organizing a protest at the House of Commons. In 1908 she was imprisoned in Holloway for inciting the public to riot during a speech at Trafalgar Square.

Pankhurst, Emmeline. *My Own Story*. London: Eveleigh Nash and New York: Hearst's International Library, 1914; reprint, New York: Kraus, 1971. Emmeline Pankhurst was a major leader of the British militant woman suffrage movement. Her authorship of this autobiography is in question; Martin Pugh, in *Women's Suffrage in Britain 1867–1928* (London: The Historical Assoc., 1980), states that the book was written for her by an American journalist. The acknowledgments do express Pankhurst's "deep obligation to Rheta Childe Dorr for invaluable editorial services performed in the preparation of this volume, especially the American edition." Pankhurst does not specify the extent of these "services." The book gives general accounts of the numerous imprisonments of suffragettes. There are detailed descriptions of her imprisonment in Holloway (1908) for demonstrating, and of another 1908 imprisonment, when she demanded that suffragettes be treated as political prisoners. In 1913 she was sentenced to Holloway for three years for conspiring to destroy Lloyd George's country house. She went on a thirst and hunger strike and, under the "Cat and Mouse Act," was repeatedly released for ill health and rearrested when she had recovered.

Pankhurst, E. Sylvia. Papers. Suffragette Fellowship Collection, Museum of London. A report on forcible feeding, April 23, 1912 (Group A: 57.70/12). The daughter of Emmeline Pankurst (*see* entry above), Estelle Sylvia Pankhurst explains the suffragettes' motives for their hunger strikes (to demand treatment as political prisoners), and describes abuses they suffered in prison. She gives accounts of cases of several individual women, including Constance Lytton (*see* entry above) and Helen Gordon Liddle (*see* Helen Gordon above).
Typed copy of a letter to her mother, Emmeline Pankhurst (*see* entry above), 18 March 1913 (Group A: 60.15/16). Sylvia Pankhurst was serving two months' hard labor in Holloway and being forcibly fed. She discusses forcible feeding in her letter.

———. *The Suffragette: The History of the Women's Militant Suffrage Movement 1905–1910*. London: Gay & Hancock, 1911; reprint, New York: Source Book Press, 1970. This history includes Estelle Sylvia Pankhurst's account of her own imprisonment in Holloway (1906) and the conditions she found there. Pankhurst was the daughter of Emmeline Pankhurst (*see* entry above) and sister of Christabel Pankhurst (*see* entry above).

———. *The Suffragette Movement: An Intimate Account of Persons and Ideals*. London: Longmans, Green, 1931; reprint, New York: Kraus, 1971. Pankhurst gives an account of her several imprisonments, among them Holloway (1906) for protesting the imprisonment of suffragettes, and Holloway (1913) where she went on a thirst and hunger strike and was forcibly fed.

Partnoy, Alicia. *The Little School: Tales of Disappearance and Survival*. San Francisco: Cleis Press, 1986, 1998. Argentinian Partnoy and her husband were arrested in January 1977 and became two of the "disappeared." She was held at "the Little School," a concentration camp. Her secret imprisonment ended in June, but her imprisonment without charges continued for two and a half more years. In *The Little School* Partnoy describes her prison experience, her companions, and her guards.

———. *Revenge of the Apple*. San Francisco: Cleis Press, 1992. Poems written by Partnoy during her imprisonment.

Peckham, Audrey. *A Woman in Custody*. London: Fontana, 1985. Peckham, the deputy headmistress of a British school, describes her eight-month imprisonment on remand

and in Styal Prison. She had been accused of attempting to hire a private detective in 1982 to arrange the murder of the woman whom her ex-lover was then seeing. She denied that this had been her intention.

Perkins, Josephine Amelia. *The Female Prisoner; A narrative of the life and singular adventures of Josephine Amelia Perkins, a young woman, who . . . for the three years last past . . . has been unhappily addicted to a criminal propensity, more singular and surprising in its nature (for one of her sex,) than can be found on record; in the commission of which she has been four several times detected, twice pardoned on account of her sex, once for reason of supposed insanity, and the fourth and last time, convicted and sentenced to two years' imprisonment in Madison County jail, Kentucky. Annexed is well-written address to parents and children.* New York: C. Harrison, 1839. (Not examined.)

Perpetua. "The Passion of Saint Perpetua." Translated from the Latin by Peter Dronke. In *Women Writers of the Middle Ages*, 2–4. Cambridge, England: Cambridge University Press, 1984. Perpetua, a twenty-two-year-old Christian martyr and nursing mother who died in the arena of Carthage in 203, tells of her imprisonment and her visions as she awaited execution.

Pethick-Lawrence, Emmeline. *My Part in a Changing World*. London: Gollancz, 1938. Pethick-Lawrence was raised in a middle class family in Bristol, Eng. She became a leader in the Women's Social and Political Union (WSPU) in 1906 and was imprisoned six times in Holloway for her suffrage work. Her first imprisonment (1906) followed an attempt to speak in the House of Commons. Another attempt to enter the House of Commons led to her imprisonment for two months in 1909; she gives a tender, admiring account of her association there with Lady Constance Lytton (*see* entry above). In 1912 she was imprisoned in Holloway and her husband, Frederick, was held in Brixton Gaol for conspiring to commit property damage; while in prison both were forcibly fed.

Phillips, Eugenia Levy. Papers. Southern Historical Collection, University of North Carolina at Chapel Hill, Chapel Hill, N.C. In 1861 Eugenia Levy Phillips, wife of Washington lawyer Philip Phillips, was imprisoned in Washington with her sister and daughters for aiding the Confederacy. Her second imprisonment was in 1862 at Ship Island, Louisiana. This collection of Phillips's papers includes her prison journal from Washington, 23 August–18 September, 1861; her prison diary from Ship Island, 4 July–6 August 1862; her 1889 account, in manuscript with clippings, of her two imprisonments; and correspondence with her family concerning her Ship Island imprisonment, 1862.

Phillips, Margaret B. "Eleven Days in the Cage." *Focus/Midwest* 10, no. 64 (1974): 24–25. Phillips was sentenced to seven months' imprisonment for a civil rights demonstration to protest racial discrimination by a St. Louis defense contractor. In May 1974 she spent eleven days in the St. Louis County Jail before her parole. She writes of her feelings about imprisonment and protests the lack of adequate medical care for the other prisoners.

Pintíg: Poems and Letters from Philippine Prisons. Hong Kong: Resource Centre for Philippine Concerns, 1979. A collection of poems, letters, political statements, and artwork by female and male political prisoners. Many works are anonymous. Included are "Letter of a Wife to Her Husband," "Letter of a Daughter to Father," "Statement on International Women's Day by Female Political Prisoners of Camp Bicutan," and a poem by imprisoned journalist Mila Aguilar (Clarita Roja, pseud.) (*see* entry above).

Pinzer, Maimie. *The Maimie Papers: Letters from an Ex-Prostitute.* Edited by Ruth Rosen and Sue Davidson. New York: Feminist Press, 1997. Ex-prostitute Maimie Pinzer wrote a series of letters from 1910 until 1922 to Fanny Quincy Howe, a respected Bostonian. In her letters, now held at the Schlesinger Library, Radcliffe College, she writes of her family's financial struggles that led to her prostitution. Her account includes a description of her brief imprisonment at the age of thirteen in the Central Police Station in Philadelphia's City Hall and in the Moyamensing Prison. She afterward spent a year in the Magdalen Home. Her offense was incorrigibility.

Poppy. The Women's Unit Newsletter, California Rehabilitation Center at Norco. Begun in 1980 in the Bright Fires Writing Workshop of California Rehabilitation Center, this newsletter publishes women's poetry, prose, artwork, and interviews with staff. (Source: Jean L. Samuel, *"Poppy," Prison Writing Review* 7, no. 2 (Summer 1983: 19–24).

Power, Katherine Alice. Poems in *Breaking Silence: Voices of Mothers in Prison,* compiled by JusticeWorks Community. Brooklyn, N.Y.: JusticeWorks Community, 1999. Poems in *In Time: Women's Poetry from Prison,* edited by Rosanna Warren and Teresa Iverson. Boston: Boston University Prison Education Program, 1995. An activist opposing the Vietnam War, Power was a fugitive who surrendered in 1993. She was imprisoned in the Massachusetts Correctional Institution in Framingham.

Priess, Anita. *Exiled to Siberia.* Steinbach, Manitoba, Can.: Derksen, 1972 (dual language edition: English and German). Born Anita Enns in 1909 in the Ukraine, Priess was living in Germany at the time of her arrest by Stalin's Russian police in 1946. She was charged with refusing to divorce her German husband and return to Russia. Sentenced to ten years in penal camps, she was first imprisoned in Torgau and then transported to Siberia, where she remained until after the death of Stalin in 1953. The book describes the other women prisoners. Priess wrote her memoirs in 1972 in Canada, where she had remarried and found freedom in 1967.

Prison Writing in 20th-Century America, edited by H. Bruce Franklin. New York: Penguin, 1998. This anthology includes work by the following women prisoners: Carolyn Baxter, Kathy Boudin, Patricia McConnel, Kate Richards O'Hare, Assata Shakur, Agnes Smedley, Norma Stafford, and Kim Wozencraft. (*See* entries above or below for each writer listed).

Prison Writing Review. (Incorporating and continuing the *COSMEP Prison Project Newsletter.*) The Committee of Small Magazine Editors and Publishers (COSMEP) Prison Project, begun in 1974, sent donated literary magazines and small press publications to prisoners and encouraged prison writing through its *Prison Project Newsletter* 1976–83, afterward the *Prison Writing Review,* and its Prison Project Chapbook Series of prisoners' poetry.

COSMEP Prison Project Newsletter 5, no. 1 (Fall 1980), contains poems by Diana Bickston (*see* entry above) and poems from the Bright Fires Writing Workshop at the California Rehabilitation Center.

Prison Writing Review 7, no. 2 (Summer 1983), contains poems by women in the Bright Fires Writing Workshop, and by women at the California Institution for Women, Frontera. Later issues contain poems by men and women from American prisons.

Quarles, Ariel. "Busted." *Moving Out* 7, no. 1 (1972): 68–71. Quarles describes her three-day stay in a county jail on charges of possession of marijuana. She notes that her purpose in writing is to describe inhumane and sexist practices in the jail system.

Qing, Dai. "My Imprisonment: An Excerpt." *Index on Censorship*. Translated by Geremie Barmé. 8 (1992): 20–27. Chinese journalist Dai Qing gives this account, dated May 1990, of her detention from July 1989 to May 1990. She had been found guilty "of the 'error' of 'supporting and participating' in what they [Communist officials] called 'political turmoil'" following the 1989 demonstrations in Tiananmen Square in Beijing. She describes her prison conditions and interrogation, and states that she had the same type of cell once used by imprisoned writer Ding Ling. Dai Qing believes that the guards' kindness and humane treatment demonstrate "that the Communists are making some progress."

Ratushinskaya, Irina. *Grey Is the Color of Hope*. Translated by Alyona Kojevnikov. New York: Knopf, 1988. Ratushinskaya, a Ukrainian poet, was arrested by the Soviets in 1982 for dissident activities and imprisoned until 1986. *Grey Is the Color of Hope* is her account of her imprisonment and the female political prisoners she knew during her confinement.

———. *In the Beginning*. Translated by Alyona Kojevnikov. New York: Knopf, 1991. Ratushinskaya gives an account of her childhood and the beginning of her political activities. She describes her arrest by the KGB in 1982 that led to her imprisonment and she gives an overview of her years in a Soviet prison camp.

Reddy, Snehalata. *A Prison Diary*. Karnataka State, Mysore, India: Human Rights Committee, 1977. Extracts from the prison diary of Reddy, imprisoned in May 1976 in the Bangalore Central Jail. A leading Indian actress, she was not told specific charges against her, but was held on political suspicion, presumably because of her friendships with socialist leaders. She suffered severe asthma attacks and developed heart problems in prison, and finally received a one-month parole for medical reasons. While on parole she learned of her release, but she died of a heart attack five days later, on January 20, 1977, at the age of forty-four. During her imprisonment and while on parole, she worked to improve the conditions of the poor women she met in prison.

Reedy, Juanita. "Diary of a Prison Birth." *Majority Report* 5, no. 2 (31 May 1975): 1, 4. Reedy's diary describes her experiences as a pregnant prisoner who delivered her only child in a hospital under rigidly supervised conditions. On April 30, 1975, she was taken from the Women's House of Detention on Riker's Island in New York to Elmhurst Hospital's "prison suite." She writes that she received poor medical treatment and was kept from seeing her baby and from breast-feeding.

Renay, Liz. *My Face for the World to See*. New York: Lyle Stuart, 1971. Memoirs of Renay, who was imprisoned for three years in the Federal Correctional Institution at Terminal Island in California. She was sentenced for perjury after refusing to cooperate with government prosecutors in the trial of gangster Mickey Cohen.

Reweaving the Web of Life: Feminism and Nonviolence. Edited by Pam McAllister. Philadelphia: New Society, 1982. This anthology of works by feminist pacifists includes some works by women who were imprisoned for civil disobedience against the Vietnam War, racial discrimination, and discrimination against lesbians and gays. These writers include Joan Baez (*see* entry above), Joan Cavanagh, Barbara Deming (*see* entry above), Charlotte Marchant, Jane Meyerding, and Juanita Nelson.

Richardson, Mary R. *Laugh a Defiance*. London: Weidenfeld & Nicolson, 1953. Memoirs of the British woman suffrage movement by a militant suffragette. She was imprisoned in Holloway several times and went on a hunger strike there. She describes in detail her slashing of the Rokeby Venus in the National Gallery to protest the imprisonment of suffragette leader Emmeline Pankhurst (*see* entry above).

———. "Tortured Women: What Forcible Feeding Means—a Prisoner's Testimony." 8 August 1914. Typed extracts from "The Woman's Dreadnought," edited by Sylvia Pankhurst, 8 August 1914. Suffragette Fellowship Collection, Museum of London. (Group A: 57.116/52). British suffragette Richardson, famous for having axed the Rokeby Venus in the National Gallery, gives details on several individual cases of forcible feeding and describes a feeding in detail.

Rickett, Allyn, and Adele Rickett. *Prisoners of Liberation: Four Years in a Chinese Communist Prison.* New York: Cameron Associates, 1957; reprint, Garden City, N.Y.: Anchor/Doubleday, 1973. An account of an American couple's imprisonment in Communist China. "Rick" and "Dell" tell their separate stories in alternating sections of the narrative, assembled in chronological order. They had traveled to Beijing in 1948 as graduate students with Fulbright grants. When hostilities broke out between the United States and China during the Korean War, they fell under suspicion. Rick was arrested as a spy and Dell was at first kept under surveillance at home and then imprisoned fourteen months later for assisting her husband in his espionage. They were imprisoned separately in Beijing. Dell was held from September 1952 to February 1955 and then deported; Rick followed afterward.

Rigby, Françoise (née Labouverie). *In Defiance.* London: Elek, 1960. Rigby, a Belgian woman active in the Resistance during World War II, was arrested in German-occupied Brussels in June 1944. Her war memoirs tell of her imprisonment in Saint Giles Prison. She was released in September 1944 when Brussels was liberated. Married and living in England after the war, Rigby founded an agency to aid refugees.

Rinser, Luise. *A Woman's Prison Journal: Germany, 1944.* Translated by Michael Hulse. New York: Schocken, 1987. Rinser, a Bavarian writer who had been banned by the Nazis from publishing and who had refused to join the party, was denounced by a friend in 1944 and incarcerated in the women's prison at Traunstein. She faced a probable death sentence had the war not ended. Her *Prison Journal* was an early postwar German publication.

Rock, Shirley. "An Introduction to the Female Offender." *Woman Offender* (March 1978): 9–15. Rock, a prisoner at the Indiana Women's Prison, Indianapolis, discusses issues in female corrections, including theories concerning the rising crime rate among women. She notes that many imprisoned women have been forced to commit crimes because of their poverty, yet few job training opportunities exist for them in prison. She also discusses the need for better health care, education, and programs for imprisoned mothers and their children.

Roland de la Platière, Marie Jeanne Phlipon. *An Appeal to Impartial Posterity: By Madame Roland, Wife of the Minister of the Interior: or, A Collection of Tracts Written by Her During Her Confinement in the Prisons of the Abbey, and St. Pelagie, in Paris.* Translated from the French original. First American edition (corrected). 2 vols. New York: Robert Wilson, 1798; reprint, New York: Woodstock Books, 1990; AMS Press, 1998. Madame Roland reflects on her childhood, marriage, imprisonment, the French Revolution, and the great leaders of the age, as she awaits her execution, which occurred in 1793.

———. *The Private Memoirs of Madame Roland.* Edited by Edward Gilpin Johnson. 2d ed. Chicago: McClurg, 1900; reprint, New York: AMS, 1976. This volume covers, in a different translation, the same material as volume 2 of *An Appeal to Impartial Posterity.*

Roohizadegan, Olya. *Olya's Story: A Survivor's Dramatic Account of the Persecution of Bahá'ís in Revolutionary Iran.* Oxford: Oneworld Publications, 1993. Roohizadegan was imprisoned in Iran for her Bahá'í faith in the early 1980s. She writes of the ten Bahá'í women who were hanged because they would not recant their faith.

*Rosenberg, Ethel. Letters. In *We Are Your Sons: The Legacy of Ethel and Julius Rosenberg*, by Robert Meeropol and Michael Meeropol. Boston: Houghton Mifflin, 1975; reprint, Champaign: University of Illinois Press, 1986. Letters written between 1950 and 1953, from the Women's House of Detention, New York, and the Death House at Sing Sing, to Rosenberg's imprisoned husband, Julius; their lawyer, Manny Bloch; and their sons, Robert and Michael. The Rosenbergs were executed in 1953 for their alleged conspiracy to give atomic secrets to the Soviets.

————. *The Rosenberg Letters: A Complete Edition of the Prison Correspondence of Julius and Ethel Rosenberg*, edited by Michael Meeropol. New York: Garland Publishing, 1994. This edition presents the complete and unedited letters, annotated and introduced by the Rosenbergs' sons, Michael and Robert Meeropol.

————. *The Testament of Ethel and Julius Rosenberg*. 2d ed. New York: Cameron & Kahn, 1954. The revised and enlarged edition of *The Death House Letters* (New York: Jero, 1953), published during the Rosenbergs' imprisonment to help raise money for their children.

Rosenberg, Susan. Poems in *Doing Time: 25 Years of Prison Writing—A PEN American Center Prize Anthology*, edited by Bell Gale Chevigny. New York: Arcade, 1999. Rosenberg was a Federal prisoner since 1984, convicted on weapons charges. Her sentence was commuted in 2001, and she was released from Danbury Federal Penitentiary.

————. "Reflections on Being Buried Alive." In *Cages of Steel: The Politics of Imprisonment in the United States*, edited by Ward Churchill and J. J. Vander Wall, 128–30. Washington, D.C.: Mainsonneuve Press, 1992. Rosenberg gives her impressions of being imprisoned in the Lexington High Security Unit.

Russell, Martha. Diary. In *The Russells of Birmingham in the French Revolution and in America 1791–1814*, by S. H. Jeyes, 61–103. London: George Allen, 1911. Extensive excerpts from the diary of Martha Russell, about her captivity aboard a French ship during the French Revolution. With her were her father, William Russell, her sister, and her brother.

*Russier, Gabrielle. *The Affair of Gabrielle Russier*. With a preface by Raymond Jean and an introduction by Mavis Gallant. Translated by Ghislaine Boulanger. New York: Knopf, 1971. Originally published as *Lettres de Prison* (Paris: Éditions du Seuil, 1970). This volume includes letters written by Russier to parents and friends from Les Baumettes Prison in Marseilles, where she was imprisoned in 1969. A teacher in a French lycée, Russier was held without trial because of her affair with one of her teenage students; this persecution led to her suicide. Her case drew public attention to the need for reform of the French criminal code, prison system, and treatment of women.

Saadawi, Nawal El. *Memoirs from the Women's Prison*. Translated by Marilyn Booth. Berkeley: University of California Press, 1983, 1986. Egyptian feminist and physician Saadawi writes of her experiences in 1981 in Qanatir Prison under President Anwar Sadat, on the charge of having committed "crimes against the State."

————. *Woman at Point Zero*. Translated by Sherif Hetata. London: Zed Books, 1983. Saadawi's novel based upon her conversations with Firdaus, a prostitute imprisoned at the Qanatir Prison in Egypt and later executed for killing a man.

Samuelli, Annie. *The Wall Between*. Washington, D.C.: Robert B. Luce, 1967. Samuelli, a Romanian Jewish woman imprisoned for espionage in Communist Romania from 1949 to 1961, writes of her association with other women prisoners from all social classes. She was held in the Political Women's Penitentiary at Mislea, the transit prison of Jilava, the secret police interrogation prison in Bucharest, and the penitentiary at Miercurea-Ciuc. She explains that her work is not an autobiography or a description of Communist political prisons, but rather a portrayal of how women from varied backgrounds endured imprisonment without admitting defeat. She recounts individual women's stories as she had heard them in the prisons, where reading and writing were forbidden, and where women maintained mental alertness by teaching each other their languages and exchanging life stories. She describes the system of wall tapping by Morse code, used as a medium of communication throughout the prisons.

Sanger, Margaret. Diary entry for 8 February 1917, Margaret Sanger Papers, Cont. 1, Reel 1, Library of Congress. Sanger, imprisoned for her birth-control activity with the Brownsville Clinic, writes of her incarceration in the Queens County Penitentiary, New York. Although the diary dates only the day of her entrance into prison (8 February 1917), there are entries for three days. She describes prison food and routine, disadvantaged women prisoners, and her resistance to fingerprinting by the warden.

———. *Margaret Sanger; An Autobiography*. New York: Norton, 1938; reprint, New York: Cooper Square, 1999. Chapters 17–19 describe Sanger's arrest and imprisonment in 1916–17 in the Queens County Penitentiary, Long Island City, for distributing birth-control information in the Brownsville Clinic in Brooklyn.

———. *My Fight for Birth Control*. New York: Farrar & Rinehart, 1931; reprint, New York: Maxwell, 1969. Chapter 14 describes Sanger's imprisonment after the Brownsville Clinic raid.

*———. "Why I Went to Jail." *Together* (February 1960): 20–22. Sanger explains her motivation for involvement in the birth control movement, and describes the events that led up to her imprisonment in the Queens County Penitentiary in 1917 for distributing information at the Brownsville birth control clinic in Brooklyn.

"San Quentin, as a Female Prisoner Knew It." Chap. 5 in *Crime and Criminals*, by the Prison Reform League. Los Angeles: Prison Reform League Publishing, 1910. An anonymous female prisoner, imprisoned for several years, gives a detailed description of living and working conditions and race relations in San Quentin. The publication of this account helped lead to some prison reforms.

Sarrazin, Albertine. *Astragal*. Translated by Patsy Southgate. New York: Grove Press, 1967. Originally published as *l'Astragale* (Paris: J.-J. Pauvert, 1965). A novel written by Sarrazin while she was in prison for burglary, about an escapee who breaks her ankle while fleeing prison, and her love affair on the outside.

*———. *The Runaway*. Translated by Charles Lam Markmann. New York: Grove Press, 1967. Originally published as *La Cavale* (Paris: Societé Nouvelle des Éditions Pauvert, 1965). A novel about an imprisoned woman's impressions of prison life and her preoccupation with plans for escape, symbolized by the recurring image of a runaway mare. Written by Sarrazin during her own imprisonment in France.

Saubin, Beatrice. *The Ordeal: My Ten Years in a Malaysian Prison*. Translated by Barbara Brister. New York: Arcade, 1991. Saubin, a French woman traveling in Malaysia, was arrested in 1981 by police at the airport for possession of drugs, which her lover had stowed in her baggage without her knowledge. Her death sentence was commuted to life. After serving ten years of her sentence, international pressure helped to secure her release.

Saunders, Barbara. Poems in *Doing Time: 25 Years of Prison Writing—A PEN American Center Prize Anthology*, edited by Bell Gale Chevigny. New York: Arcade, 1999. Saunders is a writer and artist who writes poetry about her experiences in the Eddie Warrior Correctional Center in Taft, Oklahoma, in the 1990s.

Saxe, Susan. "I Argue My Case." *Off Our Backs: A Women's News Journal* 6, no. 10 (January 1977): 4. Addressed to "Gentlemen of the Jury," this poem protests sexism.

———. "Telling Someone." In *Cages of Steel: The Politics of Imprisonment in the United States*. Edited by Ward Churchill and J. J. Vander Wall, 359–61. Washington, D.C.: Mainsonneuve Press, 1992. Saxe writes against the abuse of prisoners and calls upon readers to speak out and "tell someone."

———. "To My Friends." *Off Our Backs: A Women's News Journal* 7, no. 2 (March 1977): 5. Saxe explains why she decided to plead guilty to charges of armed robbery and destruction of government property when she was captured in 1975 and charged with acts committed in 1970. She states that she is a political prisoner who opposed sexism, racism, and the Vietnam War.

Shakur, Afeni. "Prison Women." *Ann Arbor Argus*, no. 37 (1–14 February 1971): 8–9. Black Panther Shakur, charged with conspiracy to bomb a New York City department store, describes how the court and prison systems violate the rights of poor women.

———. "The Prisons and Jails Are Filled with Political Prisoners." *Black Panther* 5, no. 2 (18 July 1970): 11. Shakur, a member of the Panther New York 21, writes of the inadequate legal counsel given political prisoners. She describes the case of a sister prisoner as illustration.

———. "To Our Black Brothers in Prison, Black Panther Party U.S.A." *Black Panther* 5, no. 4 (1 August 1970): 26. A poem expressing solidarity with imprisoned African American men.

Shakur, Assata [JoAnne Chesimard]. *Assata: An Autobiography*. Chicago: Lawrence Hill Books, 1987. Assata Shakur, a member of the Black Liberation Army, was imprisoned in New York City in May 1973 on a series of charges including bank robbery, attempted murder, kidnapping, and murder. She was acquitted of the first three charges. In 1979 she escaped and found political asylum in Cuba.

———. "Women in Prison: How We Are." *Black Scholar* 9, no. 7 (April 1978): 8–15, reprinted in 12, no. 6 (November–December 1981): 50–57. In this article, Shakur describes the other prisoners at Riker's Island Correctional Institution for Women and explains how women prisoners' dependency is encouraged.

Shanahan, Lauren. "No Winners Here." In *Harsh Punishment: International Experiences of Women's Imprisonment*. Edited by Sandy Cook and Susanne Davies, 13–15. Boston: Northeastern University Press, 1999. Shanahan, who is from Melbourne, was in and out of prison during the period 1989 to 1997 as a result of her heroin addiction.

Sharp, Evelyn. *Unfinished Adventure: Selected Reminiscences from an Englishwoman's Life*. London: John Lane, 1933. Sharp, a British writer who contributed to the *Yellow Book*, includes in her memoirs a chapter on her incarceration in Holloway Prison. Her participation in a militant suffrage demonstration in 1911 led to her sentence of fourteen days. During her second imprisonment of four days in Holloway in 1913, she participated in a hunger strike.

Sharpe, May Churchill ["Chicago May"]. *Chicago May: Her Story*. New York: Macaulay, 1928. The autobiography of Sharpe, born near Dublin, Ireland, in 1876 and christened Beatrice Desmond. In 1889 she immigrated to America, where she married Albert "Dal" Churchill and began her life in crime with their robberies. Widowed at the age of fifteen, she became active in the underworlds of Chicago, New York, London, and Paris. Her second husband was James Montgomery Sharpe. By 1927 she had been imprisoned a total of fifteen times in the United States, once in France, once in Brazil, and seven times in England, for robbery, prostitution, and blackmail. Two long sentences were served on Blackwell's Island, New York, and in Aylesbury, England, where she knew sister prisoner Countess Markievicz, the Irish revolutionary (*see* entry above). August Vollmer, chief of police in Berkeley, California, suggested she could make an honest living by writing. Following his advice, she dictated her memoirs to the stenographer of her Philadelphia lawyer, Henry John Nelson, in 1928.

Shih Ming. "In a Chinese Prison: A Girl Revolutionist Tells her Experiences as a Captive." *Asia* 37 (Fall 1937): 99–100. Shih Ming refused an arranged marriage, left her wealthy family and home in Hupeh, and entered the University at Peiping, where she edited two magazines. As a revolutionist and communist leading students in their demand for release of student political prisoners, she was arrested in 1930. This article describes her imprisonment for several months in the women's detention house and in a garrison, where she was tortured. She was released suddenly when a new warlord came to power.

*Sikakane, Joyce. *A Window on Soweto*. London: International Defence and Aid Fund, 1977. Sikakane's work includes a description of her arrest and imprisonment in Pretoria Central Prison and Nylstroom Prison in 1969 under the Terrorism Act in South Africa. Sikakane, a black journalist, was charged with membership in the African National Congress and with various conspiracies. She was finally released but was served with banning orders, which restricted her movement and prevented her from practicing her profession as a journalist.

Siklová, Jirina. "Save These Books." *Index on Censorship* 12, no. 2 (April 1983): 37–39. Prague sociologist Siklová wrote her defense statement from the Prague Ruzyne Prison, where she awaited trial for helping banned Czech writers send their books out of the country. She was arrested in May 1981 and detained until March 1982, pending a trial that was never held. Her statement explains her actions to defend the right of all Czechs to read freely.

Sisters of Inner Connections, eds. *Writing for Rights*. Newsletter. State Correctional Institution at Muncy, Pa., Summer 1981. The women incarcerated in Muncy Prison compiled this newsletter, containing poems, essays, news items, letters, and artwork. Most contributors are women at Muncy, but works by prisoners from several other states are included. One of the editors and authors of numerous pieces in the newsletter is Moving Cloud (June Boyd), a prisoner at Muncy.

Smedley, Agnes. "Cell Mates." *Call Magazine*, Sunday supplement to the *New York Call*, 15, 22, 29 February and 14 March 1920. A series of four sketches of the women Smedley met while imprisoned for six months in 1918 in the New York Tombs. She was arrested and charged under the Espionage Act for her involvement with Indian nationalists. Included are portraits of Russian revolutionary Mollie Steimer and British birth-control activist Kitty Marion (*see* entry above).

———. *Daughter of Earth*. New York: Coward-McCann, 1929; reprint, Old Westbury, N.Y.: Feminist Press, 1973. Pages 301–34 of Smedley's semiautobiographical novel describe the arrest and imprisonment of "Marie Rogers" in the Tombs for six months during World War I.

———. Letter to Margaret Sanger, 1 November 1918. Margaret Sanger Papers, Cont. 12, Reel 10, Library of Congress. Smedley wrote this letter, addressed "Dear friend Margaret Sanger" (*see* entry above), from the Tombs in New York City, where she was imprisoned during World War I. She describes her hearing, prison conditions, and her meetings in prison with Kitty Marion (*see* entry above) and Mollie Steimer.

A Snake with Ice Water: Prison Writings by South African Women. Edited by Barbara Schreiner. Foreword by Nawal El Saadawi (*see* entry above). Johannesburg: Congress of South African Writers (COSAW), 1992. Anthology of poems, interviews, and prison memoirs by women imprisoned in South Africa.

Sojourner: The Women's Forum. Monthly journal published by Sojourner Feminist Institute, 42 Seaverns Ave., Jamaica Plain, Massachusetts. Sojourner actively advocates for women prisoners through their Inside/Outside project and their frequent publication of women prisoners' writing and the names of women prisoners desiring penpals.

Songs from a Free Space: Writings by Women in Prison. Edited by Carol Muske and Gail Rosenblum. New York: Free Space Writing Project of the N.Y.C. Correctional Institution for Women, n.d. This anthology, described as "a crime of conspiracy, an informed, fully-consenting adult decision to commit poetry," contains poems and short essays by eight women: Carolyn Baxter (*see* entry above), Deborah Hiller, Fannie James, Mildred D. Moss, Carole Ramer, Juanita Reedy (*see* entry above), Gloria Jensen Rogers, and Assata Shakur [Joanne Chesimard] (*see* entry above).

Sparks Fly: Women Political Prisoners and Prisoners of War in the U.S. Edited by Out of Control: Lesbian Committee to Support Women Political Prisoners and Prisoners of War, and the Young Sisters. San Francisco: AGIT Press, 1998, 1999. Collection of brief biographies of women political prisoners, artwork by political prisoners, and a few writings by women imprisoned in the United States for political causes. Writings include an open letter from Assata Shakur (*see* entry above), a poem by Marilyn Buck (*see* entry above), and a poem by Laura Whitehorn (*see* entry below).

Spiridonova, Maria Alexandrovna. Letters. In *Spiridonova: Revolutionary Terrorist*, by I. Steinberg. Translated and edited by Gwenda David and Eric Mosbacher. London: Methuen, 1935. Russian revolutionary heroine Spiridonova became active in 1906 with her assassination of General Luzhenovsky, who had been devastating peasant villages in the region of Tambov, where she lived. This biography includes her letters from prison in Tambov (1906) and from prisons in the Kremlin and exile in Samarkand, where she was sent for later actions. In *Living My Life*, Emma Goldman (*see* entry above) describes her awe at meeting Spiridonova in Moscow.

Staal Madame de (née Delaunay). *Memoirs of Madame de Staal de Launay Written By Herself.* Translated from the 1755 French original by Selina Bathurst. London: Richard Bentley, 1877. Raised in a convent and well educated, Madame de Staal-Delaunay became lady's maid to the Duchesse du Maine. When her mistress was arrested for conspiracy in 1718, Madame de Staal-Delaunay was taken to the Bastille, where she was held until 1720. She describes the conditions of her prison, her diversions, and her prison love affair.

Stafford, Norma. *Dear Somebody: The Prison Poetry of Norma Stafford.* Seaside, Calif.: Academy of Arts and Humanities, 1975. Born into a poor Tennessee farming family, Stafford was imprisoned many times in county prisons, and she spent five and a half years in state prisons in California and Alabama for writing bad checks. In 1972 she began to write poetry as part of her work in the Santa Cruz Women's Prison Project at the California Institution for Women.

Stanford, Sally. *The Lady of the House: The Autobiography of Sally Stanford*. New York: Putnam's, 1966. Raised in poverty on a farm near Baker, Oregon, Stanford was a teenager when first sentenced to two years in the Oregon State Penitentiary in Salem for obtaining goods under false pretenses in 1918. After her parole, she began a bootlegging operation. In 1931 she began her prostitution career in San Francisco and prospered as "madam" of some of the most exclusive brothels in that city. About 1940 she was falsely arrested on charges of involvement in a kidnapping plot, when her brother ran off with an underage girl. She was held in a Livingston jail for sixteen days, until she was released on bail and later cleared of charges.

Steinheil, Marguerite (née Japy). *My Memoirs*. French edition, Paris, 1912; English edition, New York: Sturgis &. Walton, 1912. No translator named. Steinheil, a Parisian socialite trapped in an unhappy marriage with Adolphe Steinheil, a painter twenty years her senior, was arrested in 1908 for the strangulation murders of her mother and husband. She was imprisoned in the Saint-Lazare Prison in Paris until her acquittal in 1909. Her case caused a great sensation at the time, and her book criticizes the injustices of the French judicial system.

Stern, Susan. *With the Weathermen: The Personal Journal of a Revolutionary Woman*. Garden City, N.Y.: Doubleday, 1975. Chapter 16, "Jailtime, December 14, 1970–June 29, 1972," presents Stern's prison experiences. A member of the radical Weathermen group, she was the only woman among the Seattle 7, who were tried for conspiracy in 1970. She was imprisoned in the Seattle City Jail from December 1970 to January 1971; Cook County Jail, Chicago, in March 1971; and Purdy State Institution for Women from April to June 1972. Her book traces her growing involvement in radical politics.

Stevens, Doris. *Jailed for Freedom*. New York: Boni & Liveright, 1920; reprint, Freeport, N.Y.: Books for Libraries Press, 1971. Dedicated to renowned woman sufragist Alice Paul, this account of the American woman suffrage movement (1913-1919) and the jailing of its participants gives a biographical list of suffrage prisoners. Stevens, a social worker, teacher, and officer of the National Woman's Party, was arrested for picketing on July 14, 1917, in Washington, D.C. Although sentenced to sixty days in the Occoquan Workhouse, she received a presidential pardon after three days. Her account gives details of her imprisonment and prison conditions of the suffragists.

Stirredge, Elizabeth. *Strength in Weakness Manifest: in the Life, Various Trials, and Christian Testimony of that Faithful Servant and Handmaid of the Lord, Elizabeth Stirredge*. Philadelphia: Benjamin and Thomas Kite, 1810. A description of Stirredge's persecution for her Quaker beliefs. She was persecuted by a clergyman in her parish of Chew Magna, Somerset, England, and imprisoned in Ilchester Gaol in 1683.

*Strong, Anna Louise. "Jailed in Moscow." *New York Herald Tribune*, 27 March–1 April 1949. A series of six articles describing the arrest and imprisonment in 1949 in Moscow's Lubyanka Prison of Strong, an American journalist who sympathized with the Chinese Revolution and Mao Tse-tung. She was charged with spying and held five days for questioning. The Herald Tribune printed the series as an expose of Soviet police state methods.

Stuart, Lady Arbella. *The Letters of Lady Arbella Stuart*. Edited by Sara Jayne Steen. New York: Oxford University Press, 1994. Stuart, a noblewoman in line for the British throne, was imprisoned by her cousin, King James I, for marrying without obtaining his consent. She was exiled to the north in 1611 and subsequently imprisoned in the Tower of London. She died in 1615, when she was almost forty years old. A few letters from the period of her confinement survive, but scholars do not agree whether any were written from the Tower.

Suffragette Fellowship Collection, Museum of London. The Museum of London acquired this collection of papers of militant British suffragettes in 1950. Several of the longer pieces are referenced under the authors' names within this bibliography. In addition, the collection contains many shorter pieces, including brief biographical and autobiographical statements of suffragettes who were imprisoned but who are less well known. Many of these are catalogued in Group C, vols. 2 and 3. The pieces provide details on the suffragettes' experiences in the movement and their imprisonments.

The Suffragist: Official Weekly Organ of the National Woman's Party. July–December 1917. Issues from this period give extensive coverage of the American suffragists' demonstrations in Washington, D.C., and their subsequent jailing in the District of Columbia Jail and the Occoquan Workhouse in Virginia. The prisoners were released November 27 and 28, when their hunger strike forced the government to commute their sentences. Brief articles by suffrage prisoners include:
> Matilda Hall Gardner, "Occoquan," 28 July 1917
> Doris Stevens (*see* entry above),"Justice as Seen at Occoquan," 11 August 1917
> Alice Paul, " A Note from Alice Paul," 24 November 1917
> Rose Winslow, "The Prison Notes of Rose Winslow, Smuggled to Friends from the District Jail," 24 November 1917.

Sugo, Kanno. "Women and Treason in Pre-war Japan: The Prison Poetry of Kanno Sugo and Kaneko Fumiko." Article and translation of poems by Helene Bowen. In *Lilith: A Feminist History Journal* 5 (1988), 9–251. Sugo, a Japanese anarchist, was condemned to death for conspiracy to assassinate the emperor. She wrote poems in prison while awaiting execution. She was executed by hanging in 1911.

Talamante, Olga. ". . . from Olga's Prison Letters." *El Gallo* 8, no. 1 (January 1976): 14. Talamante, a twenty-five-year-old Chicana from California, describes her torture and imprisonment in Azul, Argentina. She had gone to Argentina in 1973 to work with a community center there and was arrested in November 1974 and charged with subversive activities and possession of guns. She was imprisoned for nearly eighteen months, during which time there was an active defense campaign for her in the United States.

Tassin, Ida Mae. *Proud Mary, Poems from a Black Sister in Prison*. Buffalo, N.Y.: Buffalo Women's Prison Project, 1971. (Not examined; cited in Kathryn W. Burkhart, *Women in Prison* [Garden City, N.Y.: Doubleday, 1973].)

Taylor, Mary Ellen. Letters. Fawcett Library, City of London Polytechnic, London. Correspondence of Mary Ellen Taylor, a British suffragette, with her daughter, Dr. Dorothea Taylor, 1912. In that year Taylor was imprisoned for her suffrage work. (Source: Mary Barrow, *Women 1870–1928: A Select Guide to Printed and Archival Sources in the United Kingdom* [London: Mansell, 1981].)

Tchaikovsky, Chris. "Looking for Trouble." In *Criminal Women: Autobiographical Accounts*, edited by Pat Carlen, 14–58. Cambridge, Eng.: Polity Press, 1985. Tchaikovsky describes how she began criminal activities as a teenager in 1959, and gives an account of her various arrests and imprisonments in England. She founded Women in Prison, a London-based advocacy group that works to improve conditions for prisoners, with particular emphasis upon women's issues.

ten Boom, Corrie. *Corrie ten Boom's Prison Letters*. Carmel, N.Y.: Guideposts, 1975. Letters written during Corrie ten Boom's imprisonment in 1944 at Scheveningen and Vught, a Nazi camp in Holland.

———. *A Prisoner—and Yet!* Toronto: Evangelical, 1947. The author writes of her persecution by the Nazis during World War II because her family harbored Jews in their home in Haarlem, Holland. In February 1944 she was imprisoned at Scheveningen with her sister and aged father, who died there. Corrie ten Boom was imprisoned that same year in concentration camps at Vught and Ravensbrück. She was released in December 1944, but her sister died in Ravensbrück.

Tencin, Claudine Alexandrine Guérin de. *Memoirs of the Count of Comminge.* London, 1744. Translation of "Les Memoires du Comte de Comminge" (1735) in *Oeuvres des Mesdames de Fontaines et de Tencin.* Paris: Gamier, n.d. (Not examined; source: Elissa D. Gelfand, *Imagination in Confinement* [Ithaca, N.Y.: Cornell University Press, 1983].)

Tencin, Claudine Alexandrine Guérin de, and Antoine de Ferril, Comte d'Pont de Veyle. *The Siege of Calais by Edward of England. An Historical Novel.* Translated from the French original (1739). London: Printed for T. Woodward, at the Half-Moon between the Temple-Gates in Fleet Street; and Paul Vaillant, against Southampton Street in the Strand, 1740; reprint, New York: Garland, 1974. Claudine de Tencin, a French author, was imprisoned in the Bastille for three months in 1726 for the death of her lover, La Fresnais, who blamed her for his suicide committed in her salon. In this novel she uses her prison experience to depict that of the male protagonist, Monsieur de Chalons, imprisoned by Edward II of England. (Source of biographical data and summary of book: Elissa Gelfand, *Imagination in Confinement* [Ithaca, N.Y.: Cornell University Press, 1983], 34, 111–13,121.)

Terrero, Jane. Papers. Suffragette Fellowship Collection, Museum of London.
Prison Experiences. Typescript (12 copies) (Group A: 60.15/13 and 50.87/62). British suffragette Terrero gave this paper twice, shortly after coming out of prison. "The Story of the Two Hunger Strikes" (Group A: 60.15/13). "A ten minute paper given once at Wilburn."
Letter to Mrs. How-Martyn regarding suffragette experiences, 24 January 1928 (Group C, vol. 3: 57–70/11). Terrero gives an account of her arrest and imprisonment in 1912.
Manuscript register relating to prison experience of Janie Terrero (50.82/116). "Containing scraps and extracts from letters to my husband covering the period I was in Holloway for the cause of Women's Suffrage in the year 1912." The letters are copied, in her hand, into a notebook. Also included are notes on her hunger strike and forcible feeding and on prison administration, and letters to her husband and notes written from police court while awaiting trial in 1912. Terrero was arrested March 1, 1912, for breaking windows on Oxford Street, London, and was released June 25, 1912.

Tesfagiorgis, Abeba. *A Painful Season & a Stubborn Hope: The Odyssey of an Eritrean Mother.* Lawrenceville, N.J.: Red Sea Press, 1992. Tesfagiorgis, an Eritrean mother and professional employed by an airline, was imprisoned by the Ethiopean military from September 1975 to March 1976 for her alleged support of Eritrean freedom fighters. After her release she went into exile.

Thornton, Alice. "Merely Justice." *Atlantic Monthly* 135, no. 5 (May 1925): 611–23. This is the second in a series of two papers analyzing Thornton's prison experiences. Here she discusses prison discipline and her work to start a "school" in prison, where she taught female prisoners to read and write.

———. "The Pound of Flesh." *Atlantic Monthly* 135, no. 4 (April 1925): 433–46. Thornton, explaining that she could be classified as an "accidental criminal" whose offense was isolated and "the result of sudden temptation or extreme emotional states," was a university graduate and a skilled worker when imprisoned for several years for her unnamed "one horrible mistake." Her purpose in writing her articulate essay is "to interpret certain aspects of the penal problem." She does this through a description of prison conditions and character sketches of fellow prisoners.

Till My Tale Is Told: Women's Memoirs of the Gulag. Edited by Simeon Vilensky. Translated by John Crowfoot et al. London: Virago Press, 1999. English translation of an anthology of excerpts from memoirs first published in Moscow in 1989. The writers represented here had been victims of government repression during the Soviet era and the Stalinist purges; their writings extend from the 1920s to the 1950s. They write of their prisons and labor camps in the Gulag. Writers include Olga Adamova-Sliozberg, Bertha Babina-Nevskaya, Anna Barkova, Nadezhda Grankina, Nadezhda Kanel, Tatyana Leschenko-Sukhomlina, Zoya Marchenko, Tamara Petkevich, Vera Shulz, Yelena Sidorkina, Nadezhda Surovtseva, Zayara Vesyolaya, Yelena Vladimirova, Hava Volovich, Galina Zatmilova, and Veronica Znamenskaya.

Time Is an Eightball: Poems from Juvenile Homes & the Penitentiary of New Mexico. Edited by Bob Henry Baber. Santa Fe, N.M.: Tooth of Time, 1984. This collection includes poems by girls at the Youth Diagnostic Center and prisonerss of the Women's Penitentiary of New Mexico. Lorri Martinez (*see* entry above) is one of the poets represented.

Todd, Judith. *The Right to Say No.* London: Sidgwick & Jackson, 1972. Todd, a Rhodesian journalist, was imprisoned for five weeks in Marandellas jail in 1972, while her father, the former Rhodesian prime minister, was held in a nearby prison. They were held under the Rhodesian Emergency Powers Regulations of 1970 on suspicion that they were dangerous to the public safety. Todd's book goes into detail about Rhodesian politics and describes her stay in Marandellas and later in Chikurubi Prison Farm, where she went on a hunger strike and was forcibly fed.

Trapnel, Anna. "Report and Plea." London, 1654. Wing T2033, pp. 36–53. Reprinted in *English Women's Voices 1540–1700*, edited by Charlotte F. Otten, 64–78. Miami: Florida International University Press, 1992. Trapnel, a British prophet and mystic, was imprisoned "fifteen weeks in a 'man's prison' and eight weeks in Bridewell" (Otten 58) because her "outpourings" threatened the English government. In "Report and Plea" Trapnel describes her experiences in Bridewell prison and the support given to her by female friends.

Turkow Kaminska, Ruth. *I Don't Want To Be Brave Anymore.* Washington, D.C.: New Republic Books, 1978. Turkow Kaminska, a noted European singer and actress, and her musician husband, Adi Rosner, were Polish Jews arrested by Stalin's police in 1946. Her memoirs extend from World War II to her return to Poland in 1956. At the age of twenty-six, she was first taken to a Lvov prison in December 1946, where she was held until the spring of 1947 on the charge of attempting to cross the border illegally. In 1947 she was transferred to a prison in Zolotchov, and then to prisons in Kiev and Kharkov. In 1948 she was sentenced to a five-year exile in Kokchetav, one of Stalin's Siberian camps. There, she was reunited with her daughter. They were later transferred to Karaganda, a city where she continued to live in exile until her release in 1952.

Turner, Margaret. *See* Jane Buxton.

Tyler, Mary. *My Years in an Indian Prison.* London: Gollancz, 1977. Tyler, an Englishwoman living in India, was arrested in 1970 with her Indian husband and imprisoned in Hazaribagh Central Jail in Bihar, and the Jamshedpur jail. They were suspected of engaging in revolutionary activity against the Indian government. She describes in detail her prison conditions and other female prisoners. She was released and allowed to return to England in 1975, but her husband remained in prison at the time.

Undoing Time: American Prisoners in Their Own Words. Edited by Jeff Evans. Boston: Northeastern University Press, 2001. Anthology of autobiographical writings by twentieth-century American prisoners. The majority of selections are by male prisoners. Entries by women prisoners include those by C. Kaye Ferguson, Jennifer Howard, and Darlene Nall.

Uribe, María Tila. "Notes from Inside," and "Women and Prison," translated by Charlie Roberts and Vladimir Klimenko. In *You Can't Drown the Fire: Latin American Women Writing in Exile*, edited by Alicia Partnoy, 50–70. Pittsburgh/San Francisco: Cleis, 1988. Description of women's imprisonment in Colombia by Uribe, a political activist and teacher imprisoned in 1977 for four years. She afterward lived in exile in Nicaragua.

Valâery, Nicole. *Prisoner Rejoice.* Translated. from the French by Tony and Jane Collins. London: Hodder and Stoughton, 1982. Valâery, arrested first in 1945, writes of her imprisonment by Communists in Romania for her Christian beliefs. She, like Alice Panaiodor (*see* entry above) was a follower of the Wurmbrands (*see* entry below).

Varela, Maria Elena Cruz. *Ballad of the Blood: The Poems of María Elena Cruz Varela.* Translated and edited by Mairym Cruz-Bernal with Deborah Digges. Hopewell, N.J.: Ecco Press, 1996. Cuban poet Varela was imprisoned in 1989 for her protests against the Castro regime. She was released after two years and now lives in exile in Puerto Rico.

Vasconcellos, Suzanne R. "The Tragedy of the Beast's Offspring." *Crime Delinquency* 28, no. 4 (October 1982): 518–22. Vasconcellos's essay is an indictment of the prison system and its treatment of both men and women prisoners. She explains little about her own situation, except that she has been sentenced to eleven years' imprisonment for a nonviolent crime.

Velazquez, Loreta Janeta. *The Woman in Battle: A Narrative of the Exploits, Adventures, and Travels of Madame Loreta Janeta Velazquez, otherwise Known as Lieutenant Harry T. Buford, Confederate States Army.* Edited by C. J. Worthington. New York: Arno Press, 1876; 1972. Historians dispute the authenticity of Velazquez' work. Velazquez describes her great desire to serve in the Confederate Army during the Civil War and her adventures while disguised as a male lieutenant. Her narrative contains a few brief accounts of her imprisonments while in disguise.

Vera, Marta [pseud.]. *Political Prisoners, Chilean Women No. 2: Political Prisoners in the Women's Section of "Tres Alamos" Concentration Camp.* London: Women's Campaign for Chile and Chile Committee for Human Rights, 1976. A pamphlet containing the testimony of a Chilean woman imprisoned for fifteen months in Tres Alamos concentration camp for political prisoners. She wrote from exile in 1976, relating in detail the process of interrogation, the legal situation, and prison conditions. With pride she describes the communal organization of women within Tres Alamos.

Voices from Within: The Poetry of Women in Prison. Edited by Ann McGovern. Weston, Conn.: Magic Circle Press, 1975. A collection of poems by the Bedford Hills poets: Bernadine Adams, Leonore Coons, Glenda Cooper, Clementine Corona, Susan Hallett, Theresa Simmons, Susan Smith, Constance Walker. They are members of The Long-Termer's Committee at Bedford Hills Correctional Facility, New York.

McGovern, who ran a writing workshop with these women, collected and compiled these poems.

von Meck, Galina. *As I Remember Them.* London: Dennis Dobson, 1973. The autobiography of von Meck, daughter of a pre-Revolutionary Russian landowner and railway president. In 1923, during an attempted escape into Poland, she was arrested and held until 1924 in prisons in Korosten, Zhytomir, and Kiev. She was again imprisoned in 1928 in Lubyanka Prison and Moscow's Butyrka Prison on the charge of espionage for the United States and England. In 1931 she was transferred to Siberian labor camps, where she remained until her release in 1935.

*Walker, Dr. Mary Edwards. "Hotel de Castle Thunder." *Daily National Republican* (Washington, D.C.), 25 August 1864. Dr. Walker, who served as a physician in the Union Army, was imprisoned in 1864 by the Confederates in a Richmond prison known as Castle Thunder. This article describes prison conditions and the treatment of women.

*Wallach, Erica. *Light at Midnight.* Garden City, N.Y.: Doubleday, 1967. A description of Wallach's five-year imprisonment in East German and Russian prisons, beginning in 1950. A German woman married to an American, she had entered East Berlin to find her foster parents and was arrested by the Communists on charges of spying and held at first in Schumannstrasse Prison.

Walled Garden: Poems from NSW Prisons. Edited by Rosemary Creswell. Sydney, Australia: Ball & Chain Press, N.S.W. Department of Corrective Services, 1978. This anthology of poems from New South Wales prisons was assembled with the encouragement of the Programmes Division of the N S.W. Department of Corrective Services. Most poets represented are men, but women poets include Julie Cashman (*see* Wright), Patricia Collins, Mary Farrell, and Sandra Willson (*see* entry below).

Walton, Olive. Diary during imprisonment in Aylesbury Prison, 1912 (typescript). Suffragette Fellowship Collection, Museum of London (Group C, vol. 2: 50.82/1131). The original diary is in the possession of Walton's adopted daughter. British suffragette Walton was sentenced on March 27, 1912, to four months' imprisonment for breaking windows. Her diary includes a statement given to the Women's Social and Political Union (WSPU) in London, July 1912, on hunger striking and forcible feeding in Aylesbury.

Weisbord, Vera Buch. *A Radical Life.* Bloomington: Indiana University Press, 1977. Vera Buch Weisbord was an American Communist active during the early years of the movement, in the 1920s. She worked for labor causes in New York, New Jersey, and Pennsylvania. In 1929 she was jailed in Gastonia, North Carolina, on charges of murder and conspiracy in connection with a strike. While in prison, she was encouraged by reading the story of Vera Figner's (*see* entry above) imprisonment.

Wharry, Olive. Prison notebooks. British Museum, London. Notebooks kept by British suffragette Wharry in Holloway and Winson Green prisons (1911–14). (Not examined; source: Margaret Barrow, *Women 1870–1928: A Select Guide to Printed and Archival Sources in the United Kingdom* [London: Mansell, 1981].)

Whitehorn, Laura. "Preventive Detention: A Prevention of Human Rights?" In *Cages of Steel: The Politics of Imprisonment in the United States*, edited by Ward Churchill and J. J. Vander Wall, 365–77. Washington, D.C.: Mainsonneuve Press, 1992. Whitehorn, arrested in 1985 and held in preventive detention, argues against the statute that allows this practice in the criminal justice system. A political activist, she spent fifteen years in federal women's prisons at Lexington, Kentucky, and Dublin, California, and was released in 1999.

Who Took the Weight. Weston, Conn.: Magic Circle Press, 1977. An anthology of women's prison writing. (Not examined; source: H. Bruce Franklin, *American Prisoners and Ex-Prisoners: Their Writings: An Annotated Bibliography of Published Works, 1798–1981* [Westport, Conn.: Lawrence Hill, 1982], 51.)

Williams, Evelyn. *Inadmissible Evidence: The Story of the African-American Trial Lawyer Who Defended the Black Liberation Army.* Brooklyn, New York: Lawrence Hill Books, 1993. Williams describes her efforts to defend her niece, Black Panther Assata Shakur (*see* entry above), against charges of bank robbery and murder of a New Jersey State Trooper. Williams discusses her 1975 imprisonment for contempt; she received a ten-day sentence in a maximum security unit of Westchester County jail, Valhalla, New York.

Williams, Helen Maria. *Letters containing a Sketch of the Politics of France, From the Thirty-first of May 1793, till the twenty-eighth of July 1794, and the Scenes which have Passed in the Prisons of Paris.* Two vols. London: Robinson, 1795; reprinted in *Letters from France*, Facsimile Reproductions, with an introduction by Janet M. Todd (8 vols. in 2). Delmar, N.Y.: Scholars' Facsimiles & Reprints, 1975. Williams, a popular English poet living in France during the Revolution, sympathized with the principles of the Revolution and was friendly with leading French intellectuals, including Madame Roland (*see* entry above). In October 1793, Williams was arrested with her sisters and mother and taken to the Luxembourg prison, according to a decree ordering imprisonment of the English and seizure of their property. They were released in December 1793.

Willson, Sandra A. K. "Prisons, Prisoners and the Community." In *Women and Crime*, edited by Satyanshu K. Mukherjee and Jocelynne A. Scutt, 196–204. Sydney, Australia: Australian Institute of Criminology, in association with George Allen & Unwin, 1981. Willson, released from prison in 1977, now works in the field of women's corrections. In New South Wales she worked with the Network for Drug and Alcohol Agencies, and in 1979 she founded the first halfway house for female ex-prisoners in that area. The article discusses prison conditions at the Mulawa Training and Detention Centre for Women in New South Wales. Willson criticizes the lack of a classification system, inadequate medical attention and programs for released prisoners, and poor prisoner-staff relations. She suggests halfway houses as one improvement in the system.

Winsor, Mary. Papers. The Arthur and Elizabeth Schlesinger Library on the History of Women in America, Radcliffe College, Cambridge, Mass. The Winsor Papers include "My Prisons," a typescript reminiscence of American suffragist Winsor's two prison sentences in 1917 and 1918; newspaper clippings about picketing and prison sentences (1917–18) and about the prison special train, February 1919. (Not examined; source: letter to Judith Scheffler from Elizabeth Shenton, assistant to the director, Schlesinger Library.)

Wituska, Krystyna. *I Am First a Human Being: The Prison Letters of Kyrstyna Wituska.* Edited and translated by Irene Tomaszewski. Montreal: Véhicule, 1997. Wituska was a young woman working for the Polish Underground when she was arrested by the Nazis in 1942 and imprisoned in Berlin. In 1944 she was beheaded. Her letters are to her parents and the young daughter of a friendly prison guard.

"Women Incarcerated." Special issue of *Hunt Walk Talk* (Spring 1985). This issue of the journal of the men's Hunt Correctional Center in St. Gabriel, Louisiana, focuses on articles and interviews with prisoners of North Carolina Correctional Institute for Women and Louisiana Correctional Institute for Women. Included are articles by Jeanette Parker, "The Common Bond" (pp. 95–97, 155, and Deretha Smith, "My Impressions of Prison Life" (pp. 98, 155).

"Women Locked Up." *Women: A Journal of Liberation* 3, no. 3 (1972). This special issue on confined women includes contributions by women prisoners:
Teri O'Meara. "View from Within," p. 35. O'Meara writes from a Baltimore, Maryland, prison, where she was sent on prostitution and drug charges. She describes how women prisoners are treated like children and criticizes the lack of work and training programs.
"South Vietnamese Prisoners Speak" (dated 20 September 1970), pp. 40–43. This document by several unnamed female political prisoners describes their brutal treatment in a South Vietnamese prison, beginning in November 1969. They were held in Con Son and Chi Hoa prisons and severely punished for a hunger strike.

Women's Voices from Soviet Labor Camps. Translated by Lesya Jones, and edited by Bohdan Yasen. Smoloskyp Samvydav Series: Documents of Ukrainian Samvydav. Baltimore: Smoloskyp Publishers, 1975. Included in this collection are letters to world organizations, the United Nations, and Soviet officials written by Odarka Husyak, Iryna Senyk, Stefania Shabatura, Iryna Stasiv, Nina Strokata-Karavanska, and Nadia Svitlychna. They protest the violation of human rights that occurs in Soviet prison camps, where they were sentenced in 1972-73 for "anti-Soviet agitation and propaganda."

The World Split Open: Writing and Theatre by Women in Prison, edited by Margaret Robison and Sheryl Stoodley. Northampton, Mass.: Cultural Images Group, 1986. Writings from "In Her Own Name: Workshops for Incarcerated Women," a creative writing and dramatics project at Massachusetts Correctional Institute, Lancaster, summer 1986. Photographs are included. "Journal writing was an integral part of the project."

The World Split Open: Theatre and Writing by Women in Prison. Vol. 2. Edited by Sheryl Stoodley. Northampton, Mass.: Cultural Images Group, 1992. A playscript, writing, and photographs from workshops at the Massachusetts Correctional Institutes in Lancaster and Framingham, 1986–88. The playscript was edited and written by Margaret Robison and Sheryl Stoodley, workshop instructors, "from transcribed conversations and writings gathered during a two-year theater-writing workshop program," and was produced in the Studio Theater at Smith College in 1988, with prisoner actors and a prisoner chorus on videotape. "Journal writing was an integral part of the project."

Wozencraft, Kim. *Notes from the Country Club.* Boston: Houghton Mifflin, 1993. Novel about a woman incarcerated in a federal prison for killing her abusive husband. Wozencraft, a former narcotics officer, served a sentence in the Federal Correctional Institution in Lexington, Kentucky, until 1983.

———. *Rush.* New York: Random House, 1990. Wozencraft's first novel, which contains autobiographical elements and was later made into a motion picture.

Wright, Julie Cashman. *The Angel of Death.* North Sydney, Australia: Allen & Unwin, 1991. Wright tells the story of the criminal activities that led to her series of imprisonments in Australia and New South Wales, beginning with her 1977 arrest for transporting marijuana. Her crimes included bank robberies, and she was known as "Australia's most wanted woman." Her final release from prison was in 1990.

The Writing Workshop/Bedford Hills Correctional Facility, New York. *Aliens at the Border*. Edited with an introduction by Hettie Jones. New York: Segue Books, 1997. Collection of poems by women participating in the Writing Workshop in 1996. Fourteen poets are represented, including Kathy Boudin (*see* entry above.) and Judith Clark (*see* entry above).

————. *More In Than Out*. Edited by Hettie Jones. New York: Writing Workshops, 1992. Collection of poems by women participating in the Writing Workshop at Bedford Hills Correctional Facility, New York.

Wurmbrand, Sabina. *The Pastor's Wife*. Edited by Charles Foley. London: Hodder & Stoughton, 1970. Wurmbrand and her husband, Romanian Jews who had converted to Christianity, were imprisoned in 1948 by the Russians, who had entered Romania after World War II. Her pastor husband was arrested as a counterrevolutionary and Sabina Wurmbrand was held in secret police headquarters, Bucharest, for questioning about his activities. She was sent to Jilava transit prison and then to forced labor camps near Cernavoda. In the Tirgusor maximum-security prison she worked in the sewing shop. She was released in 1953, but her husband was imprisoned for nine more years.

Zambrana, Norma. "My Experience with the L.I.F.T. Program." *Federal Prisons Journal*. "Special Issue: Focus on the Female Offender" 3, no. 1 (Spring 1992): 40. Zambrana, a Bolivian native and naturalized citizen of the United States, was sentenced to eight years for distribution of drugs. She began her sentence in 1989 in the Federal Reformatory for Women in Alderson, West Virginia. A mother of three, she describes the benefits of the Linking Inmate Families Together (LIFT) Program's courses and her work in its Children's Center.

CREDITS